Father,
Dear Father

By Arthur S. Reinherz

Elmrose Publishing
Boston • New York

Father, Dear Father
by Arthur S. Reinherz

Father, Dear Father is completely a work of fiction. Although
there are cities in Massachusetts with the same names, the
locations, institutions and people in these cities do not bear
any resemblance to locations, institutions or people in this
book.

For further information, contact the author at:
areinherz@katzmeow.net

Book design by:
The Floating Gallery
244 Madison Avenue, #254
New York, NY 10016-2819
(1-877) 822-2500

PRINTED IN THE UNITED STATES OF AMERICA

Father, Dear Father
Arthur S. Reinherz
1. Author 2. Title 3. Fiction

Library of Congress Control Number 2002117353
ISBN 0-9726779-0-9

Father,
Dear Father

Acknowledgements

I want to thank my loving wife, Eve, for her constructive comments and for her patience with me during the long hours of research and writing and rewriting.

I also want to thank my good friend and editor, Andrew Ackers, who deserves much credit for his honest criticism, advice and guidance.

This book is dedicated to my future— my children, their spouses, my grandchildren and Jacob, my great grandchild.

Chapter One

IT WAS AS COLD AS THE NORTH SIDE of a gravestone in winter. Sixteen-year-old Carl Grandee bundled up against another shrill angry blast of north wind so strong that he had to lean into it head down. His mackinaw was buttoned up to the collar. His legs struggled to keep up, pants snug against the fronts of his frozen thighs but billowing out behind them.

It was 1938, and the frigid day was typical of late February. The Montreal Express had sent a howling chill down from Canada. Snow was piled high everywhere. The previous day had brought four inches of snow to top the white tableau of unyielding crust in the Grandees' back yard.

Carl struggled to keep his footing as he continued home from school. When he finally reached the top of Las Casas Street, he surveyed his house with its peeling paint and absence of storm windows, and quietly cursed his father under his breath.

Carl sat on the front steps and rubbed his watery eyes. He removed his dark blue stocking hat and ran his hands through light brown wavy hair, but still didn't go inside. He did not want his mother to see him upset.

He tried to calm himself down, sorted through memories of his father, until he found one he liked. Two years ago, a recent softball game between the Malden Aces and the East Boston Mavericks. His father coached the Aces and they won the game because Carl had hit a home run with a man on base. His father was the first to show him how to hold a bat and how to keep swinging all the way through, even after he had hit the ball.

Carl was still lost in memory when his sister came upon him on the stairs.

"Hey, there, little brother," Louise said. "What's eating you? You hiding from Ma again?"

Carl patted the step next to where he was sitting and Louise sat alongside him. He could feel the heat radiating from her body. "There's something going on with Pa at The Chateau, isn't there?" Carl said. The Chateau was a restaurant and boarding house in Charlestown that Carl's father, Thomas Grandee, managed. "Almost every day he calls home saying he has to work late. No one works that much, and it only takes fifteen minutes to drive home from Charlestown!"

"True. You'd think if he was working so much he'd have enough money to get this house fixed. At least the heating," Louise said. "Some of my friends father's don't even have jobs—and they have heat. There ought to be a lot more fireplace logs this time of year. Pa makes good pay."

"Well, if that's true," Carl said, "the money's got to be going somewhere."

"You know about those upstairs rooms at The Chateau? I think Pa's been taking some extra naps. And I don't think he sleeps alone."

"You saying he has a girlfriend?"

"That Hannah woman. I saw her. She's very attractive and tends to hang all over the men. She's nothing but trouble."

Carl touched Louise's arm. "Maybe the problem isn't Hannah. Couldn't Pa just be pissing his money away on booze? Gambling, maybe?"

"Listen, I'm not saying Pa's a bad person, Carlie. Understand? I remember nice things about him. But he's in trouble, though. Hannah Ward. She ought to get a husband of her own. Anyway, that's between him and Ma."

"Yeah, I guess you're right," Carl said. "Pa must be in some kind of trouble. Could be booze."

Louise shook her head, managed a half smile and reached across to brush her brother's smooth cheek. At 16, he still had no facial hair, but was already six feet tall and weighed 180 pounds. "Let's go inside before Ma starts worrying where we are."

"Yeah, and it's not getting any warmer. I have to change and bring some logs in from the backyard."

The Grandee house on Las Casas Street was an old twelve-room mansion in the once wealthy West End section of Malden,

Massachusetts. The house had a broken-down heating system and only one of its three fireplaces, the one in the living room, worked. Thomas Grandee had bought the house through a bank foreclosure, a common event during the depression.

One of The Chateau's owners, Bob Morrison, was a wealthy Boston banker who knew that Thomas needed a large house for his wife, three children and his recently widowed mother. He had offered one of the bank's foreclosures to Thomas for $1,500.

Thomas' mother had a modest few thousand dollars of insurance money, and she gave it to him to help purchase the house and its sparse furnishings. She died within a couple of months of the purchase.

Carl and Louise were convinced that had she lived through the summer and fall, she would never have made it through this winter. The lack of heating in the big old house would have been more than their grandma's frail body could have withstood.

The former wealthy owners were not only unable to meet their mortgage payments during the depression, but they were also unable to properly maintain the property. It had been in a terrible state when the Grandees moved in and Thomas had promised his wife, Marie, from the outset that he would take care of the repairs. But this promise, like the others, was not fulfilled; two years later, the house was in even further decline.

Actually, many homes were in a state of decay by the time the mid-nineteen thirties arrived. Working people had lost their jobs and those who owned homes simply could not afford to maintain them. Once-wealthy families were in desperate straits due to the sudden, unanticipated business or stock market losses. Many were forced out of their homes due to inability to meet mortgage payments or to pay rent. Thomas was one of the fortunate ones; at least he had a week's pay from his restaurant job.

Carl was certain, after hearing it a few times from his sister, Louise, that his father could at least have afforded to get the fireplaces fixed and to keep their home supplied with firewood.

He was having a more difficult time with Louise's idea that his father was fooling around with Hannah Ward. Still, he had overheard enough arguments between his parents to surmise that it was a possibility.

11

Carl had gym class on Friday. It was the last class of the day and the boys were allowed to stay after class to play some basketball. Besides, it was another freezing day, and the school gym was warm and pleasant.

Carl, sometimes with Louise's help, had the job of stacking the backyard logs at the living room fireplace. The trouble was that Thomas Grandee often failed to replenish the backyard log pile.

On that particular afternoon, the family had already used all the logs that Carl had brought in the day before. There were only a few snow-covered logs left in the back yard. After about fifteen minutes of shooting baskets, Carl remembered the logs. Unless his father came home today with a fresh supply of logs and firewood, the family would be without heat of any kind. Carl reluctantly told his friends he had to leave.

It had been three days since Carl last saw his father and these absences were becoming more frequent. This ate at him, and all he could ask was, *"Why?"* Carl was also worried about the consequences that his father's disappearances had on his mother. It was not that she had ever said anything to let on that she was unhappy; Marie Grandee put up a good front for her children. They were all simply too smart not to be aware.

As far as his wife and children were concerned, Thomas Grandee was not attending to his family responsibilities for reasons only known to him. The fact that the house was not providing proper shelter during an unusually cold winter simply added to the freezing gloom, draining the Grandees of any warmth or happiness they might once have enjoyed.

Even the youngest Grandee, ten-year-old Robbie, sensed that something was wrong. That afternoon he asked Louise, as he had asked many times in the past few days, "Where is Pa? Why can't he play with me and Skip?"

Louise gently lifted Skip up. She patted the small dog and said, "Don't you worry, little pooch. You look cold, but know that we love you very much."

Skip was a brown-and-white mixed-breed with the smooth coat of a beagle and the droopy ears of a spaniel. Thomas had purchased the pup three years earlier when Robbie had asked for a dog.

Louise finished patting Skip and put him down. She took Robbie's hands into her own and explained, "Pa is working hard these days, sweetheart. He has a lot of problems, but I know he's thinking of us all. You do know Pa loves you, don't you, sweetheart?"

"Ma says I should pray for him," Robbie said. "Ma says that Pa doesn't have time to get the house fixed like he promised because of all the other work."

"Robbie, we have to be extra nice to Ma these days and help around the house, too. Everything is going to work out fine. Just you wait and see."

Louise could only hope that this would be true and everything *would* really be all right. She was not at all as confident as she tried to sound. Just then she saw Carl through the window.

"Here comes Carl, Robbie!"

Louise greeted her brother with a broad smile, relieved that his arrival would distract Robbie. Carl's hair and eyebrows were covered with icicles.

"You must be frozen!" Louise said.

"And it's not much warmer in here," Carl said as he stepped into the house. "Has Pa shown up with more logs yet?"

"Not a chance. How come you're so late from school? I've been home for over an hour."

"I was down in the gym shooting baskets with the guys. I'm getting pretty good."

"You're not thinking of trying out for the team, are you?"

"Lou, you know I want to get a job and save money so I can go to college. I just like to shoot baskets and hang out once in a while."

Robbie, who had become quickly bored with the older sibling bantering, ran upstairs, Skip fast alongside, to finish reading the latest episode of his newest interest and famous hero, Dick Tracy.

Carl looked at his sister. She was really growing up.

"Lou," he said, "I never noticed it before, but you're a lot taller than you used to be. And you've changed so much. I can't believe you were 'sweet sixteen' just a year ago."

"Carl, I have news for you. I've grown two inches in the past year alone."

"Lou, I have to do the logs."

Carl changed out of his school clothes and went out behind the house to bring in what was left of the firewood. He had to clear ice-crusted mounds off the woodpile. After he had finally gathered a pile of logs together, he headed for the kitchen door with a cloud of mist billowing from his heavy breath, icing his eyes and nose.

The still persistent howling wind thrust him through the back door and into the kitchen with his load. Louise was sitting at the large, white, enameled kitchen table where they shared most of their meals. She was nursing a mug of hot chocolate and reading *The Rains Came* by Louis Bromfield.

She took one look at her red-faced brother and protested, "Carlie, let me help. Let me have some of those logs." The next time out, she assisted him with the work.

Carl pushed her into a snow pile and they laughed as he jumped on top of her. They rolled together in the snow and laughed so much that tears came to their eyes.

Suddenly, Louise became aware that she wasn't exactly dressed for this kind of winter play. She was getting cold and wet. Her shapely legs were covered in beige cotton stockings and white bobby sox and she was wearing polished brown oxfords. All were getting wet in the snow. "Stupid me. I messed up my new shoes. I should've worn boots."

Carl laughed. "Too late." He pushed her into the snow again and they tumbled together.

She finally pushed him away and just sat down on a pile of snow. Carl joined her and suddenly both of them burst into laughter at the silliness of the situation.

Before long, their tears of laughter started to freeze, so they stopped playing and continued with their task. Carl used an axe to cut the last huge log down to size, while Louise carried a small load into the house.

After stacking the logs at the fireplace, they were finally finished. Carl looked at Louise as she walked into the kitchen.

"You really weren't dressed to bring in logs, were you?"

"No, damn it." She looked down at her clothing—a gold sweater embroidered with the letter "M" and a brown tartan plaid skirt that fell to her knees. "I hope I didn't ruin this outfit. I'm going upstairs to change."

After changing into dry clothes, she examined herself in her bedroom mirror. She wore no makeup except lipstick. She had a cute, naturally turned-up nose and the clear, sparkling blue eyes she shared with both her parents. Her light brown hair fell to her shoulders in gentle waves. Louise was a perfectly developed, nubile girl and, at seventeen, she already stood five feet, seven inches tall—as tall as her mother. Louise was satisfied with her reflection.

A few hours later, after they were both well rested, Carl decided that he and Louise both needed a distraction. Breaking into a broad smile that showed a row of perfect white teeth, he said, "Hey, Lou, Let's go outside. I want to show you something beautiful."

"Okay, brother. Lead the way."

Carl led Louise on a short walk down the street to view their house from a distance. He pointed out a row of old maples in front with branches stripped bare and glistening with ice left behind from the recent New England storm.

Louise understood why her brother was in awe of the view, which actually lined both sides of the street. She often teased Carl when he got serious, but deep down she was proud of her brother's love of nature and to his keen sensitivity about life in general.

Las Casas was an L-shaped street with magnificent old Victorian homes. The street began as a hill that gradually leveled off near the top of the "L" where the Grandee home was situated. In summer, when the trees were in bloom, they formed a canopy of shade with glimmers of sunlight dancing through the leaves. Winter was even more inspiring because of the stark, primal beauty of the branches that bent and swayed under the extra weight of snow and ice.

This section of Malden was not typical of the rest of the city. The West End of town was mostly residential, and tree-lined streets were plentiful. For the most part, homes were spacious 10 and 12-room singles with fireplaces and high-ceilinged rooms. By 1938, some were already close to a century old. They were all once quite luxurious and many boasted third floor servant quarters. Away from this area, Malden was a potpourri of shops, apartment houses and tenements as well as modest single-family as well as two and three-family homes.

After supper, Marie and the three children gathered around the fireplace in the sparse but handsomely furnished living room. There was a large, overstuffed mahogany couch with carved claw feet and two matching wing chairs—one with a footstool—aligning the two long walls of the cozy room. An out-of-tune upright piano with fading ivory keys nestled comfortably against an opposite wall. A vase-shaped porcelain and gold-painted lamp with a silk shade rested on top of the piano. The former owners had left many of the furnishings in the house when they vacated. Other valuable pieces had, of course, been sold through the years.

One of Marie's successful domestic accomplishments was preserving the few pieces left behind that they continued to enjoy. She had created the multicolored latch-hook rugs herself, to protect the polished plank floors. However, the tattered floral wallpaper—another reminder of Thomas' obvious neglect—offered stark contrast.

As Marie and her children huddled together, they watched the flickering gold and blue flames dancing in the fireplace. It was a good way to keep their spirits up and their minds off the fact that Thomas was still not home. This was not his first extended absence, but it had been happening more frequently than usual in the past six months.

Previously, Thomas would occasionally stay overnight at The Chateau for a day at a time, but recently he had been staying away for several days. He never failed to call home and let them know that he was at The Chateau. He would explain that he was taking in new guests, or had an emergency. However, these "emergencies" were happening more and more frequently.

On this particular winter night, the Grandee house was miserable. Now well after sunset, the large old Victorian mansion was getting colder by the moment. Glowing fireplace embers were disappearing into ash, allowing a sudden rush of late evening cold to pierce the dissipating warmth.

As the living room temperature dropped, the family moved into action. Marie and her children headed for their respective sleeping quarters.

The big house had two floors, which made it even harder to heat. There were five bedrooms, a large kitchen, a living room, a dining room, a bathroom on each floor, plus the bathroom attached to the master bedroom. In winter, the pipes under the kitchen sink and in the bathrooms were covered with old blankets to prevent them from freezing. Extra blankets would also be needed to keep the family warm against the wintry chill that night for certain.

A staircase with beautiful mahogany railings led up to a long, wide corridor. The master bedroom was at the far end of the hall. Marie went to the room, taking young Robbie into her bed for warmth. Carl and Louise each went to their own rooms, which were located next to each other near the top of the stairs.

Carl lay awake in bed. He had two blankets, but he was still not warm. He cried silently, thinking about how unhappy his family was. Again, he hated his father. After awhile, he started to doze off, but only into a fitful sleep.

In the meantime, Louise was also unable to sleep. She had piled an extra blanket on her bed but was still freezing. She couldn't shut out the bad feelings she was having about her father. She just could not imagine what had happened to make him act so mean toward her mother. Although they fought each other, they must have had sentimental moments. She remembered that when she was a little girl they got along much better than they did now. After all, they got along well enough to bring three children into the world.

Because of the recent arguments and the nature of overheard conversations between her parents, she suspected that her father was spending time with some "floozie," the name her mother used to refer to loose women of the times. Marie had accused him at least several times before and sometimes used pretty strong language when she was really angry. Louise simply could not sleep. She was cold and she was angry.

She conjured up an image of her boyfriend and let her hand slide gracefully down her supple body. As she tried to drift into sleep, she imagined herself as Mrs. Peter Strauss and felt secure in the thought that hers would be a marriage filled with love.

As wonderful as these thoughts of Peter were, she still was not able to overcome the freezing cold. Finally, she remembered that her mother had taken Robbie into her bed for warmth and so she decided to go into the adjacent room where her brother Carl had finally fallen asleep.

She tapped him on the shoulder and he awoke with a start and saw his sister beckoning. "Come in with me, Carl, so we can keep each other warm. It's freezing up here."

When he hesitated, she tugged at him to get him out of bed and just stood there. He was not fully awake, so Louise took his hand and led her sleepy brother into her own bed. Once under the covers, Carl was brought wide awake when Louise snuggled up close to him, rolling him over so that his back was against the contoured front of her own body.

She put her arms around him and he held her hands to his chest. It felt cozy and warm, and the presence of another body added several degrees of warmth. He liked the feeling, except he didn't think it was right to be in bed with his sister.

"This feels great, Louise. It's nice and warm and comfortable, but I don't think it's right for us to be in bed together."

"I'm not going to seduce you, little brother. I just want to keep us warm."

Carl remembered how they used to snuggle together as children. Sometimes the whole family would snuggle in bed together, in fact.

"Okay, Louise. It sure is a lot warmer than being in bed alone. I guess Ma took Robbie in her bed, didn't she?"

"Yes, she did. We're not doing anything wrong. We're only trying to keep warm, just like Ma and Robbie."

Though they had both decided that what they were doing was acceptable, especially in this unbearable cold, they were both now wide awake.

"Carl, remember when we were talking about Pa the other morning? I've been thinking about something you said. Maybe it's not that he's having an affair with Hannah or some other woman. There has to be more to it than that."

"Like what?"

"I don't know. Maybe it's money, like you thought. Whatever it is, Carl, he wouldn't have turned to booze just because he was having an affair. There has to be a lot more to it. I don't like the way he treats Ma. She has to ask him for money all the time, like he doesn't trust her."

"Yeah, I think money is what's behind it. Pa's hiding something. Why else is he being so stingy about the house repairs and making Ma practically beg for an extra penny?"

"I read about a man who started to drink like Pa does when he lost all his money," Louise said.

"Hey, let's get some sleep, Louise. I'm starting to get tired," Carl said as he rolled away from his sister.

"Good night, Carl. I'm sorry if I kept you awake."

In the master bedroom, Robbie slept soundly, warmly cuddled up to his mother. Marie, however, lay awake the whole while and couldn't help but think of her husband.

For about two years now, Marie Grandee was convinced that Thomas was seeing another woman. Not only did she smell whiskey on his breath more and more often, but she had also detected a female body scent on him that confirmed what she really didn't want to know. Recently, she began to notice the obvious fragrance of perfume, which made her even more upset.

The fact that he rarely came near her or ever became intimate was another red flag. On the one or two times that she had the nerve to confront him with the situation, he simply became silent. She was unhappy about this most of all, but she had promised herself not to bring the subject up again.

As much as she realized that she would eventually have to face reality, she was committed not to do so. Having lost confidence in herself as a woman, she was afraid that Thomas would walk out on her altogether. Sometimes she thought it would be best if he did; other times she thought of taking the kids and leaving him. These mixed feelings were wreaking havoc in Marie's life.

There were also times when she thought she still loved Thomas. Then suddenly, frighteningly strong feelings of hate would well up in her. She felt shame for those rare times that Thomas wanted sex with her and she allowed it.

Above all, she had three children to provide for, and if putting up with Thomas' behavior was what she had to do, she would do it. Poverty was so prevalent in 1938 that the modest security Thomas offered made it practically impossible for her to think of walking out. He was far from rich, but he still earned a steady week's pay.

Thomas Grandee gave Marie money on a weekly basis, and only for the barest of necessities: food and clothing as needed. Otherwise, he handled everything himself and demanded complete control. Besides, if she left him, where would she go and what would she do? She had no skills other than motherhood.

Earlier that week, Marie and Thomas had argued once more about the lack of repairs in the house. It ended as always, with a promise that, this time, something would be done. Now, for three days, he had failed to return home. If she called him at The Chateau, he would say that he was busy.

She was sleeping in an empty bed, freezing cold, and she knew that her kids were freezing with her. Perhaps it was time for her to do something about it. She vowed to summon the strength to have it out with him one more time when he finally came back from whatever it was that was keeping him away in the first place.

She got her chance early Sunday morning, when Thomas arrived with a load of logs and kindling. He unloaded his pickup truck and started a fresh fire in the freezing living room. As he turned away from the fireplace, Skip trotted over to greet him. Instead of the usual roughing up and playing, he pushed the dog away. For a brief second he felt an impulse to just kick the dog, but he didn't.

Although he had been drinking, he was aware that something else was wrong. He couldn't understand his own frustration. Although he really did know the answer, his mind, often numbed by the alcohol, refused to allow him to truly comprehend the situation.

The fireplace was beginning to give warmth but Thomas was still cold. He walked over to the burning logs and watched for a few moments, attempting to ignite new logs. He began to feel sufficient heat as he threw off his overcoat, double-breasted suit jacket and started to unbutton his vest. Thomas dressed formally for his work at The Chateau.

As he rubbed his hands together over the fire that was now beginning to burn evenly, the logs crackled and shot tiny bursts of color up into the flue. He began to pace back and forth, taking long, studied strides as though he was deep in worried thought.

Thomas was well built, muscular and well proportioned. A handsome man well over six feet tall and now 200 pounds, he could carry himself with perfect posture. Thomas Grandee showed no outward sign of the effect of the beer and whiskey he consumed. It was, however, evident in the confusion that swirled inside his mind.

After a few moments, he strode upstairs and walked into the open bedroom, where he was shocked to find Carl and Louise lying side-by-side together. They were both startled awake when he shouted, "What the hell are you two kids up to?"

Louise tried to assure her father that they were only cuddled together to stay warm, and Carl smiled meekly in agreement.

"Shit, you can't fool me!" was Thomas' reply.

Carl was almost as tall and husky as his father, but Thomas easily yanked Carl up and smashed him in the jaw. He had never hit Carl before, but this time, he hit him so hard that blood spurted out of his mouth.

"You two have been up to something you damn well should not be doing!"

Louise screamed, "It was all my fault. I was freezing, so I got Carlie to come to bed with me. Don't you hit him!" she continued to scream as she burst into tears.

Thomas turned toward Louise, moving closer. She smelled whiskey on his breath. He slapped her hard, then turned to leave.

Carl jumped up and grabbed his father's arms and yanked him around so that they faced each other. Thomas was startled, but he simply stood there with his mouth agape. Carl shouted, "I hate you. Now look at what you've done. You hit my sister for no good reason. All we were trying to do was to stay warm. It's your fault that the house is falling apart. It's your fault that we're freezing to death. All we did was try to keep warm."

Thomas' mind had not yet fully cleared from the alcohol of the night before, and he couldn't absorb what Louise and Carl were telling him. He was outraged at what he thought his son and daughter had been doing. From the sound of the fury in his son's voice, he vaguely surmised that he was guilty of something. In his confusion, he simply turned away from his children and stomped out of the bedroom.

Marie thought that she had heard noises coming from Louise's bedroom, and the next thing she heard was Thomas, shouting.

"Marie, I'm home. What's to eat in this damn place?" He was walking across the upstairs hall toward the master bedroom, and he marched straight into their bedroom while still shouting. "Get your ass the hell out of bed!"

She knew from experience that whenever Thomas raised his voice and used crude language, he had been drinking heavily. Unaware of what had just transpired, she also knew at times like these there would be no success in her efforts to suggest to her husband that he attend to anything, never mind house repairs. Yet, all she could think of was the extreme cold that she and the family had been forced to endure that night.

"We're freezing here, Thomas," she pleaded as she stepped out of bed and put on her robe. She put her hands against Thomas' chest in an attempt to pacify him.

Thomas pushed her away. "Quit whining!" he said.

"Please, Thomas, you promised you would take care of the heating and get things fixed. You don't know how cold it got last night. You have to do something."

"If I told you once, I told you a million times, stop nagging me. It'll get done when I get around to it. Now let's get some damn breakfast."

Marie could take it no longer. She swung her hand hard across Thomas' face and screamed, "You bastard. You stay out all night with some floozie while we freeze ourselves here in a house that's falling apart. We're not taking it any more. If you don't stop drinking and staying away for days at a time, you'll be coming home to an empty house."

Thomas stood absolutely still. He had been taken completely by surprise. It was the first time Marie had ever struck him. Words, yes, they had argued plenty. He didn't know how to react. Suddenly ridden with guilt, he was shocked to find that his wife could be so hurt that she would stand up against him with such anger.

Thomas Grandee had always felt somewhat uneasy about the fact that he was ignoring the necessary repairs for the house. He knew that the work had to be done, but he was afraid to spend the money to make the repairs. There were too many financial complications right now and he did not intend to discuss them with anyone, least of all Marie. He decided to change the subject.

"I caught Carl and Louise in bed together. What the hell is *that* all about?"

Marie was taken aback for a moment. She had no idea that her son and daughter had slept in the same bed. Then she looked to her own bed and saw Robbie, who was now weeping quietly out of fear.

"Oh, poor Robbie," Marie said. "Ma and Pa don't mean any harm, sweetheart. We're both just cold, too. Please don't cry." Bundling him up in her arms and putting him into a bathrobe, she turned to Thomas and said, "I took Robbie into my bed because it was cold. Carl and Louise must have done the same. I don't think there's anything wrong in trying to keep warm. Let's not argue in front of Robbie. You go on downstairs and we'll follow as soon as we're washed and dressed."

"Yeah, okay, but I still don't like the idea of Carl and Louise in bed together."

"Neither do I," Marie responded. "I'll speak to them."

Shocked and pained from their father's actions, Carl and Louise had hurried to wash and dress, and they were already downstairs in the kitchen. Louise cooked porridge while they both stood warming themselves at the stove. They pretended nothing had happened, but kept their distance from each other while neither said a word.

When Marie finally came down into the kitchen with Robbie, she saw Carl's swollen, red face. "What *happened* to you, Carl?"

"I hurt myself getting out of bed this morning, Ma. It's all right." He glanced at Louise as if to say, *"Don't say a word!"*

Marie did not believe Carl, but she didn't know what to say. Her mind was still racing after the earlier exchange with her husband. She did not believe in corporal punishment for her children and had made this point perfectly clear in the past. This, however, was far beyond any acceptable parental behavior.

She now understood that Thomas was at a stage where he could easily become violent. Although he had never struck her, Marie knew that he could become verbally abusive when he had been drinking. She was suddenly very alarmed and understood that the time had come to take some sort of action.

For the moment, she knew that it was best to let things settle down. Thomas was going through a metamorphosis of a new and unsettling kind, and the emotional situation had greatly intensified for Marie. Paradoxically, she felt an inner surge of power that she could not quite define. Her anger had already overcome the mixed feelings of fear and anguish, but her intellect told her that she needed time to think. Obviously, further rebuttal was not the solution.

Marie knew that Thomas held all the purse strings. The house was in his name alone, and so were both the checking and savings account. As the Grandee family sat around the kitchen table eating breakfast, Marie surmised that Thomas had lost control upon finding Carl and Louise in bed together. She understood why this must have been a startling sight, no matter what the circumstance. However, a physically violent response on Thomas' part was inappropriate and dangerous. She knew that she would have to talk to her children alone to learn exactly what had happened.

After breakfast, she sent Robbie to collect trash from the wastebaskets. As he always did, Thomas went into the living room to read the Sunday paper. His whiskey smell was still strong enough for Marie to guess that he would quickly fall into a sound sleep.

In the kitchen, Carl and Louise finished cleaning up. Marie sat the two children down at the kitchen table, well out of earshot of the large living room where Thomas was now snoozing on the overstuffed couch.

Marie came right out and asked the two of them if they had been in bed together the night before and if it was true that Thomas had found them that way this morning. Louise leaned forward and put her hands out in front of her on the table.

"Ma, please don't look at us that way. Don't blame Carl— blame me. I was freezing cold and worried about you and Pa. I couldn't sleep and I needed to talk to someone."

"Hush, Louise. I know you kids are upset about your father. I am, too. I expect that he's having some serious problems, but this is between your father and me. We're the ones who have to work out family matters. Now, I want you to tell me if your father hit Carl."

Louise looked at her brother, as if for permission to speak for the both of them. "Pa hit Carl—*real hard*—-and he slapped me, too."

Carl added, "Louise didn't do anything bad. We were just keeping warm. That's all there was to it. Honest, Ma.

"If Pa fixed the heating and stuff, we wouldn't have been in bed together. So what if it costs money? You need to talk to him about this darn house. If not, I will."

"Please, Carl, don't be mad at me. You know how your father is with money. Everything is a big secret. But let's not change the subject. We were talking about the two of you being in bed together. Be honest now and tell me if this sort of thing has happened before."

"Just this one time, honest," Carl said. "Because it was so darn cold."

"It's like the way you take Robbie in with you," Louise said. "I thought Carl and I could do the same . . . just to keep warm. Honest Ma, we didn't *do anything* if that's what you're thinking."

"God forbid. Not my two wonderful children," Marie responded quickly. "But next time you get real cold, you had better just get extra blankets. I don't ever want to hear that you two got into bed together again."

Carl blushed and Louise said, "Don't worry, Ma. Never again."

Marie was satisfied that nothing serious had happened and she would try to straighten Thomas out on that score. In the meantime, the kitchen clock told her that she should be on her way to Sunday Mass. She asked her children if they would like to join her as she usually did, knowing that each would make one excuse or another. Actually, it had been a long time since she was able to get either of her two oldest to attend services. Only she and Robbie were regulars at Holy Rosary Church.

Chapter Two

THOMAS GRANDEE WAS SUCCESSFUL AS THE MANAGER of The Chateau. The Naval Shipyard was close by, and the tavern catered to the thousands of workers who were employed at the yard.

Thomas' schedule was from six in the morning until four in the afternoon. Lunch was the busiest time of day, when many of the workers arrived for a glass of beer and a sandwich. Some workers also stopped by for an early morning cup of coffee and scrambled eggs and bacon. A few downed a glass of beer with an egg in it before proceeding to their job at the yard.

On Friday and Saturday, Thomas would drive home to Malden for early dinner and then return to help with the Friday and Saturday night crowds. The tavern was closed on Sunday. During the week, The Chateau usually was not very busy at the dinner hour.

There was a night assistant who arrived at four and stayed until midnight. As manager, Thomas had the freedom to work out a personal schedule to suit his needs. As long as the tavern was profitable, no one minded.

He usually sat at a table in the far corner of the dining room. From that particular vantage point he could survey the entire restaurant, the bar and the door to the kitchen. Large plate glass windows with hand-painted block lettering, along with chalkboard specials that changed daily, beckoned to locals. The bar was solid oak in a horseshoe shape, with a hammered brass top and a beveled glass back. High-backed wooden booths and a handful of round tables with red-and-white checkered cloths on top of white tile floors smothered in sawdust gave the room a familiar and comfortable feeling.

There were three waitresses and two bartenders that alternated shifts. Generally, the patrons were local workers in their twenties and thirties, couples of all ages and a handful of regulars that usually stopped in after work for an hour or two and simply drank and conversed at the bar.

Today, Thomas signaled for Victor Hermanssen to come over and sit with him. Victor was the custodian and he and Thomas often sat together and talked. Thomas pointed to the bar and signaled with a jerk of the head for Victor to bring a couple of beers.

"Feeling lonely again, Thomas?" Victor said as he put the two brews on the table and got comfortable.

"I always feel lonely in this place. All the chatter around us has nothing to do with me or with you. It's just a lot of noise."

Thomas didn't smoke. Yet, even the smell of stale cigars and the smoke from cigarettes that filled the room during busy hours somehow left him undisturbed. It was as though he wasn't really of this world.

Usually he and Victor talked about the business details of the restaurant and bar. At other times, it was just small talk to pass a few hours while they drank a beer or had a shot of scotch or whiskey together. The two men had an understanding that anything said would be held in strictest confidence.

"Hey, Thomas, I think you pay me just to sit around and talk to you. I've got work to do upstairs, you know."

"Victor, I pay you to do what I tell you to do. And don't think I don't know about that drunken fight two of our wonderful patrons had in the bathroom upstairs the day before yesterday. You get right up there after we finish our little conversation here."

"Okay, you're the boss. I'm listening. But don't blame me if my work falls behind."

"Victor, don't play games with me. The plumbing company is going to replace the broken toilet. Aside from about an hour's scrubbing, you don't have a thing to do until after closing time."

"That's because I do a good job of maintenance, right?"

"I'd fire you if you didn't. And you damn well better know it."

What Thomas didn't know was that the plumbing and cleanup of the upstairs bathroom had been completed the day before. Victor really had nothing much on his schedule except to go upstairs and take a nap in the empty room.

"What's on your mind, Thomas?"

27

"You know I've got these friends that I visit with on Tremont Street, right?" Thomas said.

Victor nursed his beer. Thomas talked a lot about these "friends," but was short on supplying details.

"What's so special about these friends, Thomas?" Victor asked, though he really didn't care what Thomas did or didn't do on Tremont Street, or anywhere else for that matter.

"I go to a brownstone there because it's stressful here and I really don't like what I'm doing."

When Victor spoke with Thomas, he did so only to get information that he could use to his advantage later. Other times, he liked to egg Thomas on, to get his goat. Most importantly, though, Victor was smart enough to know when Thomas was using him to get things off his chest. But Victor didn't mind being used. He was getting paid for it.

"So what's so special about this brownstone on Tremont Street? How does that help your stress?" Victor asked.

"It has *everything* to do with it. There are people in that brownstone that I know and that I enjoy talking to. They listen to my problems and it relieves my tension. I go there because I need a break from this place."

"I really thought that you liked what you were doing here. You certainly look happy enough when you're with the customers. Besides, you're doing a hell of a good job as a manager, Thomas. How can you say you don't like the work? Not to be too nosy, but are some of those friends of yours women?"

"Victor, I have a wife and three kids."

"I know that, Thomas. I ought to mind my own business," Victor said, though he was now very interested in the goings-on at the Tremont Street brownstone; if Thomas got into trouble, Victor could inherit his job. And women were trouble.

The brownstone that Thomas frequented was in the South End of Boston. It had once been a high-class section of town boasting mostly aristocratic residents, but had since given way, as had most of the innermost environs of prominent cities, to the changing demographics brought about by the automobile and by improved public transportation.

By the 1930s, autos had proven to be reliable for getting around. This made it possible for those that could afford to own a car and a fine home in the suburbs to easily commute to their new ivory tower offices in the heart of the city. The city's growing population and the frequent appearance, noise and pollution of automobiles were further incentive for families of means to favor expanding suburbs.

Those who could afford to had long since moved into cleaner and quieter suburbs surrounding central cities in the nation. Many former mansions in parts of urban Boston had already become rundown tenements.

Not only did Thomas Grandee not specify whom he visited or what he did, he never mentioned the sordid humanity that he often saw lurking and even curled up on the sidewalk in what was now a slum of the city. Both male and female drunks now publicly slept off their stupors after slugging down whatever mind-deadening liquid they could beg, borrow or steal in order to free themselves of the agony of growing impoverishment.

Though the government tried to help the unemployed, and Roosevelt, with his New Deal, had taken aim at relieving the state of the nation's poor, there were still thousands in larger cities who were penniless and homeless from self-neglect or mental illness, or sheer exhaustion. Thomas naturally avoided describing these scenes to Victor, since it would give away too much about where he went when he left The Chateau.

Because Victor was his subordinate at work, Thomas didn't want Victor to know too much about him. Besides, the two men were very different; even in appearance, the contrast between them was great. Thomas, as the manager, was always dressed in a double-breasted suit. Victor, as custodian, was always dressed more informally, mostly in pants, loose-fitting shirts and, in cool weather, a sweater.

Thomas was also bigger and much better looking. Victor stood only five-feet-seven. He was a man of about 40, stocky and bald with a fringe of gray hair on the back of his scalp. He had unusually strong hands and a large, bulbous nose that held up his gold horn-rimmed glasses well. His eyes were plain and black compared to Thomas' striking blue.

Thomas often teased Victor. He felt that Victor was a man without emotion because he always appeared docile and uninterested. Thomas often urged Victor to loosen up and get some fun out of life.

"Victor," he had recently asked, "you're not married, yet you show little interest in women. What is it with you?"

Victor was usually able to temper Thomas' remarks, but this particular comment provoked him. Coupled with the fact that he had already had three beers as well as a shot of whiskey, he decided to stick his neck out.

"I like women, but only when they come easy. You tell me that you go over to Tremont Street. I bet there are women over there. I don't want to pry, but it seems to me that you and Marie are not getting on well. I think you have it on with Hannah, too, if you ask me."

Usually soft-spoken, Thomas raised his voice, "You leave my wife and Hannah out of this, Victor. I'm warning you." He clenched his fist, then slowly extended his fingers, trying to work out his anger. "Let's not discuss my business. Let's talk about you."

Victor hesitated for just a moment. When it came to confrontations, Victor quickly became a white feather. "I said that I like women, but only if they come easy. I've had my share and I still get what I need. Don't forget the upstairs rooms over the weekends. Besides, some people talk about women and don't act. I keep my mouth shut."

The tavern had a few overnight units upstairs for business or government people visiting the Navy Yard. These were the rooms that Victor was referring to. Thomas also made sure that one of the units was always available for his own use. In that way, he could stay through the night when he claimed he had to be there late for business, which now turned out to be every Friday and Saturday night. The room was also always available during the week if he decided he needed it. For a moment, he wondered about Victor's remark about the weekend and the upstairs rooms.

Thomas decided to drop the subject of women. He still found Victor a good drinking companion and insisted upon his joining him for a glass of beer or a shot of whiskey at least once each day.

He felt it best to allay his anger by discontinuing the now too-personal conversation.

Although Victor had a taste for whiskey, he was the kind of person who preferred to do his drinking in private, and when he wanted to, not when someone else suggested. Victor played along with Thomas because he didn't want to alienate his boss. On the whole, Victor and Thomas got along pretty well—except when it came to Hannah.

Thomas Grandee managed The Chateau for Bob Morrison, a local banker who was also a partner in the Morrison and Braverman Realty Company. The company owned the tavern along with several other properties. While Sam Braverman was the active partner in the realty company, Bob Morrison was involved in The Chateau because he knew the previous owner's widow.

When Morrison arranged the purchase from the widow, he inherited Thomas Grandee as manager. That had been just over two years ago. Morrison and his partner were satisfied, however, because the business appeared to be operating smoothly since.

The Chateau was the only property in the realty company's holdings that Bob Morrison actually had a hands-on connection with. His daily tasks at the bank kept him preoccupied, so Morrison visited The Chateau only at the end of each month to spend an hour or so in the tavern's office perusing the books. Otherwise, he had Sam Braverman send Hannah Ward, the realty company's secretary, to collect the daily receipts. Hannah was a very pretty brunette, about 25 and flirtatious. She arrived customarily at The Chateau shortly after lunch hour.

Victor Hermanssen liked his whiskey alone. When Thomas hired him as a custodian four years ago, the thought of "on the house" whiskey that Thomas hinted at made the minimum wage job sound more attractive. That, plus a free room in the back of the tavern, and Victor was satisfied. Jobs were still scarce at the time, so in the beginning it really was a dream come true for Victor.

By the end of his first day, he found that Thomas kept his word about the booze. Thomas also liked his whiskey but he preferred company when he imbibed, which was more often than it should have been.

Victor got a kick out of Hannah's flirting. She never failed to flash him a sensuous smile. But with Thomas, he noticed, Hannah was more serious, at least in front of everyone. And when she went with Thomas into his private office to pick up the day's receipts, it took an unusually long time.

Thomas had the office well-furnished, with a walnut desk, swivel chair, nice draperies and a comfortable sofa, big and plush enough to allow for a good night's sleep. A night manager, Brad Reilly, also shared the office.

Thomas tolerated his liquor very well. If he drank during his regular working hours, he always did so in moderation, and was always able to keep up appearances and perform his job. It was only when he was ready to go home at the end of the day that he drank heavily enough to affect him. That is what his family saw.

Victor thought it was undignified for the manager of The Chateau to drink during working hours, and in front of staff and patrons especially. He had once mentioned this to Thomas, to which he had snapped, "My drinking doesn't affect me and you know it. You never saw me drunk."

"I didn't say you get drunk. I know that you can hold your liquor. So can I. A glass of beer once in awhile might look okay, but why don't you go into your private office to do your drinking? I really think some customers don't like to see you drink in the restaurant."

"No one ever complains, Victor. I like sitting at the table and having a shot. I can see everything that goes on."

After that one brief exchange, Victor thought it best not to bring the subject up again.

Bob Morrison knew that Thomas sometimes downed a shot or a glass of beer in front of the patrons. Since he didn't come in often, he had only witnessed it once or twice. He had no qualms about how the place was being managed as long as there were no customer complaints and the business continued to prosper.

Morrison was also convinced that Thomas was an attraction. The whole town knew Thomas and liked him. Some even came to The Chateau for a drink, a glass of beer or a famous roast beef sandwich, just to see what the place was all about. Thomas made it interesting for the customers. He was a handsome man and was always amiable to the patrons.

The very things that Victor objected to became the attractions that brought new patrons to the restaurant. Thomas would sit at a table in the dining area just as though he was a customer himself, enjoying a hearty lunch or dinner. He often looked up and smiled at passersby.

He would also often walk around to each table and ask the customers if they liked the food, drink and service. If anyone complained, he would deliberately add ten cents to the bill. Customers who refused to pay the extra dime were simply asked to leave without paying for the meal.

The rare few that did leave never returned, thus eliminating dissatisfied customers. However, practically all the complainers did so just to see what would happen. In the end, they actually paid the extra dime and had a good laugh. It was a fun show and it attracted business. The real money at The Chateau, however, came from the beer and booze; the drinks were always paid for as served, cash on the table.

The rapport that Thomas developed with patrons of The Chateau was unique. Once, after Victor had left to attend to his chores, Larry, one of the regulars, came over to Thomas at the corner table and asked about the small collection box that had recently been placed at the far end of the bar.

"Mr. Grandee, I'm curious. I saw a money box on the bar with 'Boy's Town' on it. Is that something new?"

"Not really *new*, Larry. Boy's Town just became popular because of the film."

"What the devil is it all about?"

Thomas knew that the box would raise the eyebrows of some regulars who would eventually ask questions about its purpose. The box served as much as a topic for conversation as it did for its cause.

"The place was started a few years ago by a priest named Father Flanagan. Boy's Town originated in Italy and is now out in Nebraska. They take in homeless boys and help them build a better life. We can all use a little of that now, can't we Larry?"

"Sure can, Thomas. Thanks for the information."

As Larry returned to the bar, Thomas wondered whether or not there really was any such thing as a better life while guzzling down the last drops from his shot glass.

Remembering a previous conversation with Victor about the house on Tremont Street, Thomas decided that he was in need of a visit later in the day. He went to the phone and called Margaret at the house.

"Margaret, it's Thomas here. I would like to visit with Glenda later today and I may want to stay the night."

"I'm sure that will be fine, Thomas. I'll let her know." Thomas was a regular at the house on Tremont Street, and Glenda was his favorite.

Chapter Three

IT WAS SATURDAY AGAIN. THOMAS THOUGHT BACK and realized how badly he had behaved the previous weekend. That was the real reason that he had made arrangements for a visit to Tremont Street; he had no desire to face his family. Thomas called home to say he would not be able to make early Saturday dinner. He told Victor to tell Brad Reilly, the night manager that he would not be in that evening and asked Victor to help out in the restaurant if needed. As usual, Victor was cooperative.

Thomas knew that he visited Glenda out of desperation, out of the need to unburden himself from feelings that needed expression. He used Glenda and he used Victor, two people who represented a safe form of otherness since neither were an integral part of his life. He knew that he could walk away from either of them and continue his place in public life. Victor was a loner, a man without roots in the social fabric of society. Glenda operated in a profession of silence and secrecy. It was the secrecy that attracted him.

Thomas also went to Glenda because he felt guilty about things that he needed to keep secret. What he refused to acknowledge to himself was the fact that each visit only added one more secret that would serve to make him even guiltier. It was a vicious cycle.

A "madame" named Margaret greeted Thomas at the handsome brownstone door.

"Welcome, Thomas, can I get you a cup of coffee or something to drink?"

"No, thank you, Margaret, not tonight."

Margaret signaled her acknowledgement with a nod and a wave of hand. She told him that Glenda was waiting for him in her room at the end of the hallway.

Just as Margaret had said, Glenda was waiting for his knock and she opened her room door promptly. Thomas stepped into a room dimly lit by several tasseled crystal lamps, ornate velvet-pillowed chairs, a small mahogany roll-top desk with matching chair, and the center of attraction, an oversized, intricately carved four-poster bed.

Heavy velvet drapes concealed windows that were usually left open, and there was always a scent of room fragrance as well as fresh perfume wafting through the large room.

Glenda was an attractive woman of about 25. She had bleached blond hair that was always curly and worn short. Tall and rather slender, the top of her head reached to about Thomas' nose. He hugged her and held on to her for a long while without saying a word. It was she who broke the silence.

"Do you want to get under the covers, Thomas, or shall we just sit and talk? I have scotch and ice cubes on the sideboard."

"A shot would be nice, Glenda. Let's sit for a while."

"Whatever you want," she said as she poured. "One neat scotch coming right up. Do you mind if I sip some wine?"

"That's fine with me. I want to talk to you, Glenda. Just let me relax a bit first."

"Whatever you want, Thomas. I gather you have lots of problems at The Chateau. Did you have a hard day?"

"It's my life that's the problem. *Me*, Glenda, I'm the problem."

"Why don't we get undressed and slip under the covers once we finish our drinks, Thomas? You know you'll be more relaxed that way, and you can just close your eyes and talk your heart out."

Thomas was one of Glenda's regulars, so there were always clean pajamas and a bathrobe to accommodate his overnight stays. She was already dressed in a pink chemise that she wore under a pale red silk robe.

Glenda draped the robe over her desk chair before slipping under the covers with Thomas. They lay now side-by-side, holding hands. Thomas didn't speak for quite some time.

Glenda knew Thomas well enough by now to know when something was bothering him. He often spent the night with her when he seemed unusually troubled. On those evenings, Glenda's bed doubled as a psychiatrist's couch. Glenda finally turned toward him and said, "Thomas, cuddle up next to me. It will make you feel better."

Thomas turned toward her and held her firmly. He was almost on the verge of tears.

"I punched Carl in the jaw last weekend. I slapped Louise and nearly kicked the life out of the dog. I think I'm losing it, Glenda."

"You poor baby. You know, you ought to give up that job of yours. I know how much you hate it. Isn't there some other work that might be more to your liking?"

"I screwed that one up a long time ago. I never should have given up on school. God, am I mixed up."

Glenda stroked him gently. "Here, honey baby, don't you blame yourself. You did it right. You were in love and you promised to marry her. Nothing was wrong with that."

"It was still a screwup. Maybe if we didn't have the kids right away it would have been different. That was the end of my life."

"Thomas, you can't go back. You have to let it go and make the best of your life now. You have a great job and a wonderful family. You are a success!"

"There's more going on at The Chateau than just success, Glenda."

"Oh, something you haven't told me?"

"Yes, something I haven't told anyone."

"Do you want to talk about it, Thomas?"

"Maybe someday. It's not important now."

What Thomas had failed to tell Glenda—though she suspected as much—was the real reason he had started to come to Tremont Street in the first place; there was something going on back at work that had distanced him from Marie and his children.

Naturally, that had only made matters worse. In reality, Thomas had found, on Tremont Street, a safe haven for airing his problems. Sex was only one small part of his original motives for his visits there. Conversation had replaced any sexual fever that was more easily dulled by alcohol.

Glenda tried what she did best. She lifted her chemise and reached over to Thomas, touching his privates. It was flaccid but she could feel it stir. She stroked to help it along. His penis became robust and firm and she thought she was about to finally get this mama's boy to put it in. But Thomas simply just pushed her hand aside. "Not tonight, Glenda," he said, weakly, as he began to flag.

Glenda sensuously stroked his hand and then his face. She stroked everything but the place she wanted to stroke the most. She held him until the scotch finally took its toll and he fell asleep. I'm this guy's mother again tonight, that's for sure, she thought.

Early Sunday morning after Thomas left, Glenda sat with Margaret, eating breakfast in the oversized kitchen with several of the other girls who were not still on call from the busy weekend night. Sometimes, the girls talked about their "Johns," which Margaret encouraged because it kept her informed of the needs of her key clients and also of any potential problems with the girls before they really surfaced.

That morning, Glenda was acting curiously and was asking the others if they ever had men that mostly wanted to be held and talked to and did not want to have sex.

"This man dresses in his pajamas *before* we get into bed and makes me keep my nightgown on as we fall asleep. During the short visits, sometimes we just sit next to the desk and talk. The guy is very moody. I never know what he wants."

"It happens," Margaret chimed in; hoping to allay what she knew would be Glenda's own fears and insecurity. "You're not the first one, Glenda, with a customer that pays for the opportunity to just let off steam. I've had men come to me who spent the entire time talking about their wives or girlfriends. I think each of us has had unusual experiences in one way or another."

"You can say that again," one of the other girls agreed.

Glenda continued, "Another thing about my guy is that he starts talking about drinking." She went on to explain how Thomas confessed that he was able to put up a good front while at work, even when he drank heavily. But, he was behaving more like a real drunk when he went home to his wife and kids.

Margaret thought for a moment and then explained, "I think that means the guy really does have problems with his wife and kids, wouldn't you say?"

"I don't think so," Glenda responded. "He hates his job. He loves his wife and kids. I think *that's* his real problem. It's hard to explain, but he just can't get it all together." She thought for a moment and then added, "*I* can't get it all together. The guy is sexy, smart, has a responsible job, family he cares for, and me! What more does the guy need?"

"Sounds like the guy needs some serious help, Glenda. More than the kind that we can provide," Margaret said.

One of the girls added, "Sounds to me like Glenda is the one who is going to need some help." They all nodded and laughed.

Chapter Four

IT WAS 1920 AND THOMAS' TIME TO be a star. He had just been voted Best High School Quarterback in Massachusetts for the second time. All the other kids at Revere High School envied him. Thomas, however, was not a happy senior. His report cards throughout high school were just barely good enough to get him promoted. He even worried whether or not he would graduate with his class in June of 1920.

His girlfriend, Marie Sullivan, assured him that he would get his high school diploma. "Maybe you can't pass a test, but you're bright and the teachers know that, so they'll make sure you graduate with the rest of us." She looked him straight in the eye, then she kissed him on the lips and stepped back and smiled. "Thomas Grandee, I am absolutely sure of it."

"Thanks for your confidence, Marie. I just wish I was as sure as you."

Marie was right. Thomas would graduate with the rest of his class in June of 1920. However, Boston College turned him down, and soon after, Thomas was hit with another piece of bad news. Marie missed her second period right before graduation.

She was a nervous wreck all through the graduation ceremony. She, her best friend Betty Herman and Thomas all graduated together. Betty Herman was her absolute best friend since they had grown up together. The two families were next-door neighbors.

Betty's mother used to persist in saying, "Maidele, why don't you play with the nice Jewish boys and girls?" After a while, though, Mrs. Herman gave up. The little girls were in and out of each other's houses all the time, and Mrs. Herman grew to enjoy Marie. She explained to her husband, "Marie is a lovely little child and the Sullivans are nice people. And, she is not a goyishe *boy*."

Both Betty's and Marie's families were waiting for the school season to finish before moving away from Revere. Betty and Marie were also both hoping that the families would move to a place near each other. The Hermans had already placed a deposit on a house in Malden's primarily Jewish Suffolk Square neighborhood.

The Sullivans had been looking to relocate in either Malden or Everett. Everett Station was a subway terminal just a couple of easy stops from City Square, Charlestown, near the Navy Yard where Marie's father, John Sullivan, worked.

It had been coincidence that the elder Sullivans and Hermans had planned to move away from Revere. While they both had similar reasons for wanting to leave the vicinity, they had not shared their feelings with each other. In fact, even though Marie and Betty were the best of friends, their parents had little contact other than to say hello and exchange polite conversation when they saw each other.

The parents were friendly enough because they had been neighbors for many years and because Marie and Betty remained closest friends. Other than Marie and Betty, the families were not particularly compatible. Mrs. Herman's friends were all Jewish and Mrs. Sullivan's friends were members of St. Michael's Catholic Church Parish. What they shared was a common desire to move from a once peaceful Shirley Avenue in Revere.

It was nice to be near Revere Beach in the summertime. The beach was beautiful and the hot dog stands and amusement concessions made for great fun. What was happening, however, was that the fun was shifting to the people who came to visit. Living in the middle of one of New England's hottest local tourist spots was becoming increasingly difficult. Revere Beach was Greater Boston's equivalent of Coney Island.

Tens of thousands of people came to Revere Beach on a nice summer day. They arrived on foot or by horse-and-buggy. Some families arrived in motorcars and a few came on tandem bicycles. For the most part, they arrived by streetcar.

Several streetcars were often hitched together to accommodate the large numbers of people as trolley excursions grew in popularity. On top of all that, the Boston, Revere Beach and Lynn Railroad had trains that ran every 10 or 15 minutes and the fare was only five cents. Everyone was traveling to Revere Beach during the summer. New methods of transportation were definitely changing all facets of urban and even suburban life.

When Marie found out that her father had settled on a house in Malden, she was pleased that she would at least be in the same city as Betty. Not very familiar with Malden geography, she hoped that she wouldn't be too far away from her best friend.

Noise and traffic were the Sullivan's main reason for deciding to change residence, but her father seemed to have another concern. One of the few secrets that Marie had kept from Betty during the moving process was a conversation that she had overheard between her parents one night in the parlor, discussing the fact that Shirley Avenue was becoming "too Jewish."

"I have nothing against the Jews," her father had explained. "I'm sure many of them are fine, upstanding citizens. It's just that I'm not prepared to live in a Jewish neighborhood. I want my kids brought up like I was, in Christian surroundings. I don't think it's right for them to mix with Jews and other foreigners."

People tended to live and socialize with others who shared their ethnicity or religion. Due to prejudice or fear, close friends of different backgrounds, like Betty and Marie, were not the norm.

However, with the growth of democratic values in America, children were being brought up together and even attending the same public schools. It was their parents who chose to impose tradition, and sometimes prejudice, upon their offspring. It was a confusing time everywhere, filled with new inventions, new ideas and mixed emotions.

As it turned out, Malden Square, the town's center, was just a short distance away from both of their newly acquired homes. The Sullivans ended up with a place just off Main Street, near the Everett border and within minutes of a trolley ride to Everett Station. So Marie and Betty would still live close to one another.

The morning after graduation, Marie called Betty. They arranged to meet for lunch at Schwartz's Delicatessen on Shirley Avenue in Revere.

After ordering lunch, Marie immediately started in. "You're my best friend, Betty. Can I ask you a serious question?"

"Marie! How can you even ask that?"

"It's about Thomas."

"Whatever it is, Marie, you can ask and you know you can trust me."

"I know. I really love Thomas, Betty. Next week is graduation and he's worried that he might not make it. I'm sure he will because he would have been told by now, but Thomas doesn't have the confidence that everyone thinks he has. Anyway, he wasn't able to get into college because he has such poor grades."

"Why is college so important to him, especially if he has such a hard time with his school work? He should have gotten in just on his athletic record, anyway. Don't forget, Thomas was voted best high school quarterback two years in a row."

"I know, but that's not good enough. His marks are terrible. He's hardly passed a test in the last four years of school. He says he just freezes in the middle and can't think. Anyway, he wasn't accepted at Boston College, where he really wants to go."

"Has he tried any of the other schools, Marie?"

"No. He was so sure he would get into BC because of his football record. He says that he might want to go back and repeat a year at Revere High with the help of a private tutor if he can get his parents to pay for it."

"Will they do that?"

"I doubt it. They don't have much faith in him as a student, and they think he ought to just get a job someplace and 'not try to be what he obviously isn't.'"

"I'm surprised. Thomas' father has a good job at the Navy Yard. They could afford to help him if that's what he wants."

"You know that his brother John was class Valedictorian and a straight-A student. They told Thomas that all the brains went to his older brother. Anyway, they're dead set against his trying to get educated. They told him not to waste his time."

"That's mean. I feel bad for him, Marie. And he's so handsome! All the girls envy you."

Thomas Grandee gave the impression to the other kids that he was always in control, and he behaved maturely. When kids got together for a game or to socialize, Thomas was usually the leader. At six-feet-two and 190 pounds, he hovered over his classmates.

Marie finally worked up enough courage to get to the important reason she wanted to talk to her friend. "Betty, I have something else I have to tell you about Thomas. Actually, it's about Thomas and me."

"What is it, Marie?"

"I'm pregnant."

"What? Didn't you guys use anything?"

"Well, kind of. We only did it twice, Betty. Thomas withdrew both times." Marie was on the verge of tears.

Betty took her friend's hand. "Does *he* know?"

"No, I haven't told anyone yet, but I missed two periods and I've seen the doctor." Marie couldn't control it any longer and burst into tears. Betty, who was a good four inches shorter than her friend, pulled Marie's head down onto her shoulder and stroked her hair until she became calm again.

"Oh, God, Marie, you're too young to have a baby. You should see someone and do something about it."

"I *can't*, Betty. My parents would *kill* me. Abortion is against our religion, and against everything I believe in. Oh, God. Whatever I do, my parents are going to murder me."

"You don't even have to tell them, Marie."

"If it was you, Betty, I guess you'd have an abortion, wouldn't you?"

"I don't know for sure, Marie. Probably. Yes. I guess I would. I'm not ready for marriage or children. Not yet."

"Betty, it's not only against my religion. It's against the law."

"I know, and I think that's wrong. The point is that I don't think the government or anyone else should decide for you."

"And what about my religion and the life that's now inside of me."

"Marie, that life inside of you is a seed right now. You can either let it grow into a baby or not. There will be plenty of time for you to raise a family after your life gets settled and you get married. As far as your religion is concerned, I can't advise you."

"But you think I'm wrong to have the baby, don't you"

"No, Marie. That's not true. I just think a woman should have the right to choose. If you feel having the baby is right for you, then you should have it."

"I have no other choice, Betty."

"Okay, then I'm with you. You're my best friend, and I'll be there anytime you need me."

"God, Betty. What about Thomas? I have to tell him, don't I?"

"You have to, Marie, and the sooner you do, the better," Betty said.

"Marie, why don't you talk to someone? Maybe you need some professional advice."

"Who, Betty? I can hardly bear talking to you, and you're my best friend. You're the only one I know that I can trust."

"How about speaking to your priest, Marie? You told me yourself that you could go to confession and the priest would keep your secrets."

"I don't have the strength, Betty," Marie cried softly. "There's another thing. We're moving to Malden in a few weeks. We went to Mass at Holy Rosary Church in Malden only once, last Sunday. We met with Father Brendan for the first time to introduce ourselves. I hardly know him, Betty. It's not like it is here in Revere. You don't know what happens in confession and I have no idea what the new priest will be *like*."

Betty took Marie into her arms and held on tight. "Why don't you go to Father Fazio in Revere, then? You told me once how easygoing he is."

After a lengthy sermon, but a not-too-lengthy imposition of penance, Father Fazio forgave Marie. He had not pried during her confession, but he suspected that Thomas Grandee was the father of the child. He hoped Thomas would do the right thing.

"Marie, my dear, you must speak to the father of your child just as soon as possible, do you hear? Don't delay any longer, because in another couple of months, you will probably start to show."

"Yes, Father. I understand."

"Now, Marie, I've known you since you were a little girl. You've made a mistake, but it doesn't mean that you are bad. You must continue to have faith in God, my dear, for He will never cease to love you."

"Yes, Father. Thank you."

"With your permission, Marie, I will speak with Father Brendan in Malden since he will be your new pastor. He's a very fine and concerned man. Since you will be living in his parish, he is the one that will lead you through what will probably be a few short-lived but difficult months. Will you do that?"

"Yes, Father. If you promise to speak to him first."

"I'll do that, Marie, and bless you. God be with you and your beautiful child. Be concerned for your child, Marie, and be certain to go as soon as possible to speak with Father Brendan. I will call just as soon as you leave today."

When Marie left the confessional, she felt surprisingly encouraged and strengthened by Father Fazio's positive outlook. She was grateful, too, when she saw Betty sitting on the church steps, waiting for her.

When Betty saw Marie, she couldn't help but blurt out, "Well, did you tell him?"

"I did, and I'm glad it's off my chest. Now I have to tell Thomas and then I have to see Father Brendan in Malden. Where do I begin?"

"Thomas first. He's the important one right now. Do it today, Marie, and come and tell me right away." Betty didn't say so, but she hoped Thomas wouldn't be too upset.

"Betty, thanks for all your help. I don't know what I'd do without you, honestly."

Marie was terrified that Thomas might not be as comforting and cooperative as the priest or Betty. Unlike them, his life would be directly affected by what she was going to have to tell him.

Thomas' first reaction was anger. "How the hell did that happen, Marie? You said you thought it was the time of month when we could. Besides, I withdrew, just like that book said I should." Thomas gritted his teeth and shook his two fists in an attempt to control his temper. "Jesus, Mary and Joseph, what the hell are we going to do?"

Marie's fear had been that Thomas would desert her. She was actually relieved that he was angry and she started to apologize as if the whole thing was *her* fault.

But Thomas quickly calmed down. "Marie, I love you. Do you want to have the baby, or do you want an abortion? Please know that I'm not pushing you to have an abortion. I'll do whatever you think is right and whatever you want."

"Thomas, I want to have our baby."

Even though Marie didn't come right out and say she wanted to get married, he knew that this was what she meant—she had used the "our" word. From that moment on, he knew he was committed.

The truth was that he really cared for Marie. She was quite attractive, with bright blue eyes, not unlike his own, and light brown shoulder-length hair. She didn't fuss with lots of makeup and fancy hairdos, but there was something solid looking, earthy and naturally sexy about her. Marie was a full-bodied woman, even though she was just eighteen. Since he was over six feet, he also liked the idea that Marie was almost five-feet nine inches tall. Having Marie for a girlfriend gave Thomas a feeling of achievement. In his mind, no ordinary fellow could make it with a girl like Marie. Everything about Marie Sullivan flattered his ego, even the fact that he was the one who had gotten her pregnant.

"I would have eventually asked you to marry me, Marie. I guess it's going to be a case of sooner rather than later."

Marie put her arms around him and tilted her head up to kiss him. They kissed for a long time and hugged each other. For the first time since she had missed her period, Marie felt less frightened.

"I love you, Marie," Thomas said. "I'm sorry I got you pregnant, but I'm glad you're going to have our baby. I think my Pa will kick the shit out of me, but my brother John may help me with the folks. John's basically a good guy. He's the one that told me all about sex to begin with. The only thing he'll be upset about is that I didn't use something. What the hell, he thinks I'm stupid anyway. He always says so."

"Oh, God, Thomas, I do love you! Now I just have to tell my parents. I don't know what they'll do!"

Thomas had a different idea. "Sweetheart, Marie, we're going to have to get married, aren't we? So why not do it *before* we tell our parents you're pregnant? We can get married right away, secretly, and then tell everyone we got married. Then we can wait a few months more before we tell anyone that you're pregnant."

Once Thomas was alone after he had committed to marrying Marie, he had mixed emotions. Had he been too hasty in offering to marry Marie? What would become of his future? He turned to his brother John for advice.

As expected, John's first words were not kind. "Asshole, you should've used a French safe! But now it's done and you got Marie pregnant. Now you want to marry the girl."

John took a few deep breaths and settled down. "Well, getting married is the right thing to do. Just remember that mom and dad will want a religious ceremony."

"Marie and I know that, and we can have a real church wedding later. I just don't want to tell mom and dad about Marie being pregnant yet. When the baby comes, we can just say it is premature."

"And I suppose Marie is not going to tell her mother and father that she's pregnant, right?"

"That's the idea, John. But we're going to have to find a place to live and I'll have to get a job. After all, once I'm married and Marie gives birth, we're going to need some money."

John relented and agreed to be present as a witness at the marriage before a justice of the peace. He also agreed to be present after the civil ceremony when Thomas told their parents.

Marie wasted no time in telling Betty about their plans for a civil ceremony. Betty also agreed to be a witness.

Several days later, Marie rang the doorbell at Holy Rosary Church in Malden and was shown in to Father William Brendan's office. "Good morning, Marie. I'm pleased that you've kept your appointment. I spoke with Father Fazio the other day about your situation."

As tall and strong a person as she was, Marie looked like a very frightened little girl. Father Brendan had seen enough young people in trouble to recognize the look. He came around from behind the glass-topped desk and took a more comfortable seat at a stuffed chair alongside the pretty white-laced second story windows.

He pointed the chair's twin alongside and said, "Please sit down, Marie. Would you care for some water or a cup of tea? You've come from Revere this morning, haven't you?"

"Yes, Father. Thank you, Father. Yes, I've come from Revere, Father." Marie was very nervous, and it showed.

"I think *I* would like a cup of tea. Won't you please join me?" Marie nodded gratefully.

Father Brendan reached for his phone and dialed the housekeeper. In the following moments of silence, Marie couldn't open her mouth. The priest sat down quietly and smiled while looking directly at the frightened young woman. He finally cleared his throat.

"Father Fazio tells me that the Sullivans have been attending St. Michael's ever since he has been there. A fine family, he says. I imagine he will miss seeing you when you move. Tell me, Marie, when do you expect to be moving from Revere to Malden?"

"In another week, Father. My brother Dan is graduating from junior high school this week and my parents want him to be able to start at Malden High in September."

"Here comes our tea."

Marie began to feel more comfortable and relaxed, and she told the priest about herself and Thomas. Her confession was received with few interruptions. He admonished her that planning a civil ceremony did not relieve her of the sin she had committed. He also stressed the need to keep the promise she made during confession about having a religious service as soon as possible.

"It sounds like you have a fine young man in Thomas Grandee. Please be sure to bring him here one day soon. I would like very much to meet him."

"I will, Father, and thank you for being so kind."

"God bless you and I wish you the best of health and happiness as well as a fruitful and peaceful marriage."

On the trolley ride back to Revere, Marie relived the visit with Father Brendan. He seemed very young—maybe about 30—to be in charge of a parish, and he was definitely warm and kind. Perhaps he won't be so harsh in confession after all, she thought.

William Brendan had only been a priest for about five years, but the Jesuit order had recognized his potential from the outset. He was a graduate of Boston College and its seminary. Not a very tall man, he had been only about an inch or so taller than Marie. He was not a handsome man, but rather friendly looking with well-defined features and deep brown eyes. His hair was wavy and also dark brown. Most of all, Marie had enjoyed his smile.

The civil ceremony took no more than 15 minutes, on the same day Thomas and Marie got their marriage license. Betty and John swore to secrecy about Marie being pregnant, and the four went out to lunch afterward.

When Thomas and Marie broke the marriage news to Thomas' parents, it went smoothly. Marie had dressed modestly. Thomas' brother had kept his word and was present for moral support. As expected, the Grandee elders insisted on a future church wedding. His parents didn't express any concern over the marriage interfering with Thomas' future, since they never felt he had one to begin with; he would simply have to take a job, any job. They probably felt that getting married was good for him.

Of course, there had been a few harsh words and recriminations in the Sullivan household. That was entirely different.

First, of course, the Sullivans objected to the haste and secrecy of the marriage. They insisted, as did the Grandees, on a church wedding.

"As soon as possible," Marie's mother hastened to demand.

Betty assured them that Marie had already told her that she was planning to be married a second time by Father Fazio in St. Michael's Church in Revere. Thomas affirmed Betty's remark, saying that Marie had told him the same thing. As expected, since the civil marriage was irreversible, the subject soon settled into preparations for a church wedding.

Marie and Thomas became Mr. and Mrs. Thomas Grandee at St. Michael's Church in July of 1920. Betty was the maid of honor and Thomas' brother John the best man. Father Fazio performed the service and Father Brendan was also in attendance.

Louise was born one month "premature" on November 10, 1920.

Betty and Marie had anticipated the need to be prepared for a very "premature" birth. They had conned both Thomas and his brother John to back them up, if questioned, regarding the date of the civil ceremony, which they backdated by four months. As it turned out, there was never a need to fall back on the backup lie; no one ever asked.

Since July, the Sullivans had been living in a house they had purchased in Malden. There were two floors, plus a three-room unused attic. Of course, Marie, Thomas and the baby took the attic, rent-free. Because Marie's father worked as a pipe fitter at the Navy Yard in Charlestown, he was able to help Thomas get work in a restaurant in the nearby City Square. He knew the owners.

The pay wasn't high, but it gave Thomas a chance to learn a trade. He actually got to do all the various jobs in the restaurant, from dishwasher to cook to waiter. This would stand him in good stead for the future.

Once he began working, though, Thomas began to regret his situation in life. He went to his brother for advice. This time he hoped John might know some way he could go on to college. John, however, shared their parents' view that Thomas just didn't have the makings of a student, so he advised Thomas to settle for the restaurant job and make his future in the business.

"I hate to give up completely. I know the senior coursework. I really think that I can do it."

"What about Marie and the baby? You have a new job."

"Marie said she can find work, and her mother said she would take care of the baby while she was at her job. I could work a part-time job on the nights and weekends. Marie and her mom think I ought to at least try, if this is what I feel is right."

"You just think you know the coursework, but you freeze because you don't know the answers to the questions."

"John, I know you don't believe me, but I'm not that stupid. I can't stand up in class and speak or answer questions easily, and I really get scared stiff as soon as I sit down to take a test." Now he was almost shouting. "I can do it if someone gives me a chance! I'm not stupid!"

"Okay, okay, calm down. You're not stupid. You're just not college material. So, what's the problem?"

"Shit. You get to go to college and get straight A's and I don't even get the chance. That's a problem right there! Will you please help?"

"For your own good, Thomas, the answer is no. I will not be party to another disappointment for you. My advice is to settle for the good job Mr. Sullivan found for you and make a career in the restaurant business."

"Thanks for nothing, John."

Once he finally decided that he had no choice but to give up his real ambition, Thomas never again brought up the subject of his poor grades at Revere High School. He never once spoke to Marie of his disappointment in not being able to go to college.

Eventually, Thomas and Marie moved into a small rented apartment of their own, not far from Marie's parents in Malden. Thomas had also found his place in a career just as his brother predicted, whether he liked it or not, in the restaurant business.

Chapter Five

MARIE HAD BEEN ACCEPTED TO BOSTON BUSINESS College in May of 1920, one month prior to her graduation from Revere High School. With Louise in the waiting room of her womb, she faced the choice of either aborting the baby or giving up school. For Marie, a practicing Catholic, it was no contest; Louise was the one who gained admission.

After Betty Herman graduated from Revere High School, she went on to Boston University, where she met Harvey Rossiter. When Betty needed help with her American history course, a classmate told her about a brilliant history major who was always willing to help fellow students. That student turned out to be Harvey Rossiter. Harvey was immediately attracted to Betty. She was very friendly and undeniably pretty. Harvey was riveted by her gorgeous olive complexion and twinkling hazel eyes that had a way of saying "I like you" whenever she spoke with him.

Harvey also liked the fact that, though he was only five feet seven inches tall, he was still several inches taller than Betty was. This boosted his self-esteem, since he felt he was not classically "handsome." His facial features, especially his nose, were just a bit too big for a small man such as himself. He felt he had a rugged face, but not a rugged build. He was, however, friendly looking.

Betty was flattered by Harvey's attention and, for whatever reason, she just liked his homely—but studious and intelligent—appearance. Maybe it was his quiet, pleasant personality that won her over.

By taking extra courses during her first two years, Betty was able to finish Boston University in 1923. She graduated with a degree in library science. Tuition was half-paid by scholarship and her parents covered the remainder of the $400 annual bill.

During her junior year of school, Betty's first job was at the Boston Public Library as a part-time assistant in the records department. Since the library was adjacent to Boston University and the hours were flexible, it fit her schedule perfectly.

After Harvey Rossiter graduated, he secured a position teaching English and history at the private Kenwood Prep School for Boys in Cambridge. She and Harvey had dated until her junior year at college and they were married during the summer vacation of 1922. By then, Harvey was earning $22 a week. That, plus the $6 Betty was paid for her work at the library, was more than enough to rent their Back Bay kitchenette apartment for $18 monthly, furnished and heated. It wasn't all that much of a place, but for the newlyweds, it was home.

When the twins were born on January 3, 1924, the private school raised Harvey's pay to $26. That made it possible for the young family to take a small apartment in Malden, near Betty's parents. With some financial help from the Herman and Rossiter grandparents, Betty was able to stop working. The twins, Nancy and David, were doted on by both grandmothers and were healthy, spoiled infants.

The most difficult financial period for the Rossiters came in 1930 when the depression forced the Kenwood School into bankruptcy. Many students withdrew when their parents lost their life savings in the stock market crash. New students were hard to come by.

Harvey Rossiter was reduced to substitute teaching at Boston Latin High School. Both Harvey and Betty's families helped as best they could, but neither the Rossiters nor the Hermans were well off at the time.

In 1932, Harvey finally landed an instructor's position at Boston University. In addition to a salary of $27 per week, Harvey was able to begin work on a Master's degree. By 1938, through diligent hours of work and study, Harvey Rossiter had earned his Masters plus a Doctorate in history and was awarded the title of professor.

By 1938, the twins had become adults. Betty was working as a librarian at the Malden Public Library to help support the family. She and Marie had remained best friends throughout the years, and Wednesday had become their regular meeting day. Marie dropped by the library to exchange whatever books she had finished and would pick up new books to read, often at Betty's suggestion. From the library, they would walk together to the Converse Restaurant for lunch and usually stop at the Palace of Sweets for a cone or sundae. After 17 years of marriage, Marie and Thomas had three children. They were now a family of five. They owned their own home in Malden. Thomas' job supported the couple and their three children, and his salary should have given them a sense of financial security. The reality, however, was a sense of insecurity and a lack of family harmony and happiness. Louise was now 17, Carl 16 and Robbie 10.

For some time now, Marie had been toying with the idea of confiding in Betty about Thomas' latest behavior. The recent series of incidents, including his violent reaction when he came upon Carl and Louise in bed together as well as her own dramatic outbursts, had triggered so much anxiety in her that she finally overcame her hesitation and decided to open up to her good friend. It was Wednesday and they were in the Palace of Sweets in Malden Square.

"I need your help, Betty," Marie said as soon as they sat down with their desserts. "Something's happening to Thomas. He's getting violent, and I'm scared."

Marie got choked up, and she swallowed hard. Betty reached over and held her hands.

"Marie, honey, calm down and sit quietly for a minute. I'm here. You know I'll do my best to help you, whatever your problem is. Drink some water." Betty picked up Marie's water glass and handed it to her. Marie took a sip.

"God bless you, Betty. I don't know what I'd do without you to talk to."

Betty smiled. "Let's start from the beginning, Marie. Tell me what happened. Go on, now."

Betty's soothing voice helped Marie to relax. She took a deep breath and spoke.

"Well, Thomas hit Carl last Friday. He never laid hands on me or on the children before. I couldn't believe it. The poor kid has a black eye and his face is swollen."

"What happened? Did they have a fight? Did Carl do something bad?"

"At first, Carl didn't want to admit that his father had hit him. Louise finally came out with it. Betty, he even slapped Louise."

Betty hesitated and wondered for a moment if she should continue.

Betty held her friend's hands again. "Marie, this sounds crazy. You didn't answer my question about Carl. Now Louise is involved. What in the devil happened?"

"I guess I better tell you."

Marie told her friend about Thomas finding the two of them in bed.

"Betty, the house was absolutely freezing. I had Robbie in bed with me for the same reason as the two kids. I swear they didn't do anything bad and Thomas should have known better."

"Well," Betty said, "at least it makes a little more sense now. I agree with you, though. I know Carl and Louise, and I'm sure you're right about them."

"Thomas is getting worse. He's nothing like he was when we were first married. Last week he was out for three nights in a row and came home with whiskey on his breath *and* smelling of perfume. Betty, I'm at wit's end. I don't have the strength to fight back. I really don't want to fight at all. I'm afraid. I just want him to be his old self again." All the talking was making Marie exhausted.

"Is Thomas in trouble at his job?" Betty asked. "Is he worried about money? You must have some idea of what's behind his behavior."

"I wish I knew. Betty, I've told you this before. Thomas won't talk to me about finances. I don't understand whether he feels that it isn't my place to know or he just doesn't trust me. Since the day we married, he's never wanted me to work. He always has to be in charge of the house, the money, his time, and just about everything else. You can't tell Thomas anything; he has to be the boss. I've always left well enough alone because I've felt that he really does love the kids and me and has always wanted what was best for us. Now I don't know what to think, except maybe he's found another woman." Marie looked away from Betty as she made the last comment.

"You told me before that you didn't like Thomas working at The Chateaun—he drinks too much there. Maybe he just has a drinking problem."

"I don't think it's that. I told you that I think he is having sex with someone." Tears came to Marie's eyes, and she wiped them away. "What I haven't explained is that he doesn't seem to want to have anything to do with me, at least not like he used to." She looked Betty straight in the eyes and then added, "I've never told this to anyone else, Betty. I'm even ashamed to let Thomas into my bed. When we do have sex, I feel like a whore." At this, Marie began to sob.

"Marie," Betty said. "Let's get out of here and go to my house. The kids are in school and Harvey won't be home until later. This isn't the right place to have this kind of discussion. Come on, let's go."

With this, they left their plates half-filled and went back to the lot behind the library where Betty parked her car. Betty had one stop to make in Suffolk Square. She parked two blocks from the grocery store. She and Marie walked up Cross Street and around the corner to Bryant where the Sunny Rose grocery was located. Young mothers were pushing their carriages and chatting with each other as they passed. An older man wearing a yarmulke who seemed to recognize Betty said "Shalom" as they approached. The street was busy with people and alive with noise.

In the 1930s, Suffolk Square in Malden, Massachusetts was very much like New York's Jewish neighborhoods in the Lower East Side, Brooklyn and the Bronx. To many non-Jews, even those that lived in the same city, Suffolk Square was as foreign as if it *were* in New York. Of the city's 55,000 or so population, more than 10,000 were Jews. Practically all of them were crammed into a congested tenement district of a little more than a half dozen small streets, the center of which was Suffolk Square.

"Is it always like this?" Marie asked.

"You should come down here on a Saturday after sundown!" Betty replied. "The Square is teeming with people when the stores reopen after Sabbath."

They passed Sher's Delicatessen, and the aroma of corned beef wafted out. Baker's dry goods store was next to the deli, and there was a drugstore on the corner. Suffolk Square actually had two drugstores, and there was also a fish market as well as a fruit and vegetable stand. Directly across the street from the Sunny Rose Grocery was the Capital Theater, where admission was five cents.

"My mother still loves living over there on Grape Street. It's near enough so that she can walk to the stores. And because she lives on a side street, she's still secluded from the noise and traffic."

"I remember when you lived there," Marie replied. "But I'm glad you and Harvey moved to Mountain Avenue. It's a much nicer house and nearer to us. I can walk to your house in less than 15 minutes."

"We like it too," Betty added, "and the area is quiet and residential. We're near Malden Square but Mountain Avenue is still set apart. It's the best of locations, which is why the houses cost more than they do in other locations. But, you and Thomas still live in the nicest part of town."

As soon as the words had left her lips, Betty regretted mentioning Thomas. The surroundings in Suffolk Square had taken Marie's mind off her unhappiness for a while, and Betty could see the sadness return to her friend's face as soon as she mentioned Thomas.

Once they arrived at the Rossiter's, Betty put on a kettle of water to boil while Marie sat fidgeting at the maple kitchen table. The room, decorated in soothing pastel blues and whites, was warm and cozy.

Betty came over and stood behind Marie and put her hands on her shoulders. She kneaded Marie's shoulders and neck gently, trying to relax her friend and urge her to talk.

"We've known each other for a long time. Is there something else that you aren't telling me?" Betty added.

"Like what, Betty? I've told you what's happening."

"Marie, you talk about Thomas and the kids and that you think there's another woman. You haven't said anything about *you* and Thomas."

"You're referring to our private life, aren't you? Our love life?"

"Marie, it's obvious that love life or whatever, things are not right between you. *That's* what you have to talk about. Either to me or a psychiatrist or to your priest."

"Come sit down with me, Betty."

Betty brought the kettle over to the table, poured hot water into flowered porcelain tea cups with Lipton tea bags already set inside, returned the kettle to the stove, and then sat opposite Marie. "Well?" she asked.

"Thomas and I had a truly beautiful love affair from the day we first dated, and I felt that it continued even after I became pregnant with Louise. Our marriage was wonderful during the first few years."

"Wonderful for you, Marie. Thomas never got to go on to college, though. Was it wonderful for him?"

"No! No, no, no, no! It's my fault!" Marie burst into tears.

"Cut the crap, Marie. *You* didn't make yourself pregnant. *He* did."

Marie wiped her eyes. "He wanted so much to take summer courses to improve his grades. Boston College would have taken him then because of his football standing."

"Thomas could have walked out on you, stupid. He married you because he loved you. Whatever is bothering him now has nothing to do with that. Marie, you've been married for seventeen years. You said the trouble only started in the past two or three."

"You're right, Betty. Then it has to be another woman."

"Maybe, maybe not. All I know is that the problem is with Thomas. It's not your fault, and you just remember that."

"So where do I go from here? What do I do?"

"Get Thomas to see a psychiatrist, or your priest, or someone. He's the one with the problem."

"I still think there's another woman. I can smell perfume on him, Betty."

"Then stand up to him. Face him with it."

"I'm afraid of him. I'm a coward."

"Marie, come stand up near me." Betty came around to stand face-to-face with her friend. "Look at that. You are a good four inches taller than I am. When I stand near you, I sometimes feel like a little girl."

"But, Betty," Marie teased, "I've always looked up to you even though I might have to look down a bit to do it." This has been the first glimmer of the real Marie all day, Betty thought. They both began to laugh.

"Well then, you mustn't feel like a midget next to Thomas. Don't let him intimidate you. He has always been able to attract women like pollen attracts bees. Maybe there's another bee trying to buzz the hive. I'd like to kick him in his behind, and that's exactly what you should do. Make him face up to it, Marie. Speak up. You owe it to yourself and the kids!"

"Thanks for your confidence," Marie replied, "but I just don't know if I can win a showdown with Thomas. I thought maybe there should be someone else that could help us, someone with authority who could make him understand how serious a mistake he's making. The only person that I can think of is Father Brendan at Holy Rosary. The problem is that Thomas hasn't been to church for almost a year."

Betty gave her friend a knowing smile. "Why don't *you* speak with Father Brendan? I'll bet *he's* not afraid to approach Thomas."

"Great idea. Betty, you've been a big help. By the way, I have been so preoccupied with myself that I didn't ask about you. You said that you and Harvey once had some problems. Do you want to tell me about it?"

"Everything is fine now. What I never told you was that Harvey became very depressed when he lost his job at the Kenwood School. He withdrew all his affection. I worried that he no longer loved me. Of course, I was wrong.

"I eventually asked Harvey if he wanted a divorce. He said he couldn't believe that I was serious. He gradually regained confidence and we've been happy ever since."

"I'm glad it worked out for you two. I just wish that I could be assured that Thomas and I will eventually be able to work things out. I just don't see how. He's cheating on me, I know it."

"You can't be sure, Marie. Thomas may just be having trouble at work. If you two were really in love once, then there is always the chance that things can work out."

Betty and Marie were standing at the sink washing cups and saucers when David came through the door, "Hi, Mom. Hello, Mrs. Grandee."

"Hello, David," Marie responded. "My, you've gotten big, haven't you? Where's your sister?"

"Here she comes now." David glanced behind him. "Hey Nancy, look who's here—Mrs. Grandee!"

"Hello, Mrs. Grandee," Nancy said.

David and Nancy indeed looked alike, and both resembled their father. Each had dark brown hair with just a hint of natural curl. Nancy wore her hair short, almost in a boyish bob. They both had striking hazel eyes.

Even though David was a good five inches taller than Nancy, he tended to slouch, where his sister was one of those posture-conscious kids. It had been drilled into her at school. Nancy was beautiful, not just pretty. Her round face had strong features: silky smooth, tan skin; full, well-shaped lips; a fine, straight nose that could almost be called haughty; and long, almost oriental-looking eyes with long lashes and deep brown pupils.

Both children were slender and healthy looking. Nancy was blossoming into a young woman, but David still appeared to be a young boy, not having yet reached manhood. They were a little over 14 years old.

"I had better be on my way," Marie said, folding her dishtowel and placing it on the counter alongside the sink. "Carl, Louise, and Robbie must all be home by now. Thank you for the tea and company, Betty. It was nice to see all of you."

Betty and the children exchanged good-byes and Marie left, relieved that she had finally had the opportunity to discuss her problem with someone, especially her closest friend. She also decided not to go straight home. Louise and Carl were old enough to take care of themselves and they knew how to keep an eye on Robbie. She often went shopping after her Wednesday lunches with Betty and the kids would not necessarily expect her to be at home when they arrived from school.

Today, instead of going shopping, she headed for Holy Rosary Church where she found Father Brendan's secretary, Leona, busy finishing the upcoming Sunday bulletin. Leona was always pleasant and especially friendly toward Marie.

"Come in, Marie," she said. "What brings you to the rectory this evening?"

"I wonder if Father Brendan might be available to see me for a few moments, Leona, or if I need to make an appointment. I would like to speak with him."

Leona could see that Marie was troubled. "Just wait right here a moment, Marie, and let me see if Father Brandon can talk to you right now. I'll be right back."

Leona found Father Brendan in his parlor office, working at his desk. "Marie Grandee is here to see you, Father," she said. "She seems a little disturbed."

"Sounds as if you had best send her in. Have you finished typing the bulletin copy?"

"Its practically finished, Father. It'll be ready by the time you're done with Marie. I'll get her now." Leona was concerned for Marie, and hoped everything was okay.

Chapter Six

WHILE MARIE HAD BEEN MEETING WITH BETTY, Carl was on his way
home from school. He walked with Charlotte Brown, a classmate.
She lived across the street from the Grandees and often walked
home with Carl. Charlotte had noticed the remains of the bruise
on Carl's face. She had wondered when she first saw him at school
how it had happened. Now she touched it tenderly. "Did someone hit you, Carl?"

Carl repeated the lie he'd told everyone at school who had
asked the same thing. "No, no. I banged myself Saturday when I
was out back chopping some logs for the fireplace."

"Carl, you know the empty house on Beltran Street? My classmate Cathy lives next door, and she says it's beautiful inside. She
says there's an unlocked window in the backyard, and they've just
finished fixing up the house to sell it. Let's go inside and take a
look!"

"Why do you want to go inside an empty house, Charlotte?"

"Because I want to go inside it with you."

Carl hesitated, but he didn't want to hurt Charlotte's feelings
by refusing.

"Well okay, I could use some excitement, I guess. Let's go see
what it looks like!"

As they approached the two-story house, it was easy to see
what Cathy had meant. It was a more modern home than either of
their own. Once inside, the polished hardwood floors beamed with
a bright, fresh coat of wax. The kitchen cabinets were handsome
oak instead of the newer but less expensive white porcelain cabinets that were more common in middle-class homes.

There were two all-tile bathrooms, one on each floor. Upstairs,
Carl called out from inside the large rectangular walk-in closet in

the master bedroom. "Hey Charlotte! Come look at this huge closet!" Charlotte walked inside to join him, carefully closing the door behind her.

They both felt the thrill of being alone in the dark. Carl didn't welcome the feeling for long. He pulled a long metal chain hanging from a naked bulb in the center of the room. The closet was instantly filled with light.

Charlotte tenderly stroked Carl's bruised face. "Does it hurt, Carl?"

"No, it's nothing, really Charlotte. It's pretty much healed by now, anyway."

Charlotte cocked her head and gave Carl her prettiest coquettish smile.

"Carl, do me a favor?"

"Sure. What is it?"

"Put your hand down the back of my blouse and scratch. I have an itch." Charlotte waited a few moments for Carl to reach the center of her back and then added, "Oh, yes, that's it, Carl."

Carl could feel that Charlotte, who didn't seem to have a bust, was wearing a bra. "Hey, Charlotte, I didn't know you had tits!"

"Hey! Shut up, Carl, or I'll smack you!" Charlotte said. She blushed and turned around to face Carl. "I do so have tits. Want to see?"

"Sure," Carl said, as he gently put his hand on Charlotte's chest and felt her small tender breasts. She didn't pull away, so Carl put his hand inside her button-front blouse and felt the smooth, firm mounds. He began to stroke her nipples. Charlotte was becoming aroused.

Putting her arms around Carl's neck, she pulled his head down so they could kiss. Carl was already erect, and he wondered if it would ever go back down.

"Hey, we better get home," Carl said suddenly. He remembered that Charlotte was a year younger than he, not yet 15, and he was a little worried about where the next moves might take him.

"Oh, all right, Carl." Charlotte sounded a little disappointed. "Would you like to come to my house tonight and listen to Amos 'n Andy?"

Carl searched for an excuse. "Well, my sister says Amos 'n Andy is a bad show. She thinks it puts the Negroes down. I think it does, too."

"We can listen to something else, then. What do you like, Carl?"

"I don't know. Maybe Bob Hope. But I can't come over tonight. Maybe some other time, Charlotte." Carl was certain that if he visited Charlotte at home, radio would not be the entertainment of choice.

After walking Charlotte home, Carl walked to his house, deep in thought. Girls really feel nice—I wonder what it would be like to have real sex with a girl, he thought. He started to picture the different girls that might be appropriate for such an occasion. Charlotte was not one of them; she was just a nice neighborhood girl. Besides, he *knew* her. He asked himself what kind of girl might let him do it. He pushed the thought aside. Maybe he would talk to his friend, Red Keating. Red had a car and he knew all about girls.

Louise and Robbie were at home raiding the icebox by the time Carl got home. "Where have you been, Carl?" Louise asked. "You're usually home before me."

"Oh, nowhere, Lou. I walked Charlotte home and she wanted to see the new house on Beltran Street."

"Did you go inside?"

"No. We just looked around and then came home," he replied. He quickly decided to avoid the issue, as he did not know how he would be able to field her questions. "Lou," he said, trying to change the subject, "I think I can get a newspaper stand from the news dealer's office in town."

"How come? How do you know?"

"Well, there was a notice at school on the bulletin board for anyone interested in working after school and on weekends. I really do need to get a job and start saving up for college, so I saw Mrs. Coffey in the administration office about it. She checked my grades and called the news distributor on Main Street. She says I should go there at four o'clock this Friday." Carl had gotten excited just talking about it.

"Oh, Carlie, I hope you get it! I know you will."

"I know I need to make some money for college tuition. I don't know if I can get a scholarship. I'd have to get my marks up in history even to get accepted."

"Weren't you thinking about Boston University?"

"Yeah, but just in case I can't get in, I'm applying to Northeastern, too. I'm good in algebra, geometry and English. History is my real problem. I think it's the teacher. She turns me off."

"Carl, you should speak to Mr. Rossiter. He teaches history at Boston University, remember?"

Chapter Seven

Luckily, Carl's bruise had completely healed by Friday. Mrs. Finkelstein was alone at the local newspaper distribution office when Carl arrived.

"So, you're the boy Mrs. Coffey told me about. My, you're a handsome devil, aren't you?" she teased.

"I don't know about the handsome part, ma'am, but I'd sure like a job."

Mrs. Finkelstein pointed to a chair in front of her desk. Carl sat down.

"I am Rose Finkelstein. I make out the schedules for newsstand deliveries for the trucks. We need someone for the corner of Main and Pleasant streets from six to eight every morning and nine to eleven on Saturdays and Sundays. The papers are left in the doorway of Joslin's Department Store, and the leftovers go inside the Pleasant Street passageway to be picked up later by the trucks. When the shift is over, you can bring the money around the corner to me, here in the office. You'll still be able to get to school on time. I promise."

"It sounds fine, Mrs. Finklestein. When can I start?"

"You can start tomorrow, but there's one more thing. I need you to have a partner. You have somebody?"

"A partner? Why?"

"We want to have two people, so if one is sick or can't work, the other still can."

"I know a few people. I'll get someone. When do I have to let you know?"

"Yesterday would be best, but tomorrow is okay. Come again tomorrow, same time. And bring your partner, okay?"

"Okay, Mrs. Finkle."

"Finklestein, boychick."

"Sorry, ma'am—I mean, Mrs. Finklestein."

Carl rushed home, excited to tell his sister Louise all about the corner newsstand job.

"How much money will you make?" Louise asked right away.

"I don't know. I didn't ask. But Mrs. Finkelstein said that I have to have a partner in case one of us can't make it. Do you think Peter would do it with me, Louise?"

"I don't think so, Carlie. He's already working after school, and he's busy with college applications, too. Maybe David Rossiter could do it! I think he's old enough, and he has good marks in school. He can probably get a work permit."

"Yeah, good idea. David's a great guy. I'll call him right away." Carl picked up the telephone and dialed David.

"Mrs. Rossiter, this is Carl Grandee. Is David home?"

"Is that you, Carl? It's me, Nancy."

"Gee, Nancy," Carl responded, "You sound just like your mother! How are you?"

"I'm fine, Carl, and you?"

"Fine. I saw you in the corridor at school today. What were you doing at the high school?"

"We were sent there for a special English class presentation. They were showing a Longfellow documentary. Why didn't you say hello, or wave? I waved to you."

"I don't know. I guess I should have. Sorry."

"No problem. Anyway, hold on and I'll get David for you."

Before long, David picked up, and Carl told him all about the job.

"It sounds great, Carl, but you know I'll have to clear it with my folks."

"I know. Can you tell me by tomorrow if you can do it or not?"

"Sure, I'll talk to them tonight."

It was nearly dinnertime when Marie Grandee finally arrived home after her rather long visit with Father Brendan.

"Sorry I'm late. The kitchen looks so clean, and something smells delicious, Louise!"

"Dinner is almost ready, Ma. Carl and Robbie helped, too. We made spaghetti and meatballs from the leftovers that I found in the refrigerator, and Carl made a salad to go with it. Where have you been? It's almost six o'clock."

"After I met Betty, we went back to her house. Then I did some volunteer work for Father Brendan at the church. I should have let you kids know that I was going to be late. It's a good thing Pa didn't come home for dinner."

"Well, he's been staying overnight even more than he used to, hasn't he? So why should you even be concerned? I'll bet he didn't even call to say he wouldn't be home."

At that, Robbie chimed in, "Pa called. I forgot to tell you. He said that he had to work late and wouldn't be home."

"Oh." Three voices mumbled in unison.

However, this was the first time since the children were born that Marie had not been home in time to prepare dinner. When Thomas came home on weekdays, he would usually arrive by four-thirty. They would have dinner no later than six o'clock. Because the Grandees were becoming accustomed to Thomas' absences, no one really expected him at *any* time.

The next morning, David called Carl. His parents had given him permission to be a partner as long as Carl worked most of the time. Dave would only be a fill-in.

"That's great David! Thanks! I just hope that's okay with Mrs. Finkelstein. Can you come with me to meet her tomorrow at four?"

"Sure, I can do that, Carl. See you then."

Chapter Eight

MARIE GRANDEE HAD BEEN A MODEL PARISHIONER at Father Brendan's church for 18 years since her first visit back in 1920 as a scared, pregnant teenager. Not until the beginning of March of 1938 did he have reason to be concerned for her again.

Father Brendan paid a visit to St. Michael's in Revere. Father Fazio greeted him warmly, with a friendly smile and a two-handed grasp of his shoulders. Looking down at the smaller, much younger man, Father Fazio invited him to be seated.

"You're here for information about some of my former parishioners. I remember the families, all right—the Sullivans and the Grandees. I remember the Sullivan girl, Marie. The Sullivans were faithful churchgoers. What did you say the name of the Grandee boy was?"

"Thomas. Thomas Grandee married Marie. He used to play football for the high school team."

"Oh, yes, a great athlete, that Thomas."

"John, you must recall that you sent Marie Sullivan to me many years ago. Her family was moving from Revere to Malden to my parish. She was pregnant at the time."

"I do remember. Now tell me what the present problem is and how I can help."

Father Brendan explained Thomas and Marie's marital problems. He wanted to learn as much as he could about Thomas' past.

"I see. I know that the Grandees had two sons, John and Thomas. I remember them both even though they didn't come to church very often. I do recall that the older brother, John, was very bright. I believe that he was class valedictorian in high school. Thomas was an athlete and a great football player. I know that much, but no more."

Father Fazio had excellent powers of recollection, but the number of parishioners and families that had crossed his path during his years in Revere were daunting. So much had changed, he thought, and in so little time.

Father Brendan said, "There must be someone you know who might have been connected to the family or to one of the two sons."

"John once had an Irish girlfriend, Mary Lou O'Brien. She married a lawyer, Robert Gallagher. She's now a schoolteacher at the junior high school here in Revere. She comes to church regularly. Perhaps she can be of some help."

Within a short while, Father Brendan had spoken with several members of the Revere parish, but the only real lead was Mary Lou Gallagher. She agreed to meet with both priests for dinner at an Italian Restaurant so they could discuss the Grandee brothers.

Upon arrival at the bright and cheerful family-style restaurant, the owner's wife greeted Father Fazio warmly. The two priests and Mary Lou Gallagher were seated at a booth in a far corner where they would have a degree of privacy. It was obvious that Father Fazio was a frequent guest at the restaurant; a quick glance at the menu confirmed the source of the older cleric's paunch and jowls.

"I recommend Angelo's lasagna," Father Fazio announced.

"Sounds good to me," Mary Lou replied.

"Fine, why not? Your choice of restaurant, John, so why not your choice from the menu!"

"Josephine," Father Fazio called out. The middle-aged, attractive proprietor's wife arrived promptly.

Father Fazio ordered the lasagna that he knew would be prepared homestyle for all three, and a bottle of Red Chianti. He smiled after returning the menus to the proud parishioner who was honored to have the pastor of her church dine at her establishment. It was also good business to keep him as satisfied as possible.

Father Fazio glanced at Mary Lou, who was now a woman of 38. She had been John Grandee's girlfriend when he was a senior and she a sophomore. She had graduated in the same class as Thomas, Marie and Betty. Mary Lou was a redhead with light complexion and freckles. Her clear blue eyes had always reflected intelligence and honesty.

Father Fazio liked her wholesome look. She was dressed in a stylish long pleated skirt and jacket and looked every bit a public school schoolteacher. Her auburn hair was neatly bobbed.

Father Fazio began the conversation. "William, Mary Lou knew Marie and both Thomas and his older brother, John. She went to school with them. I believe that you have had a chance to speak with her to explain briefly what this is all about?"

"Yes, I have," Father Brendan replied, "but only briefly on the telephone, to arrange this meeting."

Mary Lou, who had already thought about the issue to the best of her ability based upon the sketchy information from the Malden pastor, spoke up quickly. "If Thomas is troubled in any way and Marie is concerned, I don't know what I can possibly do, Father," she told Father Brendan. "But since both of you seem so concerned, I'll do whatever I can to help."

"What do you remember about John, Thomas and Marie?" asked Father Fazio.

"Marie was an awfully nice girl. I remember her well. All the girls were jealous of her. Thomas was the 'it' guy. He was a dream of a man—football hero, with good looks and all. You name it and Thomas had it. I went out with John for awhile."

"What was John like?" Father Brendan asked.

"John Grandee was an honor student. He would look down his nose at others who didn't quite measure up. When I look back on it, I wonder how I ever found him attractive in the first place. After a while, I did begin to question what I really saw in him." Mary Lou hesitated. Father Fazio smiled gently.

"Take your time, my dear," he said.

Facing the two priests, one of whom was her confessor, she closed her eyes and silently said a Hail Mary.

"John was handsome. All the girls at school used to talk about how good-looking both Grandee brothers were. John and I still saw each other even after he went to Harvard. I knew that John wanted to be intimate with me." Mary Lou hesitated again, her face reddening. "I'm embarrassed."

"My dear, you don't have to explain," Father Fazio said. "We understand. We aren't here to embarrass you in any way."

Mary Lou closed her eyes again and quickly said another Hail Mary.

"Well, I *did* become intimate with John. I thought that there was love and a relationship that could mature. I felt it was a way to continue the relationship or maybe even help John. Of course I was wrong. John was an intellectual snob who became arrogant about his abilities. I was not planning to go to Radcliffe or Wellesley. My goal was marriage. I told John that I wanted to go to Salem Normal to train as a teacher. Times were changing, and the public schools were starting to allow married women to teach. John thought that this was beneath him, or maybe he felt an intellectual competition in our relationship that he didn't care to address. We finally broke up."

"Mary Lou married a fine local businessman," Father Fazio told Father Brendan. "Unfortunately, her husband passed away recently."

"I'm sorry to hear that," Father Brendan said.

"Thank you, Father. I guess you are after information about the Grandee brothers. What exactly are you trying to find out?"

"Can you tell me something about the relationship between John and Thomas?" Father Brendan was still not certain where he needed to go with the questioning, but was pleased with Mary Lou's openness.

"That's easy. John was jealous of his younger brother.Thomas was a great football player and a high school star. John envied that. John may have been smart, but he was not well liked. He would never admit this to anyone, but it was obvious.

"He was also sweet on Marie. In fact, I was jealous of John's attraction to Marie. He never came right out and said anything, but I could tell he liked her. He made little remarks—snide remarks about Thomas and Marie that meant an awful lot because his criticism was always of Thomas, never of Marie."

"Were you ever in the Grandee's home when you went out with John?"

"Oh, yes, quite a few times. My family lived in the same apartment building on Broadway. That's really how John and I came to see so much of each other."

"I see. Then you must have known the family quite well."

"I guess I did. Poor Thomas. John was his mother's favorite, and she made it so obvious."

The waitress interrupted their conversation with the plates of food.

As Father Fazio had expected, the restaurant had prepared fresh lasagna for all three of them. The pungent flavors of oregano and cheese, tomato and peppers, fresh ground beef, and a combination of sweet and spicy sausages greeted them from the huge porcelain dish. The lasagna had just been extracted from a deep-dish rectangular pan only a moment earlier. It had been cooked in a traditional brick oven.

"Let me serve," Josephine said, and busied herself with serving heaping portions of the lasagna. The busboy brought fresh baked loaves of garlic bread and a huge garden salad, and he and Josephine hurried away to serve other diners.

Mary Lou continued, "May I ask, Father Brendan, why you are so worried about Thomas? Is there trouble between him and Marie?"

Father Brendan hesitated. "You have helped us a great deal. I feel that you must have liked Marie, and I gather that you thought well of Thomas also. Am I right?"

"Oh, yes, Father. They were such a nice couple. I really do hope that everything's okay."

"I appreciate your concern about them, but unfortunately, there's nothing much I can tell you to put your concerns to rest. You do understand that I am not free to discuss my parishioners' private lives."

"Of course, Father."

"I want you to know that we are grateful for your help, and for your confidence about our meeting with you. You do understand, of course, that you can trust us with anything you say?"

"Of course. As I explained, they were a nice young couple. Thomas was rather quiet, actually, and at times he did seem a bit stern. Most of the students looked up to him. The girls thought he was handsome and, of course, he was a football hero. His brother definitely did not like the admiration everyone had for him."

"What else can you tell us about the family?" Father Brendan asked. As he glanced over to his priestly counterpart, he found Father Fazio deeply engrossed in the enjoyment of his meal but assumed he was listening and equally attentive. Father Brendan picked up his own fork to probe at what certainly appeared to be robust lasagna.

Mary Lou smiled at Father Brendan and continued. "I felt sorry for Thomas because I knew how his mother put him down. She would always compare him to John. I personally heard her say things that must have made Thomas squirm. It was as if she delighted in her comments, which only served to fuel John's own inflated opinion of himself. Perhaps that's why she did it. It was really John who was emotionally in need.

"I once heard her scold Thomas for getting a poor report card. She practically called him stupid and she said similar things in front of me at least a couple of times. I thought at the time that she could have been more discreet or understanding."

Mary Lou paused and let out an exaggerated sigh. "Father Brendan and Father Fazio, I am dying of curiosity. I know you can't tell me any details, but please tell me if either Thomas or Marie are ill. I'm concerned. Please tell me *something*."

Father Brendan looked up from his plate. "We are not free to disclose confidences. However, I can tell you that Marie is worried because Thomas seems to be changing in character. I am sure that we will be able to help the Grandees once we learn more about what is really troubling Thomas. I thought that it might help if Father Fazio and I knew more about his background. What you have told us is very helpful."

"I do hope things turn out well. I remember Marie Sullivan. She was a very nice girl. I lost track when she moved to Malden."

Father Brendan looked up from his meal long enough to ask one question that he thought might be useful. "Can you tell us anything about where John Grandee might be now?"

Mary Lou answered quickly. "After John graduated from Harvard, he went on to get an advanced degree at MIT...something to do with sound engineering. The last I heard, he was a very important executive at one of the top Hollywood studios. He married an up-and-coming actress, but I think I read somewhere that they divorced. There was some sort of scandal surrounding the actress, and she never did make it big. I think that's what prompted the divorce. It was a while ago."

Father Fazio lifted his napkin to his face, and glanced over to Father Brendan, who was enthusiastically finishing his own plate of what had been another superb meal at the restaurant. He had been listening carefully to all that Mary Lou had been explaining and felt that she had provided more than was necessary in terms of detail about an issue that he knew little about. Determined to allow sufficient time to discuss the matter alone with Father Brendan, he brought up the time they had been together and explained that he needed to retire with Father Brendan in order to keep to his busy schedule.

Father Fazio insisted on paying the check. After all, Angelo's Italian Restaurant had been faithfully advertised in the parish bulletin for over 10 years. He made certain to ask Josephine to thank her husband for the perfect meal. Even if they didn't advertise, he had once mused, he still wouldn't miss an opportunity for the fine home cooking that reminded him of his youth.

The three said their good-byes outside the restaurant.

"Mary Lou, thank you so much for your help. I'll give you a call in a week or two to let you know how things are going," Father Fazio said. He wanted to make sure Father Brendan was going to keep him informed as well.

On the way to the rectory of St. Michael's, Father Fazio said to Father Brendan, "Now I'm curious. You asked for my help in getting background information. Now, for God's sake, man, tell me what's going on."

Father Brendan, usually a very serious man, started to laugh. "I thought you would never ask. The private lives of Marie and Thomas are, of course, confidential. However, since we of the church have had a great deal to do with the lives of these two individuals, I guess I can let you, as Marie's original priest and confessor, share some of my privileged knowledge."

The gruff older priest stopped short and shot Father Fazio a look that said, "Whom in the devil do you think you're talking to?"

"Just joking, John. I was about to fill you in."

Chapter Nine

LATER, FATHER FAZIO AND FATHER BRENDAN SAT alone in St. Michael's rectory, in comfortable leather lounge chairs facing a glowing fireplace. On the coffee table before them were some crackers and cheese, two wine glasses and a bottle of Chardonnay wine in an ice bucket. Father Fazio's secretary had prepared the spread, but after their large meal, neither man was hungry.

"Just what did you expect to accomplish by asking about Thomas Grandee's past?" Father Fazio asked.

"William, we've learned that John Grandee was not a very nice person, nor was he well liked. Thomas' mother favored—even spoiled—her older son. It seems that Thomas developed an inferiority complex."

"How in the world will the things Mary Lou told you help you understand what is going on today, at the present time? Those things happened years ago."

Father Brendan stroked his chin and looked over his eyeglasses. "Have you ever read some of G. K. Chesterton's *Father Brown* stories?"

Father Fazio shook his head. "No, but what does that have to do with anything?"

"I guess I have a little Father Brown in me. Like him, I also enjoy playing detective. The fictional Father Brown was a masterful crime solver. You ought to read the stories yourself sometime. Very enjoyable. He used psychology to solve problems."

"Will you please get to the point?"

"Right. Well, the detective priest, Father Brown, had a theory. When he was on the trail of a thief or some criminal, he believed that one often came to a fork in the road of discovery. Which way to go, left or right? The one that seemed obvious was, in his opinion, often the wrong road to take. He probably felt that if someone else knew which trail seemed most obvious, he would take the other one. It's sort of a shell game—detective and culprit each has to guess how the other thinks."

"What does that have to do with Thomas and Marie?"

"I'm also a psychologist at heart," Father Brendan answered. "I believe that how an adult behaves is often the result of his earlier, even childhood, experiences."

"Sounds to me like Freudian psychoanalysis."

"You might call it that. I just feel that the more I know of Thomas Grandee's background, the easier it will be for me to figure him out and thus help him and Marie and their children."

"I'm not sure your 'Father Brown' method will accomplish anything. But then again, I can't see that you are doing any harm and anyway, now you've got me curious."

"So, my friend," Father Brendan said, "as long as you're curious, why not join me for a bit of detective work regarding Mister Thomas Grandee?"

Father Brendan and Father Fazio were on their way to The Chateau for a casual visit—to feel the situation out without arousing suspicion. It was a bright, sunny Tuesday in the middle of June with no pressing problems or schedules to be met at either of their parishes.

When the two priests entered the restaurant, they chose a table in a quiet, private corner. However, Thomas immediately spotted them and rose from where he was seated with Victor. He greeted the two priests warmly and told the waiter that he would personally attend to them.

"To what do I owe the honor of this visit?" he asked. It wasn't often that clerics came to what was considered an upscale but still blue-collar establishment.

Father Fazio spoke first. "We were visiting St. Margaret's nearby, and when Father Brendan mentioned that you were manager here at The Chateau, we decided to come and see the place and maybe have a bite of lunch."

"Well, what do you think of it so far? We try to make The Chateau a pleasant place for a meal."

"Thomas," said Father Brendan, "I am impressed. This looks like a fine restaurant as well as a bar. I had no idea. I thought that The Chateau was, well, more of a saloon."

"The Chateau is not a saloon, father. This was originally a restaurant and still is. The first owners added the bar back in 1934, a few months after prohibition was repealed. I worked for them when it was still known as The City Restaurant. It was my first full-time job after Marie and I got married. In fact, Father Fazio here married us."

"That's right," added Father Fazio, "and then baptized little Louise." Father Fazio paused. "I understand that The Chateau rents rooms also, but I see no sign."

Although this was not atypical of establishments in New England, it could also be indicative of something else. It was the first issue Father Fazio wanted resolved, especially in light of Marie's story.

"Look just to the left of the 'rest rooms' sign," Thomas responded candidly. "That door leads to a private staircase to the second floor. Of course, the main entrance is on the street, outside. Mr. Morrison, one of the new owners, had that private staircase built when he took over the property."

Father Brendan asked, "Are there families living upstairs, Thomas?"

"Oh, no, Father. The new owners converted the apartments into small units with private bathrooms. The apartments were mostly vacant because this is not a residential area. The idea was to cater to the commercial and government people who had one or two days' business at the Navy Yard. We're located closer to the Navy Yard than the downtown hotels and the stay here is much less expensive. Actually, The Chateau has a few kitchenette apartments for longer visits." Thomas had answered the question in a straightforward enough manner, but both priests made mental notes to investigate the history of the upstairs rooms more thoroughly.

Father Brendan asked Thomas what he recommended for lunch, and asked if he would join them. Thomas agreed and they all decided to try The Chateau's famous roast beef sandwich special with a glass of beer each.

After small talk and Father Fazio reminding Thomas of earlier years when he was a football star at Revere High School, Father Brendan finally asked, "Thomas, I see Marie and your younger son, Robbie, at church every Sunday. I haven't seen much of you, lately, though. I think Easter Sunday was the last time that you attended service. I miss not seeing you at service, Thomas."

"I admit I'm lax about church, Father. I can surely try to go to church more often."

"It would be good to see you more often, Thomas. And try to get your older children to come more often as well. You know that it is a tenet of our faith to attend Mass weekly, and it is especially important to set that example for the children. Penance is important, too, Thomas. It's a sacrament. Please don't forget the graces that practicing your faith bestow."

"I understand, Father."

"Good. Now I promise that I didn't come here to preach. We do enough of that when we have to. We're here to enjoy this hearty meal and enjoy your company."

"Thank you, Father, for remembering me."

"That's part of my job, Thomas."

"Yes, I know." Although Thomas had at first wondered about the priests' unexpected visit, Father Brendan's comments about the children and his pastoral responsibility to the parish were sincere. And, both priests had gone out of their way to accommodate his marriage to Marie during some very difficult times.

Father Brendan and Father Fazio were pleased with the visit, too. "You know, John," Father Brendan said afterwards, "Thomas really is a decent person. No matter what his problem might be, I sincerely hope and pray that he doesn't ignore today's visit. Do you think that he will keep his promise about attending Mass?"

"God willing, William, it will be so. Please keep me informed."

Chapter Ten

ONE THURSDAY MORNING IN MAY OF 1938, Mrs. Finkelstein greeted Carl, upset about Adolf Hitler and his persecution of the Jewish people in Germany. After a tirade about Nazi persecution of Jews, she went on, holding up the morning newspaper and pointing to the headline. It read, "CONGRESS PASSES NAVAL EXPANSION BILL."

This was not the first time she had made her feelings clear about the Nazis, but she seemed unusually perturbed this morning. There had been hints of war ever since March when the Nazis marched into Austria, unopposed by the Fascist government in Vienna. Austria was simply absorbed in the Third Reich without a shot being fired.

Carl took the paper and read the story under the headline. The article said nothing about persecution of Jews; it was about President Roosevelt saying that the expansionist policies of Japan and Hitler's Anschluss of Austria in March required beefing up U.S. armed forces. Carl figured that Mrs. Finklestein was probably just troubled or frustrated over some personal things.

When Carl returned the newspaper to Mrs. Finkelstein, her mood seemed to change.

"Carl, would you like to earn some extra money? I have some things that need to be done around my apartment."

"Sure, if I can do them. Where do you live?"

"I'm in the apartment house on Salem Street, just a little way after the library."

"Oh, I know where that is. What do you want me to do?"

"I need new bulbs for the kitchen. Only two bulbs are good. The others already are burned up. Also, a couple of other things I need. You can do it for me, boychick?"

"I'll give it a try."

"Good. You come by later on."

That evening, after supper, Carl went to Mrs. Finklestein's apartment. The burned-out bulbs were in globes in the ceiling. Mrs. Finkelstein had a small folding stepstool that she said she was afraid to stand on. At about five-feet-two, it would be impossible for her to reach the fixtures otherwise.

"Where is Mr. Finklestein? Doesn't he help you with these things?" Carl asked.

"Oy, Mr. Finklestein, he should only hear me, is no good."

"Oh, you mean he doesn't know how to do things?"

"Mr. Finkelstein knows how to do things, boychick. He did to me plenty. All right, as long as you are asking, I'll tell you."

"That's all right, Mrs. Finklestein, you don't have to tell me if you don't want to."

"I want to, I want to. Carl, my boy, Mr. Finkelstein and I were married twenty years ago in Odessa. I was only twenty-two years old. He went to America one year later, and then I came one year after. In the beginning, it was good. Then, he started to chase after a young chippie, and that was that. If not for cousin Morris, I would maybe already go home to Russia. Morris helped me get a divorce and some money from Mr. Finklestein.

"The news company belongs to cousin Morris. He taught me, and I am a good worker in the store. Morris has three stores, and he pays me good. Oy, I am telling my life story and you are just a boychick. But such a handsome boychick, let me tell you!"

"Okay, Mrs. Finklestein, the new bulbs are in. Throw the switch."

"What!"

"Push the switch up, Mrs. Finklestein."

"I know. I know what you mean. Throw. It means push?"

"I guess it does, in a way. I'm sorry."

"Don't be sorry. Wait here. I have to go in my room to get something ready. Wait, Carl dear."

Carl placed the burned-out bulbs on the kitchen table; it was white enamel, just like the one in his own house. Mrs. Finkelstein had knotty pine wall cabinets with black wrought iron handles.

After a couple of minutes, Mrs. Finkelstein called Carl to come
into the bedroom. She was standing near her bed, which was covered in a pink and white cotton chenille bedspread. The spread
had been turned down and the blanket under it was also neatly
turned over at the end. She signaled for him to come over to where
she was standing.

Carl walked over, confused. She hadn't mentioned anything in
the bedroom that needed fixing. Just as he came close to her, Mrs.
Finkelstein opened her robe. At 42, Mrs. Finkelstein was a full-
breasted, well-built woman. She was shapely and neither fat nor
skinny. It was the first time Carl had ever seen a naked female.
His mouth opened slightly, but no sound came out. His heart
pounded. He felt a throbbing and then a sudden swelling between
his legs.

"Boychick, don't just stand there. Take off the shirt," she said
as she began to unbutton him. Carl didn't move as she undid his
belt, but he grabbed her hand when she went for the zipper. He
turned to one side and saw the two of them reflected in a maple-
framed mirror on the wall. As he looked in the mirror, he watched
as Mrs. Finkelstein opened her robe again.

Flustered, he spit out excitedly, "Gee, gosh, do you...? Geez,
I don't know."

"What is it, Carl, my young handsome man, that you don't know?
You are not such a stupid boy. I already told you, my Mr. Finkelstein
is a long time gone from me, so what you don't know is what I will tell
you," she said as she closed her robe and sat beside Carl.

"I don't want I should make you do something you do not want
to do. In my whole life, I have not had a man except with Benjamin
Finklestein. He and me did not do so good together. He wanted me
to do things that were not so nice."

"Gee, Mrs. Finklestein. What did he make you do?"

"Oy, my innocent child. He didn't *make* me do anything. He
wanted I should do what is not natural. I will not mention it even."

"Oh, you mean sex things," Carl said as he started buttoning
up.

"Now you have it," Mrs. Finkelstein said. "What I wanted you
should do for me is to come in my bed and make with me like you

are Mr. Finklestein. I am not making jokes with you, Carl. You are a handsome boychick, and when I look on you, I get goose bumps. You know what I mean goose bumps, Carl?"

"I think so, Mrs. Finklestein."

"Now you know why I made you should come to fix my bulbs. If you don't like me, I will shut up my mouth and you can go home. I will pay for the bulbs fixing."

"I like you, Mrs. Finklestein. I really do, and I understand. I said 'I don't know' because I never did it and I sometimes think I want to." He felt himself getting hard again at the thought that he could do it right here with Mrs. Finklestein. His heart was pounding more furiously than before.

"Boychick, come with me in the kitchen. I think I should have a cup of tea and we should talk some more. I don't want to make trouble for a young boy. If you were a little older, I would take the robe off again," she said.

"You would?" Carl asked with a glimmer in his eyes that prompted Rose Finkelstein to stand up and open her robe again.

This time Carl helped her when she started to unbutton his shirt. They both fumbled in eagerness. Once in the bed together, she turned to Carl and said, "Please, Carl, I want you to call me Rose, not Mrs. Finklestein. I also want you to give me a kiss and you should say you like me. I don't want I should feel like a kurveh, that's a whore."

Carl was taken aback for a second, but he knew what he had to do. "I do like you, Rose. I like you very much."

With that, he took her head in his hands and kissed her full on the mouth. His own head was swimming. There was so much heat and hardness between his legs that he thought he would not be able to control it very long.

"Thank you, Carl. Now I need you very much. Please do what you have to," she said as she reached down to help him. "Come inside me, boychick."

Carl entered Mrs. Finkelstein and felt waves of sensation surging from his pubic area straight through to the top of his head. He almost shouted, "Rose, Rose, oh my God. I'm doing it to you. I can't believe it. Oh, Ohhhhh, I'm doing it," he added, as he moved in and out, enjoying each thrust with its increasing sensation. She was just as excited as he was and her center was churning as plea-sure radiated in her own tensed body.

Rose Finkelstein put her arms around Carl and pulled at him again and again. She pressed him against and inside her with all her strength. He could hear her labored breathing as she moaned and it excited him even more. Suddenly she let out a muffled cry. He was losing his breath and nearly cried out himself as he exploded with sensuous pain and then pleasure. Wow, what a feeling!

Carl held Rose Finkelstein in his arms, hugging her and kiss-ing her again. "That was wonderful," he said when he was certain that he could contain the response. Exhausted, he lay back on the bed and smiled. He felt as if he could conquer the world.

Mrs. Finkelstein felt a release of tensions that had been building up for years. She explained, "It was better than from Benjamin. He was in and out in no time and he never said a word. He finished and turned over and went right to sleep. Boychick, you are some young lover." Mrs. Finkelstein waited a moment and then asked, "Was it good for you, Carl?"

"Oh, yes, it was real good, Rose. You were great."

When they were dressed and he was ready to leave, Mrs. Finkelstein handed Carl a five-dollar bill. "For fixing the light bulbs. My lights, they are shining bright now."

Wow, he thought, I got laid and I got paid. *What* a deal.

The next morning Mrs. Finkelstein made a phone call to her cousin Morris. She was ready for a serious talk with him.

At Holy Rosary Church, Father Brendan also made a phone call. It was the week following their visit to The Chateau. He called Father Fazio at St. Michael's.

"John, I received a check in this morning's mail from Thomas Grandee. It's a donation of one hundred dollars. That's quite a sum of money for a restaurant manager. And I didn't see him in church on Sunday, either. I think this money means a lot more than it says."

"Most assuredly, William. It sounds like we have some inves-tigating to do."

"I agree," responded Father Brendan as he hung up the phone. Neatly, he placed the check back into the envelope in which it had been sent.

Chapter Eleven

WHEN MORRISON AND BRAVERMAN REALTY FIRST PURCHASED The Chateau, their primary interest was the real estate rather than the tavern. Hannah Ward, their trusted secretary, was a smart looking young woman of 25 who made daily visits to pick up the receipts. The Bank of Commerce had a branch office in City Square near The Chateau that remained open until six o'clock. This was a convenience for important out-of-state officials and Navy Yard workers at the end of their workday.

Hannah made a deposit at the branch office each day. She brought all the paperwork back to the real estate office, which was located just a few doors away from the main office of the Bank of Commerce in Boston where Morrison was the vice president. His partner, Sam Braverman, ran the very successful realty company. During the depression years, the Bank of Commerce was mortgagor to a number of properties that were subject to foreclosure. When the bank finally did foreclose on properties, Morrison and Braverman were able to pick up some choice values. The Chateau, however, was a different story.

Morrison and Braverman purchased The Chateau from Ferguson's widow and invested money to rebuild the rundown upstairs apartments. The place had been showing a modest profit and it was beginning to show prospects for growth.

Thomas Grandee, the manager, had instituted some innovations that attracted customers. Additionally, the owners were planning to further invest in the upstairs apartments. They planned to convert the apartments into small hotel units on the basis of a development study indicating great promise for revenue and profit.

After the rehabilitation of the apartments into small hotel units was completed, the units filled to near capacity nearly every week. There were 12 hotel rooms, each charging $18 daily during the week and just $10 per day on weekends. In addition, there were two utility units with kitchenette areas.

Hannah would bring The Chateau journal that contained an entry of tavern receipts, along with government vouchers, traveler's checks and credit slips back to the real estate office. She did the bookkeeping and billing during the week and things went along so well that after two months, Morrison stopped making regular monthly visits to The Chateau. He and Braverman occasionally dropped by to see how things looked and do a cursory spot-check audit, but these visits were rare. Hannah was so capable and The Chateau so successful that the two partners were confident and knew when to leave well enough alone.

During the first few weeks of work at The Chateau, Hannah realized that there was a large amount of cash in the daily receipts. Many of the blue-collar workers, including those from the Navy Yard, paid cash for lunches and especially drinks. Hannah also noticed one particular cash record from the hotel units over the tavern.

"Thomas," she asked one day, "do some businesspeople pay cash for using the hotel upstairs? It seems odd to me."

"Oh, not at all," Thomas answered. "Government and business people are not the only ones using the rooms. One unit is rented on a continuing basis to a fellow who made an arrangement to have the place available whenever he comes to Boston from New York. Usually that's for three or four days each week. He pays only cash. He pays us $100 whether or not he uses the unit. He says that it gives him a permanent second address for guests who come up to his room when he's in town. It also gives him a mailing address. It gives *us* a steady income for one unit, so we never lose out because of the vacancy." For Thomas, this had appeared to be a win-win situation.

By the second month, Hannah had calculated that the increased revenue from the lucrative hotel, restaurant and bar was going to be greater than Morrison had anticipated. One day, when she was alone with Thomas in his private office, she went to the door and turned the knob from the inside, locking it shut. "Come here, Thomas," she said. "Let's talk for a minute."

She walked demurely to the convertible sofa, sat down and patted the sofa alongside herself for Thomas. Thomas came over and hesitantly sat alongside.

Hannah had shoulder-length titian hair and a turned-up nose. She had a smooth, light complexion that didn't need much makeup, but she used just a touch of rouge to accentuate her already high cheekbones.

Her clothing was typical of a demure late 1930s secretary, and she favored knee-length skirts. The only hint of sexuality she showed was in her form-fitting jackets that emphasized a near-perfect figure. She was stylish but always appropriately dressed for business, which made her next moves all the more surprising.

"You are a very intelligent man. May I call you Tom?"

"No one calls me Tom, Hannah. Most people call me Thomas. I guess because I've always been a tall and robust guy. I don't know the real reason."

"I like you and I like the name Tom. It fits you. You're not only smart, but you're a very handsome man. You have such intelligent eyes. Your mother must have been proud of you. Mr. Morrison tells me that you were Captain of your football team in high school."

"Well, yeah, I guess I was. I played football."

Hannah had cleverly narrowed the space between them on the couch as they were talking and she turned her face up to Thomas and said, "Tom, I'm going to kiss you. Don't say a word." With that, she proceeded to kiss him full and hard on the mouth.

Thomas didn't know what to do. He wanted to get up and run but the sensations going through him were overwhelming. Here was this pretty young woman holding him, now with arms wrapped fully around his neck, pressing her breasts against him and pushing him backwards until she was practically on top.

He started to push her up, wanting only to stop the sensations that, mixed with the alcohol from lunch, were all-consuming. Her fragrance was enticingly sensual and his head was swimming with cloudy confusion.

All the while, Hannah was unbuckling his belt and pulling down his pants. Then she abruptly stood up and undressed. She was stark naked and Thomas could only stare with a bewildered look on his face. He had felt himself harden and remained aroused as Hannah moved seductively toward him.

"Get up and let me lie down, Tom." The woman who had just told him how intelligent he was and who had kissed him and hugged him amorously soon lay beckoning, naked on the sofa. "Finish taking your clothes off, Tom, and come to me."

Something was happening inside Thomas' head. He could hear it as plain as day, "Go ahead and do it. Do it to me, go ahead and do it." He thought he recognized images of Marie.

He became like a little boy. Was it Marie's voice? Swept in a storm of confusion and heightened desire, he needed to be told what to do.

Within minutes Thomas was on top of Hannah and she was easing him inside. Thrusting deeper and deeper, Marie's voice changed distinctly to Hannah's as she repeated, "That's it, Tommy. Give me more, Tommy, give me more." He had found Hannah extremely attractive and often aloof, but here in his office, alone and inside her soft, naked body, he felt her warmth and sensual purring exciting him in a way that Marie never did.

Taken up in sexual frenzy by his own enraptured state, he wasn't certain at what point she climaxed. But, when the moment for his own orgasm arrived, he exploded with a swelling energy that seemed to make every muscle in his body come alive with sensation.

They rested for several minutes until their breathing returned to normal. Hannah whispered, "Tommy, I have a great idea for us."

Confused by the speed in which he had submitted to her desire, he could only respond, "I feel guilty, Hannah. We shouldn't have done this."

"You don't have to worry, Tommy. No one will ever know about this. I'm not the kind of girl who's going to kiss and tell."

"Sure, Hannah. I know you won't say anything. That's not what bothers me."

"What is it, then. What bothers you?"

"I shouldn't have done it. That's what bothers me." Yet something inside of him had urged him on—Marie's voice—had urged him on.

Hannah couldn't understand how such a handsome man who had obviously enjoyed their passionate interlude could so quickly become reticent. She had found him a bit pensive and thought his activity in the restaurant a little strange. Still, he had just proven more than capable and she had already determined that his business acumen was the reason for the financial success at The Chateau.

Thomas knew that something inside him was telling him to "Do it to Marie," but somehow it had translated to "Do it to Hannah." This he didn't understand. He was very upset with himself but amazed at his ability to perform so well with a virtual stranger on such short notice. It made him feel young again and reminded him of the excitement of the high school crowds screaming and cheering him on each time he ran, unhindered, toward an opposing team's goal.

Hannah intrigued him. She was the first person who had ever told him that he was intelligent. This was really what had excited him most as he saw her lying naked, vulnerable and awaiting his approach.

"Tom, I have a great idea for us."

"What's that?" he said, beginning to awaken from his daze.

"I want to help make you rich, Thomas Grandee. Morrison and Braverman are so loaded they could never mind it if some of that nice cash from the guy upstairs goes to you, my good man. I may keep a bit of it for myself, too. And, nobody has ever to know about it, Tommy."

"I don't know what you're talking about, Hannah."

"On the weekly journal that you sign for me, I just want to list 100 or so less than the total for cash revenue."

"Why would you do that?"

"No one will be the wiser and we can keep the difference."

"I don't think I like that idea, Hannah. It doesn't sound right to me."

"Well, okay, honey." She decided to let it drop for the time being. "I won't tell about today, Tom. You can count on me for doing the right thing by you whenever you want it. And, when you're ready."

Hannah was very careful to see that she and Thomas were composed and that the office, especially the sofa, was just as they had left it before their sexual stint.

The next several weeks consistently showed a larger amount of revenue on a daily basis. Not only was the cash from upstairs continuing, but the tavern was also doing more business than before. Hannah suggested to Thomas that he should raise the prices just a little. He agreed, and everything was going along very well, indeed.

Thomas thought about the journal entry idea that Hannah suggested. That meant stealing and he questioned whether or not he should tell Mr. Morrison. That could get them both into trouble he decided, in light of what had happened with Hannah. He put the thought out of his mind.

By the end of two months, Hannah was able to hand Thomas an envelope containing five hundred dollars in cash. She had kept an equal amount for herself. "Tom, why don't you open an account someplace with this money? It's a small bonus for the growth in business that *you've* made possible."

"How did you do that?"

"Very easy, Tom. I reduced the revenue totals on the journal pages that you've signed. You never even noticed it."

Thomas was shocked at what he saw in the envelope. He reached out to Hannah to return the envelope, but she just pushed it back to him. "What's the big deal, Tom? No one will ever know. Just think of all the things that money can buy. It's yours now, Tommy. You've earned it." She reached up and kissed him.

The first thought that came to him was that this kind of money could help make the necessary repairs to his house. He was also amazed at how cleverly she had hidden the money from him. Before he could find an objection, Hannah quickly added, "Remember, you're the one who has made a success out of The Chateau. It's yours, Tom. It belongs to you."

"Well, maybe it could come in handy. But I just can't put it in the bank. I don't know what to do with it."

"Open an account at a large Boston bank, Tommy. This way, no one can know."

From that first day until the beginning of June in 1938, Thomas Grandee had accumulated $7,000 in cash deposits at the Columbia Bank in Boston. Hannah continued to visit The Chateau daily, with the collection, record keeping and billing procedures left unchanged. However, after a few more brief but intimate encounters, she stopped inviting Thomas to approach her on the sofa. Other than a bit of kissing and teasing, she held the line shortly after the money began rolling in.

Theirs was a business arrangement, as she had intended all along, and she let silence continue as their code of ethics. Neither would breathe a word to anyone about what was going on for distinct but obvious reasons. Thomas' drinking increased in fervor as his bank account continued to grow.

Chapter Twelve

VICTOR WAS SITTING AT THEIR USUAL TABLE when Hannah arrived one particular Friday. After she retired to the office, he exclaimed, "Hey, Thomas, I think I like the looks of Hannah today. I bet that she can be a devil in bed."

Victor had watched Thomas' coming and going carefully, and strongly suspected that something was going on with Hannah behind closed office doors. Spurred partially by jealousy and partially by resentment that Thomas had never offered to bring him in on this confidence if it was true, he decided to taunt him to elicit a reaction. Until now, Thomas was sharp with him whenever he mentioned Hannah in terms of intimacy.

"Listen, Victor, why don't I take you over to the South End tonight? I know of a clean place there where you can get what you're looking for without any trouble," Thomas said.

"Ah, Thomas, you know I don't need it that bad. I can get it upstairs in one of the units if I need it; you know, during the weekend. Some of the women that take a place for Saturday night are just waiting. You and I both know they do a little business up there occasionally."

"Okay, suit yourself. Just keep your hands off Hannah. I told you, no fooling around with Hannah, Victor. She's part of the Morrison and Braverman team and that means work, not play."

"Okay, okay," Victor remarked, but he still wasn't convinced that Thomas wasn't saving the "play" part for himself.

Later, after Hannah left, Thomas went to the phone in his office and called the big house on Tremont Street. "Hello, Margaret, it's Thomas Grandee, over at The Chateau. I need a favor. Will you send Glenda over for the night? I really need her as soon as possible." He waited while Margaret checked.

"All set, Thomas. Glenda will be there at ten."

"Thanks a million, Margaret. Goodbye." Returning back to the bar area, he filled a shot glass with Scotch, brought it to his office and sipped thoughtfully while staring off into space. After the shot glass was empty, he sat behind his desk and put his head in his hands, thinking, "What the hell am I going to do?"

Hannah had begun to press Thomas into adding to their growing riches by letting her friend bill for fake repairs on the upstairs hotel units. She had just mentioned the day before, "Look, Thomas, the place is taking some wear and tear. Morrison and Braverman will never question it. What if the New York guy stops showing up? He's a big part of our cash flow, you know."

Thomas protested by pointing out that repairs were Victor's job and that the gentleman from New York hadn't shown any intention of not continuing to rent the space.

The units were paying $22 per day, up from $18 two years ago, and the lower cost weekends were up from $10 to $12 per day. The New York guy was still paying the same $100 weekly. Hannah wouldn't let Thomas raise him; he was too important to the operation.

What troubled Thomas more than anything else was Hannah. He had always maintained complete control over everything and everyone in his life. He was not an individual with the kind of makeup that would allow anyone else to make decisions. It took a different kind of psyche to trust others. This had been ingrained in him.

Hannah was the first person in his adult life that ever took command away from him. In the beginning, this was a challenge. Only his mother or father, and sometimes his grandfather, were ever able to tell Thomas what he could or could not do. In fact, it was his mother who convinced him that he needed someone to lead. He remembered she would say, "Thomas, you're a strong boy and a good athlete, but you need a little help in other ways. Look at your report cards. You never get better than a C or a D. You have to settle for what God gave you and what He didn't give you and learn to work with it His way."

Thomas Grandee knew that he was not stupid. Yet, he could never take a test at school without freezing up. Whenever a teacher called on him to speak in front of the class, his memory failed. Funny, he thought, in the outside world with friends and fellow athletes, he was always the leader. With Marie, when they first dated, he could do no wrong, and he took charge immediately. Things were different now. He was still in charge, but Marie was making demands on him and he could feel her looking down at him when her requests remained unfulfilled. She was making him feel that he was not a good provider. He knew for a fact that she was right, however, and nowhere did this make him feel more insecure than when they became intimate. Ever since Hannah, Thomas thought, something had become very wrong.

He wondered what he could do to stop Hannah from ruining his life. He had decided after her new requests that money was her only ambition, even though she had made him feel that *he* was the one who had deserved the gain. He had lots of money but was afraid to go near it, Marie was hounding him, the house was falling apart, and now Hannah wanted to up the ante. He couldn't handle it.

Nothing before, including the business with Glenda and Tremont Street, had ever troubled him as much as it did now. Glenda no longer represented sex to him, although she had when Hannah had first refused his advances. It was not as though he was having an affair or cheating on Marie. Glenda had actually become a link back to Marie and his children by helping to preserve his sanity. The visits to Tremont Street served to heal the alienation he felt from his family, work and friends.

He had recognized that he was talking to himself at times and since that Sunday morning when he had raised hell and smacked Carl, he was afraid to get too close to the children in case he became unnecessarily provoked. It wasn't anything Carl or Louise did as much as it was Thomas recognizing what he was doing to them. 'Damn', he thought, 'That house gets so cold during the winter. I can't even take the money out of Columbia to pay for repairs. I'm spending more than I should on Glenda. What the hell am I doing?'

Thomas sat up abruptly and decided to pour himself one more Scotch from the bar before Glenda's arrival. Sometimes it was easier to just spend the night upstairs, and Margaret was more than willing to accommodate his request at a slight extra charge.

He didn't like going back to the same house on Tremont Street and was afraid that one day someone would see him going in or coming out of what was one of the city's best known brothels. Yet, he disliked even more bringing Glenda to The Chateau, especially since Victor knew and even Father Brendan seemed to recognize that there were improprieties associated with the units above the restaurant and bar.

A sizable check to Holy Rosary had relieved his conscience and hopefully deterred the priests from their redemption mission, at least for a while. How he was going to stop Hannah, and stop Victor from prodding him for details, remained to be seen.

Chapter Thirteen

THE TWO PRIESTS HAD LUNCH TOGETHER THE first week in June. Originally curious, Father Fazio was now downright anxious about Thomas.

"William, you're right. There is something very wrong with Thomas Grandee. Everyone seems to have liked him as a teenager. We know from Marie's conversation with you that he was a dutiful and loving father to the children during the early part of their marriage. His more recent actions are not consistent with the past."

Father Brendan agreed that something was wrong. "Hundred-dollar donations from working men are quite unusual, even if he *is* the manager of The Chateau. Why should he think of contributing money at all?"

"He tells you that he will come to Mass, and instead he sends a donation. Does he think we're fools? That his donation will make him look good in our eyes? William, that man is hiding something."

"My sentiments exactly. I've already spoken with one of the loan officers at the Malden Bank where Thomas' check was drawn. He doesn't think that Thomas had very much more than a small savings and checking account. He promised to inquire, though, and I should get a call if he has any information to report."

"Do you know the names of the owners of The Chateau?"

"Why yes, I do. An executive from the Boston Commerce Bank is one of the owners of a large real estate holding corporation called Morrison and Braverman Realty Company. They own The Chateau. Marie mentioned it to me some time ago. I don't think that we want to jeopardize Thomas' position, though, by asking questions of the owners. There are too many variables yet. Perhaps Thomas is simply frugal and generous. Perhaps he feels guilty about not coming to church. Why don't I give him a call and reprimand him for failing to come to church service on Sunday like he promised?" Father Brendan was reticent about making inquiries that could backfire.

"Good idea, William. Keep me informed." Father Fazio hung up the line and smiled. Father Brendan's well-tempered manner was enough to convince him that he needn't worry about how inquiries were being handled by his younger counterpart.

When Marie heard Father Brendan's voice on the line, she thought something bad might have happened. Pastors didn't usually initiate phone calls to parishioners, and there had been little phone contact through the years between them.

"Marie, my dear, this is Father Brendan. Is Thomas at home?" It was seven in the evening on Friday.

"No, Father, Thomas called to say he was too busy at The Chateau and would be staying overnight during the weekend."

"Well, you be sure to tell him that I called and ask him to please return the call to me."

"Oh, yes, I will, Father."

When Father Brendan hung up, his phone rang at the rectory. "Hello, Father, this is Bill Hennessey down at the bank. I hope it's all right for me to call you at the rectory so late. Please tell me if you would rather I wait until morning."

"Goodness, Bill, feel free to call me at any time of day or evening if you need to. What is it? Did you learn something about what we discussed yesterday?"

"Yes, I did, Father Brendan. One of our employees picks up and delivers to a Boston Bank that we have inter-bank relations with. He tells me that he has seen Thomas Grandee at the teller's window at that bank on more than one occasion."

"And what may I ask is the name of that bank, Bill? Are you free to tell me that?"

"Columbia Bank is the name, Father. It is located in the South End of Boston, on Columbus Avenue. It's a rather small bank, sir."

"Thank you, Bill. It was very kind of you to call. God bless you, my good man, and have a good night."

Immediately, Father Brendan contacted Father Fazio. They

arranged to meet on Monday for lunch once again.

After he hung up, Father Brendan walked over to his phono-graph and selected a new Beethoven Seventh Symphony he had recently purchased. He had not yet had a chance to listen to the shiny 78 rpm recording. After setting the needle on the record, he returned and sat at his desk. The orchestra began its rich recorded strains and he leaned back in his comfortable chair to relax and listen.

The music helped, but he was still unable to get Thomas Grandee out of his mind. Father Brendan opened his desk drawer and took out a bottle of Irish whiskey and poured himself a short one. "This will relax me for sure. I have to get started on my Sunday sermon in any event," he mumbled to himself.

He started to write on a note pad. "Always look for the good in others. Often more difficult than finding fault, it can require a search that is deeper and longer than you might think or expect."

He wanted so much to find a way to reach what was good in Thomas Grandee. This week's sermon was for his own benefit and for Thomas as much as it was for the congregation.

Chapter Fourteen

THE SECOND SATURDAY OF JUNE WAS THE junior high school dance. Carl was able to borrow his friend Red Keating's secondhand 1932 Essex Coupe; it had a rumble seat. Carl had his driver's license and he promised Red that he would drive very carefully, which he did.

Carl drove to Nancy Rossiter's house and went in to say hello. He was greeted with smiles from everyone. Carl was very handsome in his best suit and tie. He felt fortunate that he was not required to rent a tuxedo.

After pinning an expensive corsage on Nancy, who looked stunning in a pink taffeta gown, the Rossiters wished them a good time. The young couple was off to the dance at the school gym.

The dance was to start at 5:30. They parked along a side street off Malden Square and looked at the clock on top of City Hall. It was a little before five, so they had time to spend together before going in to the gym. They decided to walk around the square.

Stepping past City Hall on Main Street, they commented on how attractive yet old it looked. The architects had intended for the neoclassical style building to look historical. Malden's City Hall was an honorable brick structure, but it did look more old than classical.

On the next block, Carl and Nancy passed a men's clothing store and then a shoe store. Crossing the street, they came to Mal's, a fruit and vegetable market with wood crates propped up at angles to effectively display their contents. One large crate had oranges and another, apples.

On the other side of the entrance door was an open crate of tomatoes. A young boy trotted by as they watched. He grabbed an apple and kept going. A man came out of the market and they thought that he might chase the younger fellow. He didn't. He just yelled at the kid and shook his fist. As Carl and Nancy came by the man, he tipped his cap and said, "Hello, Nancy, you look lovely."

"Thank you, Mr. Smith. Guess you lost an apple."

"No problem, when that kid's mother comes in, she'll pay me the nickel. That kid's done it before. It's a game he plays." Carl and Nancy explained that they had to get going and quickly continued their walk.

Several passersby stared at Nancy and one man tipped his felt hat and smiled. She really looked out of place strolling on Main Street in her pink gown.

They still had time, so they strolled back and turned up Pleasant Street and walked past the Palace of Sweets ice cream parlor that had a connecting door to the Granada Theatre. The city of Malden had three movie houses in the square, plus one in the Suffolk square neighborhood and another one in a section called Maplewood. The Granada Theatre was the largest.

Further along Pleasant Street, they passed a Woolworth's and two shoe stores. There were two more men's shops and several stores that sold women's clothing along the way. The biggest of all was an independent department store called Joslin's.

Shoppers came from at least eight or ten surrounding cities, towns and communities to shop in Malden Square. Joslin's was the big attraction. It was as well stocked as many of the large Boston department stores. For everyday shopping, small cities like Malden were more convenient than taking the subway all the way into Boston.

As they began to pick up pace, Carl waved as they passed the news store where Mrs. Finkelstein was still at work.

At the school dance, Nancy looked more like 18 than 14-and-a-half. Several boys asked to dance with her. Each time she obliged, Carl felt a twinge of jealousy. He liked to hold Nancy in his arms when they danced, especially when she leaned her cheek against his. After the dance, Nancy's group of friends had arranged for a dinner party at a place called The Ship on Newburyport Turnpike.

Betty Rossiter had told Carl to be certain to bring Nancy home no later than one in the morning. They trusted Carl. Carl kept the promise, but not until the very last moment and not until after he and Nancy managed to take off alone and go to the all-night Dutchland Farms ice cream parlor on Wellington Circle in Medford. They sat in Red Keating's Essex and munched their cones.

"Did you have a nice time, Nancy?" Carl finally asked.

"Of course, silly. Couldn't you tell? All the boys wanted to dance with me," she said, with a coy smile on her face.

"Yeah, I noticed. So, which boy did you like dancing with the best, Nancy? Do you have a crush on one of the boys at school?" He sounded eager for the answer.

"Mmmm, I guess so. Maybe it's a crush. Maybe it's at school." Nancy continued to be coy.

"Come on, Nance. Tell me. Who is it? It's not that lanky guy who danced with you twice, is it?"

"No, Carl. *That's* Harry Johnson. He's a nice boy, but he's not my type."

"What's your type, Nancy?"

"Oh, I'll tell you one of these days, Carl. Now you better take me home or mom and dad will be upset with us both."

Carl drove home and walked Nancy to the door of the Rossiter house. Just as he reached for the doorbell, Nancy turned her face up to his and kissed him lightly on the lips. "*You* are, silly. Good night, Carl."

Carl whistled all the way home and slept with a smile on his face all throughout the night. He knew because he woke up with a smile on Sunday morning, as well.

Like every other Sunday morning, Thomas Grandee was at home with his family for breakfast. This Sunday he was sober and more pleasant than usual. He asked Carl about the junior prom dance and his date with Nancy Rossiter.

"I had a great time, Pa. The Rossiters made me promise to bring Nancy home no later than one in the morning. Most of the other kids stayed out later."

"Well, one in the morning was late enough. Nancy's just a young girl, Carl. I hope that you got her home on time."

"I did, Pa." He looked his father in the eye and said, "Thanks for asking. Yeah, we had a swell time. I didn't know you knew about the junior prom."

"Yes, I knew. And I know that Louise has her senior prom next Saturday."

Marie smiled but didn't say a word. She hoped that this was a sign for a change for the better that could last. She wasn't sure that it would, though. This sudden change in Thomas also told her something still had to be happening to create the new attitude, especially if it continued. She made a mental note to talk to Betty or Father Brendan about this. Carl and Louise were simply pleased to see their father in a good mood.

The very next Saturday night was Senior Prom night. Peter Strauss was in his tuxedo when he arrived at the Grandee residence to pick up Louise. She wore a black satin gown with a scooped neckline and form-fitting waist. A tall young woman, Louise was absolutely ravishing, or at least she was in Peter's eyes. Peter had borrowed his father's Oldsmobile, a fairly new car, and he had another couple waiting in the back seat when he and Louise got in.

"Hi, Mary Lou. Hi there, Bill," Louise said. "My, don't you both look wonderful?"

Peter closed the door for Louise and came around to the driver's side. In a few moments, they were on their way to the high school auditorium for dancing. Afterwards, they headed for Norumbega Park for an evening of more dancing.

It was a lovely June evening, with a full moon. Norumbega's ballroom was located at the far end of Commonwealth Avenue in Waban, a very wealthy suburb just beyond the city limits of Boston. At midnight, they headed for Boston's Chinatown, where they stuffed themselves until they couldn't stomach another morsel. The four of them had a great evening as they finally headed back to Malden at three in the morning. Peter had permission to stay overnight at the Grandee house after Marie and Mrs. Strauss talked it over. The Grandees had a large enough house with plenty of extra sleeping space.

Thomas was home again Sunday morning as usual. This time he was not as talkative as he was after Carl and Nancy's Junior Prom date. He was sober, but pensive and silent and barely said more than a word or two.

Marie surmised that something new had occurred again in her husband's life. She was pleased that for the second Sunday in a row he was again sober. However, he was still staying away most of the week. She was more puzzled than ever and determined to speak to Father Brendan again.

This Sunday morning was special for Carl. He was deeply engaged in conversation with Peter. They talked about sports and then Carl asked Peter if he was planning to go to college.

"Yeah, I've been accepted at Northeastern, Carl. I understand you want to go there, too."

"I have my application already, Peter. I'm going to apply there, but I'm also thinking about applying to Boston University. I've been studying history with Mr. Rossiter, so I hope that with his help I'll maybe get a B instead of a C, like last term."

"How does Rossiter help you, Carl?" Peter asked.

Louise answered. "You should see Carl poke his nose into some of the books Mr. Rossiter sends home for him to read. He knows more than I do about the Civil War by now. Isn't that right, Carl?"

"I'm doing better, I can say that much. Besides, it's interesting to read about the real history of things and not just memorize dates. Mr. Rossiter talks to me, too, about current events. He says what has been happening in Spain since Franco invaded in 1936 is present-day history. From his perspective, it's like watching history unfold.

"Rossiter says that Hitler and Mussolini are helping Franco overthrow the legitimate government while our country and England have blockaded the Spanish coast to prevent the legal government from receiving arms shipments. He says Franco is a Fascist and Mussolini and Hitler are sending planes and pilots to help him by bombing government troops and factories."

"You really *are* learning current events, aren't you Carl? I hope you get the B you want." Peter was at a loss to keep up with Carl's stream of thought. He didn't know much about Spain and wondered why it was so important. He looked to Louise for help.

Louise stood up, walked over to Peter and exclaimed, "Listen everyone, Peter has to get on home now. I'm going to walk him to the door. We had a great time last night, didn't we, Peter?"

"We sure did. Well, so long everyone." He turned to Mr. and Mrs. Grandee, who had remained quiet as the children talked with each other. "It was nice of you to let me stay over. Breakfast was great! See you all and good luck, again, Carl."

Thomas spoke first after Peter left. "I agree with Peter, Carl. I expect you'll get a good mark in history, seeing as you spend so much time with Harvey Rossiter."

There was more than just a hint of resentment in Thomas' tone. Marie sensed it at once.

Carl received his report card that next Monday in homeroom. He had two B's, plus A's in algebra, geometry and history. The B's were in English and gym.

Carl practically jumped out of his seat. He looked over at Red Keating and gave him a big grin. Keating suspected that Carl had done well in history. He had the same history class as Carl and had noticed Carl's improvement during the past term.

After school, he walked home with Charlotte again. "Hey, Charlotte, I got an A in history. Remember how I told you it was my toughest course? I'm going to apply to Boston University now. I think I might have a chance if I can keep up the good marks. Of course, I still have to get through senior year okay, but I can get started with my applications this summer before senior year in September."

"That's great! I can't believe I'm still only a sophomore. I hate school. I wish I could quit, but my parents say I have to get my high school diploma. I don't know why. Carl, I like it when you walk home with me, but how come you never ask me for a date? I'm over 15 now. You're not even seventeen yet. It's not as if I'm not old enough." Charlotte thought Carl was the handsomest boy that she knew.

"Gosh, I don't know, Charlotte. You know I like you. I walk home with you almost every day, don't I?" he asked.

"Sure, but that's because we live across the street from each other. Otherwise you wouldn't even notice me," she explained.

"Tell you what, Charlotte. After dinner tonight, I'll take you to The Palace of Sweets for ice cream. Would you like that?"

"Sure I would, Carl, but I don't want you to do it unless you want to."

"I want to do it because I like you," Carl replied. "I'll see you at seven o'clock."

At the Palace of Sweets, Carl was sitting with Charlotte when Nancy and a girlfriend walked in. Nancy turned pale when she saw Carl and Charlotte and whispered something to her friend. They turned around and left.

Carl felt as if he had done something very wrong. He had a lump in his throat and the rest of the evening was a burden through which he forced himself to behave. He didn't have the heart to say anything to Charlotte, but he was certain that she could sense that something was wrong.

On the walk home, she asked him, "Carl, did something happen back there? All of a sudden you became a different person. I think you saw someone you knew. Did you, Carl? Please tell me the truth."

Carl thought for a moment and then decided that the truth was the best path to pursue. "Charlotte, I'm sorry. A girl that I've known for a long time saw us together and I guess she was embarrassed to see me with you. She's not really my girlfriend, though. Our families are very close and I took her to the junior high prom last week. I think that she must have felt funny to see me with someone else so soon."

"I knew that it was something. I hope I didn't spoil anything for you. I should have known you liked someone special."

"No, Charlotte, it's not like that. You didn't spoil anything; you really didn't. You know I like you. I still walk home with you from school. I don't have to, you know. I do it because I like you." Carl honestly wanted to make Charlotte feel good even though he wished that he had not taken her to the Palace of Sweets that night.

"Carl, I may be young, but I'm smart enough to know that you like whoever that young girl was that came in to the Palace of Sweets."

"You're making too much of it, Charlotte."

"Please tell me who she is so that I can call her and let her know that we are just neighbors."

"Don't be ridiculous. Forget it, Charlotte. It's not important." It was Carl who was now embarrassed and slightly annoyed at Charlotte's insistence.

The next morning, Charlotte made it a point to watch for Louise. She got Nancy's name and phone number from her. When Louise learned what had happened, she said it might be better if she, Louise, handled it. Charlotte felt a lot better about this, although she regretted that she wasn't the one Carl had a crush on.

Wednesday afternoon, Nancy telephoned Carl when she figured he would be home from school. "Carl, it's me, Nancy. Louise told me about Charlotte, the girl I saw you with at the Palace of Sweets. I guess I behaved like an idiot. I should have said hello instead of getting all upset. Will you please forgive me? I didn't mean to act jealous. I can't help it, Carl, it's the way I feel."

"Nancy, I'm glad you called. I took Charlotte out because she has been nagging me for a date and I didn't want to hurt her feelings. Gee, Nancy, I guess I would have been jealous, too, if I saw you there with some guy. I guess you could almost say you're my girlfriend."

"I want to be your steady girlfriend, Carl."

"Nancy, I think we're too young for that. You're not even 15."

"I will be soon, and they say that I'm very mature for my age. Besides, I want to be your girlfriend."

"I don't know, Nancy. It sounds a bit too formal. I mean, I really like you, but I don't know about going steady."

"We don't have to tell everyone. Girlfriend and boyfriend can be just between the two of us. I won't say anything to anyone else. Promise. I won't even be jealous if you have a date with another girl after you go to college. Maybe."

"Okay, Nancy," Carl laughed. "So long."

That afternoon, Carl went to see Mrs. Finkelstein at the news office. It was the monthly time to check the records for his newsstand.

"So how is my young man this afternoon, Carl?"

"I'm fine, Mrs. Finklestein."

"You don't remember. I am Rose to you now. But never mind, boychick. You can call me Mrs. Finklestein. I am not so glad what I made you to do for me." Mrs. Finkelstein seemed troubled. "Come with me into the back room. There is no one in the store now, so we can talk a little, Carl."

Carl figured she wanted to have sex again. He followed hesitantly.

"Sit, Carl. First, I will ask you a question. A young handsome boy like you, do you have a girlfriend?"

"Well, sort of, Mrs. Finklestein. I like this girl, but she's pretty young so I don't want to make it too serious. Anyway, I want to go to college after I graduate. That's why I took this job."

"Good boy, Carl. You're too young to be serious. Now is when you are in-between. Sometimes you are a boychick and you should have a nice young girlfriend. Sometimes you are a mench, a man. Like when you came to me the other night," she added. "I want you should know there is nothing wrong in what you did with me. It is me who is wrong. I should not spoil a young boy like you."

"Oh, I don't think you were wrong, Mrs. Finklestein. I wanted to do it."

"All right, enough. Now I will tell you something very important." She beamed, having fully regained her composure and good humor. "My cousin, Morris, for a long time has been trying to match me with someone—Mr. Golding, Harold Golding, a businessman. He is a very nice man, this Golding. But I want nothing to do again with a match, I said. 'Once was enough,' I told Morris." Mrs. Finkelstein paused and took a deep breath. "After you came to me and we did that thing, I changed my mind.

"That thing we did is a natural thing, Carl. Don't ever be ashamed. I thought about it for the whole night after. I came to a conclusion that God made man and woman they should be together. It is human nature and it is not a bad thing, as long as you don't hurt someone." She paused again and studied Carl. "I hope I didn't hurt you, Carl. I want you to know something very important to know."

"What's that, Mrs. Finklestein?" he asked, and then he said, "You didn't hurt me, Rose. I knew what I was doing and I am not hurt by it. What is it you want me to know?"

"I want you to always remember that good feelings in the heart are better than any other. In the heart and in the head, what feels good lasts forever. Anywhere else it doesn't last long, just for a little while, maybe. Then it's gone. So, what we did, you should not consider it so big an important thing. Now I want you should tell me about the girlfriend, Carl."

"Oh, she's not even 15 yet. She's two years younger than I am. Her name is Nancy Rossiter. She's a Jewish girl like you, Mrs. Finklestein."

"A Jewish girl? This could be a problem, no? Do her mother and father know about you?"

"Oh, our families are good friends. The Rossiters have known me since I was a baby. My mother and Mrs. Rossiter went to school together. They're best friends."

"I am glad the parents know you. That is good. Why don't you bring this Nancy to meet me someday, Carl. I would like to see the lucky young girl who is your girlfriend."

"Sure. Tell me about you and this Mr. Golding. Are you going to see him? Are you going to get married?"

"I have what you call a date with Harold Golding, in fact it's for dinner next Sunday. Married, I don't know yet. I think Golding will have something to say about married."

"Oh, I hope it works out for you. Sure, I'll bring Nancy in to meet you. See you soon, Mrs. Finklestein. So long."

"Goodbye and good luck, Carl. And remember, what you feel in the heart is the important thing."

Chapter Fifteen

THE MORNING AFTER BILL HENESSEY TOLD FATHER Brendan about the Columbia Bank, Father Brendan called Mr. Hennessey back and asked him if he would be able to get a copy of the Columbia Bank's financial statement. He thought the statement might give him information that could be useful. Bill Henessey agreed.

It turned out that his hunch was right. Daniel Richardson, President of Freedom Trail Travel Agency of Malden, was listed on the Statement of Financial Condition of the Columbia Bank as a member of the board of directors. None of the names of the bank officials rang a bell with the pastor. He had Leona contact Dan Richardson at the Travel Agency.

Father Brendan asked Dan if he could be of some help.

"I understand what you want, Father Brendan," was his reply. "I can't do anything myself, but Hendricks, Nathaniel Hendricks, is a teller at the bank and he might be able to help. I can ask him to give you a call."

Hendricks did call and he explained to Father Brendan that what he was asking for was confidential and that he would prefer not to become personally involved. In the conversation with Hendricks, Father Brendan learned that he lived in Medford and was a member of the Congregational Church.

Reverend Granville of the Medford Center Congregational Church agreed to meet with Father Brendan. Within a short while, Father Brendan was able to learn that Thomas Grandee did indeed have an account at Columbia Bank. The persuasive Protestant minister was able to find out Thomas' bank balance, but in quite a roundabout way.

It seems that when Reverend Henry Glanville used persuasion on his parishioner, Hendricks, the teller looked into the "G's" and found Grandee, but just next to Grandee was the name "Jeremiah Grander" which Hendricks recognized immediately as an inactive account with a substantial sum of money. What appeared in the records was that Grander's account now showed zero. To him, this was indeed suspicious. What he discovered was even more questionable.

The treasurer of the bank had recently written a charge against Grander's account for the entire sum. Since there was no Grander to receive the bank check, the bank's president put a tracer on the check and found that it was deposited in a Colorado bank, along with a number of other deposits, all in the name of James Dowd.

James Dowd was a fictitious name that the treasurer, Kenneth Jameson, used. It was discovered that he had written checks from Dowd to himself and more than $50,000 was deposited in a New York Bank account in the name of Kenneth Jameson.

Jameson was quickly arrested and would more than likely serve a sentence for embezzlement. Teller Kendricks was awarded a bonus of $5,000 by Columbia Bank for having uncovered the fraud.

In gratitude for the unexpected welcome windfall, information about Thomas Grandee was more thorough than it might have otherwise been. Kendricks attributed the award to the mysterious workings of the Lord in the course of divine justice. So, he compiled a complete history of Thomas Grandee's transactions for his minister, Henry Granville.

Granville was now interested in the case of Thomas Grandee and he arranged a meeting with Father Brendan, who invited Father Fazio as well. Since Father Brendan had originally learned about Morrison and Braverman Realty Company, he had discovered that Braverman was the more active manager of the company.

He also learned that Sam Braverman was a religious person of the Jewish faith, so he asked a Malden rabbi by the name of George Richmond of Temple Beth El to be at the meeting also. He filled the rabbi in about Thomas. Rabbi Richmond had become a good friend of the pastor's ever since the Interfaith Organization started to meet monthly three years earlier.

"Father Brendan, I am more than willing to do anything I can to be of help to you. We're good friends. But now that I have the opportunity, I have to ask you something."

"What is it, rabbi?"

"I always wondered about something. When a non-Jew meets a Jew, he or she often says, 'You must know Goldstein from wherever or Cohen from this or that business.'"

"And you think I called just because this fellow Braverman is Jewish and you are a Jewish rabbi."

"Well?"

"Guilty as charged."

"I forgive you," the Rabbi chuckled. "Who knows, I may be able to find out something. Besides, you've piqued my interest, so I may as well be at the meeting."

It was a grand meeting of local religious leaders from Malden and Medford that took place in the Holy Rosary Church rectory on Thursday evening, June 30, 1938.

Leona had ordered a catered fish dinner and made certain that every item was sufficiently kosher for the Rabbi. Since Rabbi Richmond was a reformed rabbi, Father Brendan said she didn't have to be overly fussy. "Stick to fish," he had explained.

At the meeting, Reverend Granville was the first to speak. "I have a rather complete and interesting history in front of me. We all know this information is confidential bank information. However, I was able to convince my parishioner to bend the rules just a little. He understands that it is needed to help a Catholic family in need of our assistance, which I presume is our mission. I understand from Father Brendan that we are all sworn to secrecy as to the content of the report. Am I right, gentlemen?"

All the heads nodded.

"I have had copies made," he said as he passed them around the table.

The minister continued, "Thomas Grandee opened an account at Columbia Bank in May of 1936. Cash deposits have been made every week since then. With interest, the total present value is $7,800.29. No withdrawals have ever been made."

Father Brendan exclaimed, "This is a rather amazing record for a man who earns just $55 weekly, supports a family of five, pays taxes and maintains a large house in the West End of Malden. His wife has complained to me that the house is badly in need of repair. There is never enough heat in the winter and the house needs painting, both inside and out."

"Well, gentlemen, where do we stand and what, if anything, can be done?" asked Father Fazio.

Father Brendan spoke. "We mustn't assume any wrongdoing on Thomas' part. I have the heaviest burden here, since the Grandee Family is in my parish. My first goal is to understand the issues, then to get Thomas to repair the house his family lives in before there's another dangerous winter. I need some ideas from each of you as to how I can manage to influence Thomas to come to confession, or at least explain his inability to live up to his family responsibilities."

Rabbi Richmond said, "Father Brendan, when you asked me to be at this meeting, I really didn't see at first how I could have anything to offer. However, it seems that I have learned a little about Sam Braverman from a woman in my congregation. She and her husband are friendly with Mr. and Mrs. Braverman."

"That is good news. You may be able to meet Braverman if that becomes necessary. And knowing something of a man's personality may be useful."

"I thought you would be pleased. From what I've heard, Sam Braverman sounds like a good man, one that has a kind heart. I certainly hope so for the sake of Mr. Grandee."

"A good idea," said Father Brendan. "It will be useful to have this connection. I heard from a depositor at the Boston Bank of Commerce that Morrison is a rather stern person. I think that he is also a member of the Congregational Church but he sounds like a staunch Calvinist. Braverman, however, is the one most actively involved in the realty business."

Leona quietly let Father Brendan know that dinner had arrived.

"Gentlemen, it is time to have our meal," Father Brendan announced. "Now, let us say a prayer and, if the rabbi is willing, we can have a blessing as well."

Everyone rose and Father Brendan recited, "We thank you, Father, for the food before us, and we ask that you lend assistance to the work of those here before you."

After a moment of silence, Rabbi Richmond added, "God in heaven, bless this gathering and help us all in our individual as well as collective pursuit."

"Amen," they all said in unison.

Chapter Sixteen

THE NEXT MORNING, FATHER BRENDAN ARRIVED ALONE during lunch hour at The Chateau and asked for Thomas. When Thomas joined him at the table and they ordered lunch, Father Brendan handed him back his hundred-dollar check.

"Please use this for your own family, Thomas, not for the church. Marie has mentioned that your heating system isn't functioning properly and that the house is in need of repairs. My good man, I feel that there is more need for this money in your own home than there is at the church."

Thomas accepted the check. "It was my way of apologizing for not coming to church or to confession, Father," he said. "I promise to come to church this Sunday."

"That would please me. Yes, it would please me very much," Father Brendan replied as the waiter brought over Southern style crispy fried chicken and fresh cut french fries. "My, this lunch looks appetizing. You run a fine establishment here, Thomas." Looking up at the waitress, he ordered a glass of beer.

"One for me, too, Jill," Thomas added.

"Alcohol must be a great temptation here, with it being so easily available."

"It's not that the alcohol is available, Father. It's more that the pressures of business sometimes get me a little charged. A shot of Scotch seems to calm the nerves."

The priest furrowed his brow, his mouth tightening into a knot. "With your house needing so much work, you must be hard pressed."

Thomas turned red and remained silent. He didn't know how to respond.

Father Brendan didn't press. "Why don't we enjoy lunch, Thomas? Tell me about your boy, Carl. I understand he made honor roll. Marie has also told me that your daughter Louise has graduated from high school and she has a serious boyfriend in Peter Strauss. Peter is a fine young man."

"I'm proud of my children, Father. They're all very bright, even the youngest, Robbie. I hear that he also does well in school."

"What do you mean, Thomas, when you say 'I hear'? You're talking about Robbie as if he belonged to someone else."

Thomas blushed. "That's not what I meant to say. It was just a slip of the tongue, Father. Of course I know about my own kids. About the hundred-dollar check, Father. I hope you don't misunderstand. I really want to help support the church." Thomas was trying to shift the subject away from his family. He was beginning to feel guilty.

Father Brendan saw this as a good sign. He knew that he needed to be patient and decided not to press further.

"Of course, Thomas. Father Fazio tells me that you were a fine young athlete when you lived in Revere. Tell me about that time, Thomas. I like to watch a good football game myself, you know."

Thomas began to tell of his high school years and then talked about the better professional teams of the times. The talk then moved back into the present and remained in more comfortable conversational areas. Father Brendan finished his meal and was getting ready to leave.

"I will be looking for you at church this Sunday, Thomas. I'll not press you to come to confession yet. I must leave now. It was nice to meet with you again." As he stood up to leave the Pastor said, "You will be seeing more of me, Thomas. I promise. And I intend to hold you to your promise to come to church."

"Goodbye, Father." Thomas stated pleasantly. "Thank you for stopping by." As Father Brendan left the restaurant, Thomas returned to his office to catch up with the paperwork he had left behind from the evening before. As he sat behind the large desk, he took a moment to reflect upon the meeting with Father Brendan.

Obviously Marie had been to see him, perhaps more than once, and Father Brendan was now probably aware of most of what was going on in their lives, from Marie's point of view. After all, she had confided in Father Fazio and Father Brendan years ago when she was in trouble. Why not now, even if he was the one who was really having the trouble? He wondered if Father Brendan was clever enough to figure this out and if he had been subtle enough in avoiding answers to what he thought were deliberately probing questions.

Sitting up suddenly at his desk, he returned abruptly to the work in front of him, choosing to ignore this line of self-interrogation. There were too many questions with too few answers, and now other people were beginning to ask questions, too. Thomas was confused and, without any of the answers, it was foolish to worry. He continued with his calculations, totaling the receipts, knowing that Hannah would enter them as a lesser figure in the official journal. He would sign the journal for her as he had been doing all along. Not one day had gone by when this exercise hadn't made him at least a bit uneasy. Now, he was more uncomfortable than ever.

Thomas finalized his work and rested in the high-back desk chair a second time. He wasn't accustomed to being behind schedule and would never allow work to pile up, no matter how distasteful the exercise.

Thinking again of Father Brendan and Marie, he realized that he had a complex matter in front of him and it would have to be resolved somehow. Avoiding its resolution was no longer an acceptable alternative. But complex matters sometimes have simple solutions, he thought.

He rose from the desk to return to the tavern to see if preparations were being made for the forthcoming evening at the bar. Switching the office light off and closing the door carefully behind him, he understood more clearly that his own inaction was becoming as harmful as his actions. Without a clear alternative, Thomas was still left at a loss. Yet one thing had become perfectly clear to him, no matter what the future might bring. As quickly as this started, he thought, I can make it come to an end.

Chapter Seventeen

HANNAH SHOWED UP FOR HER PART OF the bookkeeping that day at about four in the afternoon. She was seldom late for her visits. She paid little attention to Victor other than a brief wave of the hand. Victor waved back and winked. That pleased her. Let them think she was having an affair with Thomas. She thought it might even be a good idea to start it up again in order to prevent a rebellion. Lately, she could sense that he was getting nervous.

Once inside the office, Hannah locked the door behind her. "Tommy, I miss the old days. Come hold me close, honey." She was still the only one who had ever called Thomas Grandee "Tom" or "Tommy." Aware of her power over him, she smiled inwardly.

Thomas paid her no attention. He simply seated himself behind his desk and produced a canvas bag with the collection of organized receipts and vouchers.

When he stretched his hand out to offer the bag, Hannah did not take it. Instead she said, "Come now, Tom, put that bag down. I remember the day we made love right here and I've often thought how great it would be to do that again. Tommy, we've been too businesslike. Let's have some fun together. How about it?" She was seated on the sofa and had started to undress.

Thomas had only had the one glass of beer with Father Brendan, so he was completely sober. As he approached the sofa, she said, "My, you look handsome today. Have you given more thought to letting my friend bill The Chateau for repairs? The upstairs hotel rooms are used enough by now that no one will question a few maintenance invoices."

"I told you before. Victor does the maintenance, and if anything has to be contracted out, he handles that also. I have nothing to do with it."

"Okay Tom, I won't mention it again. Now come on over and make love to me, you handsome man."

"Sure, let's make love, Hannah." As he reached the sofa he pushed Hannah down roughly. "What are you, Hannah? What is it that makes you tick? I wish I could undo all the stupid things we did. Stealing is what it is. All I want now is to put a stop to it."

Hannah was startled by the outburst, but she maintained her composure. She wanted to re-ignite the erotic spark she had once started. She rose and pushed herself up against him, reaching down to his crotch. Thomas smacked her hard across the face. She took the canvas bag and headed for the door.

"Wait, Hannah. Don't leave yet," Thomas said. He knew that he was in deep and that he had to work with Hannah in some way that would get him off the hook. "I'm sorry I hit you, Hannah. I really didn't mean it. It's just that I've had a hard day. Please come back in."

Hannah was not sure that she understood what was going through Thomas' mind, so she instinctively resorted to her feminine wiles again.

"Let's not spoil it by doing it here, Tom. I have to go back to the office and take care of things and I'll come back later so we can spend the night together. How would you like that?"

"Of course," Thomas agreed. He wasn't happy with the turn that had taken place, but he was at a loss to strongly oppose Hannah at this juncture. He was simply in too deep.

After Hannah left, Thomas went upstairs to the hotel unit he reserved for himself. He downed a double scotch and sat in a comfortable chair and tried to think. He poured another double and eventually finished that one, too.

If he stopped playing her game, it would not solve the problem of two years' worth of stealing. To contact Morrison and tell all was taking a chance of being arrested and going to jail. To allow Hannah's crooked friend to submit fake invoices would simply add to the problem. How would he explain that to Victor?

Thomas filled the whiskey glass again, this time carefully sipping as he pondered. He became drowsy and didn't awaken until there was a knock at the door.

It was Hannah, smiling her familiar "come on" smile. She had them both in bed within minutes. Thomas couldn't make himself become completely awake. He just lied there and let Hannah try to stimulate him. After about ten minutes, she rolled over on her back and lay in bed alongside Thomas.

"For Christ sakes, what's wrong, Tom? I thought you'd like to make love to me."

"Sure, some other time, Hannah. Right now I don't think I can get it up."

"Oh, if that's all, lets try this," she said as she started to kiss Thomas on the chest and then quickly moved down to his private parts.

Thomas was not able to respond and he pushed her away. "I'm going home. You can stay here all night if you like." With that said, Thomas got up, dressed and walked out the door, leaving Hannah lying naked and open-mouthed.

He walked downstairs through the restaurant and was on his way out the door when Victor came into the restaurant from his back room. "Where's the fire, Thomas? You look in an awful hurry."

"I want to go home and get the hell out of here!"

"What happened?"

Thomas suddenly realized that he had burst out in anger in The Chateau for the very first time. It was too late to do anything about it, so he simply said, "I went upstairs to lie down, Victor. I wasn't feeling well. I guess I better get home." With that remark he opened the door and walked around behind The Chateau where his car was parked.

Thomas knew he had more alcohol in him than ever before and he could feel its effect. Driving five miles per hour all the way home, he was careful enough to make it safely to Malden without getting killed and lucky that he wasn't arrested for drunk driving.

Victor knew that Thomas had been upstairs with Hannah, so he could only conclude that the two of them had had some kind of a riff. He thought, Thomas is screwing around with that broad, and it must be more than just casual sex. Even the parish priest is coming around. That means there's trouble with his wife, as well.

Victor knew that Marie Grandee was a practicing Catholic and that she might go to her parish priest if there was a serious problem in her marriage. Religious Catholics don't even think of divorce, he thought. That must be why Father Brendan is coming here.

Hannah sensed that Thomas was going to give her a hard time about future cash, but she wasn't worried that he would say anything. He had as much to lose as she did.

She stood up, washed and dressed, and then headed downstairs, using the inside staircase that led to the restaurant. She could use the house telephone to hail a taxi. She didn't have her car with her tonight, and it was getting late.

It was already after closing time, and The Tavern was empty. Victor was cleaning up for the evening. "Victor, how are you?" she asked. "I was about to leave."

"I'm just fine, Hannah, how about yourself? I saw Thomas leave. He said he was going home."

"Yes, Thomas had some business at home. He won't be coming back. Would you like to spend the night with me, Victor? I don't feel like going to my lonely apartment."

"Hey, it's okay with me as long as you're sure Thomas isn't coming back."

"I'm sure. Let's go back upstairs. I locked the door to his room, but you must have a master key."

"Alright, Hannah. Let's go."

Once in the room, Victor said, "Listen, Hannah, I don't want trouble with Thomas. If he finds out I came anywhere near you, he'll kill me. I'll lose my job."

"I told you he isn't coming back. Not tonight. I'm sure."

Victor spent the night with Hannah and before it was over, she thought she might be able to proposition him about letting her friend send a couple of bills to his attention. "I won't say one word to Thomas about what we just did, Victor, Honey. I like the way you make love. We ought to do this more often."

Hannah was feeling sure of herself with Victor. She had been working at The Chateau long enough to sense that Victor was not a man with strong moral convictions. Thomas had also told her enough about him during the past several years that she had already arrived at the conclusion that he was the type of a man who cared little about anything.

Now that she held a threat over him, he wouldn't dare say a word to Thomas, or anyone else for that matter. All she had to do was threaten him with exposure to Thomas and that would be the end of his job.

She decided to chance it. Since there was now reasonable doubt in her mind whether Thomas was in a mood to continue their little game, she needed a possible replacement. She was also thinking that Thomas was starting to break down and she knew that he hated his job. Now that he was running scared about the money, he might just quit in order to get away from his problems.

The risk of starting the fake bills plan with Victor was small in her opinion, no greater than the risks she had taken throughout her life. It was a way to get Victor involved. She also thought Victor would become manager of The Chateau if Thomas left.

"Victor, I have a little proposition for you." Hannah then proceeded cautiously and explained her idea.

"I don't know, Hannah, let me think about it. It might be a good idea. I just don't want to get into trouble." He showed no surprise, or shock, or disbelief. She couldn't make out what he was really thinking.

What Victor was really thinking was far from indifferent. Victor knew that there was monkey business going on between Hannah and Thomas. The timing of her little scheme suggested more than just sex and a few fake repair bills. The Chateau handled lots of cash and he had been suspicious for some time that it was not all going where it belonged. If Hannah was the one picking up the cash and doing the bookkeeping, and Thomas was involved, there was something going on.

Victor had been playing the role of obsequious servant to Thomas long enough. If Thomas was out of the way, he, Victor, was in line for the job of manager at The Chateau. The parish priest could be his ticket to freedom from Thomas' domination and the key to a much better paying job. If he could reveal enough information to Father Brendan to make Thomas and Hannah's actions questionable, it could lead to Thomas' resignation, which would set him up for the promotion.

He was shrewd enough to be able to play the game all the way through if he had to. Let them think he was indifferent and lacking ambition. Now he had a plan.

122

Chapter Eighteen

THERE WAS SURPRISE AT THE GRANDEE HOUSE when Thomas arrived home. He was not as steady on his feet as usual. It was the first time Marie and the kids had ever seen him like this. It was actually the first time that Thomas ever visibly showed signs of being drunk.

"Just leave me alone, everyone. I'm going upstairs to bed," he said, heading for the staircase.

"Wait, Thomas," Marie said, "I think you ought to sleep in the extra bedroom. It's all made up. I'll just turn the covers down and make certain everything is ready."

"Sure, thanks. Good night, kids." He started up the stairs again, this time following Marie.

At breakfast Saturday morning, Thomas was unusually quiet. He ate slowly and seemed to be deep in thought. "Maybe I'll have a look around the house today to see what has to be done before winter sets in," he stated matter-of-factly. He remembered Father Brendan's comments about the condition of the house. His mind, however, was on the money sitting in Columbia Bank; money he had never gone near. Now he was thinking that it made no difference. He could withdraw some of it and get started on repairs. What the hell was all this misery about if he couldn't use the money?

"It would be nice to have things working, Thomas. We would all certainly like that very much," Marie mused. She was uncertain about Thomas' mood. She had gotten more than just a mild dose of whiskey and perfume upstairs the night before, even with Thomas in the other room. And, the perfume smell was still in the spare room when she went in afterwards to make up the bed. She just didn't know what to make of it.

When she had last spoken with Father Brendan, the priest told her that she should try to be patient. He explained that Thomas was having some problems but that he felt there was hope and that things would work out well in the end. She would have to wait it out, of course, but it wasn't going to be easy.

After breakfast, Louise and Robbie did the dishes. Carl left to get to his newsstand on time. He was going to meet Nancy for lunch and introduce her to Mrs. Finklestein. He was looking forward to their meeting.

At lunchtime, Mrs. Finkelstein grinned happily when the two young people walked into the news store. It was a busy time, so she asked them to wait a few minutes.

"Sit over in the corner, please. Soon the customers will be going back to work and it will be empty. Maybe in only five more minutes, I think. Here, take a magazine, Nancy. Help yourself to a candy bar from the shelf, Carl."

The store did empty out in a short while. Mrs. Finkelstein locked the door and put up the "CLOSED" sign.

"Come, let's sit together in the back room. What a beautiful girlfriend you have, Carl, and you have a handsome boy, Nancy. What is your last name?" she asked, looking in Nancy's direction. "I already forgot."

"Rossiter, Mrs. Finklestein. Nancy Rossiter."

"Such a pretty name, Nancy Rossiter. I like it. So tell me, Nancy, you are in high school with Carl?"

"No, not until next year. Well, September. That's only two months away."

"It's nice that you come to visit me. Please make it a habit. If Carl likes you, I am sure you are a very nice young lady. You both look so happy. I hope you are having good times together, yes?"

"Oh yes, Mrs. Finklestein. Carl is taking me to the beach today. In fact, we're on our way as soon as we leave here."

"So, go already. You've wasted enough time on an old lady. Go and have a good time. Don't forget what I said. Too long don't wait to come back."

As they left and were out of earshot, Nancy said, "She talks funny."

"She comes from a different country. I think she does well, considering."

"I suppose. My grandparents sometimes get the language mixed up, too."

Carl and Nancy caught the bus in Malden Square. It took them to Revere Street at the Beach. The day was beautiful. It was sunny and about 85 degrees, perfect for swimming and getting a tan.

Nancy had a blanket in her beach bag. Their bathing suits were already on under their clothing. All they had to do was strip and head for the water.

Back on the sand and lying in the sun, they turned toward each other and gazed. No passerby would ever doubt that this was a happy young couple. They kissed and then laughed. "I love you, Carl." Nancy said.

"I guess I do, too, Nancy."

"'Do too what', Carl?"

"Love you."

"Please say it, Carl. You know. Say, 'I love you, Nancy.'"

"I love you, Nancy." They kissed again. "Let's go across and see what's doing where the stands are. Want some ice cream?"

"Sure, let's go."

Carl pulled on pants and a shirt while Nancy dressed in a skirt and blouse. They grabbed their bags and ran across the boulevard to the other side of the beach where the stands and amusements dotted the ocean skyline. They walked past one interesting place after another. There were endless places to eat, amusements, exciting rides and other attractions for what seemed like miles.

Finally, they stopped to look at the passengers speeding up to the sky and down again on the Lightning Roller Coaster. The Lightning had opened for operation back in 1927 and, within two hours, a rider fell to his death. The ride was closed down for inspection, but when no structural fault was found, it reopened. No further accidents had occurred since that time.

"Carl, can we take a ride on Hurley's Hurdlers?" she asked. Hurley's was a famous merry-go-round.

"Sure, Nancy. Let's go." He bought two five-cent tickets. They took seats on colorful horses springing up, down and forward in rhythmic rotational movement on poles alongside each other. By the time the ride was over, they were ready to buy two frozen custards for a nickel each.

Afterwards, they decided to go back to the beach. It was fun to watch the seaplanes near the pier and the speedboat rides ducking in and out of the shoreline.

When Carl dropped Nancy off after walking her home, Grandmother Herman and Betty's mother were in the house.

"My, you look nice and tan, honey," Grandma Herman announced as she walked through the door. "You were at the beach with your boyfriend?" she asked, eager as usual to gather information and process it on her family's account.

"Yes! We had a great time, grandma," Nancy answered, all smiles.

"So, who is the young man, may I ask?"

"You know him. Carl Grandee. We've known each other forever."

"A goyishe boy, Nancy. I know Carl. A nice boy for sure, but he's not Jewish. I hope you're not serious about him. Are you, my child?"

"Grandma, I like Carl. I can't say how serious I am, but what if I am? Carl isn't religious or anything like that." Nancy was slightly irritated by her grandmother's incursion upon her otherwise enjoyable afternoon.

Betty, sensing her daughter's mixed feelings, turned to her mother. "Ma, why don't we have this conversation some other time. Nancy isn't getting engaged, and both she and Carl are still young enough to understand that they have lives ahead of them. They'll be going off to college soon and meeting other boys and girls. So, let's not worry so much."

Assured that she had deterred what might have become a difficult conversation, Betty changed the topic to dinner. It was getting late and she had expected her daughter home earlier. Harvey and David had been waiting and were listening without saying a word.

"I think dinner is a good idea, Betty. What can I do to help?" Harvey asked.

"The table is set. Just bring the pitcher of water, Harvey. It's in the refrigerator. Come on everyone, let's sit." Betty said. "I'll serve." Walking back over to the kitchen stove where she had been standing during her daughter's conversation with her grandmother, she cast an empathetic glance to her own mother and explained, "I made your favorite Saturday night chicken recipe, Ma."

"As if I wouldn't know what you would serve for dinner if I came," her mother responded. "I wish papa could be here but he's busy tonight. Let's eat!"

Chapter Nineteen

SUNDAY MORNING, MARIE AND LOUISE PREPARED BREAKFAST for the family. They served pancakes with crisp bacon and coffee. Leaving Louise with the dishes, Marie was off to 10 o'clock Mass with Robbie. Carl was long gone to his newsstand.

Before leaving, Marie managed to ask, "Louise, you can leave the dishes and come to church with me. How about it?"

She didn't argue when her daughter refused. From experience, she knew it would be a wasted effort. Like Thomas, Louise only agreed to go to church at Christmas and Easter. Carl wasn't much better. Well, she thought, with a father like Thomas, what could she expect?

Turning to her husband, she continued half-heartedly, "Thomas, I don't suppose you want to join me?"

"Not right now, Marie. Maybe I'll attend a later mass," was his response.

There was an early afternoon mass later in the day and Thomas intended to show his face. He wanted to make certain that Father Brendan saw him that Sunday. Maybe this would deter him from haunting him at The Chateau.

As soon as Marie left for church with Robbie, Thomas stood up and walked over to where Louise was doing the dishes.

"I'm sorry that I slapped you when I did, Louise. I really don't know what got into me. It has bothered me all the while. I feel bad that I hit Carl, too. I know you two are close. Will you tell him for me?"

"Sure, Pa. I understand. We're okay. Don't worry about it," she responded.

When Louise finished the dishes, she turned to her father and asked, "I'm going to make some phone calls now. I hope you don't need the phone. If you do, please tell me and I can wait until later."

"No, Louise, you go right ahead. I'm just going to look at the Sunday paper and maybe go out for a walk a little later."

Louise was puzzled. Her father was a different person this morning. He was usually self-confident, nearly arrogant when they were all home together, and talked loudly whenever he had anything to say to anyone, which was seldom.

Most of the time during the past couple of years, he had been nasty to the family whenever he came home, which was no more often than one or two days during the week and on Sunday mornings. Sundays were usually the worst and here he was, quiet and subdued.

Louise went into the small den where she sat down at the telephone to call Peter. They talked for about 10 minutes, then she called her girlfriend Patricia Coughlin.

"Hi, Patty," she exclaimed. "What did you find out about the Mount Auburn Hospital? You said you were going over there for information today."

"I did, Louise. They're accepting applications all this week. You asked me about the money. Tuition is $150 for the three-year course. If you're admitted, you have to pay an additional $25 for books and $25 for breakage. Oh, they explained that you have to bring an umbrella, bathrobe and boots. Everything else is provided for—room and board, uniforms, meals, *everything*."

"Sounds good, Patty. I'm going for an interview at a restaurant in Wellington Circle tomorrow afternoon. It's a waitress position and pays five dollars salary plus tips. You get to keep all the tips. I think that I can make enough to cover Mount Auburn. I already have $50 saved from babysitting and the drug store job I had last summer. How about you, Patty?"

"I can swing it! My parents said they would help if I run short. Gee, I'm so excited! What do you think, Louise? I'm ready to apply."

"Let's do it, Patty! I'm ready when you are."

Carl brought the money from the day's paper sales to Mrs. Finkelstein that afternoon.

"I have to give you notice, Mrs. Finklestein. I have a chance to get a steady job this summer and then, starting in September, they will let me work after school until five o'clock. Now that I have a driver's license, I can work in the store and then make deliveries with their pickup truck."

Mrs. Finkelstein said, "You will make more money, too, Carl. I know you are saving to go to college. That is good."

"Anyway, my class schedule calls for me to be in school earlier each day than last year. I had a study period first thing in junior year, so it didn't matter if I came a little late."

"So tell me, Carl, what is this job?" Mrs. Finkelstein asked. Her usual smile was missing. Replacing it was a sadness Carl could almost feel.

Carl was tempted to say that he would continue to work for her. Instead, he replied, "I'll be working at Mayor Lamson's place—the Lamson and Davis Wallpaper and Paint store on Main Street. They need someone. I saw the ad in the paper and I applied. Mayor Lamson hired me."

"Good for you, Carl. Don't worry. Give me one week and I will have a new boy. I got a list so long from boys who want the job. I am glad for you if you have a good job. It will help you with money for college."

"Gee, thanks, Mrs. Finklestein. I thought you'd be mad. Yes, it will help. Do you mind if I ask Nancy's brother, David, if he wants the job?"

"I will only be mad if you won't sometimes come to say hello. Call your friend, David. He's a nice boy. Only, please, by tomorrow you should let me know."

Mrs. Finkelstein smiled at Carl. Her admiration and respect for him showed in her glance. "Good luck on your new job. Now give me a big hug, boychick! I want you should know to always give me a big hug."

As she put her arms around Carl and squeezed hard, Carl held her close. It felt good, but not the same as the day he fixed her light bulbs. This was different.

Like Mrs. Finkelstein had explained, the best kind of feeling was in his heart. This was the feeling that he thought he might now be having for Nancy Rossiter after all. He was glad that he had taken the time to introduce her to Mrs. Finklestein.

The first thing he did was to make a call to David. "You can have the job if you want it, Dave, but you have to let Mrs. Finkelstein know by tomorrow morning."

"Great!" David said. "I have her phone number, and as soon as I get the okay from my parents, I'll call. Thanks, Carl, I sure can use the money. Nancy might even help me. We were just talking about making some extra money together.."

Carl's good relationship with Mrs. Finkelstein secured a position for the Rossiter twins. It was just one more perk that made him feel good about the year he had spent working for this very generous-hearted woman.

Chapter Twenty

CARL WAS AT THE ROSSITER HOUSE AFTER dinner on Monday. He was keeping an appointment he had made to meet with Harvey Rossiter to talk about his future plans for college, in particular the Boston University application that had arrived the other day in the mail.

Nancy greeted him at the door with a quick kiss that she chanced after making certain that no one was looking. "Daddy told me you were coming to see him. He's in the living room waiting for you."

Carl crossed the hall to the left and entered the large, well-furnished living room.

"Hello, Carl, come on in. How are you?"

"I'm fine, thank you, Mr. Rossiter. How are you, sir?"

"Fine, thank you. Go on into my study and make yourself comfortable, Carl. I'll be right with you."

Carl passed through the door at the far right of the living room and was astonished at the number of books he saw on the bookshelves and piled at random on a table set behind Mr. Rossiter's desk in the study. The lamp on the professor's desk was on, which meant that he was probably in the midst of reading the papers strewn in front of his leather upholstered swivel arm chair.

Carl walked over and started to read book titles. One waist-high shelf was completely occupied by the 1938 edition of Encyclopedia Britannica. Above it was a row of history books. There was a brand new two-volume edition of the life of Abraham Lincoln and next to it a volume of Ibsen's Plays. Further along on the same shelf was a four-volume set of Shakespeare's *Comedies and Tragedies. Decline and Fall of the Roman Empire* sat next to Shakespeare. In all, there must have been hundreds of volumes of books.

Dante's *The Divine Comedy* looked worn from use. Darwin, Frederick Engels, Karl Marx, Shopenhauer, Spinoza, Frederick Douglass, Greek Tragedies, O'Henry and more books than he had ever seen outside a public library lined the shelves, some slightly worn but most in good condition.

Harvey Rossiter entered the study. "I see that you're interested in my collection. If you would like to borrow anything, Carl, just ask."

The conversation between Carl and Professor Rossiter soon moved away from the application and college curriculums. After answering Carl's questions about tuition costs and the personal essay, Rossiter's suggestion on choice of curriculum was, "You have plenty of time for that, Carl. First get the application ready and get yourself accepted. We can talk about choice of subjects afterwards."

In no time, they were on the subject of the depression. Carl asked Rossiter to explain what was so good about the New Deal if the country was still in a depression.

"Your family and my own are well-off, compared to thousands of others. Your father has a job. Millions of Americans are unemployed, so for them, there is still a depression. The difference between now, under the New Deal, and back in the early 1930s can be explained very easily. I will give you an example to illustrate what Roosevelt has accomplished.

"I knew a family that was on relief in the city of Boston. They had to go to City Hall and ask for charity. The family of five was visited by a social worker. The city gave them nine dollars a week.

"Today, because of Social Security, Americans have unemployment insurance. That same family, provided the breadwinner can prove that he was previously employed, would be entitled to an unemployment check each week for 26 weeks. The different states can vary in the amount they pay or the number of weeks allowed. But, federal law requires that every American is entitled to collect compensation if they become unemployed.

"The major difference, Carl, is that now American workers have rights. Instead of unreliable charity, an American worker receives a portion of a dependable week's pay. The New Deal recognizes that workers have earned those unemployment checks. It's not just charity."

"I understand. They get more than they would from charity, too, don't they?"

"Well, in most cases they do. The important thing to remember is that the government programs can be depended upon."

"Do you know all about this because you are a history professor?"

"Not exactly, Carl. What we just talked about is current events. Like I told you once before, what happens today will be history in the future."

"No, Carl, one doesn't have to be a history teacher to know what is happening in the world. Simply look around you and be interested. Read books, newspapers and ask questions. The more knowledge you gain, the better off you will be. It's good to understand the world around you, even when that world is distressed, as it is now."

"Sure, Mr. Rossiter. I guess it pays to learn things. That's why I want to go to college. Besides, you can get a good job if you have a good education."

"Usually, and even though the good jobs may not always be there, sooner or later a good education pays off."

"That's why I want to do well in school," Carl said.

"The children of families that are living in poverty don't have as good a chance for a decent future as you, Carl. One of the only ways for them to effectively move up out of poverty is through education. That's another good point about the New Deal. Under Roosevelt, congress has put money to work building schools in poor neighborhoods as well as funding poverty programs."

"I guess you voted for Roosevelt."

"I did, Carl, and I'll vote for him again if he runs for re-election."

With that, Professor Rossiter began to explain again briefly about the politics in other countries and systems that were in conflict with American goals and ideals.

Carl began to wonder what Nancy was up to, and Harvey Rossiter seemed to read his mind. "Go on now, Carl, why don't you visit with Nancy? I've taken enough of your time."

"Oh, no, Mr. Rossiter, you've been a big help with my application and I enjoy very much learning about current events.

Maybe I'll major in history when I go to college. I never even used to like it. I hated it last year until after you began to tutor me. Now I'm able to see it all in a different light. You know I got an A in history because of your help."

"Yes, Carl. I do know. Nancy told me. Now go on and leave me to my reading, and good luck with whatever you decide to do about college."

Carl found Nancy in the kitchen and asked if she wanted to go down to Malden Square to the Palace of Sweets. She thought that it was a very good idea and went into the kitchen. "I'm going out for a little while with Carl, mom, if that's okay."

"Yes, and have fun, dear. Don't be too late, kids," Betty called out as her daughter left the room and headed toward the door with Carl.

"What were you and Daddy talking about, Carl?" Nancy asked when they were outside. "It didn't sound like your application. I couldn't resist listening. Was he telling you about President Roosevelt?"

"Yeah, I guess he likes Roosevelt. He was explaining about the New Deal. He also said that what Hitler is doing in Germany, especially to the Jewish people, is horrible and he needs to be stopped immediately."

Nancy thought for a moment and then said, "I told my grandmother that you were not an anti-Semite. She doesn't want you to be my boyfriend because you're Catholic, but I told her that I didn't care because I liked you anyway, and I said you were not a religious Catholic. You're not really very religious, are you Carl?"

"Well, I go to church sometimes, and I like Father Brendan. I guess I'm not religious like my mother, but I really do feel that we need something to believe in."

"Carl, if you really are a religious Catholic and I'm Jewish, do you think that's important?"

"I don't know, Nancy. Maybe. It's difficult for people to get married when they have differences of religion. I've never thought about it before." Carl was still speaking as they reached the Palace of Sweets.

Once inside, they each ordered ice cream sodas. Nancy's eyes were beginning to well up with tears. She wasn't crying, but she certainly did not look happy.

When their order arrived, Nancy just played with her food. Carl had lost his appetite, too. The two young lovers looked at each other and Carl said, "Hey, let's not get too upset, Nancy," but he put the money on the table to pay the check and they both got up and started to walk to Nancy's house.

They didn't say much on the way home, but the lack of conversation was eloquent in its expression of sadness for the both of them, especially Nancy, who was still on the verge of tears. Once they reached the Rossiter house, Nancy turned to Carl and said, "I love you, Carl. Please don't stop loving me just because I'm not Catholic."

"I won't, Nancy," he answered. They hugged each other as if holding on for dear life, but there was no kissing or fondling. Nancy went inside, and Carl's head was buzzing with mixed thoughts on the long walk home. He decided that he had to speak to Mr. Rossiter about the situation before there was time to let ideas like the ones that he was having get out of hand.

Chapter Twenty-One

CARL PHONED MR. ROSSITER ON SUNDAY, RIGHT after he finished his last day's work at the newsstand. They agreed to meet that evening. Carl asked if they could meet someplace other than the Rossiter house. Harvey Rossiter sensed some urgency in Carl's voice and agreed to pick him up in Malden Square after dinner. They could pick up some cold drinks and sit in his car and talk.

Carl was waiting for him at the appointed hour. Once in the car, Mr. Rossiter asked Carl if there was anyplace special he would like to go for them to talk. Carl said, "I think it would be easier for me if we were outside. Someplace where there aren't any other people around."

"And where might such a place be, Carl?"

"I don't know. Maybe we could go over near Spot Pond and just walk around. I don't really know how I want to say what's on my mind. I can't do it here in the car."

"Fine, I don't mind getting some fresh air and exercise, myself."

Carl walked alongside Nancy's father at Spot Pond in Stoneham without saying a word about himself and Nancy for quite some time. "It's peaceful here at night. I come here to run during the day when I have the time. It's a pretty sight in the daylight, but it's really beautiful at night."

Harvey Rossiter thought Carl sounded more like a grown man than a 17-year-old boy did with a problem on his mind. The pond was beautiful with moonlight shimmering across the water, forming shapes like strokes of luminescent colors from an artist's brush. He wasn't going to rush Carl into getting to the point of his problem.

"Yes, Carl. Betty and I used to come here to smooch. We called it Lover's Lane."

"Yeah, we still do. I never came here with Nancy, though. It's Nancy I want to talk about, Mr. Rossiter. I just don't know how to begin."

"Do you think the two of you are getting too serious? Is that what's on your mind?"

"Yes, in a way you could say that's it. Nancy is heartbroken because she says she loves me, but she thinks it will upset her family, especially her grandparents. Now she is afraid for me because I am Catholic."

"Because you're Catholic? Is that what she told you?"

"She asked me if I was religious and if I thought it was wrong for people to get married if they were from different religions. I didn't know how to answer her, so I just said that I thought it was good to have something to believe in." Carl paused for a moment and then continued. "The Catholic Church has its own beliefs and the sacraments, which are very important if you're a practicing Catholic like my mother. She taught me what the sacraments were. Marriage, or Matrimony, is one of them."

"First of all, Carl, let me say that both you and Nancy are great kids, but whatever you feel for each other now will still be there later on in life if you kids are really in love. Give it time, though. Nancy's not even fifteen and you're what, seventeen?"

Carl nodded and waited a moment. Then he said, "I told Nancy I thought we were too young even to be steady boyfriend and girlfriend. I think you're right, Mr. Rossiter. We *are* too young to be talking about this stuff. That's the point, I guess."

"I'm relieved to hear that, Carl. But I do have a question for you. I don't think you would be here talking to me if you didn't take Nancy pretty seriously, too. Am I right?"

"Well, yes. I certainly would never want to hurt Nancy. I guess you could say I like her very much. I've known her all my life and I get mixed up. But, I can't really tell the difference between Nancy being my girlfriend or being like a sister." Carl was becoming disconcerted now. He looked at Mr. Rossiter for help. They found a bench and sat.

"Well, there could be a special bond between you kids. It shows up in Nancy when she talks about you and it's written all over your face, too," Mr. Rossiter explained. "Now, that doesn't mean I think it's anything more than what we grownups call 'puppy love.'"

"Look, Carl, you're going to be a senior in September. Another year and you're off to college. There's plenty of time for you to live life a little, see other girls, too. Nancy should meet other boys and go on dates as well. Why, she hasn't ever had a real date except for the Junior Dance the two of you went to this spring."

Carl interrupted. "You haven't said anything about the issue of religion, though. That's the part that bothers me the most because I don't understand. I know we're too young to be serious, but I get all messed up when I think about me being Catholic and Nancy being Jewish."

"The issue of religion is confusing to many, Carl. To begin with, I have to tell you that I, personally, am an atheist. Oh, I'm Jewish all right, but I'm not religious. Betty isn't quite as far removed from her faith as I am, so let's say she's agnostic. Do you know what atheist and agnostic mean, Carl?"

"Sure, an atheist doesn't believe in God. An agnostic isn't sure if there is or there isn't one."

"And how about you, Carl? Do you have complete faith in your religion?"

"I don't especially like to go to church, and I'm not even sure if I believe in God, Mr. Rossiter, but my mother is a practicing Catholic and she taught us about the sacraments as children. It's hard to erase it all from my mind. I guess my answer is that I'm not sure of myself, not yet, anyway." Carl paused and seemed to be in deep thought.

Rossiter said, "You look puzzled, Carl. What is it?"

"Well, even though I'm not too sure how I feel about being Catholic, I can't help feeling that I have to believe in something, to have some kind of faith. So my question to you, Mr. Rossiter is..."

"Go on Carl, feel free to ask anything. I have an idea what you might want to know."

"If you're an atheist, what do you believe in or have faith in?"

"Good question, Carl. I thought that might be it," Rossiter replied. "The answer is that I do believe in something. Every human being, whether he or she knows it or not, has a belief, a philosophy. That's what a religion is to me, Carl. Each religion is based on its particular philosophy and the purpose of the philosophy is to give meaning to life, to help the believers to find a purpose and to achieve happiness. Most people believe in the religion into which they were born. It doesn't matter whether you are a Buddhist or a Jew or a Catholic or Protestant or even if you were born into a culture of Voodooists." Here, Mr. Rossiter paused briefly and took a few seconds to ponder how to continue.

"Each of the many cultures and religions, from earliest time until today, worshipped at one altar or another. Some worshipped the sun, others thought of a high mountain as God, and every civilization or culture or religion was always sure it was the one and best philosophy. I believe that for each it served the purpose of giving meaning to their lives. My philosophy is this, Carl. I believe that the purpose of life is to work for the happiness of men and women while we are here on earth, and that we must somehow find that happiness within the confines of the natural environment in which we live.

"I do not believe there is a life after death. I do believe that there is much that is wrong in the world, but I also feel that human beings are capable of eventually overcoming the wrong, as individuals and collectively. Just think of what people have achieved through thousands of years of civilization. In the same way that we learned about the sun and the moon and the planets, things that people once worshipped because they did not understand them, the mysteries that remain are not so much mysteries as they are unsolved pieces of the puzzle of life. Mankind has the power to find answers and to overcome wrongs. I do have faith, Carl. My faith is in the ability of people to help each other achieve the human goal of happiness, here on earth, not in some unknown heaven."

"Boy, Mr. Rossiter, now I have a lot to think about. Anyway, thanks for being so honest and for answering my question."

"And now, Carl, my question to you is this: If you did eventually fall truly in love with Nancy and you two had children, would you insist on raising your kids as Catholics?"

"I have never thought about it, Mr. Rossiter. I would never admit it to my mother, but I guess I really don't know. Maybe it should be up to the kids to decide for themselves. I guess I'm not really religious. Not like my mother, anyway. I never think about whether someone is Catholic or Jewish or what he or she is.

"The lady I worked for in the news company is Jewish. Her name is Mrs. Finklestein, and I think she's a great person. She speaks with a funny accent, but she's nice. She once told me that the important thing in life is how good one feels in one's heart. I think she's right about that. If I feel good in my heart about a person, then I don't care what religion they are."

"I'd say you have some pretty grownup thoughts for a 17-year-old, Carl. Now I think we better get started for home. My suggestion is for you and Nancy to meet with Betty and me and talk some of this out. I am assuming that you and I agree that you're both too young to be serious boyfriend and girlfriend. What we have to do now is get Nancy to understand that also. How about Betty and I talking first and then we'll call you to arrange a time for the four of us to get together?"

"Sounds fine with me, Mr. Rossiter. Do you think Nancy will be upset that I talked with you about this? I really was worried that I would be hurting Nancy and I didn't know how to handle it. I just want to make sure she knows how much I like her, even if it isn't love."

"Yes, Carl, that's what you've been saying all evening. Betty and I can explain things to Nancy before we all get together. I'm sure she's not going to stop liking you. In fact, the main reason I think the two of you have to have this talk with Betty and me present is to make sure that the wonderful friendship between you and Nancy is never spoiled."

"Mr. Rossiter, can I talk to you about my father? I mean, in confidence."

"Of course you can, Carl. I know there are problems with your dad. Your father and I have always been good friends. What is it that you want to talk about?"

"Well, I don't remember my father getting drunk when I was much younger. Why would he start to drink all of a sudden? That's one question. The other question has to do with the arguments between my mother and father. Pa was always the one in charge in our family. That isn't any different. The trouble now is that Ma and Pa are arguing all the time. I don't really know what I want from you. I guess I just have to talk it out a little because it's bothering me so much. Actually, its bothering my mother the most, which is kind of hurting the rest of us."

"Carl, as I said, your father and I have been good friends. You're right when you say he seems to be acting differently. I don't have a clue as to why, but I do know that there has to be a reason.

Something might have happened in your father's life to turn him upside down.

"My question to you is this, Carl. Your father was always a little strange about control and so he never allowed your mother to make any decisions about money. That, to him, must have been his way of feeling in charge. Otherwise, he was always good to his family.

"I remember him organizing a softball team with you and Louise and some other kids. Nancy and David used to watch when you kids played. They were too young to get in the game. Do you remember that, Carl?"

"Yes, I do. We used to think it was crazy that he had both boys and girls on the two teams. I guess he was good at thinking up things like that because it worked out great. We had a lot of fun. Gee, I'm glad you mentioned that. It's a good memory to have, especially during times like these."

"Well, Carl, it's that difference that tells me your father is in some kind of trouble that we know nothing about. All I can say is that Thomas Grandee is still a decent man underneath the surface. Whatever it is must be pretty hard on him. It could be pressures at work, Carl. Maybe his job is threatened and he doesn't want to talk about it. The important thing for you, Carl, is to keep remembering the good things about your father. You don't want to start disliking your father, do you?"

"No, I feel guilty because sometimes I feel real angry toward him. I don't like that feeling."

"Love and hate are often emotions that happen together, especially when you once loved someone very much and that person was important to you. Whatever is causing a problem for your father will eventually come to the surface and until then, you just have to trust your faith and the memories of the good times."

Carl nodded, and Mr. Rossiter was pleased that he was able to help allay young Carl Grandee's fears about Nancy and his father. What he wasn't pleased by was his daughter's infatuation, which was apparently serious, no matter how you looked at it. He was certain that Thomas Grandee's problem was also female-related, especially after his conversation with Betty, who had clued him in on Marie's well-founded suspicions.

Chapter Twenty-Two

FATHER BRENDAN PHONED THE OTHER RELIGIOUS LEADERS to let them know that he saw Thomas at church during Sunday's Mass. They were all pleased to hear the news and arranged another meeting for the week after next on a Tuesday evening to plan the next step. It was the hope of all that Thomas would reappear the following Sunday. Father Brendan also expressed his desire that Thomas might come to confession.

The following Sunday passed, however, without Thomas Grandee attending Mass at Holy Rosary Church. Father Brendan was disappointed. The Tuesday meeting would be an unhappy one. He saw Marie and Robbie, but neither Louise nor Carl was in church, either. He wished the whole Grandee family were like Marie.

Monday morning brought phone calls from his colleagues, who were interested to learn if Thomas had come to church. They were just as unhappy as Father Brendan to learn that he had not.

He had no sooner hung up the phone when Leona said there was a call from a Mr. Victor someone-or-other and that the man said he would call back. He had hung up suddenly, as if afraid he would be overheard.

"Fine," Father Brendan said, "I'm sure he will call again if it's important. I can't think of a parishioner named Victor. We have a Vittorio, but you would recognize his voice immediately—he has a thick Italian accent. Did he have an accent, Leona?"

"No, Father, he sounded quite Americanized, and timid. He didn't sound like anyone I know."

"Well then, Victor is the name of the man that works with Thomas Grandee. I believe I've seen him at The Chateau. Hmm. Well, as I said, he will call back if it's important."

The next phone call came at four-thirty. Victor told Father Brendan that he would like to meet with him that same evening. He explained that he worked for The Chateau and that the night manager, Brad Reilly, would be there until midnight. He started to go into detail about why it should be this very evening.

Father Brendan cut him short and said, "Can you come to the Rectory, Mr. Hermanssen?"

Victor said he could, in about one hour.

"Fine, Mr. Hermanssen. I will have dinner for both of us brought in. It will be after five o'clock when you get here, and we should both have some nourishment. What shall I order for you, Mr. Hermanssen?"

Victor hadn't given any thought to food, but was pleased with the offer. "Anything, Father. A hamburger will be fine. I'm not that hungry."

"We have a fine Italian restaurant that delivers, would that please you?" Victor said that it would.

"Good," Father Brendan explained, "I will see you later then."

The telephone conversation over, Father Brendan arranged to have the Italian restaurant send dinner to the rectory. Victor arrived at the Rectory a little after five o'clock. He poured out a story that took Father Brendan by storm. He sat silent through the whole business.

Victor told Father Brendan that Thomas had stormed out of The Chateau after spending time with Hannah Ward. He then went into detail about the proposition Hannah made to him after Thomas left.

"I suspected that they may have been having sex, but I had no idea that Hannah could be dishonest. After all, both Morrison and Braverman inspected the books on occasion and they both seemed to have complete trust in Hannah Ward."

"Now, Victor, you told me that Hannah used sex to try to entice you into allowing some bills to be sent to The Chateau for building repairs. You said fake repairs, meaning, I assume, that you would approve a bill for something that was never done and that this Hannah woman would mail a payment from the Realty Company to the fake repair outfit. Do I understand that correctly?"

"Yes, sir, you do."

"Now where does Thomas fit in? I don't understand that part of it," Father Brendan said. "You said Thomas stormed out of The Chateau after spending time with Hannah. After that happened, you said that this Hannah woman approached you, after which you decided to come to me. Please explain your motive in seeking my help. "

"Father Brendan, The Chateau is a bad place for my friend, Thomas. I've come to you because I've seen you talking to Thomas. When his parish priest comes to see him at work, it tells me there has to be a personal problem. Look, Father, I know there is something wrong with his marriage. He is not being faithful to his wife. It's the job, Father. It's The Chateau. Get him away from that place and I think he and his family will be better off."

"What do you know about Thomas' family, my good man?"

"I know that he stays away nights very often. I know he sees other women and that he is also having an affair with Hannah."

"How long has this been going on, Victor?"

"Oh, quite a while, Father, quite a while."

"And why, then, are you coming to speak to me now? Why not before?"

"Because of Hannah. I had no idea that she was dishonest. As I said, Mr. Morrison and Mr. Braverman both seem to trust her. But now that she has made this proposition to me, I know better. She may be trying to get Thomas to do something wrong at The Chateau." Victor was slightly annoyed that Father Brendan was somehow avoiding what he thought was obvious. Father Brendan simply continued.

"Is something wrong besides the fake bills you told me about?"

"Yes, father, I think that is very possible. She may have learned from Thomas that I was the one that handled repairs at The Chateau and she figured that those bills would have to go through me. In fact, she knew I was the custodian. I was thinking that she might have already tried to get Thomas to do something different. Something far more serious than a few fake bills."

"What are you trying to say, Victor?"

"I figure that she has been using sex to get something out of Thomas. If she has Thomas in her clutches, then I think that she's been pushing him to do something dishonest. Something much more than a few bills."

"Go ahead, Mr. Hermanssen. Tell me why you think something is happening at this particular time."

"Thomas has been acting funny lately. He isn't as loud or as self-confident as he used to be. That's one thing. The other thought I have is the cash. Father, a tavern doesn't get many people writing checks or running up charges that easily. Most of our business is cash money. I also know that there's cash money that comes from the hotel rooms over the weekend. Starting Friday night and all day Saturday, couples come in, sometimes just for an hour or two and then pay cash and leave. Some rooms get rented out two or three times on a Saturday, and the records are easy to play with if it's cash."

Victor thought for a minute. "Then there's this phony that pays for a room for the whole year whether he uses it or not. He even gets mail and packages delivered. This guy is up to no good, I swear, because I see unholy-looking characters sneaking up the outside entrance at times. I get to look around the building a lot. That's my job. They go upstairs and come back down and I've watched and I see another guy show up a few minutes later, like these guys have appointments, you know."

He looked straight at the priest and said very slowly, "The phony New Yorker pays cash. Never gives a check. He sometimes gives me the cash to deliver to Thomas."

"Victor," said Father Brendan, "dinner is here now." Father Brendan turned to his secretary, who had dutifully unpacked the meal and quietly set it out on a large table that she quickly cleared adjacent to the desk.

"Thank you, Leona. I appreciate your staying late for me. You may leave us now. The dishes and things can be taken care of by the staff in the morning."

"Thank you, Father Brendan. Good night. Good night, Mr. Hermanssen."

Victor nodded at the respectful secretary and then turned his gaze to Father Brendan. He didn't think that he had gone too far at all in his explanation, even though it had taken a while for him to convince the priest of the possible surreptitious links involved. Of course it was natural for the priest to protect the reputation of his parishioner. But he couldn't allow him to not understand that there might indeed be serious impropriety involved.

"Please, Mr. Hermanssen, dig into your chicken parmigiana. If there is all that cash," Father Brendan continued as he put his fork into a tender baked ziti siciliano, "There must be a record of it. I noticed a cashier at The Chateau. The owners can't be fools. There must be some way to protect a cash business."

"That's just it, Father. Thomas picks up the cash from the cashier several times each day. He counts it and it goes into a safe in the office. I sometimes bring the cash to Thomas myself. Then there is cash from the hotel rooms. It all has to be checked by Thomas and Hannah."

"Hannah picks up the money, checks and vouchers each day and enters the totals in a journal that they both sign. If Hannah can get Thomas to sign off on whatever numbers she enters, then she's home free."

Father Brendan waited until he fully enjoyed the first few mouthfuls of his tasty meal before stating with a bit of feigned surprise, "Is that what you think that she's doing? I gather you're afraid that Hannah can force Thomas to help her steal. She can either withhold sex or she can use it to expose him."

"Exactly, Father. I think Thomas has to get away from Hannah." Victor drew fork and knife to the plate in front of him and watched the chicken flake apart and onto his own fork with ease. The look of satisfaction on his host's face and the aromas from the chicken dish in front of him had aroused his curiosity and his appetite.

"So, you want me to speak with Thomas Grandee. Why not just expose Hannah to Mr. Morrison or Mr. Braverman?"

"I can't do that, Father." Victor hesitated and then continued. "I would have to expose Thomas to his bosses. I have no proof other than my word that she made me a proposition."

The two men continued their dinner quietly, having reached an impasse that both knew full well was of Father Brendan's making. Still, both had much to consider as the fate of at least several lives was resting, at least for the time being, on the outcome. Victor seemed to have talked himself out, which was what Father Brendan had hoped would eventually happen.

After they had cleaned their plates, Father Brendan leaned back comfortably in his chair. Victor asked Father Brendan if it was all right if he lit up a cigarette. The pastor nodded.

"Victor, I wonder if you might be willing to tell this Hannah person that you would go along with her idea and let this friend of hers send you a fake bill?" Father Brendan asked. "It would be in order to get the name of the person or company that is involved. That would give you the proof needed to have Hannah fired."

"Oh, no sir, I couldn't do that. Not unless I first went to the police," Victor responded. "I really think we could get into trouble without reporting this to the authorities beforehand."

"Right you are. It would be wrong to do so without proper preparation ahead of time. That is very wise of you, Victor. You're a smart man."

"If there's nothing else, Father, I had best be getting back to The Chateau." Victor saw that he was getting in deeper than he thought with this and somehow wasn't making the impression that he thought he should be with respect to Thomas.

"I do have one more question for you, Victor," Father Brendan explained. "Exactly how did you answer Hannah's request?"

"Very easily. I simply said that I needed some time to think it over. I told her the idea was of interest but I was not quite sure that I wanted to act upon it."

"Very wise of you, Victor. That put you in control of Hannah instead of the other way around." Father Brendan watched and listened carefully to Victor's reaction to what he had just said.

Victor smiled and moved his shoulders back and forth just a bit as he said, "That's right, Father, it puts me in the driver's seat, doesn't it?"

"Let me call a taxi for you, Victor. The parish has an account, and this meeting is for the benefit of one of our families. I don't think the trolleys run very often at this time of night."

"Thank you, I would appreciate it."

Victor left a bit confused but pleased that someone was able to recognize the value of his observations. Father Brendan thought that Tuesday's meeting with Father Fazio, Reverend Granville and Rabbi Richmond would be most interesting. He wondered whether or not he would be able to sleep at all that night. His head was buzzing, but his stomach was happy.

Chapter Twenty-Three

IN THE MORNING, FATHER BRENDAN ENJOYED THE opportunity of ordering lunch from a kosher Jewish delicatessen. He thought it would please the rabbi, and he looked forward to a corned beef sandwich. The men sat around enjoying lunch and talking about the Red Sox. Of course, once the small talk was over, Father Brendan was also eager to tell them about Victor Hermanssen and Hannah Ward.

After relating the story as closely as it had been told to him, Father Fazio asked, "How do you feel about this fellow Victor? Does he seem trustworthy?"

"To be honest, John, I think he has an ulterior motive. He didn't strike me at all as being the good friend to Thomas that he claimed. I have reservations as to his real motive in coming to me to talk about Thomas."

"You must have something in mind."

"Just a thought. Victor mentioned a couple of times that Thomas should leave The Chateau. Perhaps Victor is interested in Thomas' job."

"I think this may be a case for the police," Rabbi Richmond responded.

"Agreed," echoed Reverend Granville.

Father Fazio spoke up. "Now wait just one moment, gentlemen. Father Brendan's church owes its first obligation to the Grandee family. The police can wait until we decide how to handle this without causing what could be irreparable harm to the family."

"Well stated, John." Father Brendan smiled at his fellow priest. "I was up all night thinking about this. I do have an idea. It may or may not succeed. But I would like to lay it out for you."

"We're listening," said Granville. The others nodded consent and waited to hear Father Brendan's idea.

"You see, gentlemen, I never said one word to Victor about the situation, especially the money in Thomas' name at the Columbia bank. It was Victor who mentioned to me that The Chateau took in lots of cash and it was *his* thought that perhaps Hannah was using sex to get Thomas to help her to steal some of it. In other words, the only thing this Hermanssen fellow is sure of is the proposition made directly to him by this Hannah woman. And, at no point did he ever make a direct accusatory statement about Thomas. In other words, I don't think he is sure of anything more than what he himself conjectures.

"He also let me know that he had sexual relations with Hannah. I doubt that he intends to discontinue that relationship if he can possibly continue it."

"Interesting, Father Brendan," said the Rabbi. "Maybe we are premature about the police. I agree with the importance of protecting the family, as well. Let's hear more."

"Well," Father Brendan continued, "I suggest that I approach Thomas with our understanding of the situation and the money at the Columbia Bank and make our next move based on his reaction. I do not feel that we have to rush into immediate action until we know what the truth surrounding this matter really is."

There were nods from those at the table.

"Now, here comes our lunch, gentlemen."

Father Brendan arrived at The Chateau at noon two days later. Thomas was not surprised to see him this time. He had the feeling that the priest would be making regular visits. When Father Brendan signaled to him, he came over and started to lead him to a table.

"I am not here to stay for lunch, Thomas. I would like very much to see you at the rectory this evening, though. Do you think you can manage that?"

"I really have to work tonight, Father. Perhaps I can come to see you some other time. Is there something wrong?"

"There is, Thomas. I've made a discovery, and it has to do with you."

Thomas paled. Father Brendan thought he saw the big man's hands tremble. "Why can't we talk about it here, Father? I have a private office, you know."

"Fine, Thomas. In that case, I will stay for lunch. What do you suggest?"

"Ah, today's special is corned beef and cabbage, Father."

"Ordinarily that would be a delight to me, my good man, but not today. I just had a corned beef sandwich on Monday and it gave me a bit of heartburn. I'll just have a tuna salad sandwich, if you have that on the menu."

Thomas signaled the waiter and brought Father Brendan over to a table in the corner. "I'll leave you here alone while I tend to some business, Father. My office door is in the far right-hand corner. There's a small sign that says 'Private.' No need to knock. Just walk in. I will be at my desk. I've already had a light lunch myself." Thomas started to walk away, but turned back and said, "Just call the waiter and tell him to bring you anything you want. He knows you're my guest. And Father, you are not to pay for this lunch."

After a light but tasty tuna salad on rye, Father Brendan proceeded to the office. He noticed that the restaurant was again busy during the lunch hour. That alone must indeed bring in a sizable amount of cash.

When Father Brendan finished explaining to Thomas that he knew about the Columbia Bank deposits, Thomas didn't ask any questions and he didn't hesitate for more than five seconds.

"Father Brendan, I can't possibly explain this all to you, but I have thought over and over that I need to tell this to someone. Ever since you have been here, I have thought about confession. Can I simply tell my confession? It would be so much easier than having to relate the actual story."

"You may make your confession here and now, my son," Father Brendan replied. He pulled a purple cloth out of his jacket pocket that he put around his neck, blessed himself, and turned in the opposite direction to make it easier for Thomas to speak. Quietly, he whispered his own prayers and then asked Thomas to begin.

Thomas' confession went on for nearly an hour. It turned into quite a story as Father Brendan had suspected would happen, but it was much easier to use the confession format to frame the narration as opposed to simply telling details. Only several times did he need to interrupt the narrative with a question, and this was primarily to gain clarity with respect to Thomas' motive or intent. He had to be certain that Thomas was as sincere in his admission of guilt as need be not only for his own peace of mind, but to feel comfortable giving absolution.

Before offering final forgiveness, Father Brendan was reminded of a passage in St. Luke—the parable of the Good Thief, the penitent thief: "The thief crucified with Jesus who did not mock Him; Jesus promised him paradise that day."

The priest turned around to look at Thomas and crossed himself. "And finally, I forgive you in the name of the Father, The Son and The Holy Ghost. Amen. May you have serenity of conscience for your expressed and sincere sorrow for your sins."

Father Brendan then added, "Thomas, I am proud of you for having rid yourself of this business. I know it must have been difficult for you. I am certain that you must also know that you have to seek other help. Please come to see me as soon as you are able, so that together we can plan a course of action. There is no time to waste, my son. Today is Wednesday. Can you make some arrangements here at The Chateau so that you can be away for some time this Friday?"

"I think so, Father. My custodian, Victor, can handle the business. He's very capable and he gets along well with the staff."

"Thomas, I think that it is important for you to know that I learned about the fake bill proposition from Victor Hermanssen before you told me about it, and—"

"Is *he* the one who told about the Columbia Bank? How does he know?"

"Wait up, Thomas. No, Victor said nothing about that. Victor said he was looking out for your interests as well as his own. He likes his job and he feels threatened because he suspects something other than the fake bills is involved, but he never mentioned anything else. I think he contacted me because he was afraid to go to the police and he was afraid to go to you, Thomas. Don't blame Victor. The Columbia Bank information came to me very accidentally, but that's no longer important."

"All right, then, Father. Thank you for being honest with me."

"Very well, then. It will be best if you begin to talk to Marie and prepare her for what may be ahead. Tell her at least some of what is going on."

"I'll do the best I can, Father. I guess I have to let her know that there is a problem."

"Good. I will expect you at the rectory on Friday. And now, I must leave."

"Please, Father Brendan, I need another moment," Thomas pleaded.

"Go ahead, Thomas. Tell me what's troubling you."

"Father, I want you to know that I really love Marie. I'm afraid she may leave me when I tell her about Hannah and the other woman that I've told you about." Thomas was struggling to hold back tears.

"What can I do to make amends to my children for being such a bad father to them? I don't think I can talk to them about what's going on in my life. They won't be able to accept it if I tell them the truth. Still, I feel that I want to reach out to them, to let them know how much I love them."

Thomas fell silent. Tears actually welled up in his eyes. "Please help me, Father, please."

The priest took Thomas into his arms and patted his back. "You must have courage in God and courage in speaking the truth. Tell Marie that you love her and that you are sorry that you have hurt her. Tell her everything, Thomas. As for the children, by all means, tell them that you love them, too. You need to tell them nothing more than that for now. Speak to Marie about your feelings. Ask her to talk to Carl and Louise. If you would like, tell her to go easy and to call on me for support if she needs my help."

Thomas agreed, and Father Brendan took his leave quickly and confidently. He informed the other religious leaders that Thomas had made confession and maintained the secrecy expected of him, explaining that he felt that progress had been made and that Thomas would visit with him on Friday. A meeting with the other religious leaders was arranged for the very next morning. It would be a short meeting, since the others all had busy schedules.

After Father Brendan left The Chateau on Wednesday, Thomas immediately arranged for Victor to take charge for the remainder of the week. He said for him to tell Hannah that he was taken ill with a very bad cold and had to go to see a doctor.

Victor said, "Thomas, can we go into your office and talk privately?"

"Sure, Victor," he said as they moved into the office. "What's on your mind?"

"Hannah's on my mind. Don't get mad at me, Thomas, but over the weekend she propositioned me. You must have told her that I was the one who handled repair bills because she wants me to sign for fake ones. It seems to me that she must have asked you first."

Victor waited, but Thomas said nothing for the moment. He wondered if Victor knew about the money, and he wondered if Father Brendan had not told him the truth about this particular matter. He had a sudden feeling in his chest, like he was swimming in deep water and about to go under.

Suddenly, he smiled and relaxed a bit as he recalled Father Brendan's reassurance. No, he thought, Victor would not know about the money because only Hannah could have told him, and that would be admitting guilt herself.

Thomas responded, "Yes, she did approach me, and I told her that you handled the repairs. Victor, I can't talk to you about this, but I assure that this will all soon be resolved. If I were you, I would simply stay clear of Hannah. She is obviously less than honest. Promise me that you will not say anything to her about this conversation." Victor agreed.

Thomas then explained to Victor that he was to give Hannah the cash receipts, which the cashier would have ready for him, and that there would also be vouchers and other records in an envelope that he would also get directly from the cashier.

Thomas did not think Hannah would play around with the journal in his absence. He told Victor to check the cash total and initial the page.

"All right, Thomas. I have wondered about Hannah for a while. I never could figure her out. Sure, I'll take care of matters here at work. And I'll tell Hannah that you went home feeling ill and that you had a doctor's appointment, too."

"Thanks, Victor, I'll see you the beginning of next week, and I'll see to it that there's a little extra in your paycheck. I think I can manage that for you."

Chapter Twenty-Four

THOMAS GRANDEE WENT DIRECTLY HOME. HE DID not have a clue as to how he was going to tell Marie about what was going on in his life. Knowing only that he owed Marie and his children an explanation, he walked around the front from where he parked in his driveway and took a good look at their big house on Las Casas Street.

The house was situated near the top of a curving hill with maple trees in full bloom on both sides of the street, forming an archway at several places. The other houses along the block were well-kept, and it made the Grandee house stand out.

Thomas noticed the unsightly paint peeling on the old clapboards of the once-gracious mansion. The window trim was practically nonexistent because the paint on the trim had eaten away at the sizing. He felt his stomach churn as he remembered the night he had hit Carl when he found him in Louise's bed. They must have been freezing cold. The churning began to turn sour as he recalled Marie's slapping him on the face that same night. "God, what an asshole I am," he mused.

Proceeding to the front entrance, Thomas walked in and announced, "I'm home, Marie." As he entered the high-ceilinged front hall, Marie looked down from the top of the curving staircase and saw Thomas.

"What are you doing home at this time of day? Are you drunk?"

"I'm not drunk. I have to talk to you, Marie, but first I have to know if the kids are home. Are they?"

"No. Carl's working. He has a new job. Louise and her friend Patty are going for interviews at Mount Auburn Hospital, and Robbie is at my mother's house. What's going on?"

"Let's sit in the kitchen and have a Coke."

"Uh, sure, Thomas, there's cold tonic in the fridge. I'll get us both some."

Thomas sat down at the kitchen table. Marie brought the cokes and sat across from Thomas. "Please tell me what's going on," she said.

"I had a visit from Father Brendan at The Chateau this morning and he heard my confession. He wants to see the two of us at the rectory this Friday morning. We have to talk to him."

"About what?"

"I'm in some money trouble, Marie, and Father Brendan found out about it."

"What do you mean? What did he find out? You make it sound like you robbed a bank. Did you do something wrong, Thomas?"

"Yes, Marie, I did something wrong. I didn't rob a bank, though. It's a long, complicated story, and Father Brendan and I discussed it this morning. He came to see me at noon."

Marie continued, "For God's sake, Thomas, what on Earth is going on? You're frightening me!"

"First, Marie, I have to tell you that I love you. You may not believe me on this, but I honestly do love you. I've done some very bad things and I know that I've hurt you, but I love you." At this point, Thomas broke down and began to cry.

Marie took him into her arms and cradled him like a child. "I love you, too, Thomas. I love you and I've missed you. Whatever it is, please, dear God, please tell me. I don't care what you did, as long as you still love me and as long as you finally tell me what is going on! I'm a strong woman, Thomas. Please don't hold anything back. I've known for a long time that there must be another woman. Who is she?"

Thomas had stopped his sobbing by now, and Marie looked him straight in the eye.

"I'm listening, Thomas," she begged. "Please."

As Marie sat in stony silence, Thomas related his story to Marie just as though she was Father Brendan. At times, he closed his eyes and imagined the priest was sitting there rather than Marie.

Marie was stunned, but she had expected at least part of what she heard, and she was actually relieved. She had known very well that her husband was having some kind of affair. Now she knew the facts and she knew what was behind them.

There was also something else. Thomas was completely sober. There wasn't any hint of alcohol on his breath, nor perfume on his clothes.

"When does Father Brendan want us, and what do you think he will tell us we have to do? Are you going to jail, Thomas?" She was suddenly concerned for her husband. What a bastard he had been. She didn't know whether to hate him or feel sorry for him. Finally she said, "The Lord is forgiving, Thomas. As long as He can forgive you, I can try to forgive you." She didn't know what else to say.

"I don't know why," she added, stunned by the reality he had just revealed, "but I think I still love you—you son of a bitch!" Suddenly, she started to hammer away at Thomas with her fists against his chest. "Why? Why? What did I do to deserve this?"

"Go ahead, Marie. Hit me as hard as you like. I deserve it. I don't deserve the likes of you. I don't know why I did the things I did. I just don't know. Father Brendan said he thinks I need some help. I guess he's right."

Thomas stood, and pulled Marie up. They held each other, both quietly crying. "Let's not say anything to the children until we know what's going to happen," she added.

"I agree that we should not go into any detail with the kids, Marie, but I do want to let them know how much I love them. I've been a very poor father to the kids and a very poor husband to you. I want to get the three kids together after dinner and let them know how I feel. I want them only to know that I have been having problems at work but to make them aware that I love them very much."

"That sounds like a good idea, Thomas. I think you should speak to them if that's how you really feel. They've noticed and have been hurt because it is not like it used to be."

At dinner that evening there was no talk about Thomas, but Louise was very excited. She and Patty were both set to start their nursing program at Mount Auburn Hospital in Cambridge the second week of September.

"Tell us about it," Carl said. However, before she had a chance to answer, he had already asked how long it would take, and if she would be a *real* nurse, and would she be a nurse at Mount Auburn, among other questions. He sounded more excited than Louise did.

"Carl, I don't know all the answers. I haven't even begun yet. I know I'll wear a nurse's uniform, though, right from the beginning, and Patty and I will share a room. We get all our meals at the hospital, too."

"Sounds great, Louise. I'm sure that you've made a good decision. Oh, dear, I know you did," Marie said.

"I agree with your mother. I know you always wanted to be a nurse," Thomas said, "and I have always felt that you would make a great one." Thomas had seen Louise as compassionate and caring since she was a child.

After dinner, Marie said, "I'll clean up. You kids can leave the dishes to me. I think your father wants to talk to you privately. Isn't that so, Thomas?"

"Yes, yes, I would like a word with the three of you. Why don't we leave your mother here and go into the living room where we can sit and talk?"

Louise, Carl and Robbie looked at one another, puzzled. Finally Louise broke the silence.

"Come on kids, let's go with Pa. Ma, why don't you leave the dishes for us to do later?"

"Thank you, sweetheart, but no, I'd rather keep busy in here while you guys have your talk in the other room."

In the living room, Thomas and the three children sat without a word for a few minutes. Finally, Thomas began by saying that he wanted them all to know how much he loved them. He told them that he had been having some very difficult times at The Chateau and that he had let it interfere with his personal and family life.

"I even started to drink more than was good for me. I promise you that I will not ever get drunk again and that I will not let anything ever again come between me and you kids or your mother. She and I have talked about this at length. You mother is a wonderful person, kids. I wouldn't blame her if she threw me out of the house but, instead, she and I are trying to patch things up. You'll not see or hear us quarreling, either."

Thomas leaned back in his armchair after his speech and sighed with relief that he had gotten it all off his chest. He wondered what their reaction would be.

He didn't have long to wait. Louise said, "Thanks, Pa, for saying what you just did. I've been noticing that you were acting differently the past few days. I had been worried about you. I'm glad that you spoke up. I'm not going to ask why you've been so cold and mean to us because it must have been something very important. Whatever it is, I hope things work out."

"Yeah," Carl said. "I'm glad that you said something tonight, too. I was just talking to Mr. Rossiter about the times we used to play softball when I was younger. I guess you must have some big problems. I hope things get better for you so we can be a happy family again."

Robbie just smiled, and then he walked over to Thomas and crawled up on his lap.

"You're a big boy, Robbie, to be sitting on Pa's lap."

They all had a good laugh.

Marie had finished the dishes and was entering the living room as Thomas and the kids were just standing up.

Carl said, "Pa, can I have a private word with you? We can go into the kitchen if that's all right."

Thomas accompanied Carl into the kitchen. "What is it, Carl?" Thomas asked as they sat back down at the table.

Carl began to tell the story about Nancy and himself and he told his father about the conversation with Harvey Rossiter.

"Pa, do you think things could work out if two people are of different religions?"

"I'm glad you talked to me about it, Carl. I've not been much of father to you. I'm sorry you had to go to Harvey with this problem. As for what I think, it's a different story. I wish you would start coming to church again like you did when you were younger. I know that I'm not a good one to be telling you this since I have been so lax myself. There's a lot to be said for faith in God, Carl. Right now I don't know where I'd be without the help of Father Brendan."

"I don't know how I really feel about my own religion, Pa, but I would like your opinion about me and Nancy."

"She's a beautiful girl, Carl and as nice as they come. But you kids are both so young that I wouldn't take your liking each other too seriously. On the other hand, I have to admit that the Rossiters and the Grandees have a remarkable friendship. Your mother and Betty have been close forever, and I think Harvey is a good and generous man. He and I don't always agree when it comes to religion or politics, but he's a good person and a good friend."

"What about a Catholic boy and a Jewish girl, Pa? You haven't said much about me and Nancy."

Thomas felt pinned down by the question, and he was trying to ignore Carl's directness. Finally he said, "I just don't know, son. I figure it this way. If you were a serious religious Catholic and she was a serious religious Jew, it would probably not be a good idea. On the other hand, Carl, I don't think either of you are very religious, so I guess that part of it really doesn't matter. I don't know about how Ma feels, but it wouldn't bother me if you and Nancy became serious. Like I said before, she's a nice girl from a good family, and if you two love each other and get married, well, more power to you. You'll have to ask your mother what she thinks, but seeing the relationship between Ma and Betty, I can't imagine that she would mind."

Carl got up and walked over to Thomas. Thomas stood up, and the two six-footers embraced.

Chapter Twenty-Five

THE TWO PRIESTS, THE RABBI AND THE minister met on Thursday morning. They needed only a little time to agree that the next step was to inform the owners of The Chateau about the financial swindling that had been going on there. They settled on giving that job to Rabbi Richmond; one of the owners, Sam Braverman, was a Jew, and so was the rabbi. It was settled, therefore, that the rabbi would try to reach Braverman and have a heart-to-heart talk with him.

The gathering broke up quickly and Rabbi Richmond went to his office at the Temple, where he asked his secretary to get Mr. Braverman on the phone.

When the rabbi's extension rang, he answered and heard Sam Braverman's voice on the other end. Braverman said he would be only too happy to meet with him and he would just as soon come to Malden since he wanted to look into some property nearby. Things were beginning to happen rapidly. Braverman said he could meet with Rabbi Richmond that very afternoon, and so they made an appointment for three o'clock at the temple.

Three o'clock arrived and Sam Braverman was shown into the rabbi's office. He was wearing a yarmulke. The rabbi was immediately pleased by his prospects.

"Sit, Mr. Braverman, make yourself comfortable," he said.

"Please call me Sam, rabbi. You said that you wanted to speak with me about a property my company owns, The Chateau, am I right? I hope it's not too serious, but from the sound of the your voice, I think maybe it is."

"Yes, Sam, it is very serious. Why else would I have asked to meet with you?"

"You're making me anxious," Sam Braverman said, "Please tell me what this is all about." He edged forward in his seat.

"Relax, Sam. Have a cup of coffee." The rabbi asked his secretary to bring in two coffees. He had barely finished mentioning Hannah's proposition to the custodian when Sam interrupted him.

"I don't believe it. Hannah Ward has been with us for four years, rabbi. She's a very efficient worker. She's always on time, and I've never questioned her honesty. I simply can't believe this story. Maybe the custodian is making it all up."

"I'm afraid not, Sam. Father Brendan learned about it from one of his parishioners."

"What the hell are you talking about? How did the priest get into this?"

"Please listen, Mr. Braverman. I am only the messenger. Let me finish."

"Sorry, rabbi. The possibility that Hannah is dishonest makes me nervous."

Rabbi Richmond continued, and Sam sat with his mouth agape.

"If you were not a rabbi, I would think you were making jokes with me. I don't know what to say. This is unbelievable. The Chateau is one of our most profitable investments. How can anybody be stealing from us?" He had not touched his coffee. Rabbi Richmond's coffee was also sitting untouched, getting cold.

"Where do we go from here, Sam? It's up to you and Mr. Morrison to decide what to do. Please take your time and think a bit. If you wish, I will leave the office and you may use my telephone to call your partner."

"Thank you, rabbi. I better tell Bob. He won't believe it, either."

Fifteen minutes later, Rabbi Richmond returned. Sam Braverman did not look happy.

"Well, my friend, how did it go?"

"Not so good. Bob is very upset. He found the whole story hard to believe at first. He said they should both be arrested, but I was able to calm him down and convince him that it might be better to confront them with our lawyer present."

"If you don't mind some advice from a rabbi, Mr. Braverman, maybe it would be wiser to wait a few days and first figure out who this friend of Hannah's is that wants to send fake bills. It may be that you are being cheated in some of your other properties, too."

"I was afraid of that. It just never dawned on me that we should try to find that out before confronting her. You're pretty smart. Why didn't I think of that before?"

"Because you are not a rabbi, Sam."

Sam Braverman couldn't help but laugh, and it broke the tension. He agreed with the rabbi's suggestion that a meeting should be arranged with Sam and his partner, the rabbi and Father Brendan.

"Should we have our lawyer present?" Sam asked.

"I don't suppose it would hurt. Father Brendan's brother is a lawyer. He might also have some good ideas."

"I gather that you want to try to protect Thomas, or, at least to minimize any criminal proceedings against him. Am I right, rabbi?"

"Yes, in a way. Father Brendan, in particular, feels that way. As I explained to you earlier, Sam, Thomas Grandee told the entire story to Father Brendan, who also heard his confession. Besides, you have to keep in mind that Thomas has never touched the money he took. As I told you before, he is prepared to make restitution. The man has three children. Hannah seduced him."

Rabbi Richmond paused to make his next statement more effective.

"Your company, the Bank of Commerce, and The Chateau will all be headlines in the newspapers if you rush to the police. Speak to your partner again, Sam. Be a rabbi for awhile."

"Okay, rabbi. Give me the phone, please, and stay right here. I may need you."

In the end, a meeting was agreed upon. As soon as all the parties could be assembled they would set a date. In the meantime, it was decided that Sam Braverman should ask Victor Hermanssen to agree to accept a fake bill so they could find out the identity of the unknown culprit.

Chapter Twenty-Six

HARVEY ROSSITER PAID THE ATTENDANT ONE DOLLAR for eight gallons of gasoline and drove away from the gas station. The Rossiters had arranged for David to spend the evening with one of his friends. They were taking Nancy and Carl for dinner at Wagon Wheels on the Newburyport Turnpike in Danvers, Massachusetts.

At the first intersection, they were stopped by a police officer. "There's no traffic coming from right or left," Harvey said. "Why's the cop stopping traffic?"

"Harvey, there's a horse and buggy a short way down on the left."

"Damn. I hate traffic cops. They seem to wave their white-gloved hands at me every time I come to an intersection."

"Don't be so impatient. He's doing the right thing. You know how panicky some horses get when motorcars drive past them. The horse doesn't know you're not going to hit him. I read in the paper that they've had trouble this week and the cops are being extra careful."

On the 10-mile drive north from Malden, Betty noticed how much the turnpike had changed in the past few years. Originally the turnpike was part of the old Route 1 North from Boston to New Hampshire and Maine. At the beginning of the turnpike in Saugus, she commented, "Harvey, this road is twice as wide as it was a few years ago. I remember it as a country road lined with trees on either side."

In place of trees, what Betty saw was a divided highway with telephone poles on either side of the road. "We've just barely started out, and I've already seen three motels, and there's another gas station. That must be the second one we've passed already."

As they drove one more mile north, Harvey laughed and said, "Betty, never mind the motels and gas stations, we've gone past two restaurants so far. You're right about the changes, though. At this rate, this route is going to be hopping with all kinds of activity."

"The traffic is getting pretty heavy, too. They say you can get to Portsmouth, New Hampshire in about two hours, though, and that's a good 30 miles from Malden. I guess the world is making progress."

"Gee, look over there on the left," Carl said from the back seat, "That looks like a bowling alley way up here in the country. I guess you have to have a car to get around these days."

"We're here, gang," Harvey said. "It took a lot less than an hour to get here, too. I'd say that's not too bad."

Once seated in the restaurant, Nancy exclaimed, "My, it's really big, isn't it? Mom, have you and Daddy been here before?"

"Yes, dear, I think twice before. It's rather a long drive and it's not the kind of place you come to unless it's a special occasion."

"What's so special about tonight, Mom? It's not anyone's birthday or anything."

"You and Carl are special to your father and me, that's for sure." She looked at the handsome young man sitting next to her beautiful daughter.

The waitress brought menus and glasses of water. "I'll bring the hot buns as soon as they come out of the oven, folks."

"You kids order anything you want," Betty stated matter-of-factly, "and don't you worry about the prices on the menu." She paused and added, "I'm having the prime rib special. This place is famous for it."

"Me, too," Carl said.

"Gets my vote, all right," Harvey joined in. "How about you, Nancy?" and when Nancy nodded her approval, he signaled for the waitress.

The order was placed. "Hot rolls and salad coming up first," said the waitress, and she was back off to the kitchen.

"Carl, you knew my dad was going to get us together, didn't you?" Nancy said.

"Yeah, I guess so, Nancy. I asked your father for advice about us and about school and other things," Carl answered. "I was pretty upset after that night at the Palace of Sweets. I guess I should have told you, but I didn't really know what to say. I hope that you're not mad at me."

"No, I'm not mad," Nancy pouted.

"Let's not argue, kids. Now let your father and I do a little talking, okay?" Betty said.

Nancy and Carl nodded and remained silent. The waitress came back with salad and a breadboard with butter, plus a basket of sweet rolls. The smell of fresh bread and melting butter was too much to be resisted.

"There is no love sincerer than the love of food," Betty exclaimed after finishing her own tasty roll, and she added, "George Bernard Shaw."

They all had a hearty laugh, which eased the air for a few moments longer, and then Betty Rossiter continued on a more serious note.

"Nancy, you're 14 years old." Catching Nancy's look, she quickly corrected herself, "Okay, you'll be 15 in one more month, and Carl is 17. You two may feel grown up and you certainly are in many ways, but you're both going though a difficult time of adjustment. You're neither kids nor adults. One minute you are as wise as Methuselah, and the next, you're no more mature than a young child. That's only natural. Your father and I have been at the same place in time as you are now, so we understand. However, you are not in any position to make major decisions that will affect the rest of your lives."

Nancy chimed in quickly, "Well, I understand that daddy advised Carl to be sure and go to college because a good education is valuable, and he tells that to David and me all the time, too. So how come we can make decisions like that? I think getting a good education affects the rest of our lives. How come we can make that decision?"

Nancy's father spoke up. "You provide a classic example for why you shouldn't make a major decision about a relationship like yours and Carl's. Just think, Nancy, that when you go to school for an education, it is only the rare student that knows for sure what his or her major will be. Besides, I know from my teaching experience that there are many kids who decide to become doctors and change their minds and end up rabbis or ministers or history professors like myself. I never told you this before, but I used to think I wanted to become a doctor when I first went to college."

"No kidding, Mr. Rossiter?" Carl interrupted.

"No kidding, Carl, I really did. My parents always hinted that they wanted me to be a doctor."

"See, you didn't do what *your* parents wanted, did you, daddy? You just said so."

"Wait a minute, young lady. Your mother and I are not telling you to do what we want. We're just letting you know that what you think you want today may not be what you want tomorrow. Your mother is right when she says you behave like an adult sometimes and like a child other times. Right now you sound a bit like a child, Nancy."

Nancy sulked, but kept her mouth shut.

Betty felt concerned for her daughter. "Nancy, we're not telling you to stop seeing Carl. Your father and I feel that you haven't had enough experience with boys. If you never have other boyfriends, you will live to regret it. There will be a time when you think, 'Gee, what did I miss?' We don't want that to happen."

"All we ask is that you go out on dates, both of you, with other young people. Carl hasn't had much experience, either. You both need a chance to know more about your own feelings and about each other. That can only come by learning what it might feel like to be with a different boy or a different girl."

Carl was turning bright red. He sat in silence, absorbing Nancy's belligerence and Betty's contrasting assurance.

"Mom, I know you want what's best for me. I really love Carl. I'm not afraid to admit it. I think he loves me, too. I've heard you say that love is all-important. Now I'm all mixed up."

"Sweetheart," her father said. "Love is important, and I'm sure you two kids have deep feelings toward each other. But the kind of love that you feel at your age needs a chance to mature. All I'm saying is you should go out with other boys, Nancy. I don't think Carl will stop loving you if you do, and certainly not if you kids find that you still prefer each other."

"What if he meets some girl and decides he likes her better than he likes me?"

"Then I'd say it was a good thing you found that out before you got married rather than after. Wouldn't you agree, Nancy, that it would be a terrible mistake if you made a lifetime commitment and then discovered that your father was right, that what you feel now is not mature love?"

Nancy thought for a few moments. "Well, maybe as long as I don't have to stop seeing Carl. I guess I could go on dates with other boys, and Carl can date other girls. I just want to be able to kill any girl that tries to take him away from me," she said.

They all laughed. Nancy continued, "You haven't said one word about Carl being Catholic, though. Isn't that what Carl said he wanted to talk to Daddy about?"

"Right, Nancy, and it's part of the reason we think both of you should see other young people. Both of you have to be certain that religion will never become an issue. You have grandparents that will make it an issue, and Carl's mother is very religious as well. By seeing people of your own religions and still choosing each other, it would help to eliminate it as an argument from other family members who really do care, also. No one will be able to ask you why you don't go with a 'nice Jewish boy' or a 'nice Catholic girl.'"

"Are you saying that I should go out with some Jewish boys and Carl with some Catholic girls just so we can satisfy Carl's mother and my grandparents?"

Betty responded carefully, "Only in a small way, dear. It would be a way of showing respect and, like your father said, it would protect us all from anything like, 'I told you so.' It is also a good way to give all of us time to measure the results of a true test of feelings."

It was Harvey's turn to speak. "Carl has told me that religion is not as big an issue with him as with others, but he has also explained that he still isn't sure. You're my daughter, Nancy, so I know how you were brought up. Other than showing respect for your grandparents, you and David don't make a big deal out of religion yourselves. Seeing others will also give you both the time you need to sort out true attitudes toward religion."

Nancy saw from her parents' looks that they were expecting her to agree. "I know. We still need time to mature, and we still have to see other boys and girls. I really do understand."

"Thank you, Nancy," her father added, "We're glad that you really do understand and we hope that Carl does, as well."

"I do, Mr. Rossiter. I think that a little time will be good for all of us. Anyway, I still get to see Nancy!"

By this time, dessert was being served and Betty was getting ready to broach what she felt was the most important aspect to the relationship between Carl and Nancy. She waited for the waitress to leave.

"Carl's mother and I have been friends forever," Betty exclaimed. "She's a practicing Catholic and I'm Jewish, but not particularly religious. We have no conflict whatsoever. We love each other and never question each other's beliefs. We talk about controversial matters and sometimes disagree. But, these issues could never come between us. So, on that note, and at least for the time being, I agree with your father that religion is not the most important issue as far as you two kids are concerned. In fact, it's my friendship with Marie that is responsible for you two coming together, so I feel more strongly than ever that no harm comes to either of you just because you are good friends."

Betty continued, "What I am going to say now is more important than anything else that we have talked about. I know that you have strong feelings for each other. I also know what those feelings can lead to, so I'm not going to pull any punches. Date all you want, as long as you also date others some of the time. Just make sure that you don't go all the way. You're at an age where you can easily get pregnant, so *do not* take any chances. Using condoms doesn't always work, and getting fitted for a diaphragm is not one hundred percent safe either. The only way to be sure is not to go all the way. Do I make myself clear, kids?"

"Mom, we never did it. You know I wouldn't," Nancy said.

"I know I can trust both of you to be smart enough not to add unnecessary burdens to your lives. Now that I have made my parental statement, we can finish our dessert and coffee."

"Mrs. Rossiter," Carl stated clearly, "I'm glad that we had this talk. I feel a lot better now. I just want you both to know that I would never do anything to hurt Nancy. Like I said to Mr. Rossiter last week, I don't know whether what I feel for Nancy is real love or if I just love her like a sister. I just know that I feel very strongly about her, and you don't have to worry that I would do anything bad to her."

On the ride back home, the conversation drifted to school and Carl's hopes for college, and Carl and Nancy appeared satisfied and convinced that nothing really drastic had changed.

Later that evening, when Harvey and Betty were in bed, Betty said, "That boy, Carl, is really something. Weren't you surprised to see how rational he was in expressing his feelings? I think that he's an unusual kid for his age."

"Betty, Nancy is lucky to have Carl as her boyfriend. I think you're right when you tell them to date others, but down deep inside, I kind of hope that they stay together."

"Me too, Harvey. Now, let's stop talking about *them* and start thinking about *us*," she said as she nestled into her husband's shoulder. "I love you, Harvey Rossiter. Kiss me."

Harvey obliged and they lay together awake for a while, quietly snuggled in each other's arms. Before falling asleep, Harvey added, "Betty, maybe Nancy ought to see about a diaphragm."

"Shut up, Harvey. We'll talk about it under less emotional conditions. Good night!"

"Good night, Betty," Harvey answered, and soon dozed off to sleep.

When Carl arrived home, he decided that he ought to include his own parents in the evening's events. Even though he had a discussion with his father recently on the subject of Nancy, he felt a bit guilty that he was still going to Mr. Rossiter for advice and having personal conversations with him. Secretly, he knew that he had once had more respect for Harvey Rossiter's opinions than his own father's. Now that things seemed to be changing, he wanted more than ever to include his father in his life.

Marie and Thomas were both awake and sitting quietly in the living room. Robbie was upstairs asleep.

Addressing his mother and father, Carl asked, "Can we have a little talk?" Thomas and Marie exchanged worried looks, thinking that Carl was going to start asking questions about Thomas' problems.

"Sure, Carl," Thomas said. "What's on your mind?"

"Well, I think I should tell you that I was out with Nancy and Mr. and Mrs. Rossiter tonight, and we talked mostly about me and Nancy."

Marie said, "Carl, Betty and I are best friends, so I know that you spend a lot of time with the Rossiters and that you and Nancy like each other very much. I also know that you talked with your father about Nancy, and I'm glad when you bring us into your life."

"I feel guilty that I haven't confided in you enough. It's just that I know Pa is having problems and I didn't want to bring my life into it to make matters worse. I hope that I didn't make things more difficult for you, Pa, by talking about my own problems."

"Carl, I haven't been much of a father to you lately, but I promise that is all changed now. Don't you ever let my problems stop you from coming to us. No matter what happens, your mother and I are always here for you. You have to know that with all my trouble, I love you and Louise and Robbie very much. Now, that's enough about me. We both want to hear what's happening in *your* life."

Carl talked once more and at length about his relationship with Nancy. For Marie and Thomas, as well as for Carl, it was the best thing that could have happened at this time of trouble in the life of the Grandee family.

In bed that evening, Thomas turned to Marie and said, "I feel like we have our son back again. I really thought I was losing my kids, and I just didn't know where to turn."

Marie smiled. They both slept much better that night and both of them felt that at least some issues in their lives were finally being resolved.

Chapter Twenty-Seven

No SPECIFIC DATE WAS SET FOR THE meeting with Braverman and Morrison. Sam Braverman contacted Victor and told him only as much as was necessary. He authorized him to make a deal with Hannah in order to get the information that both Braverman and Morrison had decided was of first importance. They were eager to find out who was working with Hannah and how much damage, if any, had been done to their other properties.

Obtaining the identity of a perpetrator or perpetrators might not be that difficult. Determining what their method of operations was and how deep the penetration into their organization might be was another matter yet. Until they knew more, all decisions were on hold.

Victor met with Hannah over the weekend after Rabbi Richmond had his talk with Sam Braverman. He used his own room behind the kitchen area rather than use his master key to get into Thomas' hotel room upstairs. Victor was in no rush to get back to Sam Braverman. He figured the longer it took, the more fun he could have with Hannah. He did, however, keep his promise to pursue the identity of her contact.

"Hannah," he said, after they were in his room for a while, "I don't mind messing around with you, but I don't want to mess with that phony bill idea of yours unless it can be risk-free. I'll go along with you only if the bills are made to look plausible. I don't want Thomas to question major expenses for minor reasons. You better tell your friend to bill us for a major repair, like an electrical repair that requires a master electrician. Something that requires getting behind the main fuse box down in the basement."

"Fine, that can be arranged, Victor. Just make a note for a practical repair and we'll accommodate you. Now, what else can I do for you, honey?" she teased. She had been partially undressed for a while and urged Victor to help finish removing her clothing. Victor reached around behind her and unhooked her bra.

"You like this, don't you?" she said as she undid Victor's belt buckle and unzipped his pants. His shirt was already on the floor beside the bed.

By the time she pulled his underpants down, she was seated on the bed with Victor standing naked in front of her. Hannah may not have thought of it, but her routine was that of a seasoned prostitute. Victor recognized this, but it didn't faze him a bit. This was one prostitute that he didn't have to pay.

As Hannah began stroking him, Victor focused on a framed print on the beige painted wall next to his bed. He gazed at Renoir's "Bathers," a magnificent scene of several nudes. This encouraged him even further to extend his interlude. Thomas was not expected until at least Monday, so he encouraged Hannah to stay through the night.

Victor did have to get up once when his phone rang. It was a hotel guest who said that his companion was locked in the bathroom and couldn't open the door.

"Sorry the phone woke you, Hannah. Be right back honey. Don't go away."

Hannah smiled broadly while she lay waiting for Victor to return. She figured that she now had Victor in the palm of her hand. She didn't expect to get much extra money out of the fake bills. It was just a way to protect her turf in case Thomas revolted. She thought she could play Victor against Thomas and, even if she was forced to stop playing the cash game, at least she could still get a little out of The Chateau. This wasn't the only pond where she could fish, in any event.

By the time Victor returned, Hannah was dozing off. Victor didn't wake her. He was satisfied to simply get a little sleep for what remained of the night.

Chapter Twenty-Eight

At Friday's meeting with Father Brendan, Thomas and Marie learned that their fate was in the hands of Morrison and Braverman Realty Company, and particularly Bob Morrison. The priest spoke to them in detail and also made it clear that Thomas would probably lose his job as manager of The Chateau.

Thomas insisted that he was not an alcoholic, and as proof he explained that he had not touched one drop of alcohol since the Wednesday when Father Brendan approached him at The Chateau. When father Brendan asked Thomas if he would be willing to see a psychiatrist, he said he would do so, except that he didn't have money to pay for the visits.

"One of my classmates at Boston College, a philosophy major, went on to medical school and became a psychiatrist. I asked him if he would be willing to see you pro bono for a couple of visits just to make an evaluation. He thinks that I might be able to counsel you, Thomas, but I would feel better about it if you saw this friend of mine first just to elicit his interpretation of the circumstances. I know him well and I suggest you accept the offer. His name is Chase Finney, and he has a fine reputation as a therapist. He is also considered an expert in the areas of human relations as well as alcoholism."

"Father, I feel a little uncomfortable about seeing a psychiatrist."

"I understand. I will be your counselor, Thomas. Doctor Finney is simply going to see you a few times and get some background. It will make it possible for him to advise me when you and I start our own counseling sessions and he will always be available if we need his support."

The couple left Holy Rosary Church feeling a little less fright-ened about the future than before the visit. They were far from happy, but at least they knew that Father Brendan was on their side.

"It sounds as though Sam Braverman would just as soon take the money back and not press charges. What do you think about Morrison, Thomas?" Marie asked.

"It's hard to know. I don't see what he has to gain, except that he's a rather stern person; he reminds me of my father. Until he decides one way or the other, I don't think I'll be able to stop worrying. God, I'm scared stiff at the thought of prison. I feel helpless."

"Then it's a good idea to see that doctor friend of Father Brendan's," Marie interjected.

"I guess. I'll give his office a call this afternoon. I'm afraid of that, too, Marie. The idea of seeing a psychiatrist is scary. But I guess I have to go along with Father Brendan."

The first thing Marie did when she got home was to call Betty at the library. She told her that she was in trouble and asked if they could have lunch together.

"Of course," Betty agreed.

Marie told Thomas she was going to lunch with Betty and that he should raid the refrigerator when he was ready to have lunch. "There are all kinds of leftovers in the fridge. Make yourself a sandwich or heat up the leftover spaghetti. I should be home in a couple of hours."

At lunch, Marie poured out the whole story to her best friend, including the details from their meeting with Father Brendan. Then she continued, "I just don't know what to do first. God, Betty, I thought we were finally going to get the house fixed up so we wouldn't freeze this winter. Now I don't see how we can do a thing. Thomas was going to take $500 of that money to get started with the heating. It's going to take at least $2,000 to do everything, including painting and fixing storm windows. Where are we going to get all that money, especially if Thomas loses his job? Father Brendan told us to expect Thomas to be fired."

"Marie, do you think Thomas will let Harvey and I help you? We have some money put aside. We can lend you some money or even give you a few dollars if it comes to that. After all, what are friends for?"

"Oh, Betty, I don't think we could accept money from you. You've always been so good to me, but I know you're not rich. I know that teaching doesn't pay all that much. And besides which, there's Thomas' stubbornness about money."

"Marie, we have two incomes. Remember, I'm holding down a full-time job at the library. Anyway, I'm going to speak to Harvey tonight after dinner and see what he has to say. I'll call you later, okay?"

"Sure, Betty, please call. You know I always want to talk to you. I'll tell Thomas about your offer, but I think he'll say no."

"I have to get back to the library now, Marie. Tell Thomas not to be so proud. He's in a fix and we've known you both forever. Ask him what he would do if Harvey and I got into trouble. Would he turn us down? I don't think so."

After dinner that evening, Betty told Harvey about her meeting with Marie. "I said that I would speak to you about helping them with a few dollars, or lending them some money to fix their house. They're in big trouble, Harvey."

"I've known Thomas Grandee for a long time, Betty. He is basically a decent person. Thomas is not stupid, but he's been behaving like a fool. He always wanted to be the boss, to look like he was on top of everything, even when he knew he was in trouble. If anyone needs a psychiatrist, he sure does. Sorry, Betty, I guess I got off the subject. The question is whether I am willing to help out. Sure, I'll be glad to help. I just hope he sticks with the plan to see someone."

"Harvey, I don't think he's feeling like such a bigshot these days. It was Father Brendan who arranged to have him evaluated by Chase Finney. You've heard about him. He's the one that works well with Freudian analysis and understands alcoholism. If Finney thinks it's feasible, Father Brendan will take over the counseling under his guidance."

"If you want us to go up there and sit and talk about helping them, that's fine with me," Harvey said. "I just want Thomas to get the kind of help he needs and also stop trying to control Marie's life."

"I don't think that Thomas is the one in control anymore, Harvey. Not from what Marie has told me today."

"Good. And another thing, Betty. Forgive me, but what kind of counseling can a Catholic priest give to a man in trouble? He's going to end up telling the poor guy to just pray and put his trust in God."

"Harvey, Father Brendan is a very intelligent man. He's also a human being with a big heart. Look at how much he has already done. You're much too harsh and critical when it comes to religion, Harvey."

Betty never thought for one minute that Harvey would refuse to give his opinion or help financially. When Marie responded to Betty's offer to come up to the house so the four of them could talk about their problems, meaning Thomas' trouble as well as the business between Carl and Nancy, there was no hesitation on Marie's or Harvey's part.

The Rossiters picked up Chinese takeout for the four of them on the way over. Robbie was staying at his grandmother's house, and both Carl and Louise would be out late.

Harvey had always suspected that Thomas' need for control was part of some kind of inferiority complex.

"Thomas, I'm not going to try to tell you what to do." Harvey said. "You're the boss of your own life. Betty and I are here to offer whatever help we can. We're not trying to be social workers. We're here as friends."

"We're able to help you financially if you need help," Betty said, directing her remarks to Marie. "We can afford it, and it's something that both of us want to do."

"Listen," Thomas said, "I appreciate your offer, but I have pride and I don't want you to pity me."

"Who said anything about pity?" Harvey said. "For God's sake, we're your friends. If you need money, we can offer a loan. Maybe all you need is advice. Remember, I have some experience when it comes to banks and finances. The more we know about your circumstances, the easier it will be for us to help or at least advise you. Just remember what I said. You are your own master. We're not going to force money or advice on you. Let's just talk and then you can decide."

Harvey was apparently taking the right approach, because Thomas no longer hesitated. He said, "Look, as long as you both understand my trouble at The Chateau, I'm not going to keep any secrets from you. I hope, though, that whatever we talk about here doesn't go beyond this room." He looked at Harvey and then he said, "Harvey, you've already assured me that anything I tell you is in strictest confidence."

Harvey nodded. So did Betty.

"You wanted to know our financial condition, so here goes. All I have is a small checking account here in Malden at the trust company. Right now, the balance is less than $350. There's another two hundred in a savings account at the savings bank. I told Marie about it yesterday. That's about it.

"I guess I've had a problem all these years about keeping these things to myself. I've never really trusted anyone. Maybe it's because I just don't trust myself anymore. Anyway, that's it, folks. I haven't another penny to my name except for the stupid cash in the Columbia bank that I thought would solve all my problems but now may end up putting me in jail. My week's pay is up to $37.50. But, with three children and a big house, we don't really have a hell of a lot left after food and clothes and miscellaneous expenses. Then there are the real estate taxes and water bills, and excise tax, and so on and so on."

"I didn't hear you mention a mortgage payment, Thomas," Harvey said.

"Thank God there isn't any mortgage. I paid cash when I bought the place cheap because of the depressed market and the depressed condition of the house. I just haven't had the money to fix it up properly."

"Thomas, I didn't think you were that naïve! You can get a mortgage on this house today for at least three thousand dollars and maybe even more. How much will it take to fix everything up including painting, repairing loose windows and the heating system and everything else that really does need fixing?"

"Oh, that's easy. I have quotations on everything. It adds up to about $2,300."

"Thomas, you can get a mortgage today at about four and one-half percent. The monthly payments will probably be around twenty

178

dollars. Betty and I can help with those payments if you can't swing it, and if the bank gives you trouble because of your present situation, I'll be glad to endorse the mortgage."

"Jesus! Marie, did you hear that? I could never accept your charity. But, I might be able to swing twenty bucks a month as long as I have a job. Are you sure about the monthly payments, Harvey?"

"You'll have to check it out with the bank to be positive, but I think that what I said is pretty close."

Marie added, "I can get a job at the Woolworth's downtown. I was sort of thinking I'd like to be more occupied now that Robbie is getting big enough to be alone for a few hours when he comes home from school. In fact, I've already looked into it."

"You never told me this, Marie," Thomas said.

"Thomas, you and I have not been communicating that well for quite some time."

"I guess I asked for that."

"Yes, you did," she said, smiling. With tensions relieved all around, Marie felt confident that they were again on the right path.

Chapter Twenty-Nine

"CARLO CIAMPA, MASTER ELECTRICIAN" WAS THE NAME on the first bill that showed up at The Chateau at the end of August. The address was in east Boston. The bill was for $114, for rewiring and replacement of the main fuse box.

Victor was stunned. Ciampa was the electrician that Morrison and Braverman had been using for years. He knew because Ciampa had done work at The Chateau for Victor.

Victor reluctantly turned down the radio, which was playing Ella Fitzgerald's new hit, "A-Tisket, A-Tasket." He had to think. She must have someone working inside Ciampa's place, he thought. He decided to call Hannah before talking to Sam Braverman.

Picking up the phone, he called Hannah at the realty office. "Can I meet you someplace private?" he asked. "We have to talk alone."

"What's the problem, Victor?"

"I just got a bill that I want to speak with you about."

"We can talk on the phone, Victor. I'm alone. The bill says 'Ciampa,' right?"

"Right. What the hell is going on?"

"Don't get excited. Everything is under control. I know all about it."

"What the hell? You got someone on the inside at Ciampa's?"

"Victor, leave that up to me. I know what I'm doing and I told you everything is under control. Just keep quiet and leave it to me. There's nothing to worry about, okay?"

"I guess. Okay."

Victor placed the phone back on its cradle. He didn't think he would like working for a dame like Hannah. She sounded like she knew how to take control. He wondered how Thomas managed to put up with this for two whole years.

He picked the phone up again and gave Sam Braverman's private phone number to the operator. Victor had instructions to call Sam Braverman only on his private office line. Hannah could easily answer the realty company phone, and that would unearth their plan.

"I want to see that bill," Sam said immediately. "I'm on my way over before Hannah gets there." After he hung up, he called Bob Morrison, who was just as stunned as Sam.

"Sam, we've know this guy forever. He even banks here at Commerce. I recommended him to you years ago. The guy also does work here at the bank. It makes no sense whatsoever. Sam, you better call Carlo. Ask him what in hell is going on."

"I agree. I've already left a message for him to call me as soon as possible." Sam became impatient when the whole day passed without a call from the electrician. He called the shop again, and this time the worker who answered told him that Carlo was home sick and had been out for the week. He expected him to come to work again in a few days. When Sam asked about the bill to The Chateau, the man said he didn't know anything about it. Not wanting to bother Carlo at home, especially if the guy was ill, he decided to wait a day or two more.

Two days later, Victor put in another call to Sam Braverman. Sam didn't answer, so Victor decided to call Bob Morrison at the bank instead.

When he finally got through to Morrison, he said, "Good morning, Mr. Morrison, this is Victor down at The Chateau. Yes, Thomas is here and he seems to be fine."

Only when Bob Morrison had established that matters were still under control did he let Victor continue.

"The reason I called, sir, is to tell you that another bill just came in today's mail. No, sir, it's not from the electrician. This bill is from a company called Wilson Plumbing and Heating Service."

Morrison literally screamed over the phone. "What in hell are you saying? The Wilson Company is an old, reliable firm. Victor, don't do a thing. I'm on my way to The Chateau. You tell Grandee to take the day off. I don't want him to see me. Make sure we can use his office, though, and you keep trying to get Sam Braverman and tell him to meet me there."

"Mr. Morrison, may I remind you that Hannah comes in at about one o'clock each afternoon? It's already noon, so you had best wait until after she leaves. I'll call you then."

Bob Morrison reluctantly agreed, and Victor hung up the phone.

The second bill was dated "September 1, 1938." Today was the third of the month. Sam arrived a few minutes after Bob Morrison, and they went into a huddle in Thomas' office.

"Victor," Sam Braverman asked, "What time does Hannah show up for the collection?"

"Usually about one o'clock," Victor answered.

Sam said, "Hell, she works in my office so I ought to know. I could kick myself for not staying on top of the details. I can't tell you how stupid I feel. I thought Hannah Ward was the best thing that ever happened to the business. That young woman could do anything. She was a speed typist, a damn good bookkeeper and smart as they come. I should have known she was too good to be true."

"Victor," Bob Morrison said, "I think you'd better leave us alone. Oh, and tell Grandee that he should be back here in time to make the money transfer to Hannah. I gather he's home by now."

"I will, Mr. Morrison, but in case I can't reach him, I'll tell Hannah that he had to do an errand and I'll get the cashier to give me the deposit and the receipts. I guess one of you will have to okay it with the cashier. Thomas gave his okay the last time I handled it for him."

Morrison thanked Victor and said he would check with him before leaving. "Oh, tell Thomas we will be out of here by two o'clock at the latest. Can't take a chance on Hannah finding us here."

"Will do, sir," Victor replied as he closed the office door.

"For God's sake, Bob, why are you so hard on Thomas?" Sam said when they were out of earshot. "The man is obviously going through hell. He's admitted his wrongdoing and he's trying his damnedest to be helpful."

"Sam, I don't give a damn about his admissions and I'm not interested in his personal reformations, religious or otherwise. Where I come from, when a man commits a crime, he pays for it."

182

"I know how you feel, Bob. I have my own doubts, too. But, when you stop to think about it, if it wasn't for Thomas having a conscience and owning up about the money, we might never have found out about Hannah."

"I suppose that's true, but how is it that he never used his conscience to let us know first? How is it that Victor is the one who told us about the bills? I find it hard to forgive that man."

"All right. Let's talk about this later. Right now, I think we have to make a call to Larry Wilson. His plumbing outfit has always been fair with us. I wonder if Hannah has some phonies working at both Ciampa's and Wilson's?"

Sam called Wilson Plumbing. They knew nothing about a bill to The Chateau. He then made a call to the electrician's place of business and was finally able to speak to Carlo Ciampa, the boss.

"No, Sam, we never did no work for The Chateau last month. I think, maybe two years ago, we done a small job. I think that Victor fellow needed us for something."

Sam hung up the phone. "Damn, I can't even check my own records without going through Hannah. What a mess, Bob."

Bob thought for a moment. "Yes, but I think that we can do an audit, Sam. Why don't I have the outfit that audits the bank's records look into this. They can have Hannah open the books on a routine check without arousing suspicion. We've had audits done before, haven't we?"

Sam thought and then responded, "Yes, and that's just the problem. They won't find anything out of order. Hannah will have a bill for everything that she's paid for. How the hell does she and her friend get hold of the money if she sends the checks to the contractor? These skilled contractors do the work and send out bills. The ones we use on a regular basis don't even send monthly statements."

He paused and then added, "Another thing. Carlo's wife prepares his bills. And Wilson's old maid daughter does his. Are they in on this, too?"

"I don't think so, Sam."

Bob continued. "Hannah makes a check out directly to each company, never to an individual. The check gets mailed to a business address. She could never take a chance of paying a fake bill and mailing the check because the chances are that the owner of the business would see a check for a job that he didn't do. That would be too risky."

He thought again for a moment and then added, "Maybe she delivers the checks in person and then figures a way of cashing them."

Sam said, "We need a private detective agency with experience in solving these kinds of problems."

"I guess you're right, Sam. All I know is, we better get to the bottom of this before I have a heart attack—or before Hannah gets wind of what we are doing."

"Bob, The Chateau is still doing well. We're still showing more than a decent profit. I think you're getting too upset because you have high principles. I wish you would think hard about Thomas Grandee. Underneath this whole business, we're continuing to do well in spite of Hannah Ward's manipulations."

"You have a more pragmatic approach than I do, that's for sure," Bob said. "I hope you're right, Sam, but I have my doubts. Let's see what an investigator comes up with."

Sam Braverman agreed and determined to continue his campaign to discover the real culprits as well as remove Thomas Grandee from Morrison's immediate line of fire. Grandee had become a scapegoat for his partner's own inability to come to terms with Hannah's crime and also to deal with the problem in an unemotional manner in order to resolve their own professional situation. Putting the company back on track without publicly exposing the partners' own managerial ineptitude was much more important than trying to place blame where it obviously no longer belonged.

Chapter Thirty

SAM BRAVERMAN WASTED NO TIME IN CONTACTING a detective agency. He asked the detective to meet him at The Union Oyster House in Boston for an interview. Harry Cohen, proprietor of the Holmes and Watson Agency, was happy to oblige. At the restaurant, when a small man with black hair and sparkling black eyes walked over and introduced himself, Sam was taken by surprise by his smiling, outgoing, almost jolly manner. He hardly looked or sounded like a detective. Harry Cohen had the demeanor of a used car salesman.

He told Sam that he worked alone most of the time. "I used to have several employees, but with the depression and all, I had to let Sherlock and Doctor Watson go. They were too expensive for me."

Sam smiled, but wondered if he hadn't hired the wrong agency. He decided not to mention the detective's sense of humor to his more stalwart partner, Bob Morrison.

After explaining the problem and listening to Harry Cohen carefully, Sam decided. "Mr. Cohen, I'll give you a chance, but if I don't get some sort of report in a week or two, I'll have to reconsider and perhaps go to the police."

"Mr. Braverman, I'm good." He paused briefly and then added, "Please call me Harry. I prefer that to Mr. Cohen."

"Fine, Harry. But my partner, Bob Morrison, does not conduct business in the same manner that I do, so please be more circumspect when speaking to him. By the way, you can call me Sam. My partner, however, is Mr. Morrison."

"I understand, Sam. I guess it's a good thing I spoke with you first. I'm informal in the way I do business. Actually, that's often the way business is conducted with detectives. We can be a pretty rough bunch. If you're soft, you don't make it in this line of work."

"Right. As I explained, the reason I asked you to meet me here at the Oyster House is because my bookkeeper is a thief. If you come to my office after six o'clock tonight, I will show you the records and we can go into detail."

"It's a deal, Sam. I'll be at the office after six. Maybe we can have dinner together. Naturally, you'll treat," he said and gave Sam a big grin, showing his perfect set of false teeth.

Sam Braverman felt that Harry Cohen would somehow get to the bottom of the situation. The main hurdle would be to investigate Hannah while she still did the company's bookkeeping and billing. There was no doubt that it was going to take some time to get answers. Keeping her unaware was quite a different matter.

At the end of his first week of investigating, Sam Braverman informed Harry Cohen that another contractor had submitted a bill. This time it was to provide two new doors in one of the hotel rooms at The Chateau. The contractor was John Romano. The billhead said, "J. Romano, General Contractors". Romano's place was in Chelsea, a small town bordering Charlestown. Braverman also explained that Romano had never done any work for The Chateau.

Out of curiosity, Sam called Victor and asked him if he had any information about a bill for two new doors. Victor told him that Hannah did mention that such a bill might arrive. "She told me that if anyone questioned the bill to say that a guest had broken two doors and they had to be replaced," Sam told Harry.

Sam then asked Harry what he had learned thus far.

"I know this much. That Hannah broad is a smart cookie. She has got some con game going, and if she wasn't so greedy, she might have gotten away with it. I'm almost ready to make a full report, Sam."

"Why didn't you just let me know if you have information?"

"I'm sorry, but I still have a few more facts to gather before anyone will be able to take action. Look, you guys already know she's dishonest, right?"

"I guess we do, Harry. That's why we hired you."

"Then give me a little more time and I'll give you what you need to nail her. Okay?"

Sam agreed.

Two more weeks went by before Harry contacted Sam Braverman again. "Sam, I think we have the goods on Hannah, finally. I also think that you should arrange for a complete audit and, if I'm not mistaken, I believe you have been suckered for a lot more than just the bills to The Chateau. I bet you're going to find that you've paid a small fortune for fake bills submitted to Braverman and Morrison Realty, and every penny of it went to Hannah Ward. Or, Henrietta Wadsworth, which is her real name."

"I guess you better get your ass over here, Harry, and let us know what the hell is going on."

"We can't do it at your place, Sam. We need a neutral location where we can lay things out without Hannah around. It looks like this broad really suckered your manager.

She's quite a pro. He didn't have anything to do with the fake bills, and Victor was smart to tell you about it before getting involved."

"Let's talk about that when we meet. I'll call you back in a short while after I've arranged a meeting place. You don't have any objections to a church, do you?"

"A church? Hell, I guess not, Sam. What church?"

"Wait for my call. Stay where you are, Harry, and I sure hope you're not joking when you say that you have Hannah's scheme figured out."

Chapter Thirty-One

SAM BRAVERMAN ARRANGED TO MEET AT FATHER Brendan's rectory at the beginning of October, on a Wednesday evening. The other religious leaders were also present. With Sam Braverman, Bob Morrison and Harry Cohen, it made a party of seven. The meeting started after dinner.

Harry Cohen spoke first. "You people are not going to believe this, but Hannah Ward is a loner. She has no known accomplice. I've been following her. It was just that simple. I shouldn't tell you how easy it was to figure this thing out because you might balk on the charges. But a deal's a deal, and I'm certain that you'll live up to your part of the bargain. I've lived up to mine."

"Harry, get to the subject," Sam Braverman said, "and never mind the defense. You'll get your money. We are more interested in getting to the bottom of what sounds like a very expensive crime."

"Okay. Well, I said that I followed her. On the second day, she headed for the post office in Waltham and went directly to a P.O. box. It took several phone calls to some important connections to learn that the box was issued in her name, Hannah Ward."

"That doesn't sound too mysterious, Harry," Bob Morrison stated.

"It is when you learn that Hannah Ward lives on Commonwealth Avenue in Brookline," Harry answered. "I found out where she lives, also by following her. I'm pretty good at getting into other people's apartments, and I had a perfect chance to look the morning after I found out where she lived. It isn't always that easy. Anyway, now hear this," Harry said with increased excitement, "this dame has two typewriters in her apartment. One is a Royal, similar to the one at Ciampa's, and the other is an Underwood, like the one at Wilson's place. That took a little more unearthing to discover. I'll bet my last buck that this other outfit, Romano, has either a Royal or an Underwood.

"Anyway, she has blank bills printed with billheads that look just like the ones those companies use for their billing. I saw a couple of samples of what I think were real bills. Anyway, I had a trace put on our clever Hannah, and I won't bore you with the details, except that her real name is Henrietta Wadsworth and she's from Altoona, Pennsylvania.

"She also has a record of arrests for soliciting, and she was once arrested for forging a check. The most she ever got was a couple of night's sleep in a Philadelphia police station holding cell. She was young and pretty, and the judges always just gave her a slap on the wrist. So she moved to Boston and answered the ad for a bookkeeper that Morrison and Braverman ran in all the Boston newspapers."

He stopped to take a breath. "Oh, I forgot to tell you, she's not twenty-five years old. Would you believe she's thirty-three? And she went to business school after graduating Altoona High School with honors. Her mother's boyfriend raped her when she was sixteen. Her father was a drunk. Mrs. Wadsworth threw him out shortly after Hannah—or Henrietta—was born. The mother wasn't exactly the wholesome kind, either."

Father Brendan was absorbed in the details. "How did you learn about all this, Mr. Cohen?" He said.

"Police records in Altoona and Philadelphia, Father. That's how."

"But Mr. Cohen, those records are confidential."

"Yes, I know, Father Brendan, but the police have to get information, so they rely on informers. I use the same informers as the police. Can I help it if the information I get is confidential? I don't ask any questions unless I want the answers, and I never ask about confidentiality. In my line of work, 'confidential' simply means that some information is always available."

"Quite a story!" Father Fazio chimed in. The other religious leaders also expressed similar amazement.

"Anyhow, I also have some photos here for you. These show Hannah walking into three different banks, two in Rhode Island

and one in New Hampshire." Harry placed the photos on the table in front of him. "Hannah has several sets of identification. At one bank, she is Hannah Ciampa, d.b.a. Ciampa Company. In New Hampshire, she's Wilson, and the Rhode Island bank knows her as H. Romano."

Bob Morrison asked Harry, "What is the next step, Mr. Cohen?"

"I think it is my obligation to either report a crime to the FBI, or to ask that your people do so. This woman used the United States mail to do her business, and she crossed state lines. This is a case for the Feds."

"Since you have the facts before you, I think it's best for you to report her, Mr. Cohen," Father Brendan said.

"Well, how much do you know about Thomas Grandee, Mr. Cohen?" Morrison asked.

"Not very much, other than the fact that Mr. Braverman explained that Thomas Grandee knew of Hannah's desire to submit fake bills. It seems odd that Thomas would not report Hannah's proposition to you or Sam if he did know about it." He continued after a pause. "I'm curious, myself, as to Thomas' role here. Can I ask that I be informed?"

"You can ask, Mr. Cohen, but I suggest we limit this to an inquiry into the real culprit, Hannah Ward—or Wadsworth," Father Brendan responded.

"Father Brendan," Bob Morrison asked, "I cannot for the life of me understand your tolerance for Thomas Grandee. Hasn't he been a bad actor in this whole dirty business?"

"Yes, Mr. Morrison, you are right. He has. However, Thomas came forward and related his story to me and made his confession. His penitent behavior since then has been commendable. The man has earned God's forgiveness, and so I recommend that he be treated with the respect due to a person who has proven that he has a conscience. Besides which, Mr. Morrison, Thomas has not benefited in any way. Remember, he never touched the money. And he has suffered emotional harm and guilt through some four years of doing Hannah's bidding."

Father Brendan caught himself with that last remark. He looked at Harry Cohen and explained, "Mr. Cohen, I have given part of a secret away to your trained ears. I wish I had not, but it will be for the best if you know the rest of the story. Otherwise, you may draw incorrect conclusions."

Father Brendan looked around and saw that all present were waiting for him to tell Harry about the Columbia Bank and the cash theft.

When the priest finished, Harry said, "Father, you may not believe this, but I'll tell you anyway. I'm a good Jew. I was Bar Mitzvahed, and I go to synagogue on the High Holy Days. But this is what I want to say. It's obvious to a guy like me that if you're going to steal from a place like The Chateau that does mostly a cash business, the cash is what you would steal. It also seems to me that this Hannah dame got caught in her fake bill scheme because she became too greedy.

"Yeah, I'll report this to the FBI. I've reported many a crime to them, and they'll take my investigative report quite seriously. However, I suggest that you do nothing until you hear from me. I'll need to get the information together tonight, and I'll report it to the Feds in the morning. But, if this guy Thomas never used the money and has offered to reimburse the realty company, I say let it go. The world is full of really bad people. This guy doesn't sound like one of them."

All eyes were now on Bob Morrison. He glanced over at his partner. "Okay, I'll go along with you, Sam. We don't have to press charges against Thomas, but I don't want him working for me any longer. As soon as Hannah is arrested, he's out of The Chateau, with no questions, no severance pay, nothing."

Sam didn't need to wait a moment. "Fine, Bob. I'll go along with that."

This time, it was Reverend Granville's opportunity to ask a serious question. "Mr. Morrison, are you a churchgoer? I gather that you are not Catholic or Jewish. From your name, I also imagine you come from a Protestant family. Am I right?"

"I attend church sometimes. I can't say every Sunday. My family belongs to the Congregational Church."

Granville smiled broadly and added, "Well, we have something in common. I happen to be a Congregational Minister. If I may, I will now act as one for your benefit, Mr. Morrison. There is a memorable saying in James; in fact it's James chapter five, verse nine, that states as follows: 'Do not complain, Brethren, against one another, that you yourselves may not be judged; behold, the Judge is standing right at the door.'"

Bob Morrison smiled and said, "I guess I've heard that a number of times, Reverend. In fact, I've heard several different renditions of the same verse throughout the years. I get the message, but I still can't help how strongly I feel about Thomas. I had faith in the man and would have trusted him with anything. It just makes me feel like a damned fool."

Granville smiled. "Your feelings are understandable, but I ask you to please think carefully before condemning Thomas Grandee. What Thomas Grandee did is not to be condoned, but he was willing to explain and repent. Our faith, in fact many of the world's faiths, are supposed to be based upon God's forgiveness."

"Amen" was heard all around. Bob Morrison remained silent. He simply nodded approval.

Sam Braverman said, "Before we leave, I'm curious about one particular matter. Harry, this is a question I thought to ask earlier, but I didn't want to interrupt. I can understand the aliases and the separate bank accounts. I guess Hannah must have taken us for plenty, so it was worth her while to travel out of state. What I don't understand is why she needed that Waltham post office box. Why would she need it to mail checks to herself? Why not just put the checks in her purse and deposit them later at the appropriate bank?"

"Good question, Sam. Maybe she was afraid someone would look into her purse or, more likely, she needed time and didn't want the checks lying around in her apartment. Don't forget that Hannah put in a full day at the realty office and spent time at The Chateau. She must have visited the out of town banks on Saturday mornings or when she found an excuse to leave work early." He thought for a minute. "At first, I thought it was a bit strange myself."

With that, the meeting was over. When everyone departed, Father Brennan relaxed into his easy chair and sighed with relief. Thomas wasn't going to be pleased that he would soon be out of a job. However, he and Marie would certainly be relieved to know that jail was not in his future.

Chapter Thirty-Two

SOON AFTER THE FBI PICKED UP HANNAH, Thomas found himself out of work. He applied for a job at several restaurants. Father Brendan and Marie had both asked him to avoid places that served alcohol. He agreed, but explained that if nothing turned up after a while, that he would have to broaden the search.

Marie landed a job in the local Woolworth's as a clerk. The pay was eight dollars per week for a 40-hour week. They were waiting for the Malden Savings Bank to notify them on their mortgage application so they could get started on the house repairs. Since Thomas was unemployed, Harvey and Betty Rossiter co-signed the mortgage application.

Carl was able to get a discount price on some paint at the store where he was now working, and Thomas was spending some time each day scraping and priming 18 storm windows to get them ready for installation.Both Thomas and Carl were early risers, so they would both get up at five in the morning and go downstairs to the basement where they worked together on the storm windows.

Thomas was hurting. He felt guilty for his misdemeanors. He lacked confidence and was still fearful that Bob Morrison's high moral standards would surface and that he might decide to bring charges against him. Guilt, feelings of inferiority and fear of imprisonment would have caused a weaker man to give up and become depressed. Some, with Thomas' problems, might have even considered suicide. However, beneath the surface, Thomas Grandee had great strength. Now, he turned to his son, Carl, who reminded him of himself in his youth. Carl looked so much like his father.

Thomas spoke up one morning as they were downstairs together. "My biggest regret, Carl, is that I've lost touch with the family. You and I haven't had much in the way of a father and son relationship. We haven't shared very much at all recently, have we?"

"I guess not. But Pa, you've had so much trouble that you didn't really have the time," Carl said, being polite.

"Thank you for being nice about it. You really have the right to be upset with me. Sometimes I actually hate myself."

Thomas was unconsciously beginning an expurgatory. Since it seemed to make him feel better, he eventually opened up a bit more.

"I did some bad things, Carl. I hurt Ma and I hurt you kids, but I've come to my senses. I'll be able to make it up to you."

"You will, Pa, honest." Carl was beginning to have a good feeling that things were going to get better for the Grandee family.

"I understand that you spent some time with Red Keating, last week. You didn't get home until the early morning hours. What happened?"

Carl remembered the night before with Red. They had gone across Main Street to Joe Nemo's hot dog stand, where they each had a hot dog for a nickel apiece. They shared a nickel bottle of coke.

"Pa, Red asked me to do him a favor, that's all."

"Do you want to tell me about it?"

"Red has this girl he really likes. She said he could do something with her." Carl hesitated. "Pa, I don't think you want to hear all the details. It's hard to talk about this stuff. You know, sex stuff. Red Keating is different than I am. He acts more grown up, I guess."

"Carl, you can tell me about these things. I was young once, myself. Besides, maybe it's about time you and I talked about the things fathers and sons really should talk about. Go on and tell me about Red. Maybe that will get us someplace."

"Well, all right, if you want me to." Carl then proceeded to tell the story of the previous day's adventure with Red.

"Red said that the girl told him he could get in bed with her if he came up to her bedroom after one in the morning. She sleeps in a front bedroom with a door leading to the porch, and she said her parents would be sound asleep by midnight. Red had to shimmy up to the porch on the second floor. The girl was supposed to raise and lower the window blind to make sure it was safe to come up."

"So what did that have to do with you, Carl?"

"The girl didn't want his car parked in front of her house. There's no nighttime parking allowed, for one thing, but she was also afraid her neighbors might notice. He needed me to drop him off and then pick him up at two o'clock in the morning. I didn't like the idea, but I owe him, so I agreed to do it."

"Sounds like a crazy story," Thomas responded, wondering if he was missing the point.

"Well, it gets even crazier," Carl added with a smile.

"What do you mean?"

"That's the funny part, Pa. Wait 'til you hear this."

"I'm all ears," Thomas Grandee added.

"Well, when I returned, Red was sitting on the curbstone in front of the house. He'd been out there for three-quarters of an hour. Red said, 'It's a good thing the weather's nice, but my ass hurts from this damned curbstone. I was afraid to sit on the steps.'"

"What happened? I'll bet he got caught. He took an awful chance getting in bed with a girl in her father's house."

"Yeah, he sure did get caught. Red told me the girl's father wanted to kill him, but all he did was pull his daughter out of bed and smack her across her backside. Red said that he just grabbed his clothing and jumped out the window. The way he tells it, he only got his pants on halfway and then had to shimmy back down from the porch."

Carl did not tell his father what he and Red had also said in the car on the way home.

"I got laid, though," Red had said, "before the old bastard heard us and pounced into the room. Jesus, Carl, it was great. But really scary."

"Well, I'm glad you got laid, Red. I don't think I could do what you did. It's okay for a guy who wants to very much, but I don't know. Maybe I'm too serious about doing it. I think I'd like it to be part of a relationship."

"Hey, you haven't ever been laid, have you?"

"Why do you say that, Red?"

"I don't know. You're too nice a kid, I guess. I just like to have fun, Carl. You're the studious type. But you didn't answer me. Did you ever get laid?"

"I did, once. It was an older lady. She seduced me."

"Not that old bag you worked for at the news office, was it?"

"Oh, no. Mrs. Finkelstein is a very nice person. She would never do a thing like that. It was someone you don't know. She's not around here anymore."

"I think you're full of shit, Carl. You're still a virgin. That's what I think."

"Have it your way, Red. I don't care whether you believe me or not." Carl was glad Red hadn't found out about Mrs. Finklestein. He felt guilty. He'd already said too much.

Carl hadn't gotten home until three in the morning. Thomas and Marie were at the top of the stairs, wanting to know what had happened. "I'm sorry I'm so late. I was with Red Keating and his car broke down," Carl had lied. "I'm okay. You can go back to sleep. I'm bushed."

"We were worried, Carl. If that ever happens again, please call the house if you can get to a telephone."

Carl made a date with Charlotte Brown. They went to the movies at the local theatre. Tickets at the Granada in Malden were 15 cents each, and they saw a double-feature plus Pathe News.

On the walk back home, Charlotte asked Carl if he had broken up with Nancy. He explained, "I still see Nancy. We go out sometimes, but she's not my steady girlfriend anymore." Charlotte was satisfied and felt that she might still have a chance to make Carl her steady. Carl liked Charlotte, but he thought it would have been more fun to go to the movies with Nancy.

Nancy dated a boy whose family was friendly with the Rossiters. His name was Jack Gould, and he, like Carl, was a senior at Malden High. Jack had the use of his father's car, and all he wanted to do was park at "Lover's Lane" in Spot Pond. Nancy spent an entire evening there pushing Jack's hands away from her body. When he asked for another date, she flat-out refused.

Nancy thought it funny that Jack, a so-called "nice Jewish boy," wasn't really very nice. Nancy did see Michael Levenson, another Jewish boy, for another date. They went to a movie and to the Palace of Sweets for ice cream afterwards. He was very pleasant and they had a nice time. Nancy thought he was intelligent and polite, and she really liked him, but she thought it would have been more fun to be with Carl.

Two days after the application for the mortgage was signed, the Grandees were approved and the contract was signed for the heating company to replace the old furnace. A chimney cleaning company would be coming the next week, and everyone would have to be out of the house for a full day.

Thomas made an arrangement with Victor Hermanssen to spend Sunday afternoons at the house, helping him chip away cracked putty from around the windows and to tighten up loose hardware as well as replace any worn insulation. Victor also agreed to help him hang the storm windows. Carl said that he would pitch in, too, in any way that he could.

The outside scraping and painting would have to wait until spring; the painter Thomas had contacted was finishing up on current jobs and didn't want to take a chance on starting the big house on Las Casas so close to winter.

Thomas was finally hired to work in the kitchen of the Apollo Restaurant in Chelsea, a small city just over the bridge from Charlestown. His salary would be $14 per week, which included breakfast and lunch. Between Marie and Thomas, their combined weekly salaries came to $22. The mortgage payment on the $2,500, 15-year loan was about $19 per month. When the real estate tax and their food bill and other expenses were all added together, the Grandees just barely broke even.

There was still some money in the checking account at the trust company and, because of Victor and Carl's help, they would have more than $500 left in the bank after all the contractors were paid. In the meantime, the money for the painter was sitting in the savings bank, earning a little interest.

Victor was now managing The Chateau, and since he was unfamiliar with some of the policies and procedures there, Thomas gave him a lot of guidance in exchange for his help with the house repairs.

Actually, now that Victor had accomplished his purpose in becoming the manager, he didn't think Thomas was such a bad guy after all. He felt sorry that Thomas was in trouble, and the only thing Victor really missed was the game that he had played with Hannah. On the one hand, he was glad she was gone. He knew she was bad news. On the other hand, the game was something he enjoyed, and he had to admit that she had also provided him with quite a good time.

Chapter Thirty-Three

DR. CHASE FINNEY INTERVIEWED THOMAS AND SET up a schedule of four weekly visits. He explained to Thomas that he was requested to give a report to Father Brendan, but he wanted Thomas to understand that anything he said would be held in strictest confidence. His report to the priest would only cover the type of counseling he would recommend. None of the details would be disclosed unless Finney felt it important to do so, and then only if Thomas agreed to such disclosure.

After the four weekly sessions with Dr. Finney, Thomas was to start counseling with Father Brendan. Finney arranged to meet Father Brendan at the rectory the first week in December on a Wednesday evening.

"Well, it's been a long time since we've seen each other, Chase," the priest said as he greeted his school chum.

"I'd say a good 15 years, if not more, Bill." Chase Finney was a tall man who had once played forward on the Boston College basketball team. He had gone on to Harvard Medical School afterwards, where he became interested in treating drug addiction.

Finney was not only a medical doctor, but he was also board certified in psychiatry. He had a number of patients to whom he provided psychotherapy in multiple session programs. After the Volstead Act was repealed in 1933, Finney added Alcoholism to his list of areas of practice and was known nationwide for this particular expertise.

"I don't think that I've been called Bill since my college days," Father Brendan replied. They both laughed.

"Would you rather I address you as Father Brendan?"

"No, 'Bill' is fine. I like it. Now, take off your hat and that Mackinaw and make yourself comfortable."

"It's so cold outside. I like the warm feeling I get being inside without having to have all this clothing on." Dr. Finney proceeded to strip down to a sweater and slacks. He was not one to dress formally unless he was forced to do so, and he almost never wore a tie. Once the stocking hat was peeled off, he brushed his thick red hair back with two good-sized hands. "It's always good to be out of the cold."

His smile was a wide grin that made him look like a large friendly kid rather than a medical practitioner of 50.

"Getting to the point of this meeting, Bill, I believe Thomas Grandee is a highly intelligent man. He has a fairly classic inferiority complex. Anything I tell you about the details has already been discussed with Thomas. I promised him that I would respect this confidence.

"Thomas knows that I am meeting with you and that I have his permission to discuss certain issues. Beyond that, it is up to him to provide you with any other information. Do we understand each other?"

Father Brendan nodded.

Chase Finney then explained that as a teenager, Thomas' ambition was to work in the athletics field with young people. He had a very strong desire to become a gym teacher and coach. Thomas was one of those very bright youngsters who froze when he needed to speak in front of class or was faced with important written tests. There are a number of reasons for this type of reaction to pressure as well as other manifestations that carry through in the decision-making process in life. Had there been proper therapy back then, Thomas Grandee's life might have taken quite a different course.

The priest asked, "Why would Thomas still have a strong inferiority complex? After all, he held a very responsible job and appeared to be in total control at all times."

"Not so, Bill. Remember, he quickly capitulated under the pressure of Hannah Ward. Thomas had three very special obstacles as a youngster, which he was never able to resolve. A stern father, a mother who thought Thomas was as stupid as his report cards indicated, and an older brother, John, who was a brilliant student.

"The brother went on to college on scholarship, and now lives in California and has had nothing to do with Thomas since their parents died. From what little Thomas knows, his brother John has always been very successful and has prominent connections with one of the major Hollywood film studios."

Father Brendan added, "Thomas' wife also tells me that he needs to feel in control. He has to be in a dominant position at all times in their relationship. That has been the situation throughout their marriage until the present. It seems that since he has assumed responsibility for the malefaction, he has been acting somewhat childlike, depending on Marie for support as though she was his mother.

"There was an implied dependency on me, as well, in my role as a priest and someone that he could finally confide in. I seem to have become not only his symbolic father through the church, but his substitute real-life father as well."

Finney waited for Brendan to continue. After a moment, Father Brendan remarked, "I guess my question is about Thomas and the need to be in control." Finney thought for a minute or so. "It's a most difficult question to answer, and only time will tell if my guess is right. The one area in which Thomas has always been confident is in his own physical dynamics."

"Bill, I can try to tell this to you in layman's language, or I can talk about Thomas in more professional terms. It is easier for me in the latter, but if you prefer, I will try layman's language."

"Chase, make believe I'm a colleague in psychiatry. I've studied more than my fair share of psychology through the years. I'll let you know if I need you to interpret."

"Thank you," Chase responded, and he began his report. "Thomas was good at sports and he has always attracted women. Whenever he sensed that he was losing control, he turned to a control area. Without active sports in his life, sex became an alternative. He also equated the ability to take charge with control.

"That's the reason that Hannah's personality became an immediate problem to him. She was the only woman besides his mother that could actually dominate him. So, he turned to using other women, prostitutes, to prove his own sexual prowess and convince himself of his ability to dominate. This is what I think.

"Deep down, Thomas has used his physical strength and appearance to control the people around him. He resorted to this more superficial approach out of fear.

"You see, if you have little real confidence in yourself, you can't have someone else ordering you around. Why? Because you may end up not being able to do what the other person wants you to do. In other words, you can fail the immediacy of a test, just as Thomas failed his school tests and then was chastised by his mother.

"This is a classic example of human dialectics, Bill. You see, logically, he thinks that by demanding control, he can avoid responsibility. Avoiding responsibility reduces the likelihood of failure. On the other hand, because he is unsure of himself, he really does need someone else to take charge. Such a need can only revert back to a mother or father image. If I am right in this particular analysis, then we need to stimulate an internal synthesis of these two opposites, something that a naturally evolving psyche creates for itself as it matures in life. Such a synthesis should eventually resolve itself as a reasonable balance between self-confidence and trust in others. Thomas has a way to travel to reach this goal."

Father Brendan looked puzzled. "Chase, I have promised to counsel Thomas. I need your advice as to how to proceed. I'm beginning to feel a bit insecure. I'm not at all sure I have the training for what appears to be a difficult theoretical task. And, there are very real issues such as his drinking. We have to discuss that too, Chase."

"You'll do fine. I believe that you are in the best position to help Thomas. First of all, he has faith in you. He trusts you. And remember, you have also recognized that he sees you in a 'father image' role."

Finney then went on to explain that Marie's new influence upon him was every bit as good a defense against Thomas' drinking as anything else could be. As long as the couple was getting along and stayed together, Thomas would have enough reason to have concern and even develop a willingness to abstain.

Finney did not think that Thomas' drinking had ever been completely out of control and it was certainly not at its worst. To Finney, it was a symptom of a more deep-rooted illness that could be eliminated by that particular illness' cure. That illness was an instilled feeling of inferiority, plain and simple.

Furthermore, Thomas could never have been a true alcoholic because he hadn't touched a drop of alcohol in months; no true alcoholic, dependent on the drug, could stay away from drinking for even a day or two.

Finney's suggestion was to put Thomas back in touch with the inclinations of his youth to step him up through time again to better reconcile the present. Putting him in contact with young people in some sort of athletic activity would subliminally encourage the process.

He felt that Thomas, from the outset, revolted against his work because he had accepted a career path that remained in conflict with what he had most wanted to achieve in life. That was dangerous. Thomas Grandee, down deep inside, still had ambitions to remain a physically active professional entity. This could mean becoming a coach or even a gym teacher, as long as he kept a link to the place where he knew he could always remain in charge because of his ability. That security to Thomas might still be found in the athletics field.

Father Brendan interjected, "But you still haven't told me where to start a counseling program, Chase."

Finney replied, "Concentrate on catharsis at first. Get Thomas to tell you about his brother, John, and his parents. Just get him talking, Bill, and I think he will gradually cleanse himself of guilt feelings. We will also remove the seeds of ineptitude that these very destructive influences in his life insisted on nurturing.

"The other thing you must do is to begin to build a sense of self-confidence and self-esteem. Bolster him as much as you can, particularly in the areas of inherent ability. He thinks he is stupid, but he is very intelligent. He is trying to prove to himself that his mother was right and that she really loves him. It's as if her telling him that he was stupid was for his own good, so that he would not have to try hard to pass a test. In his mind, his mother was saying that he should be happy just because he was big and strong and a good athlete, as if brains were not important."

"I'm beginning to see where you're coming from," Father Brendan responded. "I am puzzled, though, that his inferiority feelings were strong enough to cause this much trouble in other people's lives. What brought you to this line of reasoning to begin with? Was there a clue in his own behavioral patterns that might have suggested all of this to you?" Father Brendan wondered.

"Funny that you should ask about a clue, Bill. You gave me the clue. Remember telling me that Thomas played a silly game with the patrons of The Chateau, asking customers to pay 10 cents if they didn't like the food or service?"

"Yes, I recall that. It seemed a strange way to build goodwill, but apparently it worked."

"Oh, I can understand that it might work. Thomas must have handled it diplomatically enough to make it seem like fun. What was really going on, though, is that Thomas hated what he was doing. He was a severely frustrated individual. He blamed Marie for getting pregnant; blamed himself for his early school failures; blamed his parents and brother for not supporting his career goals. The final straw was his choice by default to marry Marie. He knew that he was never going to make it to college if he had to raise a family. This was a first morally influenced decision on his part, which proved that Thomas always did have strong conscience.

"I challenged him on that game he played with the customers. He responded by saying that the idea of him spending a lifetime working in a restaurant was an unimportant achievement that he was determined to laugh at. Making someone else pay for either the restaurant's shortcoming or their own misjudgment was a way to shift the blame into another arena. He could prove superiority, right or wrong, on his own shaky turf."

"I still don't understand. Please explain," Father Brendan asked.

"Thomas made it clear that he had been totally and extremely frustrated that he could not achieve his ambition. I think that if Marie did not get pregnant, he would have managed in some way to get into college and pursue a sports career. At the least, he could have remained in the field of physical education. He would have succeeded, in any event.

"It was a feeling of obligation for getting Marie pregnant that caused him to give up the very strong desire for the future that was his very real dream."

Finney continued after a thoughtful pause. "I believe his success in the restaurant business just enabled him to repress the frustration. The problem was that an increasingly unfulfilled and underlying emotion was transferred into hostility; hostility toward those he loved most, like his wife and children.

"Sex became a weapon, even against himself. Hannah's perverted goals also became part of the regression process. I can only guess, but I think that when the money at the Columbia bank was exposed, it opened a floodgate of repressed feelings that brought Thomas back to his very real sense of failure and frustration. This would account for his childlike behavior in the aftermath toward Marie."

"If you're right, Chase, than that explains a lot," Father Brendan postulated. "I've heard about regression and transference before."

"One other thing, Bill. Thomas is decidedly concerned about the effect of his behavior on his children as well as Marie. I suggested that he open up about his situation with the two older ones, Louise and Carl.

"He doesn't have to go into the details of his affair with Hannah, but it would be good for all concerned if the children were aware that there was a serious problem with someone at The Chateau. They are a logical substitute for Hannah in the reforming of Thomas' character, and somehow should be brought to understand the importance of that role."

"I'm glad that you bring this to my attention, Chase. I've felt pretty bad about the development process for these children during Thomas' escapades. I'll talk to both Thomas and Marie and make certain that they discuss matters with the children.

"However, I wish that I had a better understanding about this ambition to physically excel. After all, if he needed it so badly, why didn't he try harder to achieve it at the time? In fact, now I'm surprised that he ever agreed to marry Marie. Not every young man would have chosen that course of action."

Chase Finney grinned boyishly. "I didn't think it was necessary to go into that aspect of Thomas' unique psychology, Bill. However, since you asked, I shall."

"Please do."

"The spirit, the energy, the eagerness to overcome obstacles and to reach what was being supported by his family as an unreachable goal, all of this was subdued by a powerful conscience. It may also appear farfetched that something as simple as a college education for a failing student can evoke such a spirit of energy and ultimate challenge.

"The power of a strong conscience became the moderating factor in this particular decision-making process. However, there was an even stronger need to achieve another ambition based upon education. This further ambition, the desire to accomplish in the physical arena, in the end, surpassed the logic of the situation at the time. In other words, his consciousness sided only temporarily on the side of logic. Eventually, his emotions kicked back in.

"This ambition for Thomas was an all-powerful wish to remain physical, either as an athlete, a teacher or a coach. The strength of his conscience he owed to his love of Marie Sullivan, a love so great that it took precedence over his ambition. From the time of Marie's announcement of her pregnancy before the marriage, these two powerful emotions, love and ambition, have been in conflict. This conflict was so overwhelming that love at times became hate and ambition turned into unhappiness. In the end, they led to confusion and self-punishment with unhappiness being the ultimate victor."

Father Brendan was open-mouthed. "That was some analysis, I must say. I'm not certain that I understand or agree with all of it, but it sounded very professional."

"Well, Father Brendan, I must say that there are Catholic doctrines that I have difficulty in comprehending, so it seems as if we're even. Besides which, I am an intellect, not just a professional."

"Thank you, Chase, for giving freely of your time."

"Call me anytime that you have a question. You know how to reach me, and let's see each other more often!"

Finney left, and Father Brendan had Leona place a call to Captain Casey at the police department. Casey headed up the Police Athletic League, also known as PAL at the time. He wanted specific information before Thomas' first counseling hour scheduled for the next week.

Chapter Thirty-Four

WITH NEW YEAR'S EVE JUST A SHORT while away, Carl called Nancy to discuss details of the plans they had been making to celebrate the arrival of 1939. When they finished making arrangements, she asked him if they could get together that evening. She wanted to talk to him in person.

They met in Malden Square. It was a pleasant evening, and not too cold. When he saw that she was dressed in a heavy jacket and woolen slacks instead of a skirt or dress, he suggested that they walk to Glendale Park in Everett, one of their favorite places. The park was bordered on two sides by a tree-lined walking path with benches where older people often sat during the day, and young lovers at night. In the center of the park, there was a huge playing field for baseball games. Children often congregated in groups when there were no competitive games taking place. Beyond the large field was a steep rise to the top of a hill with tennis courts. When the hill was snow-covered in winter, as it was today, the city sponsored toboggan rides.

They began walking along Ferry Street toward the park, about two miles away. Ferry Street began in Malden Square at the high school. They passed a furniture store, a photographic supply store, a tavern and a carpet store.

Crossing over a busy intersection with newly installed traffic lights, they stopped to look in the display showroom of a Cadillac and Oldsmobile dealer. The long black Cadillac in the showroom was elegant. As they continued along the brick sidewalk, they passed by a funeral parlor and then came to a residential area. It seemed that every other large house was either a doctor or dentist's office.

The practitioners lived in these homes and had their offices in what were once very large reception halls and dens or other formal living areas. The interiors had been remodeled to accommodate their offices and waiting rooms. Most of the doctors practiced family medicine. Since the houses were really very large, they could be redesigned to allow families privacy while still having sufficient space for their daily lives.

"Why do I have to date other boys when I really want to go out with you?" Nancy asked. "I don't think it's fair, and I don't like it when you go out with other girls."

Carl had suspected she might bring this up. "Nancy," he responded, "you know that I like you. You can even say that I love you. I love you like a sister for sure, and I would do anything for you."

Nancy pouted. "You don't kiss your sister like you kiss me, do you, Carl?"

"You're not even 16, Nancy, and I'm not 18 yet. We're both planning on college. We both have our whole lives ahead of us."

"So what? It's not like we're getting married. Lots of kids our age are steadies, Carl."

"I've thought a lot about it, and I agree with your mother and father, Nancy. We have to see other people or we'll regret it later. If I never go with another girl and you never go with another boy, then if we get married we are bound to think back and wonder what it would have been like. We need to grow up and live a little before we make this kind of major commitment."

"Ha, you just said we're going to get married. I think that's good enough so that we can go steady."

"I didn't say we *are* getting married, I said *if* we get married."

"Anyway, Carl, I *do* see other boys. I saw Jack Gould, remember? And besides, I didn't like going out with him."

"You told me that, Nancy, and I get jealous when I think about it, but I know it's something you have to do."

"What about you, Carl, are you seeing other girls?"

"You saw me at the Palace of Sweets with Charlotte. Sure, I see other girls. I go out with my friend Red sometimes. He wants to introduce me to girls."

"I'll kill him. I don't like it. I'd rather you went steady with me." Seeing the look on Carl's face, she added, "Okay, I know, but I still get jealous when I think about it."

"Nancy, I told you, I get jealous, too, when I think of you and that Jack Gould kid."

"I hate him. He's the one with 10 hands," Nancy said.

"Okay, but what about Michael Levenson? I get jealous of Michael because I visualize him kissing you. I guess I have to accept that, though. Like I said, you can't go through life having never kissed more than just one boy. We have to grow up and live a little before we make any major commitments, Nancy."

"Gosh, you sound just like my father, Carl. All right, I'm convinced that we need to date other people for a while, but will you please kiss me when we get to Glendale Park?"

"How about right now?"

"No. It will be better if we wait and think about it first," Nancy teased.

Once beyond the long block of large houses with the doctor's offices, they went by several blocks of tenements and then came to a less affluent neighborhood.

They finally passed through Glendale Square in Everett and came to the park. After the long walk, they sat on a bench in the walking path.

After they were seated, they glanced at each other and simultaneously reached for each other. Carl tilted Nancy's chin up and said, "I do think that I love you, Nancy."

He kissed her in a way they had never kissed before. Her heart was racing and she held his head and wished the kiss would never end.

The happy couple remained on the bench for a fairly long time and hugged and kissed and then they just sat and put their cheeks together.

Finally, they stood up and headed up the hill to take the next toboggan ride. There must have been about six young people already on the one they were assigned. Nancy climbed on first and Carl held up the rear. He was seated on the very end.

When the toboggan reached bottom, Nancy realized that no one was behind her. Carl was laughing and running down the snowy slope. "I fell off halfway down." They both shook the snow off and started the long walk home to Malden.

THOMAS HAD HIS FIRST TWO counseling sessions with Father Brendan in early January of 1939.

It was too soon for Father Brendan to know whether or not Chase Finney had made a good analysis of Thomas' situation. Finney had seen Thomas only four times. Father Brendan knew that he needed more time for a proper evaluation.

However, both Father Brendan and Marie were optimistic about Thomas' drinking. He no longer drank anything other than an occasional beer or a rare glass of wine. On that account, it appeared that Chase Finney was right.

After Thomas' first session with Father Brendan, he asked Marie to contact Louise and ask her to get some time off from school to come home for an overnight evening on a day that Carl would also be home. Within several weeks, he and Marie sat down with their two older children and Thomas began to discuss some of the difficulties he was facing.

The Grandee family was much better off as a result of these few hours spent talking about what had been a very serious problem. It didn't mean that the family was happy, but it was obvious that it was becoming a stronger unit. Even Robbie, at his young age, sensed the improvement, and he was often included in the family discussions.

Life went on, and the world continued to deal with its problems in its own frustratingly difficult and complicated way. The political situation in Europe had worsened and Franco's Falangists, aided by modern air power provided by Nazi Germany and Fascist Italy, marched into Madrid in April of 1939, putting an abrupt end to the Spanish Civil War. Five months later, after Hitler and Stalin signed a non-aggression pact and agreed to divide Poland, Germany invaded Poland, and World War II was now well under way. President Roosevelt declared United States as neutral at the outset of the war.

Nancy Rossiter was now a junior at Malden High School. Louise Grandee had completed more than a full year of Nursing School, and Carl was a freshman at Boston University.

By the end of 1939, Thomas had already been working as a volunteer coach with the local Police Athletic League. Captain

Casey of the Police Department told Father Brendan he could use all the help he could get.

Casey was pleased with the way Thomas handled the kids. Malden's PAL Basketball Team, The Shooters, won a game against the Everett CYO's team for the first time in three years.

At the next counseling session with Father Brendan, Thomas asked the priest what he thought about his idea of going back to school.

"It may not be a bad idea, Thomas. What do you have in mind?" Father Brendan asked.

"I've been talking to my friend Harvey. He's a professor at Boston University. I asked him what he thought about my getting a degree from Boston University's Sargent School. They have a very good athletics program. Harvey explained that I would have to pay and that I would be required to take an exam since my Revere High School Grades didn't qualify me. Harvey offered to help me study for the exam, but I don't know. I was never good at tests."

"What about the cost, Thomas? Can you afford it?"

"We still have several hundred dollars left from the mortgage money and all the contractors have been paid. Besides, Marie got a raise to $10 a week, and I'm now up to 20 myself. The Apollo likes the way that I've reorganized the kitchen, and they've used some of my suggestions for recipe changes as well. The cost at Sargent is $300 a year. It would be tight, but Marie is also willing to give it a try."

Father Brendan was concerned for the children. "I suppose Louise is taken care of. She gets everything paid for by the hospital, but how about Carl? Isn't there tuition and other costs, like books, at Boston University?"

"Carl still works for Lamson and Davis. He makes enough on weekends to cover expenses. The boy is ambitious. He works at the store from six o'clock Friday until closing at nine. Then he stays until nine-thirty to clean up.

"Saturday is an all-day affair. He's in at nine in the morning and stays until five. He reserves Saturday night for dates or whatever. Carl's a good kid, Father."

"Yes, I suppose all of your children are fine, Thomas. I wish Carl and Louise would attend church, though. You and Marie and young Robbie are coming to church regularly and that gives me much pleasure."

Getting back to the subject of school, Father Brendan responded, "Thomas, I don't see why you can't go back to school. As long as you feel you can afford it, then by all means, try. You're nobody's fool, and if Rossiter is willing to help you study for the exam, go for it. You can always count on me for support if you need it.

"By the way, remember your evaluation with Doctor Finney last month? He called just a few days ago. He was out of town for the two weeks after you spoke with him, so it was his first chance to get back to me. Finney thinks you've made remarkable progress. His comments made me think of your family. Your mother would be proud of you if she were still alive."

"Please don't mention my mother. I loved her very much and certainly I don't hold anything against her, but she was the most negative lady in the world when it came to me. I know that she had a hard life, but she never did give me the right time.

"My brother John always received the credit. The only way I could ever have gotten my mother to pay attention to me would be to pretend that I was John instead of Thomas, which I could never do. I would have to stay out of sight, disguise my voice and then call out, 'It's me, John.' Maybe then she'd respond.

"Don't be too harsh on her, son. At any rate, you have made much progress, more than we thought possible in such a short time. Keep me informed about sergeant."

Harvey gave Thomas several study guides to help prepare him for the special examination that Harvey had convinced Boston University to allow Thomas to take. Harvey was on the admissions committee at the college and was in a very good position to advise Thomas. The only problems Rossiter had with Thomas Grandee were personal and in the area of contemporary politics.

As with Carl, Harvey tried to talk about current events with Thomas. He explained that until the Hitler-Stalin Pact was signed, he had been a staunch supporter of almost everything the leftists in America stood for. After Stalin agreed to cooperate with Hitler, he explained that he was not nearly as confident in his support of leftist rhetoric.

"I've become far more cautious about my politics, Thomas. I believe people have to think very carefully about what political leaders tell them."

Harvey remained adamant about the Spanish Civil War. He was opposed to Roosevelt's support of the blockade, which helped make the Franco victory a certainty. The trouble was that many Catholics were supporters of Franco as well. Some Catholics felt that because the church supported Franco, they had to be for him and against the elected republican regime that many considered communist.

Thomas Grandee was one of those who saw Franco's victory as good. Harvey didn't ask Thomas if Father Brendan felt the same way, but he suspected that he probably did. He never really argued with Thomas, but they did get into some passionate discussions.

Thomas was not a particularly political person like Harvey, so there could never really be an argument between those two. Harvey tried to show Thomas the bigger picture.

"Thomas, don't you see that Hitler was able to invade Poland just a few months after the end of the civil war in Spain? The Nazi war machine is no longer concerned with Spain. All through the years since 1936, Germany's Wehrmacht has been increasing its military capability. If America and England had lifted the blockade and prevented the overthrow of the Spanish government, Hitler might have been prevented from starting this new war."

Thomas meekly replied, "I don't know, Harvey. I'm not up on the stuff like you are, but they say Franco is good for the church in Spain. That's what I know."

"Okay, Thomas, then let's get on with the exam you have to take. Have you looked at any of the study guides?"

"Yes, Harvey. I think I'll be okay with the math part if I don't completely freeze up when I'm sitting at a desk with the paper in front of me. My biggest problem is with English."

"Right, so let's get to work."

For the next month, Harvey and Thomas spent several hours a week together. The exam itself would take place that December. If he were accepted, the spring semester would begin at the end of January 1940.

The sargeant schedule would require him to be at the school during daytime at least twice each week and the rest of the curriculum could be evening classes in Boston University's main building. Thomas had already made arrangements at The Apollo in the event that he was accepted. Thomas would work two nights a week and the rest of the time during the day. He worried about when he would have time to study, but decided to cross that bridge when he came to it.

Carl joined a current events club at Boston University. He didn't have a lot of extra time between his studies and his job, but he had been stimulated by his conversations with Harvey Rossiter. He was taking a keen interest in world events, especially now that a major war was under way in Europe. He figured that he could always attend some meetings of the club and assumed that other members had constraints for free time, as well.

He found the discussions at the club exciting, especially when members took sides and ended up in firm disagreement. In fact, that's what appealed to him the most. The discussions were almost always in the form of arguments between left and right. Carl was leaning more to the left, probably because of Harvey Rossiter. He wished that he had Rossiter for history and he thought he might ask to be transferred. His professor was stodgy and dull, nothing like Mr. Rossiter used to be.

Carl was doing well in school and enjoyed the challenge that an intensified education brought with it. He was also broadening his perspectives about life in general, and anxious to explore new opportunities.

Chapter Thirty-Five

CARL HAD ARRANGED TO HAVE NO CLASSES on Friday afternoons so that he could go home for the weekends. He would have an early light supper and get to his job at the paint and wallpaper store by six. This particular Friday, his mother explained to him that there had been a call from Mrs. Finklestein. She asked Marie to have Carl drop by the news store Saturday morning on his way to work.

When Carl came into the store, Mrs. Finkelstein was all smiles. "Good morning, my handsome young friend, Carl, and how is going everything with you?"

"Mrs. Finklestein, you should say, 'how is everything going with you?'"

"What did I say?"

"It's okay, I guess, Rose. Is something happening? You asked to see me this morning."

"I would like that you and your lovely Nancy should come to my wedding. I am getting married to Harold Golding. You know. He is the one my cousin Morris introduced me."

"Hey, that's great." Carl was pleased that she would have a companion to replace Mr. Finkelstein after all. He added, "When's the wedding?"

"I will be Mrs. Harold Golding, God willing, on February tenth. My cousin is making ready invitations and I want to know should I send one invitation to you for both or I should send to Nancy one, too?"

Carl reflected for a moment. "Just send the invitation to me. Tell your cousin to write to Carl Grandee and Nancy Rossiter. You still have my address, don't you?"

"I have the address, Carl. So you will come, and you will be sure to bring that beautiful girlfriend. She is so nice."

Carl looked beyond Mrs. Finkelstein to a table just behind her desk where she had a lamp and some file folder racks for keeping the different magazine and newspaper records separated. He spotted a framed photograph that looked familiar. "Where did you get that photo of me and Nancy, Rose?"

"Your Nancy gave it to me. She said a friend took the picture at some party on New Years Eve. You both look so nice. She stops in to say hello every once in a while."

"That's great. Thanks, Rose. I have to get to work now. Bye."

"Goodbye, Carl. Tell her she sounded like a nice lady, your mother. I talked on the telephone with her."

Father Brendan and Chase Finney had started to meet for dinner occasionally. The situation with Thomas Grandee had renewed their college friendship. Dinner tonight was at Rosoff's near South Station in Boston. Father Brendan had a taste for Jewish delicatessen food, even though it often gave him heartburn.

Finney began the conversation after they were seated. "Bill, you ought to go to confession and tell your priest that you have no willpower. Why do you eat this stuff if it makes you sick?"

"Ah, Chase, my friend. It doesn't make me sick. It just gives me heartburn. I eat the food because I enjoy it. Besides, what makes you think that priests always have willpower?"

From the look on Finney's face, Father Brendan continued, "Alright. Maybe the answer is that I eat what I shouldn't because I like it. Otherwise I would be tempted to do what I shouldn't because I'm dissatisfied. Does that answer the question?"

"Much better, Bill. Much better."

"On a more serious note, Chase, I think you and I have done a good job with Thomas. He is taking his exam for Boston University's Sargent College program tomorrow morning. This Professor Rossiter was able to get him set up for consideration. I think that Rossiter is on the Admissions Committee." He paused and looked as though he didn't know how to proceed.

"There is something bothering you, Brendan. Am I right?"

"I would say you are, Doctor Finney. For the love of God, I have worked hard to help Thomas and I have bent over backwards because of his problems. His wife is a good practicing Catholic and it seems that Thomas is becoming one again as well. Their youngest, Robbie, never fails to come to church and he is now in the choir. I seem to have lost the two older children."

Father Brendan hesitated and then continued, "You know, Chase, I think that fellow Rossiter is to blame. I know that he's a radical. I've heard it from several Boston University students and I've read his published letters to the papers. He even got his name on an editorial for the Boston Post about the Spanish Civil War. It read like the Communist Manifesto.

"The boy, Carl Grandee, spends a lot of time with this Rossiter family. He goes out with the daughter, one of their twins. I know Harvey Rossiter's kind. He's a big shot history professor who thinks he knows more than God. I am also certain that he does not go to his synagogue. The fellow is an atheist."

"Hold on, there, Bill. You're going to pop a blood vessel if you keep on. In the first place, I've read work that Rossiter has written, not only letters to editors, but he's published some articles in the Academic press and the Atlantic Monthly. It's true that his name has also appeared on a couple of pieces in The New Masses."

"You see? He's a communist. I thought so."

"Not so fast," Finney said as he held up his hand to stop Father Brendan from starting another tirade. "Rossiter's position on the Spanish Civil War is no different than my own and you can't say that *I'm* a communist, can you?"

Chase Finney took a deep breath and sighed before continuing. "You've agreed with me that both Hitler and Mussolini were behind Franco, and I know that you hate what Hitler stands for. We've talked about this before, Bill. We also both understand that the conflict between Protestants and Catholics complicates the situation in Spain. Liberals and all manner of leftists, from intellectuals to communists, supported the Loyalists in Spain against Franco. You also know that many Protestant leaders are also against Franco. Does that make communists out of Protestants? This Spanish issue is a problem for you because it's more religious in your mind than it is political."

Father Brendan said, "Religion and politics do not often mix well. I'll admit that much. Maybe Harvey Rossiter isn't a communist, but I think that he is an atheist and that can have a very negative influence on young Carl Grandee." He paused and looking thoughtful said, "Professor Rossiter is far too liberal for my liking."

As he held up his hand once more to stop the priest from beginning a discussion on liberalism, Finney said, "Rossiter is a darned clever man. I doubt that he's a communist. He is obviously leftist in his political outlook, but I understand that he is often at odds with doctrinaire left-wingers."

Finney waited to see if Father Brendan was calm enough for what he was about to say next. He appeared to be, so Finney continued, "Rossiter is the one that made it possible for Thomas to have a chance at this exam that he's about to take. Thomas has also told you that Rossiter has spent many hours coaching him in readiness for the exam. He has not asked for payment, and this is according to what you have told me, Bill. You said that Rossiter has even given him test papers to practice on in simulated conditions to help him overcome his hysteria about testing. Isn't that true, Bill?"

"Yes, it's all true, but damned if I can understand how Carl and Louise, brought up in a Catholic family, got lost to our church."

Finney said, "Because they did not have a suitable role model in Thomas Grandee. Marie was so distraught during important, value-forming years in their lives that even though she was a practicing Catholic, she had little influence over them. I don't know too much about Louise, the older sister, but Carl has been exposed to a brilliant role model in Harvey Rossiter."

Finney thought for a moment and then went on, "Another thing I believe you told me is that Marie, who is Catholic, is best friends with Betty Rossiter, who is Jewish and is married to Harvey Rossiter."

"True, Chase. I did tell you that. Actually, it puzzled me that those two women have been really close friends since early childhood. Apparently, from what I could learn, Betty Rossiter is not any more religious than her husband. Now that's a mystery. How could Marie be so close to a non-religious Jewish woman? Aren't there conflicts in impressions and opinions between them?

Both religions are meant to encourage values that affect judgements throughout a person's lifetime."

"I know that you are not a prejudiced man, Bill. You and I go back a long way. We both had Jewish friends in college and even before that in high school. But, it's more than that. You're a good man, Father William Brendan."

"Well, Chase, maybe you're right about Carl and Louise. Thomas and Marie Grandee have been in no position to compete with an educated man like Professor Rossiter, as much as I disagree with much of what he stands for. I just had to express my dissatisfaction about the spiritual well-being of the family. Everything else has to play a secondary role. Still, I have to admit that Marie Grandee and Betty Rossiter are probably good for each other. I admit there is a lot of love between them. Yes, from what I have learned, this Betty Rossiter woman is a fine person even though she doesn't seem to be religious."

"That's a better attitude, Bill."

A similar argument ensued at the Rossiter house. Harvey was telling Betty how nervous he was about the examination that Thomas Grandee was about to take the next morning. "As much as Thomas has studied for the exam, you still have to remember that he has psychological blocks to overcome. I sincerely hope that the counseling he has been getting works. As I explained before, I have little faith in religious counseling. Thomas would have done much better to get professional help."

"Harvey, the priest *is* a professional. They get excellent training in psychology. You know, you and Father Brendan are really alike. I doubt that he has any more use for you than you do for him."

"And just what do you mean by that?"

"Harvey darling, just think of what Father Brendan has done for the Grandee family. He devoted endless hours counseling both Thomas and Marie. He hasn't tried to stop Thomas from coming to see you for coaching. That priest is a good man.

"Remember what he did several years ago in that racial incident at one of the public schools. He fought like a tiger for a Negro boy, and if I remember correctly, the Negro student was not from a Catholic family."

"All right, all right, Betty. Yes, I'm prejudiced. I know Father Brendan has helped beyond the call of duty. He has my respect for using his influence to help Thomas get the PAL coaching job. That ought to help build his self-esteem a good deal. Let's hope that it helps him pass that exam. I feel as if I was taking the exam myself and that my own life depended on it."

Chapter Thirty-Six

THE DOOR CLOSED, AND ALL EIGHT CANDIDATES for special college admission were seated at their respective student desks. A teacher's assistant passed two eight-page examination forms among them and gave instructions about maintaining silence. They had exactly two hours to complete both segments of the examination. One segment was on science and math, including algebra and some geometry. The other was composed of multiple-choice questions on English and history, and the remainder was a short essay on why the candidate wished to attend college.

Each candidate was given two sharpened pencils with erasers and a few sheets of scrap paper on which they could make notes. The official then went to the front of the class and said, "You start when I say go and you stop when I say time is up. If you are finished before the end of the two hours, you may pass your papers in and leave. If you are not finished when time is up, you must pass your papers in, regardless."

Thomas eyed the large clock with roman numerals in the center of the wall behind the official. Just as the large hand reached 12 she said, "Go."

Thomas stared at his paper. He wrote his name and address at the top of the cover page and looked down at the first question. His hands started to tremble and he froze. His mind began to wander and he instantly pictured his mother telling him how stupid he was. He thought of standing up and leaving, but he knew from what Father Brendan told him that he might expect exactly this reaction.

What the hell did he say to do? he asked himself, and then he remembered. Thomas thought to himself, I'm an intelligent individual and I understand the course work. I'm an intelligent individual and I understand the course work. He kept repeating this to himself as he quickly flipped through the examination pages.

Father Brendan had also told him to remind himself that was he not competing with anyone, especially his brother. "Just take the test and do the best you can." Thomas realized that whatever the outcome, he would know that he had done the best that he could. That was what he was learning life was really all about. At this point, the pencil began to steady in his hand and he started to answer the first question. One hour and fifty minutes later, he reached the end. The big clock read 11:50.

Thomas Grandee stood up and walked proudly to the desk, smiled and dropped his paper in front of the official. She smiled back at him and said, "Good luck!"

As Thomas headed for the subway, he began to worry. How was he going to get through the days before he found out how he did on the exam?

Several weeks later, on her way home from her job at Woolworth's, Marie Grandee walked up the hill toward the Grandee house on Las Casas Street. She looked at the clean white clapboards of their house, and the dark green trim and shutters. The front steps had accumulated a light coating of snow that either Carl or Thomas would clear away later.

She remembered how she and the kids had practically frozen to death in that same house only a couple of years ago. The temperature this first week of January, 1940, was only 20 degrees Fahrenheit. She smiled with pleasure as she bundled up against a sudden burst of wind.

It was warm and cozy inside. Carl was on school vacation and Louise had the weekend free. They'd both be there for dinner.

Marie greeted them, hung her coat in the hall closet and headed for the downstairs bathroom.

"The mail came, Ma. It's on the hall table," Carl yelled after her. "One of the envelopes is from the college."

"I'll get it as soon as I come out, dear."

While at the bathroom sink, Carl's reference to the envelope from Boston University finally registered, and Marie was out of the bathroom in a flash, her hands and face dripping wet.

She fingered the Boston University letter open as she ran for the kitchen, screaming for Carl, Louise and Robbie to join her.

She read the acceptance letter out loud. They all started yelling and hugging.

Marie went to the phone and asked the operator to ring the number of the Apollo Restaurant in Chelsea. It was just four-thirty and Thomas worked until five. The man who answered told Marie that Thomas had run out for supplies and would be back by five.

The next call was to Betty. "He's in, Betty. He passed the test! The letter came, and it says Thomas can start school on the third of February, which begins the spring semester."

"How wonderful for you!" Betty replied, also thinking how pleased her husband would be when he heard the news. "How does Thomas feel about it? He must be jumping for joy!"

"He doesn't know yet, Betty. He'll be coming home at about six tonight. Oh, God, I'm so excited."

"Marie, Harvey is home now. I'm going right in to tell him. Congratulate Thomas for us, will you? I'm hanging up now, but I'll call you again in a little while."

When Harvey heard about it, he grinned and asked, "What kind of grade did he get on the exam, Betty?"

"Gosh, I didn't ask. All I know is that he passed and he's going to college. Isn't that wonderful?"

"Yes, it is. It's simply wonderful. You know what I'm going to do, Betty, and I've been thinking about this for a while. I'm going to call that priest of his, Father Brendan. In all fairness, the man worked hard for Thomas and he ought to be one of the first to know the good news."

When Harvey called the Parish House, Leona answered. When he told her the news about Thomas, Leona told him to hang on while she ran to get the priest.

Harvey began as soon as he heard the priest at the other end of the line. "Father Brendan, this is Harvey Rossiter. I'm calling to tell you that we passed the test."

"You mean Thomas is being admitted to Sargent?"

"Yes, Father, he made it. I don't know the grade, but it really doesn't matter, does it?"

"No, Professor Rossiter, it doesn't matter at all. Nothing matters but the success Thomas has achieved. I have to give you credit, Professor. You did a great job of preparing Thomas for this examination. My congratulations."

"I think that you deserve more credit than I, Father," Harvey explained. "I believe Doctor Finney gets a lot of credit also. But you're correct in saying that the true success was earned by Thomas himself."

"Yes, well, my good man, thank you for letting me know. I appreciate it."

Rossiter had a sudden notion and then added, "Father Brendan, my wife and I are going up to the Grandee house to wait for Thomas to come home. It's just about five now and he is expected home by six or six-thirty. Would you like to join us in greeting Thomas when he arrives? He doesn't know the good news yet. Marie just opened the mail when she came home from work today."

"I really don't want to intrude," Father Brendan said, "but I would enjoy seeing Thomas' face when he finds out. If you don't mind, Professor, yes, I would be pleased to join you."

"My wife and I will pick you up at the parish house if you would like."

"That's not necessary, but thank you for the offer. I have my own transportation. What time do you think I should be at the Grandees?"

"Not later than six. Thomas may come home any time from six on."

At the Grandee house, while waiting for Thomas and Louise, Professor Harvey Rossiter and Father William Brendan sat in the den just off the living room. They were there alone while the others were busy getting things organized for dinner.

"Professor, I owe you an apology," Father Brendan stated politely. "You and I have many differences of outlook, but I must say, you are a good man. Not a Catholic, unfortunately, but even though I can't go along with many of your views, I admit you must be a good man in spite of our differences."

"Well, I thank you, Father Brendan, and I must also apologize. My attitude toward religious leaders has been less than favorable. During this past year, I have learned through you that spiritual advisors can be remarkably well-educated and informed, as well as selfless and giving. You have devoted an exceptional amount of time to Thomas Grandee. This has not gone unnoticed. I am humbled by what I have seen happen to Thomas as a result of your efforts."

The priest smiled like a cat that had just caught a canary. "Now, professor, will you admit that it would have been wrong if Marie had listened to the advice of liberals and had an abortion? After all, the family is getting straightened out, and you must admit that Louise and Carl and Robbie are fine children."

With a smirk on his face, Harvey Rossiter wasted no time in his rejoinder. "Had Marie and Thomas used birth control, many years of grief and harm would have been avoided."

"Blasphemy! That is against God's will."

"If that's the case, Father Brendan," Rossiter said, "then they should not have allowed their natural sexuality to lead them astray. They should have abstained.

"That, however, is not the real issue here. God's will aside, whether it was birth control or abstention, everyone would have been better off if Thomas had gone ahead with his original plan to take tutoring courses and entered Boston College as he had planned. Marie would have completed her studies as well. They would then have been able to marry under far better circumstances. Their children would also have benefited."

The priest's face turned purple. "Poppycock. You're a dreamer."

"You're entitled to your opinion, sir, but I believe that one day abortion will be legal in America."

"Is that what you want? Abortion? Killing babies?"

"No, not really, Father. I personally don't believe in it. But until young people are better educated, until good jobs for everyone are guaranteed, young couples, God's will or not, will engage in sex. If the conditions of a pregnancy are intolerable for economic or social or health reasons, then abortion may just be the better alternative."

"I still say poppycock. But, as you say, we each are entitled to our opinions."

The two men looked at each other and shrugged. That argument had more or less talked itself out, with each man feeling that his philosophy had won.

At that moment, the front door opened and Thomas arrived. It was a few minutes past six-thirty.

Marie and the children, The Rossiters and Father Brendan all gathered together and shouted "Congratulations" and applauded.

The gathering of so many people who loved and respected him and for whom he in return had genuine care and concern startled Thomas, but he knew their congratulations meant that he had been accepted.

Thomas read the letter of acceptance out loud. When he repeated the grade, he received more lively applause. He had scored 85 out of 100 points. For a 40-year-old man who had been just barely able to get good enough marks to graduate from high school, an 85 earned under pressure so many years later was exceptional.

The next morning, Father Brendan placed a call to Doctor Finney. He used his new dial telephone, the latest improvement in telephone technology. When he told Chase Finney the good news about Thomas, Chase exclaimed, "Wonderful! I really am pleased. Abraham Maslow would be delighted to hear about Thomas. He and Rollo May base their existential analytic philosophy on the theory that a man's past is not as important as the present and where he is headed. It looks like Thomas Grandee is about to prove them right. I hope Thomas also proves that every human being has the potential for actualization, to achieve the maximum of his or her ability at any given point in time."

"Chase, you helped a great deal. But now that this is all fairly resolved, I wish you would stop using all those big words. I hope that you aren't beginning to take yourself too seriously?"

"Coming from you, Bill, that's quite an admonition!"

At that they both laughed, and Father Brendan was still smiling as he hung up the neat new phone.

Chapter Thirty-Seven

THE MARRIAGE OF ROSE FINKELSTEIN TO HAROLD Golding was scheduled to begin at noon, February 10, 1940 at the Aperion Plaza in Roxbury. Meanwhile, meetings of the Boston University students' current events club began on February 5 and were scheduled to take place once during the first week of each month in a room located in the School of Journalism. The club also began to organize group activities and plan special events for the whole club or select groups of members.

One such event was an appearance that coming weekend of Paul Robeson at Boston's Symphony Hall. It was the topic of conversation throughout the first meeting.

Robeson was going to sing and make some introductory remarks. Florence Luscomb also planned to say a few words on behalf of the United Office and Professional Workers Union. Florence Luscomb had been a leader in the women's suffrage movement in earlier years and was a union activist. This event was a fundraiser for the newly formed CIO United Office and Professional Workers Union.

When the club members arrived at Symphony Hall, Melanie, Carl's date, took Carl's arm and held onto him as they entered Symphony Hall. They looked at each other and smiled as they found their seats in the rear of the balcony. Neither Carl nor Melanie had ever heard Robeson sing before. They were in for a rare treat.

They paid more attention to each other than to the speeches, but once the concert began and Paul Robeson's voice rang out, all eyes and ears were focused on the stage. His rendering of "Ol' Man River" was magical. It was true what the newspaper reviews had said—that Robeson "had one of the greatest voices ever heard in the city of Boston." The audience was enthralled by the power and vibrant sound that filled the hall.

Paul Robeson had gained a worldwide reputation as a singer of folk music and Negro spirituals. Listening to his magical voice, Carl and Melanie understood why.

After the concert, the eight members of the current events club headed for Chinatown, where late-night chow mein and chop suey were all the rage. They pooled their money and came up with eight dollars. That much money in Chinatown paid for more than they could eat. A whole char-grilled sea bass, shredded beef chow mein and a large vegetable chop suey were all served homestyle at an enormous round table. Wonton soup with crispy fresh fried noodles and individual bowls of white rice accompanied the meal.

Carl walked Melanie home to the apartment near Boston University that she shared with three other girls. Carl kissed Melanie goodnight and headed home to Malden. Living as close as he did, Carl was able to commute. Students like Melanie, whose family lived in New York, were able to share the cost of apartments so that the price for room and board was manageable. On the way home by subway, Carl remembered that he and Nancy were supposed to go to Mrs. Finklestein's wedding in just a few days.

The afternoon before the wedding, Betty Rossiter suggested to Nancy that she and Carl might enjoy breakfast at the G & G Restaurant on Blue Hill Avenue in the Grove Hall area. It was not far from the Aperion Plaza and it would be a special treat for Carl, who had probably never had a real Jewish breakfast. For that matter, David and Nancy seldom enjoyed an ethnic early day repast. It wasn't the kind of American cooking Betty did and, although Harvey's mother was good at old-fashioned Jewish cooking, she mainly prepared dinners and traditional holiday meals.

Clear, cool weather greeted Carl and Nancy on the morning of the Golding wedding. Carl and Nancy rode the subway to Dudley Street and then took the trolley up Blue Hill Avenue to Grove Hall. They strolled down the Avenue to the G & G hand-in-hand.

Nancy's cheeks were pink from the brisk February air, and glints from the sun reflected from her hair. Carl couldn't help but notice how very beautiful she was. Melanie was blonde and pretty, but Nancy was just naturally beautiful. There was no other word to describe her looks.

Nancy started to pull at him as if she wanted to run. Carl played along and the two of them skipped halfway toward the entrance of the restaurant. Carl held back and they slowed to a walk. They passed two kosher butcher shops, a grocery store, a synagogue and a dry goods store.

Once inside, they spied an empty table and seated themselves. Carl looked around and said, "I guess this is like the Converse Restaurant in Malden. It's really a cafeteria. We have to order at the counter." The menu board was visible from where they sat. "Did your mother tell you what we ought to try here for breakfast, Nancy?"

"Not exactly, Carl, but it's breakfast, so I think we might try one of the egg dishes. We could each order something different and share. Then we get to taste two different things."

"Sounds good to me. Nancy, what are cheese blintzes?" he asked.

"You'll like them. My grandma Herman makes them sometimes. They're something like Chinese egg rolls, but instead of meat or vegetables inside, they're filled with a cheese mixture and they're usually sweet. I like them dipped in sour cream. Have you ever had sour cream, Carl?"

"Of course. Our moms share recipes, remember? So we get to try some Jewish dishes at home. Besides, where my dad works, they cater to a large Jewish clientele. He had to learn about Jewish dishes."

"Hey Carl, see the top of the second column on the middle menu board. See where it says, 'lox and onions and eggs'?"

"Yeah, I heard of it from my father, but I never had it. Have you?" Carl asked.

"No, I know what it is, though. It's supposed to be good. Let's try that, okay? I want some coffee and orange juice, too."

Carl went up to the counter, placed his order, and returned to the table.

"Carl, tell me about the people you've met at school. You said you joined a club."

"Yeah, I joined the current events club, and there are twenty students in it, mostly freshmen and a couple of sophomores. We have ten boys and ten girls. No, Nancy, I haven't slept with any of the girls...yet."

"I didn't ask if you slept with a girl, Carl, and you don't have to tell me if you do. That's the rule for us, isn't it? Anyway, as long as you mentioned it, I'm glad you didn't, unless you're a liar and you really did." Nancy looked questioningly at Carl.

"The guy behind the counter is signaling me. I guess our food is ready," said Carl, as he proceeded to pick up the order.

"It's ten-thirty and we're just having breakfast. I hope we don't get a big lunch or dinner when we show up for the wedding," Carl said.

"My mother says that we don't get to eat until after the ceremony. First you socialize, and then after a while they serve hors d'oeuvres. We'll probably be starved by the time we get to eat anything," Nancy replied. After a while of sampling from both dishes, she inquired, "Do you like the eggs and lox and onions, Carl?"

They were seated side by side, which made it easier to share. Carl said, "Yeah, it tastes good to me. I like the blintzes better, though. How about you, Nancy?"

"I love the blintzes, but I don't think I care too much for the eggs and onions and lox. I can only eat a little of it. If you like it, you go ahead and eat all you want. I could never eat half of it."

"Let me tell you some more about the current events club. We choose articles from the news and then vote on which subject to discuss first. If we finish and have time left over, we vote on the next news item. We assign just one subject for an evening.

"We've already assigned the Wagner Labor Act, and it sounds like it's going to be interesting. We asked Professor Morse if he would come to our next meeting and lead a discussion. I think that this is going to be a great meeting. This guy Morse is brilliant. He teaches history at Boston University, like your father does. Morse specializes in the economic-related aspects of history, so that's why we asked him to talk about the Wagner Labor Act."

Carl told her more about the club and he explained how they had arranged with the journalism department to always have a room available for their meetings. "It seems that there are times during each week when the class schedules always seem to leave one or two rooms unused for a couple of hours in the evening. There are not as many evening classes in journalism as there are in the language or English or writing departments. We take whatever classroom happens to be unoccupied when our meeting night comes around."

By this time they had finished breakfast and were now standing up and putting on their coats to get started for their walk to the Aperion Plaza. On the way over to the wedding, Carl and Nancy talked about Carl's father.

"I think it's wonderful that your father is going back to school at his age. It must take a lot of guts to do what he did, Carl."

"It sure did. We're all very proud. You know he had a hard time when he went to high school in Revere. He probably got passing grades because he was an all-star athlete in practically every sport. According to my mother, he could never pass a test. She told us it was psychological.

"My Uncle John in California was older than my father. He was one of those brilliant students that got straight A's. My mother said that my father was always afraid he couldn't compete with John, so he just froze up and didn't even try. Your dad helped him a lot, and so did Father Brendan at Holy Rosary. We were all worried that he would freeze when he took the entrance exam for Boston University. But I guess your dad had something to do with his success."

"Maybe he did. Daddy is on the admissions board at Boston University. He argued for a special trial program for older applicants who had been out of high school for many years but wanted to come back to earn a degree later in life. He said it was on account of the depression that some people missed the opportunity for further education.

"He pointed out that a person out of school for 20 years probably could not remember many of the details of their high school course, but he also said that some of those people had life experiences that were of more value than high school classes. The exam your father took was designed for that special group of people. It was a trial to see how those folks that passed the exam would make out during the next four years. Daddy thinks they should do even better at college than the young high school kids."

"Gee, I knew there was something special about the exam, but I didn't realize just what it was all about. It sounds like a great idea, though."

When they reached the Aperion Plaza and went inside, they felt out of place for the moment. Nobody looked familiar. As much as they both searched, there was no sign of Mrs. Finklestein. Carl went over to one of the other guests and asked her where Mrs. Finkelstein was.

"Rose Finkelstein is the bride. You won't see her until the ceremony."

Nancy exclaimed, "Oh, look, Carl, isn't that Mr. and Mrs. Rosen from Malden? He owns the menswear store in the square."

"Yes, Nancy. I think there must be a few Malden people here. Maybe we'll have someone to talk with. I wonder who we get to sit next to?"

"Let's go look at the cards on that table. I think they should have our names on them with an assigned table number," Nancy suggested.

They finally located their names. They were at table number seven. When they walked over to the table, Carl said, "Hey, look at that, Nancy. That's my boss, Mayor Lamson. I should have known he would be here. Their stores are right near each other."

Mayor Fred Lamson was a popular mayor with a record of fairness. He was a pleasant-looking man about 30 years old, with a ready and honest smile. With very light brown hair perfectly groomed and eyes that twinkled when he spoke, he had the appearance of cleanliness and honesty that helped make him a successful politician as well as retail businessman.

Mrs. Lamson was an added attraction to his career. She had a round, pretty face that also suggested sweetness of character. As they came up close, Mayor Lamson introduced his wife, and Carl introduced Nancy. The mayor then turned to another couple at the table and introduced them as Mr. and Mrs. Charles Hanley.

Hanley said, "You can call me Charlie, and this is my wife, Martha." Martha was as small as her husband was big.

The guests at table seven were all looking attentively at Nancy. She was breathtakingly beautiful in a white tailored dress that dropped just to her knees. It was trimmed in dark brown, which matched her eyes. The white of her dress against her tan skin was striking. Carl, tall and handsome, made the couple complete.

After some time of conversation, Mayor Lamson spoke up and remarked to the young couple, "You two are absolutely charming." He looked around the table and said, "Don't you all agree?"

The complimentary comments poured forth from all at the table, making both of the young people blush.

There were still two empty seats, and Nancy wondered if other Malden people would be sitting with them. The big man, Charlie Hanley, finally said, "Let's walk around a little. It looks like they're starting to serve hors d'oeuvres. I think I see knishes." He stood and waved at Carl and Nancy to follow, which they did.

When they reached the waiter, who was carrying a tray of hors d'oeuvres, he explained that they were just setting up the appetizer table, and that there would be no food service until after the ceremony.

By the time they returned to the table, two people were occupying the other seats. Charlie apparently knew them. He said, "Hi, Stanley. You know Mayor Lamson, I'm sure. I want you to meet Mrs. Lamson, and these two gorgeous young people are Carl Grandee and Nancy Ross."

"That's Rossiter, Mr. Hanley," Nancy said.

"Sorry about that, Nancy. Please meet Doctor and Mrs. Gordon, Stanley and Sylvia. Doctor Gordon is an optometrist, and I gather that he's the groom's eye doctor. Is that right, Stanley?"

"Yes," Doctor Gordon said, "Harold Golding is also a good friend. Golding brought Rose Finkelstein in for an exam last week, so the bride is now also a patient."

Doctor Gordon turned toward Carl and Nancy and said, "I'm pleased to meet you, Nancy and Carl."

"How do you do, Doctor Gordon?" Nancy said.

"I'm very pleased to meet you, Doctor Gordon and Mrs. Gordon," Carl said. "With all the studying I've been doing, I may need glasses soon. I will surely come to you, doctor, if that happens."

Stanley and Sylvia Gordon smiled. They were older than the others, in their late fifties, and were both rather heavy-set, almost obese. Doctor Gordon was almost completely bald, and wore eyeglasses. His wife looked robust, with very black straight hair. She wore a pair of pale pink high-fashion glasses with gold filigree edging.

Charlie's wife, Martha, asked Nancy, "Nancy, is your father Professor Rossiter at Boston University?"

"Yes, Mrs. Hanley, he is. Do you know my dad?"

"I don't know him personally," Martha Hanley answered, "but I heard him speak at a rally for President Roosevelt last year."

"My dad is a strong supporter of the President," Nancy said proudly. "That must have been him."

Mayor Lamson said, "I'm also a supporter of Roosevelt, Miss Rossiter."

"I thought you ran for state Senator on the Republican ticket, Mr. Lamson," Carl interjected.

"I did, Carl, but I'm what you call a Roosevelt Republican," the former mayor and now state Senator replied. "It's funny, though. In Malden, I'm neither a Democrat nor a Republican. People still know me as Mayor Lamson, and that's what they call me."

The band was just starting to play "Here Comes the Bride." Everyone sat down, and the hall fell silent. Carl saw what looked like an open tent supported by four poles. Inside the tent was a table with an open book and a Rabbi standing alongside. What must have been the groom and another man walked along a carpet to the tent.

Mrs. Finkelstein now entered from the side and stepped onto the carpet. A man, who Carl assumed was her cousin Morris, accompanied her. He whispered to Nancy, "What's the tent?"

She whispered back, "It's a canopy. In Hebrew, it's called a hupeh."

The ceremony proceeded with what sounded like a lot of mumbling of prayers or wishes. Then, at the end, the groom stomped down on a cup and broke it under his heel. The Rabbi then said proudly, "I now pronounce you man and wife." Harold Golding kissed his bride.

Carl turned to Nancy and asked her to explain the canopy and the broken cup.

"According to what I've heard from my mother and my grandparents," Nancy explained, "the canopy is a symbol of the future home of the married couple. It signifies that they will live together under one roof. The poles stand for something, too, but I don't really remember what."

"What about the cup?"

"I know about that. Tradition says that a glass or similar object is broken to symbolize the destruction of the ancient Jewish

Temple and to remind the newlyweds that a marriage can also break unless it is carefully protected by love and respect on the part of both husband and wife."

Carl noticed the bride signaling for them to come over. "Nancy, I think Mrs. Finkelstein wants us to say hello."

"Remember, she's Mrs. Golding now."

Carl and Nancy walked over to where Rose Golding was standing and congratulated her.

Rose replied, "You look beautiful, Nancy, and Carl, you are so handsome all dressed up. Come, kids, I want you should meet Mr. Golding. Oh, there he is." She waved to her new husband, and he walked over. Introductions were made.

"So you are the young man that Rose tells me about all the time? She thinks that you are some special young fellow. I understand you are a student at the university in Boston. Is that right, Carl?"

"Yes, sir, it is, Mr. Golding. I'm a freshman at Boston University. Mrs. Finklestein—I mean Rose—has told me so many nice things about you. I think that you're very fortunate, because Rose is the best. Don't you agree, Nancy?"

"Oh, I certainly do, Mr. Golding. She is such a nice lady. I love to stop by after school sometimes and visit with her," Nancy said, and she continued, explaining, "Carl and I are honored that you invited us to your wedding."

"So, one day soon, you two will be making a wedding, I'm sure," Mrs. Rose Golding said. "Now I think you should go back to the party. Harold and I, we have to mingle."

The canopy was removed, and Carl and Nancy walked back to their table just as the Rabbi started to say a prayer over the challah, a ceremonial bread, and almost all the guests were up from their seats and headed for the appetizers. The center floor was now cleared and the band was playing hora music.

"Let's join in, Carl," Nancy said as she pulled him toward the hora line.

Some guests had already formed a circle and were going around in time to the music. Carl and Nancy had no trouble breaking in.

Someone shouted, "How come the dancing started? We haven't had a chance to get the appetizers."

Someone else called out, "Never mind appetizers. The dancing isn't supposed to start until after dinner."

A waiter passing by with some more appetizers for the table said, "The kitchen is behind, so the chef asked the bandleader to start the music. Pretty soon they'll catch up and the music will stop."

"I don't have the time I used to have, Nancy. There's a lot more studying and homework and don't forget, sweetheart, I spend an extra hour each morning and another hour each evening just on public transportation. Some days it takes even longer. A few of the other commuting students are talking about getting together and renting an apartment near the school."

"I suppose you do have less time. Carl, do you know that it's the first time you ever called me sweetheart? I like it, Carl."

"Gee, did I? I never even knew I did. I guess it is nice that we can call each other by a special name. It sounds nice, but just don't go getting any serious ideas."

"Okay, I know you still don't want to be boyfriend and girlfriend. I can understand that as long as you're just getting started in college and you have so much on your mind. Remember, we talked about what you wanted to be when you finished school. Have you made up your mind yet?"

"Not really. I spend a lot of time thinking about the future, though. I haven't decided on my major. Sometimes I think I'd like to be a history teacher, but then I have to admit, the idea doesn't seem to fit like it must have with your father."

"You once said that you thought biology was an interesting subject. Do you still feel that way about it, Carl? See, I still call you Carl. Would you rather I called you something else?"

"It sounds natural to me, Nancy. I don't know why, it just does. Yes, I love my biology class. Maybe that's why I can't get comfortable with being a history major. We should be thinking seriously about our major field of study soon so that we can make curriculum choices for next year, I mean all the Freshman students should."

"Well, here we are Carl, at my house. Want to come in?"

"Sure. I can say hello to David and to your mother and father if they're home. By the way, how is David? I haven't seen him for quite a while."

"Oh, Dave's great. He never gets anything but A's in his classwork. He's a conscientious student and everybody likes him, too. We think he has a great future ahead of him."

The Rossiters gave Carl a warm greeting. Betty invited Carl to stay for a light supper. "Gee, thanks, Mrs.Rossiter, but we just had a big wedding dinner. They didn't serve us until after two o'clock."

"Carl, it's six-thirty already and we won't be eating until after seven. Why don't you stay and visit? It's been a long time. You can call home and tell your parents where you are. I'm sure your folks won't mind."

"Well, yeah, I guess I could do that, as long it's a really light supper. Right now, I couldn't eat a thing. Could you, Nancy?"

"God, no. We ate ourselves sick."

"Good," Betty said. "Carl, go right to the kitchen and call home."

When Carl returned, they all sat around in the living room and discussed Mrs. Golding's wedding. Carl propped himself up along the armrest of a comfortable damask upholstered sofa with a mahogany coffee table in front. There were some snacks on the table and a vase with flowers.

Carl looked across the room to a large fireplace with a mantle above it that held small framed family pictures. Above the mantle was a huge, handsomely framed print of Georges Seurat's "La Grande Jatte." It was one of Seurat's more famous paintings that was compounded from studies he had made on the island of La Grande Jatte in the Seine river near Paris.

It was7:30 by the time Betty called everyone into the dining room for some food. When she brought out cheese blintzes, Nancy and Carl laughed and simultaneously exclaimed, "Oh no, cheese blintzes again!"

Chapter Thirty-Eight

CARL HAD JUST WALKED INTO HIS MONDAY morning biology class when Larry Green and Hank Johnson greeted him. They said that they needed a third guy to take a furnished apartment on Bay State Road. Larry explained, "Carl, it's in the building next door to your girlfriend. One of her roommates told me about it and they suggested that we take a look. It sounds terrific. If we can each put up $11 a month, we've got it!"

"It sounds great, but I haven't heard about my scholarship application yet. It's not just the eleven dollars, guys. Don't forget, I still have to go home for dinner and I have breakfast at home, too. I don't know. Can we have a few days so I can find out if my scholarship money is coming through?"

"Can you check administration today about the scholarship, Carl?"

"I can try. I don't want to screw things up, though, by sounding too anxious." He thought a minute and added, "Yeah, I'm sure that there's nothing wrong in my asking."

Professor Manley entered the room and the students all scrambled for their seats. The notes Carl was making on a scratch pad had nothing to do with biology. He was figuring out his expenses. Even with his salary, he was still short and would have no spending money.

I need that scholarship, he thought. Shit, I better pay attention to Manley. I can't afford not to get an A or at least a B-plus. Professor Manley was talking about the anatomy of the frog. Carl opened his textbook.

After biology, Carl had 20 minutes before English class. He checked administration. A clerk explained that letters had been sent to him on Friday, but there was no way of knowing whether he was on the scholarship list or not. He was apprehensive for the rest of the day.

When he called home before his next class, there was no answer. Robbie was at school and his mother was working. He didn't know whether his father was at the Apollo or nearby at some class in Boston University. Initially, he had a funny feeling about his father being a fellow student, but eventually, it made him feel good.

It so happened that Thomas was at school, entering his English class. The class consisted of older students and the course structure was geared to life experiences, concentrating primarily on composition.

Rachel Wolfson, the English professor, was part of the special program structured for this particular group of students. Thus far, she was reporting better results than originally anticipated. The older students were more serious than many of the younger. At the beginning, they had some syntax problems in composition, but they all responded well to correction. Thomas was the only student aiming at an athletics program. The others, mainly men, were interested in journalism, education and political science. Of the eight students, only two were women, and both wanted to be journalists. Professor Wolfson felt she'd never taught an easier class.

Thomas' biggest problem was that at 40, he wasn't in good enough physical condition to participate at the level of the younger people in some of the gym classes. He did a minimal amount of actual physical activity compared to the other students, and he was the only older student there.

Frank Clark, the mentor assigned to Thomas, explained that since Thomas was not here to become an athlete, but rather to coach or instruct young athletes in the future, his active participation was not as necessary as it was for the younger students. Thomas insisted on trying and continued at the best of his ability. Clark thought he looked pretty good playing basketball, considering his age. He was strong and experienced. As long as the coach limited his playing time, Thomas was competitive. With his aim geared to teaching rather than doing, his principal courses were in the area of education.

When Thomas walked in, Professor Wolfson called him over before he reached his seat. "I have your son, Carl, as a student. In fact, he just left a few minutes ago. His class is just before this one."

"Oh, my God, that really gives me a funny feeling, Miss Wolfson. It is Miss, am I right?"

"Yes, Thomas, it is. My life's work is teaching. I suppose that I am part of a very small minority here at Boston University, and it would be the same at any university in the country. Most women in the teaching profession end up in elementary schools or high school. I do believe, though, that the status of women will change for the better in the future. What do you think?"

"Oh, absolutely. I think women are a lot stronger and smarter than men think. There are some outstanding female students over at Sargent. I've seen them at practice and I envy what they can do. The women in my classes are often better students than the men are. I'm impressed."

"Glad to hear you say so, Thomas. You're a pretty good student yourself. I hope that this older student program will be successful. I believe it will be," she added.

"What about my son? Does he do well?"

"Like father, like son. Carl takes his studies seriously and he does well. He's young, so I wouldn't tell him that I said so yet. It might make him feel so self-assured that he becomes complacent."

She thought for a moment and decided to say more. "His friend, Melanie, is a fine student also. They seem like a fine young couple, Mr. Grandee."

"Melanie?"

"Oh, my goodness. Did I speak out of turn? You mean you haven't met Melanie? I sincerely hope that I haven't made trouble for Carl."

Thomas laughed. "No, you haven't made trouble. It's just that I automatically picture Carl with a girl he grew up with, Nancy Rossiter. They played together when they were children and they went on dates as teenagers. I have to get used to Carl being more grown up. It figures that he would meet a girl once he went on to college. This Melanie, is she a pretty girl?"

"Oh, she is pretty. And smart, too. A nice girl, but I should have minded my own business. Rossiter? Professor Rossiter?"

At this point the classroom was filled and the other students were wondering what was going on between Miss Wolfson and Thomas Grandee.

"We better tend to business, Thomas. Take your seat, but please come up after class for just one more minute, won't you?"

"I sure will," Thomas answered.

After class, Miss Wolfson inquired about the connection between the Rossiters and Grandees. Thomas let her know some of the details and she was impressed. "That explains a lot, Thomas. It shows me where Carl and you get some of your moorings. It's interesting how environment affects the future of all of our lives.

"Harvey Rossiter is one the University's treasures, and I believe both you and your son have been enriched by contact with him. However, I believe that I have let the cat out of the bag about Melanie."

"Please, Miss Wolfson, you did nothing wrong. If this Melanie thing is serious, Carl will tell us about her. I think he's grown up enough that he doesn't have to tell us about every girl he meets. Actually, I'm glad you mentioned it."

When Thomas walked out of Miss Wolfson's classroom, he saw Carl walking toward him. "Well, fancy meeting you here, Carl."

"I left my jacket in Wolfson's class. You have her, too, don't you, Pa? One of the kids said he heard that Wolfson conducts a special older student class in English."

"Yes, son, I do."

"Pa, I don't have any classes from noon until two-thirty. Can we have lunch together?"

"I can do that, Carl. Where shall we meet?"

"How about the student center? I'll bring my lunch."

"Fine, Carl, I'll do the same and we can talk."

Thomas and Carl enjoyed lunch hour together at the center. They were both bringing lunches with them most days in order to keep expenses down.

"Carl, this is something, isn't it? A father and his son both students at school together must be pretty rare."

"Does it bother you, Pa?"

"Not in the least. I kind of like the idea. How about you?"

"No problem. The kids know about you, and I think they admire you for what you're doing. Anyway, that's what they say. I'm sort of proud of what you're doing, too, and I hope it works out the way you want it."

"I hope so, Carl. I hope so."

"In fact, one of the students in my current events club is interested in the older students program and she said she would like to meet you."

Thomas suspected that the student Carl referred to might be the girl, Melanie. He said that he would be happy to meet her.

"Why don't you bring her around for lunch here at the student center. Will that work out?"

"I'll have to ask her if she can pick up a lunch and join us. I'm not sure of her class schedule. What about yours?"

"Monday is always good for me. I have no classes at noon. I can meet for lunch on Thursdays at one o'clock. Which is better for you?"

"Thursday works best for me, Pa. Today is unusual. I don't usually have Monday free until much later. But let me talk to Melanie and then I'll get back to you. How about making a date for this Thursday?"

"That's fine with me, son."

"Great. I'll meet you here either alone or with my friend from the club."

When Carl got home that evening, the letter from Boston University was waiting for him. He had been awarded a scholarship based on his straight-A average during his first semester. The superior average plus his financial situation plus recommendations from teaching staff were all favorable for the award. The only contingency was that he maintain a minimum B average during the 1940 spring semester. The scholarship was worth one full year's tuition and was subject to renewal upon application if warranted.

Carl showed the letter around, and the Grandees celebrated by toasting and sharing a bottle of wine. Even Robbie, now 12, was given a small glass of port so that he could share in the toast with his mother and father and Carl.

Louise would have to drink her wine at the Mount Auburn School of Nursing. Marie had called and asked the office at the hospital to tell Louise to call home. After dinner, Thomas took Marie aside and told her about his session with Professor Wolfson. They decided to call the Rossiters and arrange to get together. Marie wondered if Nancy knew about Carl's new friend, Melanie. She seemed to be of the same opinion as her husband. Both maintained that it was just as well that Carl had finally found another girl besides Nancy. Still, they felt that the Rossiters should also know what was going on. Anyway, it had been a while since the two couples had been together.

The next day Carl showed the letter to Larry Green and Hank Johnson. The three freshmen went to see the apartment on their lunch break. Melanie came along with them.

There was a living room with convertible sofa, two bedrooms, a bathroom, an eat-in kitchen and a modest sized dining room. By converting the dining room into a bedroom, each boy would have privacy, although they would have to figure out how to seal off the dining room from the living room, since the two rooms opened to each other without a door.

Larry wanted to know if they should flip a coin to see who got the dining room. Hank pointed out that there was no closet in the room.

"Boys are dumb," Melanie said as she walked over to the opening between the two rooms and put her finger into a slot. She pulled a sliding door from one side of the partial wall halfway over to the center. "Do you want me to close the other side, too, or do you think you three dummies can figure it out all by yourselves?"

"Jesus," Carl said. "The closet is no problem. We can buy one of those portable ones over in Harvard Square. A closet, a mattress and some sheets and a blanket are all we need. How do we get rid of the dining room table and stuff?"

"Ask the landlord. That's what we did. In fact, he's a nice guy, and you might be able to talk him into helping you make the change. The landlords here have connections to used furniture places. They rent mostly to students, so they know how to work things out. You may have to rent a U-Haul for a day. That's what we girls did."

Hank Johnson said, "I guess it takes a girl to make a boy happy." He laughed out loud at what he considered his great sense of humor. Then he looked at Melanie and asked, "Is there an underground tunnel between this place and yours, Melanie?"

Melanie threw a fake punch at Hank and they all had a good laugh. "So it looks like you guys are going to take the place, right?"

"Right," each guy said after the other, as if in perfect marching order.

Carl added, "Let's see the landlord and seal the deal."

"Do you mind waiting one more minute, fellows?" Melanie asked.

"Sure, Melanie," Larry replied. "What's wrong?"

"Nothing's wrong," she said. "Carl, come with me. You two stay put."

She pulled Carl into the dining room and added out loud, "I just wanted to see if we could close the doors from the inside," and she pulled on one door and Carl pulled on the other.

Larry and Hank started to whistle as the doors closed. Behind them Melanie and Carl hugged and kissed. "It's going to be great having you next door, Carl. I can't wait. When do you plan to move in?"

"Maybe by next week."

"That's when we have spring break and I guess I have to go to New York, but soon we can see more of each other, and I'd like that. Wouldn't you?"

"Of course. You know I do, Melanie." They opened the doors to see Larry and Hank staring. "What did you two do, have sex while we waited outside?" Larry asked.

"Naturally. We do it all the time, didn't you know?" Melanie responded, grinning. They all had a good laugh.

Chapter Thirty-Nine

HARVEY AND BETTY ROSSITER PLANNED TO HAVE dinner with Thomas and Marie Grandee at Durgin Park in Boston. Robbie was with his grandmother for the evening. It was the Friday before Carl started spring break and he told his parents that he had made a date with Nancy for that same evening. He had promised to see her as soon as Spring break started. It was the third week in February and he had 10 days off.

"Where are you and Nancy going, Carl?" Marie asked.

"The weather is pretty nice, so we thought we'd go dancing at the Spanish Gables on Revere Beach Boulevard and then have a bite to eat at one of the nearby restaurants."

"That sounds very nice, dear," Marie said. "I hope you have a lovely evening."

The Rossiters came by to pick them up for the drive into the market in Boston. Durgin Park was famous for being one of Boston's oldest restaurants. Equally famous was Durgin Park's roast beef. The restaurant had originally catered to farmers who brought produce into the market place.

Harvey had just bought a two-year-old Chevrolet for $400. On the ride, Harvey discussed the Nazis and worried that, having conquered Poland, the war would spread to the rest of Europe. He also denounced Stalin for signing a non-aggression pact with Hitler the previous year.

"Harvey, for heaven's sake, this is the thousandth time you've brought up the Stalin-Hitler thing. We've all heard it a million times before. Let's not spoil the evening talking politics and war all night long," Betty complained.

"Do you think America will get into the war, Harvey?" Thomas asked.

"Here we go again," Marie said. "All you men want to talk about is the war."

"I give up," Betty said.

"I don't know, Thomas," Harvey responded. "The American people are against this country getting involved. My personal opinion is that Roosevelt is not going to let Great Britain fall to Germany. A lot depends on what happens in the next few months. It's really impossible to predict, but my educated guess is that we will get involved one way or another before too much time passes."

They reached Durgin Park and found a place to park the Chevy within walking distance. "Congratulations on your new car, Harvey," Marie announced. "It rides nice and smooth. Don't you think so, Thomas?"

"I do. I do. Thirty-eight Chevies are great cars," he said as Harvey shifted gears on the way into town.

Betty said, "Promise me, Harvey, that once we go inside, all talk of war and politics stops. Is it a promise?"

"I promise. There will be no talk about war or politics. I think I'm getting sick of hearing myself complain anyway."

Betty suggested that they walk a bit and first see the interesting historic sights like Faneuil Hall and then cross the street to the open market. It was a mild winter evening, the sun had just set and the busy North End neighborhood was well lit by street lamps. Horse and wagon drivers, some wearing three-cornered hats, were offering tours along Freedom Trail.

The two couples walked first to Old North Church, built in 1723. It was from the steeple of this edifice that the signal was flashed that informed Paul Revere of the direction of the British on the night of April 18, 1775.

Then they walked past Faneuil Hall and crossed over to inhale the tantalizing smells coming out of the Olde Union Oyster House. Marie and Betty persuaded the men to walk across to the open-air market, where they meandered through throngs of shoppers bargaining for fruits and vegetables. The stalls were laden with oranges from Florida, potatoes from Idaho, local onions and tomatoes and a thousand varieties of other good things to eat.

There were stores with open doors offering meats and poultry and fresh fish of every kind. The smells from sidewalk stands sell-ing grilled sausage, hot dogs and hot roasted chestnuts whetted all their appetites.

"Let's go to Durgin Park. I'm getting hungry!" Thomas exclaimed. Harvey agreed.

Betty was not too sure that Durgin Park was the right place for them that night. "Durgin Park is a great place, people, but if I remember correctly, they seat you at long tables with other people. It gets noisy and it's very hard to carry on a private conversation."

"Their prime rib is the best, though," Harvey said. "It's done to perfection and they give you so much it hangs over the plate."

"All the more reason to stay away. None of us need the extra calories."

Thomas suggested that they go to the Union Oyster House.

"The Oyster House sounds fine to me," Harvey said. The others were satisfied, and so they headed for the famous seafood restaurant.

Once they were seated, Betty said, "Marie, you called and told me that you think Carl has a new girlfriend, someone he met at college."

"You both seem to feel guilty that Carl is seeing someone other than Nancy. Why? It's what we have been urging both kids to do all along. Carl isn't doing anything wrong. He wasn't engaged to Nancy. I wish she would get a crush on another boy. She goes out on dates, but she still seems to be infatuated with Carl."

The waitress brought water and asked if they were ready to order. Harvey looked at the waitress and said, "I guess we need another couple of minutes." Then he turned his attention to the table. "Let's look at the menu and order. Then we can get on with this other major world calamity," he said.

There was silence while they studied the menu. Finally each looked up, indicating their readiness. Harvey signaled the waitress, who came over to their table and told them the special of the evening was a 12-ounce prime rib with corn on the cob and coleslaw for a $1.25 that night.

"I thought this was a seafood place?" Thomas said.

"It is, but the manager is offering the prime rib dinner to compete with Durgin Park."

Harvey ordered first. "I'm sticking with seafood in this place. Boiled lobster platter for me."

Betty and Marie also ordered lobster, but Thomas decided on the fried seafood dinner. Piled high with clams, shrimp, scallops, haddock and onion rings, it was a specialty of the Union Oyster House.

The interior was dimly lit with wide wooden plank floors and dark wood-paneled walls. There were seafaring trophies mounted on the walls, and the atmosphere was decidedly intended to impress the patrons with the sturdy character of the old Boston sea town.

Harvey said, "Betty tells me that Marie thinks Carl may have a girlfriend at Boston University. That could well be, but it doesn't matter. Carl isn't the problem, Nancy is. She has gone on a couple of dates with a kid named Michael Levenson. He's a nice boy, but she doesn't really go for him.

"Nancy is a very attractive girl, and she has many opportunities to go with other nice boys. but she always makes excuses and turns them down. She just sits home and waits for Carl to call. Last week, before we heard about this girl Melanie, Nancy said she thought about it and decided she would start to go out with other boys. I hope she does."

Thomas said, "I guess I made a bigger thing out of this Melanie than I should have. Maybe because of the mix-up I got myself into, I worry about Carl. I'm sorry that I even mentioned this new girl's name."

Betty said, "Thomas, you reacted naturally, and that's understandable. How do you feel about it, Marie?"

"Oh, I think it's great if Carl has met a girl at college. I don't know that he has, though. All I know is that Thomas heard a rumor that Carl had a girlfriend at college. Carl and Nancy are too young to be going steady. Isn't that what we all agreed? My only concern is that I don't want Nancy to get hurt."

Harvey held his hands up, a habit he had developed to gain attention in his classroom. He said, "Tonight Nancy is at the Spanish Gables dancing with Carl. Let the two kids work out whatever problems they have. Carl may not be in love with Nancy, but it's pretty obvious that he respects her and will always be considerate of her feelings.

"I trust Nancy to use her intelligence and good instincts no matter what the situation is. I think we have two good kids, and they're smart and level-headed. So why don't we just let nature take its course?"

"Amen," said Thomas. They raised their glasses of white wine and Thomas said, "Here's to the happy future of two fine young people, Nancy and Carl."

However, Thomas could not let the matter drop. "I have something to tell you all. I met Carl's friend, Melanie. Carl said she was interested in the older students' program. He said she wanted to meet me and ask some questions. Anyway, she joined Carl and me for lunch at the student center yesterday.

"I can't really tell if they're boyfriend and girlfriend yet or just school chums. They did seem to get along well together, though. She said that she wanted to learn about my program for a paper she was writing for a sociology class."

"Is she pretty, Thomas?" Betty asked.

"Yes, very pretty. She's an attractive girl and she seems bright. I really don't know much more."

"You should have been able to sense if they have something between them, Thomas," Betty inquired.

"Maybe *you* could have, Betty, but all I can tell you is that her name is Melanie Boudreau and she's a student at Boston University. Her family lives on Long Island, and she belongs to the current events club, along with Carl."

"Well, I guess we'll just have to wait and see," Betty said.

Thomas was pretty sure that it was serious between his son and Melanie. He just didn't want to say so, especially in front of Nancy's parents, or even Marie.

Chapter Forty

IN THE MEANTIME, CARL AND NANCY WERE having a good time at the Spanish Gables. They were both good dancers and because they had spent so much time together, they knew each other's dance moves.

There was only one another couple on the dance floor besides Carl and Nancy. A contest for best dance team of the evening was drawing to a close, and as soon as the foxtrot was over, whichever couple got the loudest applause would win a $10 gift certificate to Barney Scheff's Delicatessen.

Carl was tall and pretty husky, but he had played enough basketball to be light on his feet. Nancy had filled out more during the past year. She was tall, with a gorgeous figure, and she moved as gracefully as a swan. The music stopped and the other couple was signaled forward to a hearty applause, but most of the sound came from one corner of the onlookers.

When Carl and Nancy moved to the center of the dance floor, the place erupted. They had easily earned their dinner at Barney Scheff's.

Nancy reached up to Carl in front of everyone and he bent to kiss her full on the lips. There was more applause as they waltzed off the floor and to the box office to collect their prize.

Within a half hour, they were at Barney Scheff's. Carl said, "Look at this menu, Nancy. I don't see how we can spend $10 tonight. We may have to come back here a third or fourth time. Corned beef sandwiches are 15 cents. Hot dogs are a nickel. And you can order a hot brisket plate with all the fixings and coffee and dessert."

"How much is that, Carl?"

"A dollar twenty-five," he answered. "I wonder what the fixings are?"

"Probably coleslaw and potato salad or something like that," Nancy replied.

"Hey," Nancy pointed to her menu. "They have cheese blintzes, Carl. How about that?"

"I'm getting the brisket dinner, Nancy. What about you?"

"Same. We have to use up some of the prize money. Wasn't it great winning a dance contest? I knew we were good, Carl, but I never thought we would win a prize. Did you?"

"Sure. We always danced well together. We could do it professionally, I think."

They placed their order and sat back to relax after the rather vigorous dance routines they had just put themselves through at the Spanish Gables.

After a while Carl said, "I got the scholarship I applied for in December. So, two other guys and I have rented an apartment in Boston close to Boston University. We'll be moving in right after spring break and should be set up by the first of March at the latest."

"Oh, I'm glad you got the apartment. I heard about the scholarship, Carl. My father told me about it the day your family heard and you told me about it tonight on the streetcar. Don't you remember?"

"Oh, yeah, I did. When we get the place set up, Nancy, you ought to come and see it. It's really a nice apartment. We have three separate bedrooms and a good-sized living room and a big kitchen. I think you'll like it."

"What about furniture, Carl?"

"Oh, the place is completely furnished. We paid an extra $50 for the first month's rent and the landlord sent over a bed and all the stuff that goes with it. I guess he gets to keep the bed when we leave, but he did all the work to make a bedroom out of the dining area."

"You'll still be coming home for the weekends, won't you?"

"I have to, Nancy. I need the money from my weekend job. Besides, it's the only chance I get to see my parents and Robbie. I'd like to see my sister Louise, though. I really miss her."

"How about me, Carl? Will I see you at all now that you'll be living in Boston?"

"Of course you will. Didn't I just say I want you to visit the apartment? Besides, I can call you when I'm home over the weekends."

"Tell me about your roommates. Who are they?"

"Well, there's Hank Johnson. He's a member of our current events club. Hank is a fun guy. He has a weird sense of humor sometimes, but he's really a very bright person. Hank is a freshman, like me. His family lives in Revere. He's a heavy-set fellow with blond hair. Hank Johnson is Swedish."

"You said there were two others. What about the other guy?"

"Larry Green. He's a very good student who comes from Chelsea. He's also in our club."

At this point, having finished their meal, Carl abruptly stopped talking about his roommates. He asked Nancy if she would like to walk along the beach or the amusement side of the boulevard.

She chose the beach side and they left the restaurant to go for their walk, but as soon as they got started, she asked again about his roommates.

"Carl, you were starting to tell me about Larry Green. Remember?"

Carl wondered why girls were always so interested in the details about people.

He obliged her and went on to tell her about him. "Larry's almost as tall as I am. He received a double promotion back in grade school, so he's a year younger than Hank and me. I guess Larry is not eighteen yet. He has black hair and he's good-looking. Larry is usually serious but he can be a lot of fun, also. He wants to be a doctor. I guess that was always his ambition ever since he was a little kid.

"His father is a kosher butcher in Chelsea. Larry hates working in the butcher shop, which he does part-time, like I do at Lamson's. I once asked him why he hated the butcher shop so much. He said because he doesn't like looking at bloody carcasses."

"How come he wants to be a doctor if he hates the sight of blood?"

"I asked him that very question and he explained that he didn't want to be a surgeon. He knows that he will have to see blood during medical school, but he thinks that it won't be like working in the butcher shop. Anyway, his interest is Pediatrics, so he doesn't think it will be the same as working in a butcher shop. I hope he's right."

During the second week of March, Nancy took the subway into Boston and met Carl for lunch at a restaurant in Kenmore Square not far from Carl's apartment. After lunch, they walked to Back Bay Road to see the apartment.

Hank and Larry were there, so Carl introduced them. "Nancy, this is Larry Green and my other friend here is Hank Johnson. Larry and Hank, meet my best friend, Nancy Rossiter. We grew up together. Nancy and I just won a prize for best dancers at The Spanish Gables in Revere."

"Hi, Nancy," Larry and Hank said.

"I'm really very pleased to meet you guys. Carl has told me a lot about you both."

"Hey, Nancy, is your father Professor Rossiter here at Boston University?"

"Yes, he is. Do either of you have him as your teacher?"

They both shook their heads no.

Larry and Nancy made and held eye contact. Nancy's head was swimming in a cloud and she was wondering why she felt tingling sensations.

She spoke to Larry as if he were the only other one in the room, "Carl tells me you come from Chelsea, Larry. I have friends who live there." As she spoke, she and Larry started to walk away from Hank and Carl and into the kitchen.

They stopped before they left the living room, looked at each other, and laughed at what they had just done. Nancy put her arm through Larry's and they kept walking away. Carl and Hank just looked at each other, speechless.

Chapter Forty-One

On June 22, 1940, France surrendered to Germany and the Nazis marched triumphantly into Paris. There were demonstrations in the United States against America getting involved in the war in Europe. There were also "Letters to the Editor" starting to show up in newspapers by those demanding that the U.S. step up its aid to Great Britain.

Business was starting to pick up because of increased defense spending. War industries were not only providing equipment to U.S. armed forces, but shipments to Europe were feeding the war machines on both sides of the conflict. Unemployment was beginning to drop, but there were still close to ten million Americans out of work.

Carl got to see Louise in Harvard Square at the end of June. She had one more year of nursing school, and she loved it.

Her friend Patty was still in school with her and enjoying it too.

Carl told his sister he really missed her and she explained that she felt the same. When they left to go their separate ways, they hugged each other as they said goodbye.

By September of 1940, Carl was able to use his scholarship to go on to his sophomore year, and Nancy was now a junior at Malden High School. Thomas Grandee successfully completed his first year at sergeant with an average grade of 3.5, which pleased everyone.

Thomas was also continuing his volunteer work for PAL, the Malden Police Athletic League. The league had significantly improved its win record since he had been working with them.

He saw Father Brendan and showed him his grade record from Boston University. The priest called Harvey Rossiter to thank him

once more for the good job he had done. Brendan also dropped a
note to Doctor Chase Finney and asked him to come by and visit.
He chided him because he had not been in touch for several months.

Carl had been seeing Melanie regularly and had also continued to date Nancy from time to time. Larry Green called Nancy
and was now dating her, to the relief of both families. Carl felt a bit
of jealousy, and he had remained somewhat annoyed by her actions the day he introduced her to his friend.

Melanie visited her family in New York during summer vacation. She and Nancy had met, and now each girl knew that Carl
was seeing the other. Melanie seemed more concerned than Nancy.
Larry told Carl how pleased he was that Carl had introduced him
to Nancy, and eventually Carl accepted the situation.

Nancy entered her senior year at Malden High School and
was already beginning to think about college. Catalogs were arriv-
ing in the Rossiter mail and Nancy seriously considered going to
Barnard in New York. As the daughter of Professor Rossiter of
Boston University, she would not have to pay tuition if she went to
her father's school. As catalogues and application forms piled up,
she began to feel guilty about making her parents spend money for
school unnecessarily.

"Nancy, it's your life, and your dad and I want what's best for
you. If you decide on Barnard or Berkeley then we will find a way
to pay the tuition. We want you to do what's best for *you*, dear."

"Mom, that makes me think of something you once said about
your own mother."

"What did I say, Nancy?"

Nancy replied, "Word for word, this is what you said, and if
you've said it once, you've said it a million times. 'My mother always told me to do what's best for me and not to worry about her. It
was like she had a bankbook filled with my guilt.'"

"You're right, Nancy, I guess I did sound like Grandma
Herman. Regardless… "

"…I want you to do what's best for you," Nancy interrupted.
They laughed.

Suddenly the phone rang. It was Larry Green. "Nancy, I can
get away this week on Friday night if you're free. My schedule is
light on Friday. Last class is over by one in the afternoon. I can get

most of my homework done later Friday afternoon. If I keep Sunday night available for last-minute studying, it gives me Friday and Saturday nights."

"Sounds good to me, honey. I have nothing planned for Friday or Saturday."

Nancy's senior year went along smoothly. She was seeing a lot of Larry, and Carl kept in touch as well. She and Carl even went on a couple of dates together and they often talked about Larry and Melanie.

"Are you going out with Larry again this weekend, Nancy?" Betty asked.

"Yes, mom. Why do you ask?"

"Just wondering. Not that I mind, dear. Larry is a very fine young man, and I'm glad that you have someone besides Carl that you're interested in. It's just that we used to see a lot of Carl, and I sort of miss him."

Nancy was about to say she missed him too, but she was surprised by her own thought and she simply said, "Well, you and daddy thought I was seeing too much of Carl. Now you sound like you regret saying it. You say you like Larry, but maybe you think I'm seeing too much of him, too. Do you?"

Betty said, "You're right, Nancy. You're a big girl now and I think I better start minding my own business. Daddy and I trust you. You must know that."

"I know you do, and I love you both very much. Besides, with Christmas vacation coming up, soon Carl will be home and he always comes around to visit us during the holidays."

By January of 1941, British troops had moved into Ethiopia. In early April, Germany invaded Bulgaria and Yugoslavia. The Croatians welcomed the Nazis but Tito's Yugoslavia put up resistance to Hitler. The war in Europe was beginning to involve practically every country except Franco's fascist regime in Spain, which remained neutral. There was no need for Germany or Italy to be concerned with Spain.

German rockets were still hitting England, and night flights over London destroyed both military and civilian targets. Many Londoners lost their homes. Air raid sirens were becoming common and underground shelters were filled regularly. The British people were showing great courage and patriotism under the able leadership of Winston Churchill.

Malden High School's graduation was planned for June 20th. Nancy graduated with high honors and finally decided to go to Boston University.

Two days after Nancy's graduation, on June 22 of 1941, the Nazis invaded Russia. The United States landed troops in Iceland in July, and unemployment was dropping by the millions while the war in Europe was spreading rapidly.

At the beginning of September, Thomas Grandee received a phone call from Sam Braverman. "Thomas, do you think you could possibly take the time to have lunch or dinner with me over at The Chateau?" he asked.

"I might be able to arrange it. What's going on?"

"I think it best if we talk when we see each other. I believe you will be pleased with what I have to say to you."

"Sam, you do know that I have became a student in my old age, right?"

"Yes, I know all about that, and I understand you've been doing quite well. Rabbi Richmond told me all about it."

"Yes, I have done well, much better than I could have hoped. If I'm going to meet with you, it should be tomorrow because I start classes the day after Labor Day."

"Fine. Be at The Chateau in the morning, say ten o'clock. By the way, how is your son, Carl, doing? I understand he's also studying at Boston University."

"Carl is fantastic. He gets straight A's. He'll be entering his junior year at Boston University next week."

"Great, Thomas. I'm looking forward to seeing you tomorrow morning."

Ten o'clock Friday morning found Thomas at The Chateau for the first time since he had been fired two years previous. Sam Braverman was waiting for him. He was sitting at Thomas' favorite corner table talking to Victor Hermanssen.

After the morning greetings, Thomas asked what the meeting was all about. Sam explained, "First, you might be interested to learn that Hannah was recently released from prison after serving a two-year sentence. She never did reimburse any of the money she stole. Bob Morrison and I estimate that she took more than $10,000."

"You know," Thomas said, "no one ever told me that Hannah was sent to prison and I never asked because I tried to wipe that whole fiasco from my mind. I figured that she would have to do time, though. I don't imagine she'll ever return to Massachusetts, let alone the Boston area."

"No, as a matter of fact, I heard that she was going to live with some aunt in Hawaii. But I think Hannah is behind us, and that isn't what we want to discuss any more than you do," Sam Braverman said.

"So, what do you want to talk about, Sam?"

"You, Thomas. The Chateau is not pulling in as many customers as it did when you were running the place. Oh, we're more profitable, all right, but that's because we don't have Hannah dipping into the cash. Business in general is better everywhere because of the war." Sam leaned back and looked at Victor before continuing.

"Victor doesn't feel that he has your touch with the customers. He explained that you used to think up new ideas for getting people to talk about The Chateau, like charging an extra nickel or a dime when someone complained. Victor doesn't seem to have that kind of imagination. When he tried the dime thing it made a problem for him, so he gave up on it."

"I'm sorry to hear that. I thought Victor was very capable."

"I'm good as a custodian, Thomas. I wish you would come back, and I'd be happy to have my old job again. As much as I envied you when you were the manager, I think that I liked it better than I do now. I don't think I'm cut out for being manager."

Sam Braverman said, "That's what we wanted to talk to you about. Victor is here with us so that you'll understand that if you return it will not hurt him. In a way, this was his idea. Morrison has agreed as well."

"Sam, I'm flattered, but you know I've turned my life around and I want to continue what I set out to do. I'm sorry that I have to say no."

"Before you turn this offer down, Thomas, consider that your salary will be double what it was when you left. In other words, you will be paid $75 a week to start, and if the place starts to pick up as we hope will happen, Bob and I will consider a raise above that."

"Sounds like a lot of money. I still feel that I want to stay with my school and my job at The Apollo, but with the offer you made, I guess I owe it to Marie to see what she thinks. Can I have a few days to think about it and to talk it over with my wife?"

Of course, Thomas, and I hope you accept."

There was silence.

Victor said, "Have you guys noticed that there are so many Negroes around these days?"

"I don't like the way you said that, Victor."

"Thomas, you're high class now that you go to college. Do you find many colored people in school?"

"There are some. I think there will be more as time goes on. Listen, Victor, it's just that I was never in any way prejudiced. Education helps people to be tolerant, though. I've always judged people on an individual basis and not by their color or race or religion. The Nazis in Germany are white. Never forget that, Victor."

"Okay, but I still notice more of them than before. I wonder why?"

"I think that it has to do with better job opportunities here in the North because of military equipment and armament orders."

Sam Braverman said, "I read that movement of Negroes from the South to the North is increasing. *The New York Times* had an article about it last week. They claim that it's a combination of less discrimination up here and better job opportunities, like Thomas says."

"Whatever the reason, I'm still not comfortable with it," Victor said. Thomas and Sam Braverman decided to drop the matter.

When Thomas left The Chateau, he was debating whether or not to tell Marie. *What if she wants me to take the job offer? I hate that place.* He went directly to Marie at the Woolworth's in Malden Square.

Marie asked the store manager for a half-hour break and he told her to take the rest of day if she wanted. "You won't be docked, Marie. You never take time off, so I think you've earned a free day. Are you on this Saturday?"

"No sir, I'm not. I'll be back here Tuesday morning. Monday is Labor Day."

On the ride home in Thomas' old pickup truck, he told Marie about Sam Braverman's offer. Marie didn't hesitate.

"Don't you dare go back there. You have to be crazy to even think about it."

"I love you, Marie. I was hoping you wouldn't let the money make a difference. It's just that I would feel guilty if I turned dow 75 bucks a week without telling you first. I hate that place more than you, sweetheart. It almost ruined me *and* our marriage."

Thomas was silent for a minute before he said, "It wasn't The Chateau that nearly wrecked my life. It was my own doing, Marie. What a weakling I was. That damn Hannah got under my skin. Jesus, I can't believe what I did to myself and to you and the kids and…"

Marie interrupted, "Stop it, Thomas, we've been all through this and we both agreed that what happened is in the past and that's where it stays. The change you made in your life makes me proud, Thomas."

"I could never have done it without you, Marie, you know that, don't you?"

"I went along because I knew, down deep, that the man I married was a good man despite everything that had happened. Father Brendan told me that he was amazed at how hard you worked to overcome very difficult problems. He's proud of you, too, Thomas."

"I've got the day off from the Apollo, Marie. You've got a day off, too. Let's drive over to the beach and have lunch somewhere and then let's go to The Spanish Gables and see if we can win a prize like Carl and Nancy did."

"We're really not dressed for it, but let's go anyway," she said. "I'm willing to give it a try." They both laughed, and Thomas was finally relaxed for the first time since Sam Braverman had called.

The day after Labor Day, Thomas and Carl went to school together. During the last week of August 1941, Nancy had moved into her room at the dormitory with a roommate named Grace Quigley. The new freshmen spent the first week before classes at orientation.

Nancy called Larry and asked him about the current events club. He didn't see any reason why she couldn't join, but said he would mention it when the other members got back.

"You know, most of the members are sophomores or juniors."

"Of course I know that, dummy. You were all freshmen once, remember?"

By new agreement, the current events club met the first day back at school. There was no special topic. All twenty of them showed up because they wanted to be together. After all the hand shaking and hugging, the war in Europe soon became the discussion of the evening.

Larry Green said, "Hold it for a moment everyone, my girlfriend Nancy Rossiter would like to join the club. She's a freshman this year."

"Who's Nancy?" one of the girls asked.

Melanie told them that Nancy was Professor Rossiter's daughter and that she was a great girl. "Carl grew up with her and she was once Carl's girlfriend for a while. She's a good friend to Carl and me, as well."

All members indicated approval, and the conversation returned to the war. Larry said that he was thinking about signing up for ROTC. "I think we're eventually going to get into this war, and I'd rather be an officer than an infantryman."

"Are you thinking about it or are you actually going to do it?" Hank asked. "Personally, I don't want to be an officer or an infantryman. I just don't like the idea of being a soldier and shooting people.

How about you other guys?" Larry asked.

A couple of fellows said that they had already signed up for ROTC. Carl said that he would wait and see how things developed. "I agree with Hank to some degree. I don't like the idea of aiming a rifle at someone I don't know and killing him. War stinks, but if I have to, I'll go and I guess I'll take my chances on whatever they ask me to do."

One of the girls said that if America gets into the war, she would volunteer to do whatever women volunteers do. "It's our war, too, you know, just like the men."

Someone finally said, "Let's get off the war, people. Right now America is not in it, and I hope it stays that way."

Larry said he wanted to make a suggestion before breaking up for the evening. "There's a lot of talk about Hitler and persecution of Jews. I heard some terrible stories about what the Nazis are doing to the Jews in Poland. My suggestion is to have a meeting where we invite someone to lead a discussion on that subject."

Carl agreed and suggested that either Professor Morse or Professor Rossiter be asked to lead the discussion. There was unanimous agreement to have Larry and Carl work it out, and then the meeting ended.

Carl and Melanie said that they were leaving, and they went to Kenmore Square for coffee and doughnuts.

"I missed you this summer, Carl. New York is hot and sticky in August and my folks just wanted me to hang out with them on Long Island."

"I missed you, too," Carl said, "but I wasn't really bored. Don't forget, I have a full time job during the summer months. With my scholarship, I can really have extra money to spend for the first time in my life."

"My folks take care of my expenses, so I don't have your problem about money. I guess my family is pretty well-off."

"You're lucky. You don't know what it's like not to be able to do what you want or buy the things you need. My family has a very complicated work situation since my father decided to go back to school to get a degree. He works odd hours and my mother works at Woolworth's. Both of them together make less than he made in one good job. Anyway, it's funny. We seem to have more money for things than before. I don't understand it."

Melanie wanted to know more about Carl's family now that the subject had come up. Carl told her a little about The Chateau, but he said nothing about any problems. He started to tell her about Thomas being offered his old job back at double the pay but decided that he didn't want to get into The Chateau thing any further. After a while, he changed the subject because he was starting to feel uncomfortable. He and Melanie went back to the apartment and they spent some time in the privacy of Carl's room.

The first serious current events club meeting took place in October with Professor Rossiter as the guest moderator. Nancy was there, and so were nearly all the members of the club.

Harvey started by telling the students that much of the anti-Semitism that took place in Germany during the thirties was common knowledge.

"There are anti-Jewish laws that we can read about in the newspapers. By now, everyone has seen news photos and movies of Nazi troops singing the Horst Wessel song and smashing the windows of Jewish-owned shops during Kristallnacht. Am I right in thinking that you all know this much?" he asked.

"I think that's probably true of this group," Larry Green said, "but I've met people who don't believe the stories. How do you explain that?"

"Not very easily, Larry. Unfortunately, much of what people call anti-Semitism is also ignorance, even here in the United States. But we can't deal with that subject tonight if we're going to talk about Nazi Germany."

"Since I am a history professor, I believe the best way to understand what is happening is to look for the causes. Recent German history will help us.

"The defeat of Germany in World War I, together with the worldwide depression of the 1930s, wreaked havoc upon the German economy. The Versailles treaty had already imposed economic ruin on the nation.

"The early 1930s completed the disaster. When Hitler came to power in 1933, he blamed the Jews for Germany's misfortunes and he began his campaign against them. With Aryan superiority as the theoretical excuse for anti-Semitism, many Jews left the country. Some Jewish refugees managed to flee to other countries, but there were immigration restrictions that finally trapped others inside the Nazi nightmare."

One of the girls asked Professor Rossiter about the Nazi persecution of others besides Jews. Rossiter explained, "A good question. Of course, there is widespread discrimination and persecution of Gypsies, and many Catholics have also suffered at the hands of the Nazis. There is also a campaign waged against homosexuals. I haven't talked much about this because I was asked to lead a discussion regarding anti-Semitism. Socialists and Communists have also been arrested and interrogated by the Gestapo. Many were simply killed."

Carl asked the Professor why there wasn't an uprising or even a revolution after the depression.

"It seems that there was industrialization and American loans to Germany after World War I. With the onset of the depression in America, the consequences in Europe were devastating. Because the Americans called in their debt, Germany suffered the most. Sudden poverty made the situation ripe for the rise of a radical alternative before there could be an uprising.

"Hitler was named chancellor. If the Communists had formed a coalition with the Socialists, they might have been strong enough to succeed in taking power. However, the left wing groups simply argued against each other and the National Socialist Party of Hitler was able to take advantage of the disunity. At this point, it really doesn't matter how or why Hitler came to power. The fact is the Nazis took complete control."

Larry said, "My mother still has family living in Germany. A cousin of hers, a man in his sixties, was killed on Kristallnacht. I didn't want to bring up anything personal during the discussion, but there is something I'd like to say."

"Go ahead, Larry," Professor Rossiter urged.

"It just really bothers me. Hitler and his Nazis are a menace that have to be eliminated. I feel guilty that we have it so good in America by comparison."

One of the girls said, "I agree that it's terrible, Larry. What we hear they do to Jews in Germany is absolutely horrible. I think that this country should declare war on Germany and stop Hitler immediately."

The discussion picked up for a couple of more minutes, but they were all pretty much talked out. It was a thoughtful and preoccupied group of students who left the current events club meeting that evening.

Chapter Forty-Two

ONCE CLASSES BEGAN, THE STUDENTS QUICKLY FELL into their new routines. The fall semester was approaching an end when news came on December 7 that the Japanese had bombed Pearl Harbor. On December 8, 1941, America declared war on Japan. The country was shocked into the reality of what would become World War II.

Guam surrendered to the Japanese on December 10, followed by Wake Island on December 23. On Christmas Day, 1941, British troops surrendered at Hong Kong. The Japanese occupied the Philippines at the beginning of January 1942.

Thomas called Harvey Rossiter at the end of the first week in January and told him about a bulletin he had seen from the Coast Guard's Commercial Street headquarters in Boston. They were looking for part-time civilian volunteers. The two of them decided to go to the meeting. After learning what the responsibilities were, they signed up for one four-hour shift each week. Both men chose Sunday evening for volunteer duty.

Both were trained to patrol the waterfront adjacent to the Coast Guard station. It was a patriotic thing to do, and the time involved was not too great a sacrifice.

They were also asked that if at any time they could not be on duty, they should give advance notice and the Coast Guard would get substitutes to cover for them. They had special uniforms that made them both feel pretty good about having volunteered.

Thomas Grandee received a call from the board president of the Malden YMCA. It seemed that the assistant athletics director had enlisted in the Army, and the board wondered if Thomas would consider taking his place. The president understood that Thomas would have to arrange special hours, but he was willing to meet and talk about it.

A meeting was arranged. After talking with his mentor, Frank Clark, he was advised that a daytime schedule at the University would be best, but he could arrange for some evening classes just as he had for the past year-and-a half.

He met with the director at the YMCA and learned that he would have to be available at least some daytime hours, but that evenings could also be useful. In other words, he could maintain the same schedule as the one he had with the Apollo. When he was told that the salary would be $55 per week, he immediately accepted; his Apollo salary was $42. He arranged to give the Apollo two weeks notice.

Carl had been given a raise to $14 for his weekend job at Lamson's. Since he was still on scholarship, his bank account was growing. He now had close to $300 in a savings account.

After looking into ROTC and thinking that he would like to volunteer for the service, he decided to talk it over with both his father and with Harvey Rossiter. Both men advised against rushing in, and he decided to at least complete the semester that ended in June. If he was called, he would probably be entitled to a student deferment. The current events club was already down to six men and ten women. Larry had still not enlisted.

Carl was seeing a lot of Melanie and very little of Nancy. Larry Green was occupying much of Nancy's time, and Carl figured this was the reason why Larry hadn't joined the Army. He started to feel guilty that his own main reason for not joining was Melanie, but he quickly pushed the thought into the back of his mind. Whatever the real reason, time passed and before he knew it, he was back in Malden, working his-full time vacation job at Lamson's.

Louise came to visit him at his apartment right after the start of his senior year at Boston University. Hank had left for the Army during the summer, but rather than get a replacement, he and Larry decided they would manage the rent between them. When Melanie found out, she gave them an offer. "Why not let me take Hank's room? Quite a few of the apartments are now co-ed, and we have a waiting list of girls for a vacancy in case one of our rooms is taken."

Larry said that it was okay with him and left it up to Carl to decide. It took Carl about half a second to say yes.

"I think I ought to move to the middle so you two can't get too cozy at night," Larry teased.

"I can always walk around you if I have to, Larry," Carl quipped. Melanie just grinned happily at their banter.

When Louise came to visit, she explained to Carl that now that she was a registered nurse, she was thinking of signing up for the service. After graduation, she had taken a job as a nurse at the Peter Bent Brigham Hospital on Huntington Avenue in Boston. Her friend Patty was working back at Mount Auburn Hospital in Cambridge and they had both considered signing up. Obviously, this was a major decision for two young women to make.

"Why we think it will be better if we wait is unclear. I don't think it makes any difference. They need nurses, and we know that in the end we're going to sign up. Anyway, Patty thinks we ought to wait until the end of this year. Are you signing up, Carl?"

"I am, but I might wait the year out, too. I wish I had my degree already, but I guess I'll have to postpone it until after the war. I don't know what I'm waiting for, because I don't earn my bachelor's degree until June of forty-three, and I know I'm going in before that. I'm starting to feel guilty, Lou."

"I don't see why you should feel guilty, Carl. Lots of guys are using their student status for deferments. You're not even thinking of that."

"Well, sister, it looks like we'll both be going in at about the same time."

And that was how it happened. Louise volunteered and was asked to sign a paper saying that she was willing to serve overseas. On December 15, 1942, she left for Fort Devens in Massachusetts, where she spent three days being indoctrinated and issued regulation clothing. She was then shipped to Fort Dix in New Jersey and was immediately assigned to ward duty while waiting for her next orders. Her duties at Fort Dix made her proud, and she began to realize how vital the Nurse Corps was to the army.

Carl enlisted right after the first of the year. After three days at Fort Devens in January 1943, he was on a train bound for Camp Hood in Texas.

Larry was planning to enlist as soon as he finished an overdue paper from the past semester and had it approved. Melanie regretted having left the apartment next door with her girlfriends. A new young lady now occupied her former room. Even though the Boudreaus told Melanie she could afford to stay there by herself if she so chose, she was not happy about being alone. With so many of the boys leaving for the service and most of the girls she knew either in dorms or commuting, she asked Larry if he had any ideas.

"Sure, why not ask Nancy if she's interested? She might even know of someone else if she isn't."

By the time Larry resolved the paper issue, Nancy and another girl had agreed to move in with Melanie. Larry Green enlisted at the end of January.

Chapter Forty-Three

IT WAS HARD FOR THOMAS GRANDEE TO believe that he was a senior at Boston University. He was now 43 years old. He also thought it remarkable that he was an assistant program director at the Malden YMCA.

Financially, he and Marie were fairly comfortable. Marie was still working at Woolworth's, but with several young men having gone into the service, Marie had been promoted to a supervisory position and was now earning $27 per week. Thomas was up to 60 per week. With that plus the money that Carl and Louise were planning to send home, the Grandee family income would be about $100 per week.

Marie suggested that the deposits the Army would be crediting to them for Louise and Carl be set aside in separate accounts for each of them. Both Carl and Louise protested this; they felt that they owed their education to the whole family and they didn't really need the money. They had arranged that respective portions would be used while serving and that the rest would be sent to their parents.

"I agree with them, Marie. The accounts are already in place. Louise and Carl each gave me their bank books and they signed some papers the bank gave them so that I would have power of attorney until they came home."

Marie smiled at Thomas. "I could never have imagined five years ago that my life would be this good. I do worry, though, because of this damned war. I hope Carl and Louise come through it safely. Last night I had a dream that Carl was wounded. Do you worry about the kids, Thomas?"

"You can say that double, Marie. I haven't slept a wink since Louise left in December and here it is, February of 1943. I'm worried that she may be shipped overseas. "Remember what she said in the letter about having to sign papers again about being willing to serve overseas. She doesn't go into the details, but it seems that she was one of 11 nurses chosen for some special assignment. I guess the Fort Dix people wanted to keep all the nurses in New Jersey, but they got orders from above, and now Louise is getting ready for another move."

Actually, Louise was already at Camp Shanks in New York, starting six weeks of training in preparation for overseas duty. Her name on her return address now read, "2nd Lt. Louise Grandee, RN." Louise and Patty had started out together, but Patty was sent to California while Louise was at Fort Dix.

In the meantime, Carl had written several letters home from Camp Hood in Texas. He explained that the basic training was fairly straightforward, but he complained that he had a dumb hick of a sergeant whose only qualification was his size. He was big and he liked to pick on the little guys. Carl hated him because he ordered the recruits to do unnecessary work after supper that he referred to as "chicken shit."

He was especially angry with this Sergeant Jones because he picked on a kid that Carl had become friendly with. The guy was Murray Halpern, a Jewish boy from Brooklyn, New York, who Carl thought was a really nice guy. In the second letter he wrote to his parents, he explained that Murray was really smart and good-natured and that everyone took advantage of him.

"Apparently Carl has taken a liking to this Jewish boy," Thomas said, as he handed the letter to Marie. In exchange, she gave Thomas back the letter from Louise, who had also received mail from Carl. She wrote a little "P.S." at the bottom saying she had sent a letter back to Carl in response and she hoped that he would receive it. The postscript also explained that some of the nurses thought the mail sometimes got "screwed up," but that she didn't really think that was true.

By the time basic training was over at Camp Hood in Texas, Sergeant Jones had taken significant privileges away from Murray Halpern. Murray couldn't complain or he would get into even bigger trouble. Carl knew that Murray had not been guilty of anything other than being Jewish.

Not many of the guys at Camp Hood were fond of their sergeant. Almost every private had something to complain about. Quite a few of the new recruits were given latrine duty as punishment for things they knew they had never done. Jones also had the recruits filling in mud prints soldiers had left during drills. The next day the boot prints would return after the morning drill.

One particular day, Carl had been playing chess with Murray in the dayroom when Sergeant Jones called Murray outside. He said, "Listen, you prick, I don't like the way you looked at me this morning. You're on 'no privilege' indefinitely, and you start KP tonight." KP meant kitchen duty from three in the morning until eleven at night for one full day. Carl overheard the orders, and he saw Murray walk back to the barracks.

Carl walked over to Sergeant Jones and grabbed him by his collar. He stood tall enough so that he was nose-to-nose with the sergeant, who wasn't in the same physical condition that Carl was in. Jones may have issued the orders, but the recruits were the ones to do the pushups and the running. Carl wasn't going to stand for it.

Carl threatened, "Jones, you are one son of a bitch, and if you don't stop picking on my friend Murray, I'm going to kill you. So help me God, I will literally kill you." He pushed Jones back so hard the big man nearly fell down.

Jones staggered for a minute, retrieved the cap that fell off his head, and turned and walked away. Murray Halpern was back with privileges by the end of the next day.

Not long after the incident, Murray and Carl's company were transferred out to Camp Bowie, Texas for advanced infantry training. Jones never had the chance to pick on Murray again.

Carl and Murray were now in the 66th Infantry Division and were among the few soldiers selected for Weapons Training. They were given intensive training in all weapons, from .22 caliber up to 3 inch, including 81mm mortars and machine guns.

Carl and Murray were never promoted beyond the rank of private. Some others were at least private first class or corporal. Carl once asked about it and was told that the Army often screwed up with respect to rank. "It's just another snafu," their new sergeant explained, "because I already put you guys in for promotion. The paperwork sometimes gets fouled up because of the transfers from one outfit to another. I'll see what I can do."

Nothing ever happened, though, and both he and Murray were transferred again, this time to Special Forces. They now wore Tank Destroyer patches that depicted something like a Black Panther with a tank in its mouth. The training in the Tank Destroyer Unit was extremely intensive and went on for many months.

Chapter Forty-Four

THOMAS GRANDEE RECEIVED HIS BACHELOR OF SCIENCE in physical education at the end of 1943. The university arranged a ceremony for the seven graduates of the innovative program for working adults that had begun in January of 1940. Only one of the original eight was no longer present and that was because he was in the Air Force Reserves and had been called to active duty shortly after Pearl Harbor.

Thomas was the only candidate for the physical education degree. The others all received Bachelor of Arts degrees in one discipline or another.

Marie and Robbie attended the ceremony, along with Father Brendan, Father Fazio, Rabbi Richmond, Reverend Granville, Doctor Finney, and Betty and Harvey Rossiter.

Father Fazio called Father Brendan aside to explain to him that he would like to meet privately after the graduation ceremony. "I heard from Mary Lou Gallagher just yesterday, William. She filled me in on some interesting information about John Grandee." Father Brendan agreed to meet.

Frank Clark was mentor to the original eight students. He addressed the graduates and their families and friends.

"It is my privilege to have spent the past four years with one of the finest groups of students I have ever worked with. I believe that I have learned more from them about discipline and hard work than they have in terms of curriculum. To the students I say, 'Very well done. You have pursued your studies as actively as Romeo pursued Juliet and you have done Romeo one better by achieving your goal.'

"To the families and friends of these wonderful students I can only say that I envy you the productive years ahead that you are certain to see from these dedicated men and women."

Thomas had never felt more proud in his life. After the speech, Frank Clark came forward and handed each student a framed diploma. Thomas was awarded his degree magna cum laude.

Marie met Thomas as he approached his seat, diploma in hand. They hugged each other with genuine love and respect. There was applause from the small audience that lasted long enough to show that everyone present must have been aware of just how great an accomplishment this was for Thomas Grandee, former bartender, waiter, chef, and individual able to overcome more than a handful of very serious difficulties.

Rabbi Richmond approached Thomas and Marie after the ceremony and asked that Thomas please call him at Temple Beth El. Thomas promised him that he would do so within the next few days. The rabbi handed him a card with his name and the temple phone number.

Thomas and Marie wondered what the rabbi would want to talk to him about. "Maybe he wants you to coach the Temple's softball team if they have one," Marie said.

"Maybe he wants to convert me to Judaism," Thomas joked.

When Thomas met Rabbi Richmond at the Temple, he discovered the real reason for the meeting. The city of Columbia, Massachusetts, which had a growing Jewish population, was building a YMHA, a Young Men's Hebrew Association. Columbia's YMHA would be the equal of Malden's YMCA and they would need a capable athletic and physical education director. Rabbi Richmond said, "I told them about you, Thomas, and they're interested. I think you can probably have the job if you want it. Naturally, you will have to meet with the administration at Columbia. I think that it's a great opportunity for you. The position pays a substantial salary and probably carries valuable benefits as well.

"Columbia has a fairly wealthy Jewish Community. The YMHA will be part of an expanded Jewish community center and, as athletic director, your duties will include community center exercise classes."

"I'm honored by the opportunity, Rabbi Richmond, but I was hoping for a teaching job at one of the high schools, combined with coaching or gym classes."

"That sounds like a good goal for you. What subject did you have in mind?"

"I'd love to teach English. It was a difficult subject for me in high school, but in college I had the most wonderful English professor. She made the subject come to life for me, and I think I am capable of doing the same in a classroom of high school kids."

"Does that mean that you don't want to meet the Columbia people for an interview?"

"Oh, no, not at all. The opportunity is attractive and I'm not certain that any teaching jobs are available. I would just like time to think it through. If I go to the interview and accept, I want it to be a commitment that I'm honestly prepared to keep."

"Fine, Thomas. Let me know what you decide. Oh, and Thomas, please understand that no matter what your decision, I wish you all the success in the world. You certainly have worked very hard to turn your life around."

"Thank you, rabbi," Thomas said.

At home, Thomas told Marie about the Columbia job opportunity. They decided to ask the Rossiters for advice. It would also be a chance to talk to Betty and Harvey Rossiter about the latest family developments.

Marie and Thomas didn't have to worry about leaving Robbie home alone, since he was now 16. Robbie was beginning to date, and soon he would be taking Charlotte Brown's younger sister, Jackie, to the movies. He was also working afternoons at the Smoke Shop in Malden Square. He relieved the owner so that he could have a late lunch, use the bathroom and restock the shelves. In return, he earned a few dollars and got free cigarettes.

Thomas and Marie headed for Wagon Wheels Restaurant in Thomas' new car. He had traded in the old one for a 1940 Oldsmobile sedan. This time, the Grandees picked up the Rossiters.

After ordering charbroiled sirloin steaks with all the usual fixings, the conversation quickly came around to their concerns for their children overseas, especially Louise and Carl. David had just been called for his physical the very next week. He was also a student at Boston University, but he commuted. David didn't like living away from home. His first year at a dorm was not a happy one for him.

"Why doesn't David try for a deferment to finish college?" Thomas asked.

Harvey answered, "For the same reason Carl didn't. They feel guilty if they don't go. I sometimes feel guilty myself, don't you, Thomas?"

"Yes. I definitely do, and don't think I haven't thought about enlisting. I don't think they want a guy my age, Harvey. After all, I'm going to be 45 in a couple of weeks."

"Well, anyway, what's this about wanting to teach, Thomas? I thought you were finally pleased to have a chance to be in athletics."

"I am, but look at all the high school coaches that have teaching jobs. In fact, I think some schools require it of the coaches."

"I'm not so sure about that, but you may be right. What subject would you want to teach?"

"Rabbi Richmond asked me the same question. I'll tell you what I told him. I spent a year at Boston University with Professor Rachel Wolfson and realized that a good teacher is worth a million bucks. That woman didn't just teach English. She taught me how to teach, really. I learned more about teaching from Wolfson than I did in my education courses. I can probably teach several subjects at the high school level, like algebra or geometry, for example. What I think, though, is that no kid can learn any subject until he or she knows how to read with understanding. I really believe that in this country, the most important thing we can do is to teach our kids how to read and comprehend. Since English is the language of our textbooks, it's essential to be good at English in order to be good at any other subject."

"Well, you have a point, " Harvey said, "but I don't think you have to be a linguist to study history. I will agree, though, that you have to be literate and so, yes, English is of primary importance."

"The dinner is coming, guys. Let's be still for a minute or two about Thomas and his English mania," Marie said. "How is Nancy, Betty? Carl says that they correspond. He gets letters from her as well as from Melanie."

Betty answered, "Nancy is doing great at school and she's already had several works published. She says she wants to be a writer. That kind of supports Thomas and his mania for English." They all laughed.

"Thank you, Betty. You're kinder than my wife," Thomas said.

"There happens to be an opening at Arlington High School for an English teacher, Thomas. I don't know about a coaching job, though. There was a notice on the bulletin board at the University about it. I suppose you could look into it. I doubt that you can earn as much money teaching as you could at this YMHA job that Rabbi Richmond told you about."

"I've talked to Marie about that. We know it will pay less, but it's what I want to do if I can find a place that will take me. I just think I can be a good teacher, Harvey. It's a gut feeling."

Marie added, "Well then, I guess it's settled. If you want it that badly and Harvey seems to feel that you have the qualifications, then I say go for it, Thomas. I'm with you all the way. Now let's concentrate on these still sizzling steaks before they all start to get cold."

Betty said, "I think that you might be making a mistake, Thomas, by passing up this YMHA thing. If you're so keen on teaching English, there's a large need for English for new immigrants at the high schools in the local communities. Even if you did it as a volunteer, you probably would come out way ahead financially and you would be able to set your own hours. Being a volunteer gives you a lot of flexibility because no one is paying for your time. Quite a few Jewish people have come over here from Europe, at least the ones who were able to get away. I think when the war is finally over, there will be a lot more people coming to live in this country who have to learn the language."

"You have a point, Betty. If they hire me, I'll have a well-paying job just a few miles out of town. I'd still have time to put in some evening volunteer work and try out my skills as a teacher."

Marie said, "I like that idea, too, Betty. I just hope Thomas doesn't go off half-cocked and volunteer every night of the week."

Thomas wasted no time in calling Rabbi Richmond to say he would like to arrange an interview with the YMHA in Columbia.

"They know about you, Thomas, just give them a call. Ask for Jack Berger. He's expecting to hear from you."

Thomas met with Jack Berger in February of 1944 and once more in March. At the March meeting Berger said, "The board has decided to hire you, Thomas. The new construction is complete, except for some last-minute details. We would like you to come on board by the beginning of May. In that way, you will have time to get schedules organized for our grand opening July first. Does that work out all right for you, Thomas?"

"It does, Mr. Berger." Thomas looked on the wall calendar and said, "I'll be here on Monday, May first."

"Thomas, you can call me Jack. They tell me that no one ever calls you Tom, only Thomas. Am I right?"

"That's right, Jack. For some reason, everyone has always called me Thomas. Maybe it was because I was bigger than most of the other kids when I was a teenager. My wife, Marie, says it was because I was a star athlete in high school and the other kids looked up to me. A nickname wouldn't bother me though, as long as it's not Tom."

"Why is that, Thomas?"

"Well, it's a long story, but the only one that ever called me Tom was a woman that made nothing but trouble for me. I just can't abide being called Tom."

"I think I heard something about that," Jack Berger remarked. "I would like you to come over to the new building and inspect the facilities. You can do that now; Thomas or we can set a date convenient for you. I think it best if you have a look before you start your new position with us."

"I'll be happy to do that right now, Jack."

Thomas Grandee, newly appointed athletic director of the Columbia YMHA, spent the next three hours making notes about the beautiful new building. He was amazed at the amount of space allotted to the gymnasium. The swimming pool facilities, both indoor and outdoor, were the best he had seen locally. The playing field for outdoor sports was more than he could ever have hoped for.

"What do you think, Thomas?" Jack asked.

"I'm glad I decided to accept the opportunity to come up to Columbia. I'm very impressed."

Thomas gave notice to the YMCA in Malden and started his new life on schedule, May 1 of 1944.

Chapter Forty-Five

IMMEDIATELY FOLLOWING THE SMALL SPECIAL COMMENCEMENT SERVICE
for graduates of the Older Adult Program, Father Brendan and
Father Fazio met for coffee and a friendly visit at a cafe in nearby
Kenmore Square in Boston.

Father Fazio cleared his throat and said, "William, I am more
than full after having those sandwiches and God knows how many
cups of coffee back at the graduation celebration. If you don't mind,
I will just have a glass of red chianti."

"You said it, John. Everything was delicious. A double Irish
whiskey will help me wash it all down." Father Brendan was anxious to learn more about what Mary Lou Gallagher had told Father
Fazio about Thomas' brother, John.

Father Fazio began, "Thus far, I know very little. Mrs. Gallagher
called me about John just yesterday, William. She claims that the
scandal surrounding John's former wife was really a scandal involving John. I have no idea what it was all about, though."

"Curious. Do you intend to look into it further?" Father Brendan
asked.

"I most certainly will do that. I'm as interested as you are. In
fact, I will confess to you that in this case I feel downright nosy.
What I would like to do is arrange a meeting with Mrs. Gallagher."

With a knowing grin on his face, Father Fazio, who knew very
well that Father Brendan was even more anxious than he was to
hear Mary Lou's story, looked at his colleague, straight-faced, and
said, "I don't suppose that you'd like to join us?"

"John, for God sakes, you know I would."

"Relax, William. You are much too serious."

Both clerics then spent over an hour talking about the successful redemption of Thomas Grandee, complimenting each other

on their contributions to that end. During that hour, they each imbibed more than they should have while making toasts to their success and conjecturing about Thomas' brother John.

Fortunately, they had each arrived by public transportation rather than attempting to drive through Boston's traffic.

Standing up to leave the cafe, they looked at each other and burst into laughter. Father Fazio said, "We had best call for a taxi and try to look sober so the cab driver will not notice our condition."

"Agreed." Father Brendan was unable to control his laughter. "Imagine the headlines if we walked out into the street like this— 'Two Drunken Priests Arrested in Kenmore Square.'"

The laughter now caught on to the few others in the cafe and the waitress, having overheard, said, "I'll place the call for a taxi myself, right this minute." She crossed herself and, still laughing, went to the telephone to make the call.

She then admonished the other patrons to keep their silence, knowing full well that they, like she herself, would never forget what they had seen.

Father Brendan may not have been able to walk straight, but he was not so inebriated that he could not think straight. He had made sure to ask Father Fazio to arrange the meeting with Mary Lou Gallagher at Angelo's Italian Restaurant on Broadway in Revere. He could already taste Angelo's wonderful lasagna. Father Fazio also thought Angelo's was the perfect place in which to meet.

When the taxi arrived, Father Fazio and Father Brendan each blessed the patrons of the cafe who were still attentive to them and started toward the door. As the patrons wished them a safe journey home, the two men walked as soberly as they had when they first arrived. Most of the physical effect of the alcohol had worn off during the time it had taken for the taxi to arrive. What remained was pleasant.

When they finally met with Mary Lou Gallagher two weeks later at Angelo's, Josephine personally waited on them and took their orders for lasagna. The atmosphere was inviting and the aromas still wafted from the kitchen, immediately whetting their appetites.

Getting down to the reason for the meeting, Mary Lou told them that she read about Thomas attending college to earn a degree in physical education. "I was thrilled to see that John's brother actually succeeded in getting into college and that he was about to get his degree."

"And I gather, Mrs. Gallagher, that you wanted to let John know how wrong he was about Thomas. Am I right?"

"Yes, Father Fazio. I did think John ought to know how wrong he was about Thomas. I suppose that is a bit wicked of me, sort of like rubbing it in."

"Your feelings are very understandable, my dear. Now tell us how you found John and what it is that you learned."

Mary Lou then explained that she had remembered a classmate that was one of the few friends that John Grandee got along with in High School. She contacted him, a man by the name of George Lazarre. It turned out that George had maintained contact with John and had, in fact, attended his wedding in Los Angeles.

"George told me that he had lived in Los Angeles for several years and had once worked with John. He was now living in Revere, having at one point decided that he didn't like Los Angeles. At any rate, he gave me John's address and said that his present contact with John is limited to an exchange of birthday cards."

Mary Lou then went into the story of what had actually happened to John Grandee and his marriage to Anna Maria Papazian. Anna Maria had managed to obtain a few small parts in films under the name of Annette Page.

"George had renewed his friendship with John in the late twenties when he learned that John was working on the new sound systems in Hollywood prior to the innovation of 'talkies.' George was a sound system engineer who had studied at MIT with John Grandee and, when he heard about the work being done in Hollywood, he contacted John about the possibility of helping him get a job. Well, John hired him because he knew that George was well-versed in sound engineering. That was how George ended up living in Los Angeles."

The priests were well into their lasagna as Mary Lou continued to explain. She told them that George was best man at the wedding and that he had related to her that Anna Maria Papazian was a lovely and beautiful girl. George worked as assistant to John and he said that John was brilliant at his work. His genius was helpful in surmounting many of the problems related to bringing sound into the movies. While the heads of the studio that employed them respected John's virtues as a scientist, the people that worked under John hated him. He looked down at people and was often rude to the staff.

"George also started to find John difficult to work for. He said that after the first few months he began to regret having taken the job. The pay was so good, though, that he was hesitant about resigning. However, he told me that several of the best staff people left and went to work at other studios, taking much of what they learned with them."

Father Fazio told Mary Lou to slow down and start eating her lasagna before it got cold. There was a pause in the storytelling while she obediently took the time to enjoy her own food. Once absorbed in eating, the scrumptious Italian treasures hidden among hand-rolled pasta layers were too enticing to leave. The heavenly dish silenced Mary Lou for the rest of the meal.

When all three plates had been cleared Josephine came over to their table and asked if they would like anything else.

"A cup of cappuccino would be nice," Father Fazio said. "Would you like some, too, Mary Lou?"

"Oh, indeed, and I seldom have dessert, but I thought I saw cannoli in the pastry display."

Josephine left to bring Cappuccino and cannoli for all three. Father Brendan asked Mary Lou if she had sent a letter to John informing him of Thomas' success in gaining admission to college and earning a degree.

"No, Father, I'm not sure I want to do that anymore. Let me tell you more about John and you will see why I am now hesitant about telling John about his brother."

She went on to relate that John had alienated so many of his staff that the CEO of the studio called him in to his private office for a talk. When the CEO, Martin Faber, told John that he was concerned about the loss of so many capable staff people, John turned on his boss and told him that he didn't need a lecture on how to run his department. John was fired on the spot. When he told Anna Maria about it, she asked him what he was going to do.

"Why, I'm going to take a job for another studio. Martin Faber and Liberty studios will soon regret losing the best sound man in the industry."

John moved to Hudson Sound Systems and a higher paying position than the one that he had held at Liberty. George chose to stay on at Liberty. He never told John the real reason he did not want to make the change. He was hoping that Liberty would promote him to replace John.

"And did that happen?" Father Fazio asked.

"No, he was kept in the second place role, and Liberty hired a bigshot engineer. But George liked his new boss much better than he did John. He stayed on for several years and only chose to move back to Revere because he finally decided that Los Angeles was getting too big and he missed old friends and the more tempered pace back here in the east."

"I like your friend, George. He sounds like a fine man."

"Oh, he is. George is really a nice person."

Father Brendan asked, "Is John Grandee still with the new company? I believe you said the name was Hudson Sound Systems."

"No, Father Brendan. He did the same thing at Hudson that he did at Liberty. He disenfranchised the staff and he made the management so angry that they asked him to resign."

"The man is in need of counseling."

"I believe that's true, Father Fazio. At this point, John started to mistreat Anna Maria also. Because of his failure to maintain a decent job and his mistreatment of her, she finally asked for a divorce. That's the real story behind that unhappy marriage."

"You said there was a scandal. Is it a scandal to divorce in Los Angeles or in Hollywood? It seems to me they do it all the time."

"No, the scandal had to do with John's failure to meet the terms of the divorce settlement. He refused to divide their joint holdings. George told me that the proceedings were all over the Los Angeles area newspapers and that John ended up looking like a scoundrel."

She went on to say that George thought there was eventually an out-of-court settlement because Anna Maria decided to settle for less than the court had ordered in order to put the situation at rest. She couldn't take the pressure of her ex-husband's refusal to abide by the rulings nor afford the expense of constant non-payment actions against him. This is what also infuriated the general public at the time. Everyone knew he had more than enough money to satisfy the decrees. By now Hollywood was also well aware of his seamy employment history. Hollywood itself is really like a very small town.

When Father Fazio asked what John was doing now, Mary Lou said that George told her that John Grandee had taken a job teaching Physics at a small high school. No film studio wanted to have anything to do with him.

While teaching high school is a laudable goal for some, including his brother Thomas, for John Grandee it spelled complete failure. George said that the last time he saw him, John was a very depressed person and that he had turned completely gray and looked at least ten years older than he really was. He said John was living in a rented apartment in a poor section of Los Angeles not far from the school where he was teaching.

The saddest part of all is that he told me that John has no friends. He is a lonely, unhappy man. That's why I decided not to tell him that his brother Thomas was a very successful college graduate with a good family and good friends.

The two priests and Mary Lou Gallagher finished their meal and said little else until exchanging pleasant good-byes outside the restaurant. The sadness of the situation weighed heavily upon each of them. Indeed, misfortune had run in the Grandee family.

Chapter Forty-Six

FIVE WEEKS AFTER THOMAS STARTED HIS NEW job in Columbia, he received a phone call from Rabbi Richmond on a Monday evening. It was June 5, 1944.

"I'm sorry to have to tell you this, Thomas, but I just received a call from Sam Braverman. It seems that Hannah Ward was found murdered in the apartment that you once used at The Chateau in Charlestown. She was apparently strangled to death. Sam asked me to contact you. I just told Father Brendan, and he recommended that we have a meeting to discuss the situation. I imagine that you will be one of those that the police will want to interview. I expect that Braverman will be at the meeting and we will learn more at that time."

"My God, rabbi. I didn't think much of Hannah, but this news is horrible. Who do they think did it?"

"They have no idea at present. The police are starting an investigation. I believe they're also calling the detective, Harry Cohen. He's the one who originally notified the FBI about Hannah. I'll try to have a little more information for you tomorrow morning."

"Where will we meet?"

"At Holy Rosary Rectory. Tomorrow, Tuesday morning at nine o'clock."

Thomas brought Marie with him to the meeting. He was surprised to see Victor Hermanssen talking to Father Brendan when they arrived. A few minutes later, Rabbi Richmond entered the conference room with Sam Braverman.

Marie was holding onto Thomas for dear life. He could feel her trembling. "Marie, calm down," he whispered, "I haven't done anything wrong. Let's wait and see what the others have to say."

Father Brendan opened the meeting since it was in his bailiwick. He soon asked that Sam Braverman take over, since he was the one that the police had contacted after Hannah was found.

"I'm not too clear on how the police found out about Hannah in the first place," Sam Braverman began. "I asked and the officer said for me to wait. When he came back on the phone, he explained that he thought that one of the hotel guests heard sounds of a fight upstairs at The Chateau and called the station. He said that he wasn't really sure how they learned about it. He knew they had responded to a call and found Hannah alone in bed in the apartment that Thomas once used and that now was being used by Victor."

Sam explained that they had asked Victor a few questions, and when they learned about Hannah and the FBI, they called in the federal investigators again. "Right now we're waiting for Harry Cohen because he was also called."

The door opened suddenly. Standing at the entrance was the small, almost comedic but very clever detective. Sam continued as everyone turned to look.

"Here he is now. Harry, come right in. That empty chair is for you."

"Sorry I'm late. I never was an early riser. My kind of work keeps me up late at night quite often. I rushed over as soon as I realized I had overslept. Is there some hot coffee, Father? I think I need it. I skipped breakfast."

Father Brendan used his intercom to ask Leona to get coffee for everyone.

"Do you want some muffins, Father?" Leona's voice beamed back. "I can get them over in a hurry."

Enough nodding heads told him to say yes. "But please bring one cup of coffee right away, Leona."

"Thank you, Father," Harry said. "Mr. Grandee, I know that you won't want to hear this, but I have to tell you that the FBI called me in immediately and I needed to turn all the records over to them as well as explain everything. I had no choice, Thomas. One doesn't hold back information from the Feds.

"They know you had dealings with Hannah and that she made trouble for you. I guess that makes you enough of a suspect that

286

they said they would be contacting you. Just be prepared to have witnesses as to your whereabouts when the murder took place.

"Victor is in a much worse predicament than you, but you both will be bothered by agents and possibly by the police. In the meantime, I advise you both to talk to no one outside of this room until this matter is settled. I did what I had to do, but I'm not acting in any capacity whatsoever other just than being a witness if and when called upon."

Father Brendan thanked Harry as Leona arrived with donuts and coffee for everyone. He said grace and told them all to take a break and enjoy the light breakfast.

Leona said, "I'm sorry, they were all out of muffins so I got donuts instead. Hope you like them." No one objected and she quietly left the room.

Sam Braverman spoke. "I understand from the police and the FBI that they are still investigating. They said that they will be asking for fingerprints from both Victor and Thomas but that doesn't mean they think either of you are guilty. They really have no clue at this early stage of the game. I guess they want to know how Hannah happens to be in Boston rather than Hawaii where she had gone after her release from prison."

Victor said, "She came to Boston to have a go at me because she knows I was the one who originally turned her in. She just walked into The Chateau and came right up to me. She played her usual stupid game, flirting and asking me to come upstairs with her.

"At first I told her to go to hell. Oh, excuse me, Father Brendan and Rabbi. Then I figured, in my own stupid way, that I might as well go up and see what happens. Big mistake, I guess, but I didn't strangle her. I should have known better but I let myself be seduced into getting into bed with her. I hate to be telling all this, but I guess it will be better if I do. We were making out in bed when Hannah tried to stab me. She must have hidden her knife under the pillow before we got into bed. Anyway, I managed to catch her arm before she could finish me off."

Marie stood up and Victor paused. She said, "May I be excused? Thomas obviously had nothing to do with this awful crime. I would like to wait outside with your secretary, Father Brendan."

"Fine, Marie. We understand."

Marie left the room.

Victor then undid his shirt and showed the place on the back of his left side where the knife had left its mark. "We fought and I got the knife out of her hand. I grabbed the blade part and tossed it out of reach. Then I quickly grabbed my clothes that were all in one heap and left the apartment. I'm lucky no one saw me, because I was stark naked running through the hall. I headed for the staircase that leads down to the restaurant. I got dressed on the stairwell."

Harry asked Victor why he hadn't called the police after Hannah had pulled a knife on him. Victor said that he was afraid to get involved and decided to keep his mouth shut. "I knew that she was up to no good, and I figured that the best thing was just to stay clear of Hannah."

"Do you have any idea who might have done it?" Harry asked.

"I don't know. It could be that guy Prescott from New York. He must have been in some kind of racket. I remember that Hannah asked me about him when she learned that he was paying cash for a room all year long even though he only showed up once in a while. I know he had some strange-looking characters coming up to see him when he was in town."

Everyone agreed that the best thing to do would be to wait for the police and the FBI to continue the investigation. When the meeting was over, everyone offered their support to Thomas; they all believed he was innocent.

At home Marie looked so sad that Thomas thought she was going to start crying. "Marie, honey, you look like this business is taking a terrible toll on you. It's really going to work itself out, you'll see. I'm not guilty of anything, and the police will find that out once they realize that I was at the Columbia YMHA during the day and home in time for dinner with you and Robbie. On top of that, I answered the phone when the rabbi called on Monday evening to tell us about the murder."

"Oh, Thomas, I'm not really worried about you. It's Carl. Maybe this business with the murder made me think of it, but I keep worrying that something is going to happen to Carl."

"I'm concerned for him, too, Marie. Carl's a smart kid, though. He knows how to take care of himself. I wish you wouldn't worry so much about him."

When Sam Braverman learned about Hannah Ward's murder on Monday, he knew that Thomas Grandee was going to be questioned by the police or the FBI. Rather than call Thomas, though, he thought it best to call Rabbi Richmond. Braverman and the rabbi had become close friends, and Sam thought Thomas and Marie could use some emotional support when they heard the news. He was right in thinking that Rabbi Richmond would inform Thomas' priest.

Thomas Grandee's remarkable progress over the past four years had earned the respect of all those who knew him. The Tuesday meeting at the church was planned to show support for Thomas and to try to avoid a possible emotional setback.

By the time the Tuesday meeting was over, everyone was comfortable with Thomas' alibi; on the day of the murder, he had been at work at the Columbia YMHA all day and had arrived home for dinner at the usual time, around six. He had answered the phone when Rabbi Richmond had called half an hour later. There was no way he could have been at The Chateau when Hannah was strangled.

Tuesday and Wednesday newspaper articles told the story of the murder. The Wednesday papers carried a front-page story revealing the actual time of Hannah's murder—Sunday night between 10 and 11 p.m.—as well as the suspects, Victor Hermanssen and Thomas Grandee.

Thomas had been on Coast Guard volunteer patrol from six to ten on Sunday evening. Marie remembered that he had arrived home at around eleven, as he usually did. However, since the Coast Guard station was just minutes away from The Chateau, Marie's statement would be of no help as far as the police were concerned.

Thomas called Rabbi Richmond as soon as he finished reading the Wednesday newspaper article. He asked him if the publicity and the estimated time of the murder would affect his job at the Columbia YMHA. He also asked him how the time of the murder could be Sunday when he had just heard about it on Monday.

"I saw the paper, Thomas. The mix-up on the Sunday or Monday business is probably my fault. I never asked Sam Braverman for specifics. He may have gotten the call on Sunday and waited to call me the next day. At this point, it's no longer important. The facts are the facts. Even so, as far as I am concerned, nothing changes. I can't speak for the Columbia YMHA, but I doubt that anything will change as a result of a newspaper story. Jack Berger told me that he is very pleased with your work."

"Well, thank you for saying so. It does make me feel better. I didn't feel comfortable about calling Jack Berger. After all, I've known him for only a short while. I'm sorry to bother you with my problems, rabbi."

On Thursday, June 8, 1944, the police fingerprinted both Thomas and Victor.

Victor told the police about Hannah's connection with the New York guy, George Prescott, who rented the year-round apartment at The Chateau, and the suspicious characters that came and went whenever Prescott was in town. The police informed the FBI, and they started an investigation into the New York connection.

After both Thomas' and Victor's fingerprints were found in the apartment, the police lost interest in that part of the investigation. They reasoned that both men had actually lived and slept in that apartment over a period of years. Fingerprints on furniture and doors and walls did not indicate anything other than both men's presence in the apartment at one time or another.

Prescott's fingerprints were not taken, so they had to wait until he was located. Besides, if there were dealings between Prescott and Hannah, it could have been in his apartment. Victor criticized the police and said that Prescott could have still come into Victor's apartment when Hannah was there and simply worn gloves. Victor's problem was the fact that, at the present time, the apartment was his.

The woolen scarf that Hannah had been strangled with had been found around her neck, but it revealed no clues about the murderer.

Mr. Prescott had not yet been located. His office in New York seemed to represent a respectable small import-export business in Manhattan. His one employee, a secretary, said that Prescott was on a trip to Mexico and she was unable to reach him.

The FBI, in the meantime, had discovered that Victor's story about Hannah's connection to Prescott was correct. They found telephone call records that suggested a dope smuggling link in which Hannah may have been involved. That information took a lot of pressure off of Victor and Thomas. The newspapers had dropped the story after about a week when Mr. Prescott could not be located.

Two months later the FBI learned that Prescott was doing business under the name of George Pressman at a Newark, New Jersey import-export office. The New York office had been abandoned and the secretary had disappeared. Pressman was picked up on drug dealing charges. Although his lawyer got him out on bail, Pressman was now the most likely suspect in the murder.

In the meantime, the apartment where Hannah had been found had remained sealed. When Pressman was located, his fingerprints were taken and, as expected, none of the prints from the apartment matched his. Although predictable, it was still another dead end.

Chapter Forty-Seven

IT WAS THE SPRING OF 1944 BEFORE Carl's unit was shipped over-seas to England. By the time his company arrived, the tank destroyers were no longer needed for Africa. German resistance to the British and Americans had ended in Africa more than a year earlier. The tank destroyers, M10s, were converted to artillery use, and Carl's company was sent across the channel on June 8.

Their unit was one of the later waves to hit Omaha Beach. Murray was still with Carl's company and he started to vomit when he saw bodies floating up to the surface of the water as their LCI hit the shore. Carl pulled Murray with him onto the beach where crews were at work carting bodies and debris away. Bodies continued to drift onto the shore almost as fast as the crews could remove the remains of the D-Day dead. It was an ugly scene, and the men all thanked their lucky stars that they hadn't arrived two days earlier.

The cliffs ahead showed the remains of German pillboxes. The company trudged up through the debris and finally reached the top, where the sergeant waved them on as if to say all was clear ahead. They finally climbed on board a transport truck in a convoy that was headed for the front. The sergeant said they were headed in the direction of the city of Rouen.

Within the next hour, the truck convoy moved about 100 yards and the men were ordered out. There were 10 men in the group Carl and Murray were herded into. A tent was erected, and it served as headquarters for a temporary command post. The lieutenant in charge told them that they were now going to a Replacement Depot and they were being reassigned to General Patton's 80th Division, 3rd Army, 318th Battalion, Company H. The H, they later learned, stood for Heavy Weapons. Carl was no longer with a tank destroyer unit. He had become a foot soldier in an ordinary infantry outfit. He carried a 30-caliber M1 rifle.

The Germans had been turned back on the Eastern Front. Stalingrad was in Russian hands since the winter of 1943, and the siege of Leningrad had been broken in January of 1944. Hitler was desperate and ordered his troops to fight to the last man on the Western front. Patton's 80th Division had the tough job of taking Normandy back from the German army that was concentrating all of its energy on what seemed like a face-saving effort in France.

From this point on, Company H traveled north and east on foot. They had to fight for every inch of Normandy soil. Germany artillery was constant and slowed their progress to a snail's pace.

During the third week in their eastward advance, Murray Halpern was one of a three-man team that had just finished setting up an 81mm mortar. The shell was loaded and two soldiers moved back out of the way. Murray now had the job of pulling the firing pin at the base of the barrel. Suddenly, a German mortar shell landed within an inch of the base. Murray was blown into the air and landed in several pieces. His war was over.

Murray Halpern had given his life to stop Hitler and his insane attempt to impose Nazi rule. When Carl saw Murray's remains, he broke down. Carl was taken out of action and sedated by the medics. He was now 50 yards behind his company. The sergeant told him to rest for 10 minutes before returning to the front.

Marie was getting one letter after the other from either Carl or Louise. When she received Carl's letter about Murray Halpern, she started a crying tirade that lasted for more than a week. Carl had described Murray as a gentle, intelligent, likeable man. Each time Thomas came home she took one look at him and started weeping again. To her, it could just as easily have been Carl.

Louise's letters didn't help much to make her feel secure about either of her precious children. Louise wrote about the soldiers she treated. Many were suffering from tropical diseases, but others were brought in beyond repair or in such pain that they came in screaming until they ran out of strength.

In one letter, she said that she thought war was worse than hell. Louise wrote that she couldn't believe that human beings could do such damage to each other. Marie thought about Robbie, who was now almost sixteen. In two more years, if the war continued, her baby would be drafted into the army. How can you let this happen, God, she asked herself. She was beginning to question her very foundations of faith and spiritual belief.

On the Wednesday after she read the letter about Murray Halpern, she took a sick day off from work and went to Holy Rosary Church in search of solace. The weekday service was sparsely attended, and Father Brendan was at the pulpit leading prayers. When the service ended, she moved forward to catch his attention. He led her to his small office within the sanctuary.

"Father, I feel like a sinner. For the first time in my life, I am uncertain about my faith in God," Marie said.

"Please sit down, Marie. Tell me about it," Father Brendan said.

"I just received a letter from Carl telling me that his dear friend was killed. Louise is in the Pacific and tells us about the horrors of treating the wounded. I can't understand how God can allow this war to go on. Evil men seem be in charge of our lives. Please, Father Brendan, help me to regain my faith and my sanity."

The priest smiled and nodded. "My dear, I sometimes feel exactly the way you do. My own brother's son is in the Navy, and I am just as concerned about him as you are about your loved ones. We must have faith, Marie, or we stand to lose our objective appreciation."

"I always thought that prayer would make me feel better, but I've tried without success. The Lord simply is not answering my prayers."

"I know what you mean. We must keep trying, and we must never stop asking the Lord for his love and forgiveness. Marie, I've known you for a long time and I know you are a strong woman. Do you remember how desperate you were about Thomas five years ago? Just remember what faith and prayer did for your husband, and how much better his life and your own became once Thomas regained his own faith and belief in God."

Marie sighed and said, "Oh, Father, you are so right. I never thought of the connection between those days and the present. I'm glad I came to see you. Thank you for helping me."

While her own prayers seemed to have little effect on the final outcome of such a tragic war, having her faith restored certainly helped Marie to feel at least a little more secure. Father Brendan was well aware that both Marie and he had to keep hoping and praying that their own loved ones were lucky enough to be spared during this nightmarish conflict. This he felt confident the Lord could provide.

Chapter Forty-Eight

At about five in the morning on August 30, 1944, the 66th Infantry entered the Argonne. The sound of heavy artillery fire was coming from behind, in front and on either side of the unit. There was utter confusion until they heard Sergeant Pete Cooper yell, "Down and spread out. I'll signal if I want you to move ahead."

Carl heard the clatter of a machine gun. That must have been why Cooper gave the order. Cooper held a grenade up to indicate that H Company should get their grenades ready.

The sergeant crept over near Carl and asked three of the soldiers within hearing range if one would volunteer. He pointed toward the machine gun emplacement just over the edge of a nearby hill. "Listen, guys, we can't stand up and set up a mortar. We'll get gunned down. We can't even dig a ditch without exposing ourselves. If we don't knock the machine gun out, we are in deep shit. Someone has to crawl up while the rest of us cover with our M-1s."

Carl started to crawl forward very slowly. There was a section of brushwood to their right, just a few yards beyond a clearing among the pines. The machine gun emplacement was about fifty or sixty yards up ahead and there were trees all around. Once Carl started his move, Pete Cooper moved toward the other troops of Company H to alert them to protect Carl if he came under fire.

Carl crawled from tree to tree until he came to the clearing. He looked back and nodded to Cooper, who was watching his every move. Cooper signaled for rifle fire from the left to draw attention away from the clearing. Carl slithered across to the cover of the thick growth of brushwood. Once he was beyond the clearing, he maneuvered forward, using the thick brush for cover.

He reached the end of the brush and now had to rely solely on the cover of trees. With less than fifteen yards to go, Carl once again heard rifle fire aimed at the machine gun nest from far to his left. This time, Cooper maintained a steady barrage so that Carl could get close enough to toss the grenade. He even had a backup grenade; Billy Jackson had handed him his own when Carl had volunteered.

Carl crawled to a point within a few yards of the machine gun emplacement and heaved the first grenade. It went off just to the left of the gunner. He heaved the second one and it hit the target. He held his breath and waited, motionless. If he hadn't knocked the gunner out, he would not live to see the next minute. His heart pounded until he heard Company H running forward.

Pete Cooper was screaming, "Let's move up to the top of the hill and dig in." As he passed Carl, he grabbed hold of him and hugged him. "You son of a bitch. You're a fucking hero!"

As they were pretty well dug in to make the hill safe, Billy Jackson was just about to drop into the trench when he got hit in the thigh and fell to the side.

Cooper grabbed him and pulled him down into the trench. "Someone radio back for the medics while I try to stop this Goddamned wound from bleeding. It doesn't look too bad."

Meanwhile, Company H set up its own machine gun emplacement not far from where the Germans had theirs. Carl and the sergeant and one other soldier were getting the mortar ready. It took three men to set up the mortar.

With Billy wounded, the sergeant stepped in to replace him. From the noise and confusion around them, they had no way of knowing how effective the 80th Battalion's artillery was. They knew that American artillery was firing over their heads at the German troops who seemed to be retreating into Belgium, Luxemburg or Germany.

Cooper wasn't positive about their exact location, the direction of the German retreat or of the American advance. What he did know was that the 66th Infantry Division's objective was to reinforce trapped American troops in Bastogne, a part of Belgium.

The 66th Infantry was in the Battle of the Bulge but they didn't know it; no one but the Germans knew that they had been allowing American forces to penetrate the middle into a bulge-like shape. It wasn't going to be much longer before they learned more about the trap they had fallen into. In a matter of two more days, American forces secured the Argonne Forest area.

The 66th reached Sedan the first week in September and crept slowly forward, fighting every inch of the way to the outskirts of Bastogne. In early November, it started to snow and they trudged through slush and mud. German artillery fire never ceased.

During a break when the front seemed deserted of enemy soldiers, they dug trenches with a view, where they would rest for a few hours before proceeding. Carl looked up over the edge of the trench and saw a figure in a gray uniform. It was a young German soldier apparently separated from his outfit and unaware of the Americans' presence so close by. He was walking away from the direction of the trench. Automatically, Carl aimed his M-1 and fired. Not being the greatest marksman, he missed, and the young soldier turned and saw him.

The German aimed his gun at Carl, and Carl fired again, this time hitting the soldier. The German slumped over and lay on the cold, muddy and wet ground. Carl foolishly left the trench. He felt guilty, as though he owed something to the young German who had just tried to kill him.

He got to the soldier, who was now moaning and holding his chest where the bullet had entered. His rifle was on the ground beside him. Carl dragged the soldier back to the trench as he were a wounded American and dumped him in, saying, "This kid is wounded. Call for the medics."

Just as Carl started to climb back into the trench, an artillery shell burst nearby. Shrapnel hit Carl, and he fell to the ground, half-in and half-out of the trench.

The war was over for Carl. The medics arrived and carted him and the wounded German back to the hospital tent and then onto an ambulance headed for a hospital west of the front.

Carl had suffered face and body wounds from the shrapnel, as well as a severe concussion. He was treated in a French village and, one week later, shipped to a United States hospital in England. After two weeks there, he was on a ship headed back to the United States. Carl never did find out the exact name of either town where he had been treated.

Chapter Forty-Nine

MARIE'S COLLECTION OF LETTERS FROM LOUISE DATED from late December of 1942 when she first arrived at Fort Dix, New Jersey. Peter Strauss was accepted by the Navy in the fall of 1942 and was stationed at Staten Island, New York. They got to see each other pretty often on furloughs, and Peter was sometimes able to ask permission to go into the city to meet her.

Her letter about Peter sounded as though they were really serious about each other. It didn't surprise Marie one bit. "She always was sweet on the Strauss boy," she said to her husband.

From Camp Shanks, Louise had traveled by train to New York Harbor to board a new small ship—part of a convoy on the way to the Pacific, or at least that was what the warrant officer had said. The nurses were told to pack their winter clothing, even though it was late summer in New York.

Once on board, the doctor in charge of the unit informed the nurses that they were headed for the tropics, and he hoped that all or at least some of the nurses in the company had been schooled in tropical diseases. He acknowledged that he himself had never been taught much on the subject.

After several weeks on board the ship and a number of stops along the way, they finally reached the small Tahitian Pacific island of Bora Bora. It was only a stopover on the way to Australia, but Louise and several others were anxious to stretch their legs on real land. They took advantage of one of the small tenders that took them ashore.

In a letter, dated in the fall of 1943, Louise wrote that her group was almost stranded on the island because they were late and missed their tender back to the big ship. Fortunately, they were missed and a tender was sent out to find them.

After leaving Tahiti, they moved on to Brisbane, Australia. Louise was on temporary duty, assigned to casualties of the CBI, or China Burma India Theatre. Her company was assigned to hospital duty located in a children's school.

Three months later, Louise was transferred north to Townsend and, in October, she was sent to a more permanent position where she became part of 62 Station Hospital in Oro Bay, New Guinea. Louise remained in New Guinea for 21 months.

Louise continued to write home to her parents. In every letter, it was clear that she was still alright and still enamored of Peter Strauss. She also mentioned Peter in her letters to Carl, which Carl relayed back to his parents at home.

At Oro Bay in New Guinea, Louise was in the dayroom reading her mail when the ambulance screamed in. She heard "Nurse Grandee to O.R.!" over the loudspeaker. She hurried over to the operating room, where Captain Jenkins was already scrubbing.

"Hurry, Grandee, the medics called in a woman in labor with a breech. They've been trying to help her give birth with no success. Get scrubbed and ready. Mosely is on his way." Doctor Mosely was an anesthesiologist.

"Who is the patient? Where did she come from?" Louise asked.

"She's Papuan. The medics were on patrol when they drove past a group of villagers standing around this woman. She was on the ground, clutching her abdomen. One of the medics managed enough pidgin English to learn that they were on their way to meet a group from another village for a *kula*, an exchange of gifts, or at least that's what he thinks. Anyway, this one is pregnant, and I guess she didn't expect the baby to be coming so soon."

Louise said, "Here they come."

Doctor Jenkins let out a whistle and said, "God help me. I'm no obstetrician."

They laid the woman out on the table and got her feet into stirrups. "Are you in pain?" Doctor Jenkins asked.

The Papuan was actually a girl of not much more than 13 or 14. She looked blankly at the doctor.

"Captain, she doesn't speak English. How do they know the baby is in breech?" Louise asked.

"I don't know. Let's have a look. Grandee, you probably know more than I do about delivery. Get inside and tell me what you think."

Louise probed and wasted no time in saying, "She's in breech, alright. She's presenting buttocks."

"Mosely, I want an epidural rather than a general. What do you think?"

"I agree, let's go. Get me ready, nurse."

"Ready and waiting," Louise said.

"Grandee, I can go up-and-down or bikini. What do you think?"

"Bikini would be my choice, doctor. I think it's safer."

"That's what they say. Okay, scalpel," Jenkins said. He made the incisions. Nurses Hanley and Peters were assisting by now, and they held back the opening. Louise handed instruments to Doctor Jenkins, who seemed to look to her for guidance; he didn't know where to make the uterus incision.

"Down low is what I think they prefer," Louise said, hoping she was right.

A messy, smelly baby's bottom came into view, and the infant girl was in Nurse Peters' hands in seconds while Nurse Hanley smacked the baby's bottom. The infant's howls brought joy to everyone. Louise and Doctor Jenkins proceeded to close the wound.

The mother had been pretty much "out of it" throughout the procedure, but she smiled at the sound of her baby's crying.

"Jesus, Mary and Joseph," Louise said. "I haven't seen a newborn baby since I left Mount Auburn in Cambridge. I'm exhausted, but I feel good."

Nurse Peters asked, "What the hell are we going to do about the baby?"

Mosely said, "Nothing to worry about. The whole group is waiting out front. These people love new babies. They'll take her back to their village and have a great celebration." The new mother recovered well, with no serious complications.

A couple of days later, Captain Doctor Jenkins came to Louise in the dayroom and said, "I need you, nurse." His smile told her that this was not an emergency.

"Yeah, I know what you need me for, and the answer is still no."

While the story about assisting in the delivery of the Papuan girl's baby filled a good part of one of Louise's letters home, it was unusual for her to say much about her surroundings or her day-to-day work. She wrote about the doctors and nurses and tried to assure them that she was safe and well. She didn't want to worry her parents.

The Station 62 base hospital building in Oro Bay had a raised floor to protect against rot from the jungle ground. There was only a four-foot high wooden framework and a tin roof suspended on poles. The space above the wooden framework was open. Doctors and nurses had practically no protection from mosquitoes; however, the necessary mosquito netting was attached to each patient's bed.

One situation that Louise failed to report to her parents had to do with a nurse who was bitten on her bottom by a scorpion when she was using the latrine. She nearly died of the fever caused by the bite.

Casualties arrived to Station 62 from the battle of New Britain. The nurses often spent harrowing hours giving injections, anesthetizing, ripping off clothes, and stitching gaping wounds. They witnessed amputations, sterilized instruments, comforted the young wounded soldiers in their beds, set up IV's and, too often, covered with sheets the wounded that they couldn't save. They never grew accustomed to the sight of young boys torn apart, bleeding and dying.

Louise sometimes got mail from Leona, Father Brendan's secretary at Holy Rosary church in Malden, Massachusetts. She mentioned that the priest said a prayer for the men and women in the service at almost every mass.

Louise answered, saying that she prayed for the war to end.

Chapter Fifty

By THE SUMMER OF 1944, BOTH THE police and the FBI conceded that they lacked sufficient evidence to bring charges against anyone. Victor's story raised eyebrows, but since he admitted having contact with Hannah, it was not possible to charge him. His fingerprints alone or the fact that he was the last one known to have been with her did not prove him guilty. Still, the police had picked him up for further questioning.

Victor hired a lawyer who argued that Thomas Grandee had more of a motive than anyone else to murder Hannah. "After all," the lawyer said, "Grandee was seduced into serious trouble by Hannah, and he had a key to the apartment."

When the police called on Thomas, he explained that he had turned the key in but admitted that he could have had a copy made. He was told he was still considered a suspect.

Pressman was being ruled out as the murderer. There was no evidence that he was anywhere near the apartment on Sunday, December 19, 1943, when the murder was committed. Of the three possible suspects, only Victor or Thomas could have been there on that particular night.

It was already November of 1944. Time had passed and nothing seemed to be happening. Thomas and Marie were able to go on with their lives mainly because those who knew them were convinced of Thomas' innocence. However, neither Thomas nor Marie would rest comfortably until the real murderer was identified and Thomas was completely cleared.

Marie suggested that Thomas call Harry Cohen to ask if he could help to resolve the mystery of the murder of Hannah Ward. Harry agreed to do so and he worked out an agreement with the Grandees that would cost them only his expenses and a small fee. "I'm convinced that you're innocent, Thomas, and I know you can't afford a lot of money. Besides, I have some ideas on who the guilty one is."

Harry Cohen didn't tell the Grandees that he had been quietly studying copies of documents he was able to get hold of through his police connections. He even had permission to scrutinize some FBI records based on his early cooperation with the federal investigators and on his help in convicting Hannah four years ago.

Harry visited Victor and asked him if they could go into his office at The Chateau. Victor didn't like the idea and said he wanted his lawyer present, so Harry said that he would come back.

"I'll call your lawyer, Victor. I know him, and I'll make the date for the three of us to meet. But before I do that, I'd like to ask you one question."

"Go ahead, ask," Victor said.

"What are you hiding that you are so afraid to let me talk to you for a few minutes? All I want is to learn a few things to help clear Thomas' name. You're his friend, aren't you?"

"Of course I am. Okay. Come on into my office now, and let's get this over with."

Once they were both seated comfortably in Thomas' old office, Harry said that he only wanted to ask Victor one question.

"Go ahead with your question," Victor said.

"You said that you suspected that Hannah had dealings with Pressman and that he came into the apartment and used gloves to avoid fingerprints. You seemed convinced that Pressman was the real murderer. I think you're right. He could have taken a plane, using another alias, and returned to Mexico a day later."

Harry had studied the reports at police headquarters thoroughly, so he knew that the FBI had positive proof that Pressman was still in Mexico on the day of the murder. He continued on the ruse.

"Victor, if I knew how Pressman could have gotten in through the locked door, it might help both you and Thomas."

"Yeah, that's right. I think he's the one. He could have just walked down the corridor and maybe picked the lock."

"You mean that when you ran out naked, holding your bundle of clothes, you stopped to lock the door?"

"Oh, no, that's right. He could have just come right in. I left the door open."

"You've been very helpful. That's all I want to know right now, Victor. I'll see you again if I need you."

Harry left and immediately headed for police headquarters. By now he was convinced of Victor's guilt. He had put Victor off his guard by convincing him that his only interest was to clear Thomas.

At police headquarters, Harry came prepared. He asked for Detective Sergeant Scott Perry, the one who was on Hannah's case and the Detective with whom Harry had a good relationship. The sergeant was in and he asked Harry into his office. "What's up, Harry. You on a new case?"

"No, an old one, Scott. The Hannah Ward case."

"Oh, hell, we gave up on that one. We can guess that Victor did it, but we can't charge the guy. There's just not enough evidence."

"Well, how's this, Scott? I just left Victor, and he's trying to convince me that Pressman came into the apartment right after he had just run out into the hallway naked, holding his bundle of clothes, and leaving the door open. But first he said maybe the guy picked the lock on the door."

"So what does that prove?"

"Nothing, really, except that he's reaching for straws, because I told him I only asked him a question because I wanted to clear Thomas Grandee. So I'm thinking Victor is the guilty one. No question."

"Come on, Harry, what you're telling me means nothing. We need real proof."

"How about this?" Harry said as he reached into his briefcase. He showed Scott a copy he had made of a bookkeeping page that Hannah Ward had written. He found it in his four-year-old "closed cases" files.

"What the hell does this mean? It's just a page of bookkeeping entries."

"It's not an ordinary page, Scott. It was written by Hannah, and it's one of hundreds like it that are all written by a left-handed person."

"So?"

"So Hannah's fingerprints on the knife are made by her right hand. The blade with Victor's blood on the tip has Victor's left handprints on it. He was very clever in making sure to get clear prints of both his left hand and Hannah's right hand on the knife."

The detective continued. "I don't think Hannah ever saw that knife in her lifetime. I think it's Victor's switchblade knife that he used as a prop after strangling her. Hannah was in town for a week after meeting with Pressman. The FBI found that out. They also found out that Pressman left town on Sunday night, a week before the murder. He showed up in Mexico three days later and stayed in Mexico for three weeks. They have evidence. Victor knew about that. Why was he trying so hard to point the finger at Pressman when he knew it was impossible to prove the guy did it?"

"You tell me, Harry."

"Because he's scared. It was wishful thinking that made him fall for my ruse about Pressman flying up from Mexico. He knows Thomas is innocent and he knows that he's guilty. That's why. Hannah being left-handed proves it."

"What was Victor's motive?"

"I think Hannah wanted revenge and picked a fight with Victor as soon as she enticed him to come up to the apartment. There must have been a struggle, and he ended up strangling her."

"You're right, Harry. That could be the motive, and the fact that Hannah was left-handed could very well be our proof. We'll have Victor picked up within the hour."

"Thanks, Scott. I'll be seeing you."

Victor was arrested by the police and charged with the murder in mid-November of 1944. When he was presented with the facts, he broke down and confessed.

Between the police and FBI records, Victor's signed confession and his oral testimony, the following facts were established:

During their investigation, the FBI had learned that Hannah had been with Pressman in his apartment the previous week. She had been dealing drugs for him. She decided to stay on and get her revenge on Victor for having turned her in to the police four years previous.

When she came to The Chateau on Sunday, December 19, the restaurant was closed and Victor was alone. Hannah enticed him into going upstairs to his apartment where she continued her seduction until she got him into bed. Once in bed, she pulled a knife out from under the pillow where she had apparently managed to hide it while she got undressed.

She grabbed the knife in her left hand and Victor heard the snap of the switch. He was alerted by the sound and instantly caught her hand and jerked the knife away and threw it on the floor. An angry, vicious fight ensued. He was able to pin her down, and at that point it was easy for him to strangle her with her own scarf. He had used a handkerchief to tie the scarf around her neck to avoid hand contact.

He didn't have to run out into the hallway naked. He had plenty of time to get dressed. He picked up the switchblade knife, made a small stab wound on his own back, wiped the knife clean of prints and then decided that had been a mistake. He then carefully put the knife handle in Hannah's right hand, holding the blade in his left. While Victor could not establish self-defense, there was sufficient basis to find him guilty of manslaughter rather than first or even second-degree murder.

Harry's only mistake was to think that the knife belonged to Victor. Victor's big mistake was to wipe the knife clean. If he had not, the case might never have been solved.

Later on, Detective Sergeant Scott Perry wanted to know what had prompted Harry to investigate Hannah's left-handed handwriting. Harry answered him by reminding him that he had worked on the original case involving Hannah. He remembered going through stacks of bills and records that Hannah had worked on. The handwriting, obviously that of a left-handed person, was memorable. When he read the report about Hannah's murder, it mentioned perfect right-hand prints on the knife handle.

Chapter Fifty-One

CARL GRANDEE ARRIVED AT CAMP EDWARDS IN Massachusetts a week before Christmas. When he called home, Robbie answered the phone and thought the call had come from England because that was the last place from which they received mail from Carl.

Thomas drove down to Camp Edwards to bring Carl home on furlough for the holidays, accompanied by Marie and Robbie. Carl would have to return and spend a few months to be properly mustered out. He was wearing a bronze star, Combat Expert Infantry badge and three battle stars. He had also been cited for heroism in the Argonne Forest and at Bastogne.

When he arrived home in Malden, the Rossiters were there with Larry Green, Melanie Boudreau and Nancy. It was a sunny winter day, and they all came out in front and stood on the sidewalk alongside the driveway. When Carl emerged from the car, they erupted into cheers. Then silence fell as he and Nancy made eye contact.

She stepped forward and Carl stepped toward her and they embraced for what seemed an endless few minutes. No one said a word until Melanie looked at Larry. She smiled, shrugged and said, "Larry, we should have known."

Once in the house, everyone started to speak at once. They all had a million questions. Things finally quieted down and Carl said he didn't really feel like talking about his future right now. He had to go back to Edwards to be out-processed, and that could take weeks or months. He wasn't sure.

About finishing at Boston University, he said he intended to complete the remaining semester and would not talk about anything beyond that.

"What do you hear from Louise?" he asked his mother.

Marie said Louise wanted to come home as soon as the war was over. She and Peter Strauss had definitely decided to get married when she returned to the States.

"How do you like your new life, Pa?" Carl asked Thomas.

"It feels wonderful. The people at the YMHA are easy to work with and they seem to like me. I'm doing what I always dreamed of, and I have Betty to thank for suggesting that I volunteer to teach the English classes. I'm doing that at Malden High School one night each week. My life is good, Carl."

The next day, when Carl had a chance to be alone with Nancy, he told her he was going to go on to medical school after getting his bachelor's degree. He asked her what her plans were.

"Carl, I'm going to love you for the rest of my life, and I am going to continue writing. I have less than a year to earn my B.A. and since I'm already writing and earning some money, I can be at home and still write."

"What does that look in your eye mean?" Carl asked.

"It means I can stay home and make money while you go to medical school, silly." She laughed a little and continued. "What do you think it means?"

"I think it means I love you and we can get married. Maybe we ought to wait for Louise to come home and we can have a double wedding."

"Sounds good to me, Carl, but I can't wait to get you really alone, if you know what I mean."

"I know what you mean, Nancy, my sweetheart. I know what you mean."

In January 1945, the Germans were finally driven out of Bastogne. On May 7, 1945, the Germans surrendered to the Allies. In August of that year, atom bombs fell on Hiroshima and Nagasaki. Japan surrendered and the nuclear age was upon us.

One year later, Carl was in medical school and Nancy was living in the apartment with Melanie. She was taking a course in journalism and writing a book about the role of women in World War II.

The End

About the Author

ARTHUR S. REINHERZ began writing more than 40 years ago. A recipient of numerous awards, his career has spanned the fields of graphic design, advertising and healthcare. He is the founder of Intercity Home-maker Service, Inc. of Malden, Massachusetts. He has spent the last 19 years as a volunteer member of the board of directors of the Tri-City Mental Health Center. He makes his home in Massachusetts with his wife Eve.